I0678829

ABOUT THIS BOOK

Emeline by Katie M. John

Emeline Fairchild couldn't imagine a more perfect match for herself than Drayan Bishop. Her real-life Prince Charming, a powerful mage, freed her from a curse, awakening her to a new world in 1913. But as the much anticipated wedding approaches, Emeline soon finds the magic turning dark. Is her light enough to defeat the darkness of a jealous and insane mind? Or is it too late to save the true love of her life?

Released From a Curse by Brynn Myers

Sequel to *Trapped Within a Wish*—Nathan found more than he bargained for when he came to Havenwood Falls in search of his father's camera, and freeing Amani was only the beginning. Now, they spend time getting to know each other in the town that's become a safe haven, while awaiting the goddess's judgment that will determine Amani and her nefarious sister's fate. Khalida knows her time is limited and everyone adores her sister over her, but she has discovered a way to show them another version of Amani—a version that could possibly destroy them all.

A Pack of Lies by Kallie Ross

Gaby Kasun, alpha of the Kasun Canyon Pack, is responsible for protecting her people and the magical falls hidden in the mountains in the Wild West, but she's struggling to ensure her pack's survival. In 1820, as the pack prepares for winter, Gaby receives a message of hope from an old acquaintance in St. Louis. But when Gaby and her mate Ric arrive at the gussied up, gun-slinging city, they're met with obstacles at every turn. The Creole Elite, a group of tycoons led by Benedicte Trudeau, have other plans for Gaby. She must unravel a pack of lies to save herself and her pack.

LEGENDS OF HAVENWOOD FALLS VOLUME THREE

A LEGENDS OF HAVENWOOD FALLS COLLECTION

BRYNN MYERS   KALLIE ROSS   KATIE M. JOHN

Copyright © 2018 *Emeline* by Katie M. John, *Released From a Curse* by Brynn Myers, *A Pack of Lies* by Kallie Ross, Ang'dora Productions, LLC

All rights reserved.

Published by

Ang'dora Productions, LLC

5621 Strand Blvd, Ste 210

Naples, FL 34110

Havenwood Falls and Ang'dora Productions and their associated logos are trademarks and/or registered trademarks of Ang'dora Productions, LLC.

Cover design by Regina Wamba at MaeIDesign.com

Except as permitted under the U.S. Copyright Act of 1976, no part of this publication may be reproduced, stored in a retrieval system, or transmitted in any form or by any means, electronic, mechanical, photocopying, recording, or otherwise, without written permission of the owner of this book.

Please do not participate in or encourage piracy of copyrighted materials in violation of the author's rights. Purchase only authorized editions.

This book is a work of fiction. Names, characters, and events are either products of the author's imagination or are used fictitiously, and any resemblance to actual persons, living or dead, is entirely coincidental.

LEGENDS OF HAVENWOOD FALLS BOOKS

Lost in Time by Tish Thawer

Dawn of the Witch Hunters by Morgan Wylie

Redemption's End by Eric R. Asher

Trapped Within a Wish by Brynn Myers

Blood and Damnation by Belinda Boring

Fated Beginnings by E.J. Fechenda

Emeline by Katie M. John

Released From a Curse by Brynn Myers

A Pack of Lies by Kallie Ross

Kiss the Ashes by Desiree Lafawn

Hidden Truths by Colleen Nye

War and Retribution by Belinda Boring

Changing Fate by Char Webster

Also try the signature New Adult/Adult series, Havenwood Falls, and the YA series, Havenwood Falls High

Stay up to date at www.HavenwoodFalls.com

EMELINE

BY KATIE M. JOHN

~ A Legends of Havenwood Falls Novella ~

HAVENWOOD FALLS

LEGENDS

EMELINE

KATIE M. JOHN

ALSO BY KATIE JOHN

THE KNIGHT TRILOGY

The Forest of Adventures

Immortal Beloved

The Star Fire Sisterhood

THE MEADOWSWEET CHRONICLES

Witchcraft

Vengeance

Devilry

Angelicus

Haunted

BEAUTIFUL FREAKS

Season 1

To all my author tribe. I couldn't do it without you
xox

CHAPTER 1

SPRING 1913

*I*t's spring, and I'm sitting in the garden with the man I'm going to marry. He's perhaps not the first man you'd think I'd be marrying. We're almost entirely different in every way. He's tall and straight, with dark brooding blue eyes that can read your soul for all its desires, and I'm petite, with snow-blond hair and green eyes that dream of meadows and woodlands and home.

He is witch, and I am fae, and our magic is real, but not entirely compatible. I am the early summer day, and he the storm that follows it. He has the power to destroy me, and I have the power to redeem him. Our love is a battle between the two, and it is fierce and full of passion in a time when passion is a secret activity, executed in brief moments, of crushed velvets and satins against library cases, in smoldering looks in the candlelight, in the touch of leather gloves against my skin. Stolen pleasures. Divine moments.

We are to be married in two months, on the night of a full moon, by the great falls. The ritual will be conducted by a member of the Court of the Sun and the Moon. Then we will be left in the woods as children of Nature, and when we return, we will be man and wife under the eyes of all the gods and goddesses; of Father Sun and Mother Moon, of Holy Creator, and all other universal energies.

We will be married in the humans' church on the following Sunday, for the sake of appearance; me dressed in pure cottons and carrying summer flowers. The town of Havenwood Falls will be there to witness the joining of our two powerful bloodlines. Founding families. The folks from the big houses. Mr. and Mrs. Bishop.

~

"TELL ME OUR STORY AGAIN," I say, resting my head on Dragan's burgundy-velvet-covered shoulder.

He stretches out his legs and crosses them at the ankle, luxuriating in the weak spring sunshine. His smile could melt the sun. His dark blue eyes dance with secrets and promises. They are eyes that threaten to take me to dark places I've only just begun to imagine.

"You really want to hear it again?" he asks, cocking his brow.

I thread my arm through his and push myself closer to him. He smells of rich spices and faraway lands. It is through his stories I have come to love him. Stories of his home, of his magic, of the ravages of war and the terrors of the Ottoman invasions; of his Serbian mother, Anika, who was burned at the stake for being a witch, and his father's return to his native England, where he established a coven in Glastonbury, who worshipped at Stonehenge. And then, the family's flight across the big ocean to the New World on the promise of gold, mountains, and freedom—only the dream fast became a nightmare when the New World started burning their witches like the Old World had.

"I want to hear it all—right from the minute you stepped off the boat," I say, knowing Dragan will not spare the details like my parents do when I ask them about those times.

He's still looking at me with eyes so intense I can almost read him, but not quite. Dragan is dark waters.

"Okay, all of it, but in chapters, and not all today as I have to be somewhere in an hour," he says, taking a deep breath and checking his pocket watch. "Also, maybe a few little omissions." He smirks, making a gesture with his thumb and finger, and in a flash, I see the boy he once was and all the potential for delightful wickedness he holds.

"Yes, perhaps you should leave out the saloon fights and the brothels," I say, trying to shock him with my worldliness. He doesn't rise to the bait. His eyes have already filmed over and he's traveled into the past; a place that I both inhabited and didn't. A time I was both alive and dead, but more on that later.

CHAPTER 2

"We had arrived in New England and made our way a little south, not yet sure where we would settle, for the land was far less hospitable than we had thought it would be. Everything seemed set to push us back out of the country, and we were seriously thinking about returning home to continue our father's coven in England.

"But just as we were about to give up, Rodavan had a vision while scrying that sent us south. We'd find a group of travelers who would lead us to home. I thought the idea was absurd, to go traipsing halfway across the nation on the basis of a vision, but Rodavan was adamant it was our destiny, and when Rodavan gets an idea in his head, there's no shaking it. To be honest, I was more than happy to leave.

"We had made a reasonable amount of money peddling potions and lotions and cure-alls, which in a land of new diseases and poisonous animals, made for rich pickings. We continued to make our way south, me riding our wagon with all of our worldly possessions and Rodavan following with our trade wagon. It made for slow progress, and the sound of rattling bottles soon became maddening.

"By the late 1840s, we had made it as far as Mississippi and were heading toward St. Louis, having heard rumor of other powerful witches and medicine men practicing a form of magic not too dissimilar to our own. It had been a hard journey, but we were used to a life of hardship despite our wealth and privilege. The war back home in Serbia during our childhood had not discriminated, and no amount of money could protect us entirely from the bloodshed.

"Nevertheless, Mississippi was unlike anything we had seen, and it certainly wasn't what we had hoped for when we had traveled to the New World with the hope of making a life in a new land without prejudice.

"When we traveled the banks of the Mississippi, we saw many a rich white man, 'civilized' and finely dressed, whipping his slaves, or placing them in shackles as if they were no more than animals. We were haunted by the songs of African slaves, their magic speaking to our own; their persecution and subjugation a song all too familiar to us —so that although we were different, we were the same.

"The horrors we witnessed in the cotton plantations flanking the river bank were enough to blanch even our hardened souls. Rodavan and I quickly came to the understanding we had swapped one ethnic cleansing horror for another. We were again wondering if we should return to England and see if we could find sanctuary there, when a caravan of wagons approached us.

"There was nothing novel about this. We had seen a great many caravans on our travels. The whole nation was in a flux of settlement and motion, but what was unique about this caravan of wagons was the powerful magic surrounding it. Whoever was coming, they weren't human—and they weren't just witches either."

Dragan pauses with the flair of a practiced storyteller.

"The Old Families?" I ask, knowing this part of the story well. "My mother and father?"

He nods.

"They told us how they had originally come south, with some hopeless hope of freeing some slaves, but the scale of the situation was beyond even their wildest nightmares. The overwhelm, even with their combined magical powers, had been too much. They had done everything they could along the way, petitioning and campaigning anyone who would even half listen, but in doing so, they had made many powerful enemies, who were only too keen to spread vicious rumors that they were a band of Satan-worshipping criminals and outlaws. They had been forced to flee and were now traveling, looking for a place they could finally call their home.

"The hardship of our circumstances meant friendships were made fast and firm with the group. My brother and I were keen to travel to a place where we could settle and make a world of our own, one based on freedom and possibility, one where we could practice our magic and our beliefs without fear. It was a notion that bonded us all deeply."

Dragan stops his narrative, and I look up to see Harriet, our maid, walking toward us with a tray of lemonade and plate of scones in one hand and a collapsible tray table in the other. Dragan removes my hand from his arm, and we straighten up into respectability.

"Your mother thought you might be in need of some refreshment," Harriet explains, putting up the table with a skilled flick of the wrist.

"Thank you, Harriet," I say, smiling.

I see the way she glances at Dragan from under her eyelashes and the blush on her cheek, and I know exactly what she thinks about when she's laying in her bed at night, because they are my thoughts, too.

"Your mother says not to be too much longer," she says. "She needs you to go over some of the menus for the wedding breakfast so we can start planning."

I nod and tell Harriet to assure my mother I'll be in within the hour, but to my disappointment, Dragan has already drunk half a glass of lemonade and is standing.

"Actually, I'm afraid I need to go," he says, checking his pocket watch. I have some business to attend to in town."

"Oh," I say, unable to hide my disappointment.

He sees my smile fall, but doesn't offer any kind of promise or apology. I stand up too and walk him back toward the house, leaving a disgruntled Harriet to gather up the lemonade and tray.

CHAPTER 3

other sits in one of the soft blue velvet chairs in the morning room, the sunlight making her pale hair glisten like spun gold. She is still so beautiful, and I can see why father is still completely captivated by her. He has always loved her. There has never been any doubt.

She looks up when she sees me enter.

"Good morning, Emeline," she says, dropping her eyes back to the pamphlet she is reading. "How was your night?"

"It was good. I slept."

Her head jolts up, and she frowns. "You slept?"

I nod and sit down in the chair opposite her. "Yes, and it feels so good. I feel like new this morning."

She lets out a full sigh, and I can see the worry etched around her eyes. "And you had no problem waking?"

"No."

"This is wonderful news, Emeline."

There's a period of silence as she returns her attention to the pamphlet and I sit, enjoying the way the morning sunlight is falling on my face.

I look over to her and ask, "What really happened to me, Mother?"

She freezes, closing her eyes as she inhales deeply, trying to center herself. "Let's not talk on this," she replies. "Those times are past."

"But I need to know."

She puts down the pamphlet on the side table and picks at imaginary lint on her skirt. "Why, Emeline? What purpose does it serve?"

"Because not knowing is creating a whole host of monsters and quiet fears inside my head."

She swallows, glancing away from me, unable to meet my eyes. I can tell she's trying to decide what to tell me.

"Okay, I'll tell you what you need to know and then you must promise to be satisfied and talk no further on it."

I nod, resigning myself to the idea that is about as good a deal as I'm likely to get. Mother straightens her back and begins with deliberate words.

"It was your sixteenth birthday, a day we had been approaching with dread. You had wanted a party so badly. You were so full of life and the whole world was in the palm of your hand. Do you remember?"

I nod. "I had begged you for a green silk gown," I say.

Mother smiles. "Yes. You were quite set on it. Green has always been your favorite color. It was a big day for you, not only because you were turning sixteen, but because you were in love, too, and I think you hoped that might be the night you finally had your first real taste of love."

This memory brings forward a stab of pain I didn't expect. His name was Jasper, and I had been besotted. We had grown up together, and it had always been meant to be. I had spent months hoping that my birthday party would be the night we shared our first kiss, but then . . .

"I cried the entire night before your birthday," Mother continues, "promising that if somehow you were spared, I would happily take your place. As you know, you had been cursed at birth, it being foretold that on your sixteenth birthday you would ingest a poison that would place you into an endless slumber."

She stops with a sense of finality I'm not willing to accept.

"And the rest of the story?" I ask. "All of this I already know. I want to know the reason for my curse. I want to know what it was that poisoned me."

Mother sniffs. "You were cursed because your father made a terrible mistake—a mistake he has never forgiven himself for."

"What mistake? What did he do?"

She starts to shake her head.

"No, Mama, I need to know," I insist.

The discussion is evidently painful, enough to bring tears to her eyes.

"Before your father met me, he was in love with a girl called Felicity. There was an accident, and she died. Felicity's father was a powerful mage and vowed vengeance on your father. The first daughter your father produced would face a fate worse than death—an eternal slumber that would start on the day of her sixteenth birthday, the age Felicity was when your father killed her."

My heart is pulling tight and my head swimming. I had known there must be some terrible secret to have caused such a vow of vengeance, but my father killing a young girl!

"What happened? How did Felicity die?"

Mother shifts in her chair, her hands knitting together with anxiety.

"It was Christmas and his parents were hosting a party, like they did every year. At some point in the festivities, your father and Felicity had snuck away to be alone together. Her father had grown suspicious when he couldn't find his daughter and had gone looking for her, knowing the two of them were stupidly in love and probably up to no good.

Hearing his approach, they panicked, and your father encouraged Felicity to hide in an oak linen chest, shutting the lid. Felicity's father, on finding your father alone, took the opportunity to give him a serious talking to about his daughter's virtue and warned him that should his daughter be discovered ruined, your father would pay a high price.

Eventually, Felicity's father left, and your father rushed to the chest to release her, only the locking mechanism had triggered, and she was locked in. Your father tried desperately to free her as he listened to the decreasing cries and her desperate thuds. By the time he found the key, hidden on top of the wardrobe, Felicity was dead."

I let out a cry of anguish, tears springing to my eyes. "Poor Felicity. Poor Father! How horrible. I can't imagine. . ."

"Your father set about a period of self-punishment, but it wasn't enough in the eyes of Felicity's father. He wanted your father to feel the grief he felt, and so you were cursed."

We sit in stymied silence, letting the truth wrap around us. My father killed the girl he loved—I can't even begin to imagine the anguish and the suffering—and because of that, we had all suffered.

And no one more than me.

Dragan freed me from my curse just over a year ago. No one understood how hard it was to adjust. They were just happy I had returned, but I'd not only woken into a new world, but a new time.

My last memories from before are of being at the Fae Court on my sixteenth birthday, hoping to kiss the boy I loved. All that was over a hundred years ago. Now, I am in a town full of other supernatural beings, and humans, with their strange technological contraptions and weapons—and I've acquired a sister, Beatrice, who is now my elder sister. The whole thing is enough to send anyone insane.

But thankfully, there is Dragan. He was the first face I'd seen in over a hundred years, and his eyes were so full of love that I held no doubt that regardless of everything, I had found home.

"I think I need to go and get some air," I say, standing and making my way to the French doors and the garden. I need to escape the walls, which suddenly feel like they are sliding inwards.

*D*ragan has missed our usual morning coffee. I have been waiting all day for him to call and it is already late in the afternoon. I'm just about to give up hope, starting to worry something might have happened, when the doorbell rings.

I spring to my feet to answer it before Mother sharply instructs me to sit down and act like a lady, something I often have difficulty with. I straighten my hair and pull my skirts neat, anticipating his arrival any moment. When his brother walks in, my heart skips a beat, and I know immediately something is wrong.

"Good evening, Roseline," he says, reaching out for my mother's hand to give the customary kiss. "Emeline."

"Is Dragan well?" I ask, skipping the formalities.

"He is the reason for my call."

My hand flies to my heart space, preparing myself for bad news. "What's happened? Is he hurt?"

"There was a situation in town earlier. A brawl broke out in the saloon when a game went south. Dragan got caught in the action and was knocked out cold when he got hit on the head with a chair."

"Oh, my goodness," Mother exclaims. "How shocking."

My heart begins to settle when I see Rodavan break into a smile.

"He's fine, Roseline. His ego is hurt more than his head. However, the doctor said he had to rest up for a couple of days."

"But he's going to be okay?" I ask, still panicked.

Rodavan nods. "He's going to be fine. He's sent me round to ask permission for Emeline to go and see him for a couple of hours. He's feeling a little sorry for himself. I'm very happy to chaperone her."

Mother is uneasy. She and Father have been quite clear about the boundaries when it comes to their daughters spending time alone with gentlemen, even those whom they are due to marry.

"And you will be accompanying her?" she asks for confirmation.

Rodavan nods. "You have my word I'll keep her safe, Roseline."

I'm blushing, not able to quite believe that my mother and future brother-in-law are so openly discussing the protection of my virtue.

"She must be back before eight," she says eventually. "Her father will be home shortly afterwards, and I don't want him to come home and find her out."

"Certainly."

I've already stood, ready to go when Rodavan asks me if I need to prepare. I shake my head.

"I just need to get my coat, and I'm ready," I say, keen to get to Dragan's and see for myself that he is all right.

The walk to Dragan's house with Rodavan is strange. It's a little difficult to know what to talk about, so we pass the ten-minute walk talking about the weather and various town news, like the new statue they are putting up in the gardens in the town square. It's causing quite a stir. Everything seems to cause a stir at the moment.

When we arrive, Rodavan tells me he'll come back to collect me in a couple of hours. I turn to him, surprised he's leaving me after his promises to Mother. He's taking a little too much joy in my anxiety.

"Just push the door," he instructs, waving me on with his hand. "Dragan has dropped the ward."

I stand at the bottom of the imposing stairs looking at the large oak door, with its Green Man door knocker. Butterflies flutter in my stomach. I look back at Rodavan, who smiles with encouragement.

"You'll be fine, Emeline. He's in no fit state to be a rogue, and besides, you're practically married already." He chuckles.

I take the first step with hesitation and then skip up the rest of them, my heartbeat increasing with each step, and slip in through the door.

His house is the perfect mirror of him. It's all solid wood, dark rich colors, and full of shadows.

"Emeline?" I hear him call from a room on the right.

I follow his voice and find him in the library. We have an impressive library, but it's nothing compared to Dragan's, which is large enough to fit two overstuffed leather chesterfields as well as a large imposing desk and work table. It smells of him, and my blood quickens at the scent.

"You survived your bar brawl then?" I say, smiling.

He's reclined on one of the sofas, dressed in navy silk house pants and a dark green velvet dressing gown. He's not wearing a shirt, and I can't take my eyes off his exposed sculpted chest, which is decorated with several tattoos. Most are symbols, but above his heart space is an owl in flight. I bite down on my lip with sparked appetite. The room suddenly feels very warm, and he's examining me, curious about the unexpected results he's elicited in me.

"Do you see something you like, Emeline?" he teases, slowly pulling at the cord of his gown and causing it to fall open further, exposing the tops of his hips. I'm caught in the doorway, my throat constricting with desire.

"I thought you were incapacitated?" I say.

"I am. I'm terribly injured. The doctor said I might not even make it through the night," he says, smiling wickedly.

"Did he now?"

"Maybe I just need some really attentive nursing?"

I'm trying to keep a straight face, but I can't help the grin that sneaks across my face.

"Dragan," I scold, sitting primly on the opposite sofa. "You can get all those impure thoughts out of your head right now. I'm going to sit right here, and I might, if you're lucky, make you a cup of sweet

English tea and place a blanket over you. You're in danger of catching a chill from overexposure."

He laughs. "Actually, I think it's gotten quite hot in here, don't you think?"

I press my lips and raise my brow at him. "Clearly that knock to your head was harder than we first thought. It's made you crazy. Cover yourself up, or I'm leaving. I can't concentrate—and you're meant to be resting."

He pulls the folds of his gown together and ties it loosely, knowing it's still leaving just enough visible to keep me on the edge of preoccupation.

"How do you feel? Do you have a headache?" I ask.

He shakes his head. "Rodavan gave me a little something to take the edge off."

"So you're feeling quite well, then!"

"Hmm," he says, pulling his lips between his teeth as he's thinking. "I have an idea," he says, standing.

"You're meant to be resting," I say, seeing the cut on the side of his head properly for the first time. "You look pale."

"I told you, it's serious. I might not make it," he says, extending his hand out, inviting me to stand, "which is why I have decided to seize the day. Carpe diem!"

I resist him as long as possible, but I know he's going to kiss me, an invitation that is almost impossible to refuse. I stand, bashfully turning my eyes away from him, because I'm scared of the power he has over me, of the way he makes me feel. His finger strokes the side of my cheek, soothing me.

"We're behind closed doors here, Emeline. In our own world, where we are king and queen. We can do as we please."

He places his finger under my chin and lifts my face so that my eyes meet his. "You don't need to hide your desires from me."

"We are not yet married," I say, trying to find reason amongst the encroaching madness.

"A kiss isn't going to corrupt your soul, if you worry about such things. You can't get pregnant from a kiss," he says, his other hand holding my waist. "Trust me to look after you, Emeline."

I offer the slightest nod, and he moves closer, his hot breath on my lips. His lips touch mine for the briefest of moments before returning again. Teasing, tempting, inviting me to respond, even if I don't quite know how to. He places his hand behind my head, and my hands fly up, pressing against his chest to brace myself, my fingers tracing the soft down across his muscles. Then it's as if he unlocks me, and I'm pressing forward as he pushes back, his lips crushing mine, his tongue deliciously invading my mouth, filling it with hot muscle and intent—intent to steal all the air from my lungs and leave me swooning under his spell.

His hand slips down from my waist and cups my bottom, stroking it, pulling me closer so that there is no space between us, and my body and his body are separated by only the thinnest pieces of fabric.

"Stop," I gasp. "I can't take any more."

He laughs against my lips, enjoying the results of his labors, then he steps back, taking both my hands in his as he falls onto the sofa, pulling me with him so that I topple and only save myself by slamming my hand into the back of it.

"What are you doing?" I ask, giggling as loosened strands of my hair fall over my face. I will have to fix my neat chignon before I leave, or Mother will be alarmed.

He pushes back into the sofa. "I'm resting, like you told me to," he says.

I smile and look at the sparkle in his eyes as he pats the space beside him.

"Sit with me," he says, indicating I should lie down beside him. I sit on the edge of the sofa, and he pulls me backwards.

"Put your feet up. Relax. Make yourself at home."

His arm is around me, and I'm held in a crook, my head leaning against his shoulder, feeling soft velvets, silk, and firm skin. He places his chin on top of my head, and his fingers trace circles on my hand, sending skitters up my skin. We're quiet for a while, relishing the sensation of such close intimacy, and for a moment, I think maybe

Dragan has fallen asleep. I turn my head under him and see that he is awake, his eyes dreamily staring out the window.

"I could stay like this forever," I say quietly, not wanting to break the spell. It feels like we are a million miles away from real life.

"When we are married, we can do this every day," he says.

I snort. "Won't the servants mind?"

"They're paid not to mind."

I fall quiet for a moment, deciding whether or not to tell him what went between Mother and me, and the story behind my curse. Not yet, I decide. Not until we are married.

"Will you continue our story?" I ask. "We were up to the part where the Hungarian Hunters had been defeated and the Luna Coven established."

"Ah, yes," he says, leaning his head against the back of the sofa. "The Luna Coven and our hopes of finding a home we could call our own."

"And my picture?" I ask. "What did you learn about my portrait?"

"I knew your mother was sad, even though she tried hard to hide it amongst the busy activity of mothering your brothers, which was no easy task when undertaking such a journey. However, there was always a sense she was about to set one more place at the supper table, or that she was waiting for one more child to fall into line. She'd have this way of hesitating before closing a door behind her, as if ever hopeful, by some trick of time, that her missing child would come bounding out. I'm not sure the others noticed it so much, but there was something about her melancholy I found inexplicably curious, and really rather beautiful.

"Several times, I had observed her nursing a small doll, the fabrics of the dress worn thin with time and tender touches. Each time I had prepared to ask her about it, I saw the warning flash in her eyes—there was something slightly savage in them. Grief can do that to you.

"We were on a particularly hostile stretch of the trail when the wheel came off their wagon, one of many trying incidents along that section of the journey. We all did everything we could to help. The motion of the sudden de-wheeling caused the wagon to pitch wildly, and it careened toward the edge of a small gully, tipping with the threat of sliding. Only fast-acting magic prevented it from crashing all the way to the bottom and taking the horses and your family with it.

"With time and motion stopped, we managed to combine forces and stabilize the wagon, but not before several items had started their gravitational journey downward. Rodavan's quick casting of a suspension spell meant everything was saved, although we had to work quickly to pull the objects back to safety. As Rodavan, Thorne, and Judson worked on getting the wagon back onto the trail, it was left to me to summon the objects from their perilous suspension and into my hands, the last of which was a cloth-wrapped painting. As the painting traveled toward me, the movement loosened the strings and caused the cloth to fall away. By the time I clasped it between my hands, my heart had stopped.

"The painting was of a young woman, the beauty of which I had never seen. She was so exquisite that at first I thought it must be a painting of an angel."

His head lowers so that his lips are right by my ear, his breath sending shivers over my neck. His voice quiets and thickens.

"In that very moment, I knew . . ."

"Knew what?" I ask, turning to him.

"That I had to have you," he says, planting the softest of kisses on my stretched neck and sending another wave of sensations through me that travels right down to my toes.

"To this day," he continues, "I can't work it out. It was as if I had been placed under some kind of powerful charm. Your mother came hurrying over to me, weeping with relief.

"'Emeline,' she whispered through her sobs. That was the first time I had heard your name, and it etched upon my heart. I watched in a kind of shock as Roseline snatched the painting from me and held it to her body, embracing it. I can't tell you the loss I felt at the sensation of my empty arms. It was then I understood just a fraction of your mother's grief, and the fact the painting was imbued with an extraordinary level of dark magic, which disconnected entirely with the purity of your image.

"I knew the painting was somehow cursed, and I spent the hours afterward in a kind of tempest of thoughts and emotions."

"Did she ever tell you how I came to be cursed?" I ask.

Dragan shakes his head. "Do you know why?"

I can't force the lie out of my mouth, so instead, I shake my head and hope that will be enough for him. Emotion is welling up inside of me. She must have hated my father, I think. To have paid such a price for his stupidity. And yet, in the year since my waking, I had never suspected they didn't love each other with full hearts.

"She carried me for all that time and for all that way," I say. "Never letting harm come to me." I find it remarkable we should have all survived such a journey. "She never gave up on me."

"No one could ever give up on you, Emeline."

CHAPTER 5

A lot of people in Havenwood Falls are a little afraid of Dragan and his brother. They're an enigma and a bundle of contradictions. The Bishops are so ingrained in the history of Havenwood Falls, and so intimately connected with the founding families, that they're long beyond public criticism or mistrust, but there's something about them that makes people gossip concerns in low voices.

I understand it. Dragan cuts a foreboding presence. His Eastern European aristocratic features inherited from his mother, and his British reserve from his father, create a sense of something not entirely familiar. His dress is on the edge of luxurious and always impeccable. He is a man with exacting standards, which often makes others feel inadequate. He exudes a latent power that people can feel like subtle vibrations. It is this power that makes my toes tingle and my stomach flutter.

His brother Rodavan is a respected member of the Court of the Sun and the Moon, as well as being a leader of the Luna Coven. I think Dragan holds a certain amount of admiration for the way Rodavan has managed to politically position himself in both the human and supernatural world of Havenwood Falls.

Dragan may, in many ways, be the prince to his kingly brother, but his monstrously large house and his not-so-secret and very exclusive private supper club, which he holds on the last Friday of every month, have made him a powerful figure in his own right. I don't know much about Dragan's supper club, but from what little I've managed to extract from him, I know it is more like a small coven, which also welcomes some of the richest and most influential humans who align themselves with a more pagan world view, as well as some of the fringe supernaturals.

I also know Rodavan and Dragan are in conflict about it. I've noted the way Rodavan bristles every time it is mentioned, and seen the look of disapproval in his eye. I don't think Rodavan likes the idea of a splinter coven, especially not one that muddles the ground between human and supes, which is what the supernaturals have become known as.

However, despite these differences, the brothers are close, and Roman, Rodavan's son, looks up to his Uncle Dragan with a level of admiration that is borderline hero worship. Like Dragan, Roman is a character formed of shades.

I'm seated with Dragan, Rodavan, Roman, and my sister and brother-in-law in the library of Fairchild Mansion, waiting for a party of Father's guests to arrive. My father likes a busy house, full of interesting people.

He has spent the day hosting an old friend, whom he met somewhere during the early stages of their journey from New England. The man is a scientist who specializes in the use of electrical energy to bring spirits forward from the afterlife and also to supercharge natural energies in the environment. His name is Professor Gleinheart, and he's agreed to give a short talk and demonstration to Father's friends later this afternoon.

Father has invited half the town in his enthusiasm, and Mother has been worrying all day about how we are going to fit all the guests into the reception room. Dragan is unusually animated with excitement, which has caused more than a few glances of entertainment from his brother.

"Have you met this Professor Gleinheart before?" Dragan asks, his eyes twinkling.

I shake my head. "No, but I know he and Father have been corresponding since they met, when Professor Gleinheart was a young man just out of the University of Oxford, in England. He was already making quite a name for himself because of his work with energy sources."

Dragan nods sagely. "Won't he think it strange that after all these years, your father still looks the same?"

"People see what they want to see, especially when it comes to fae folk," Beatrice, my sister, says. "We have the glamour, don't forget."

I have never been close to my sister. She was born whilst I was sleeping and seemed to resent the fact that I came back to life and ruined her only-daughter status. However, Mother adores her and has struggled since she moved out after the wedding.

Dragan smiles directly at me. "So, do I see you as I want to see you, Emeline, or as you really are?"

I sip my tea, looking at him over the rim of my cup, buying myself time to answer his question. "When you're in love," I say, "you only ever see what you want to see. Love is its own glamour."

Father comes bustling in, flapping his hands about and giving directions, clearly confusing us for a bunch of willing volunteers. For some reason, he tells Dragan and me to remain behind. I exchange looks with Dragan, who is clearly as bemused as I am. When the library is empty, he looks to me and shrugs, and we share a quiet, nervous laughter. My father's behavior is becoming increasingly eccentric.

Now that we are alone, Dragan's eyes darken and stare into mine, his teeth pressing into his lips mischievously. They are lips I have kissed. Lips I have gently bit and pulled between my teeth. Lips I have momentarily bruised with blood rush.

"I can hear your thoughts," he says.

I look to the door and listen hard to the distant, busy household as I begin to slowly unbutton the pearl buttons of my striped cotton dress one . . . by . . . one, taking my time, teasing him.

Dragan sits back in the chair, his eyes barely blinking, his hand stroking his chin with both appreciation and agitation. I've taken to purposely not wearing a shift or camisole underneath my boned dress in order that I can tease Dragan like this, in fleeting, secret moments, knowing it gives me a kind of power that can match his, if only for a moment or two. His tongue darts over his bottom lip, and his nose wrinkles. He's doing his best to keep control, but the heat is rising in him, causing a blush on his cheeks.

When footsteps approach, I hurriedly button my dress up, and Dragan sits bolt upright in the chair, crossing and then uncrossing his legs and looking distinctly uncomfortable. I flash him a victory smile, and he coughs with poorly concealed embarrassment when my father returns, by which time, I am demurely drinking tea and Dragan has repositioned his angle in the chair to utilize a well-placed cushion.

My father is wily and can feel the energy in the air. He scans the room but can't see any evidence of misdemeanor and so is forced to ignore his instincts. He clears his throat before asking, "Dragan, Emeline—I have a slightly delicate matter to discuss with you, and I'm sorry that I haven't had a chance to approach this with more warning."

Dragan flicks me a look, and I can tell he is concerned our increasingly bold behavior has been noted.

"What is it, Father?" I ask as innocently as I can.

He looks between the two of us with rising agitation, and I'm just about to blurt out a full confession when Dragan flashes me a warning look, telling me not to say anything.

"It's a somewhat delicate matter surrounding the history of your curse," my father explains, "and I'm not sure if Dragan is aware of all the details—I know your mother spoke with you about it a few days ago?"

I nod, slowly placing my teacup down. Of all the things I thought he was going to discuss with us, this wasn't one of them.

"I haven't had a chance to discuss this with Dragan," I say, glancing at him.

Father nods. "Well, being as Dragan was instrumental in breaking the curse on our family, and that he is soon to be your husband, I think it is only right he is party to the following discussion. As you know, Gleinheart has discovered a pioneering way to use electrical charges in order to manipulate energies and electro-magnetic fields in the paranormal realm. Spirits are able to use this energy to manifest and come forward to interact in a sentient manner with the living. To speak to us from beyond the grave."

Like a blinding flash of light, realization sparks in my mind. My father's obsession with Gleinheart and his experiments, all those years of detailed and lengthy correspondence, it's all to do with Felicity, the girl he loved and killed.

"Felicity!" I whisper. "You want to reach out to Felicity, don't you?"

Dragan looks to me for clarification. "Who is Felicity?"

My father knits his hands together. "Felicity is the girl I killed. We were to be married."

Dragan's eyes widen with shock. "You killed your fiancée?"

Father nods, and the pain and sorrow that emerge in his eyes are enough to make me want to spring from my seat and hold him, but I don't. There is a strange energy running between my father and Dragan.

"It was a terrible accident," my father mutters. "A moment of stupidity, which I have regretted every day of my life since."

"And it was her father who was the mage who cursed your blood?" Dragan asks, connecting all the pieces. "Why didn't you tell me this when we were working on breaking the spells?"

"I was ashamed to tell you," my father says. "I'd hoped to keep that particularly ugly part of my history a secret. However, it's been increasingly evident Emeline is not the kind of woman to settle for half-truths."

I can't help but feel a level of accusation in his voice, and I don't like it. None of this is my fault, and furthermore, I don't like the idea that now some potentially vengeful angry ghost is going to be brought into our home.

"Grief and anger turned her father mad with vengeance," my father explains. "He didn't care that my daughter was innocent. He knew cursing her was the worst possible punishment he could execute on me."

Dragan shakes his head as he clasps his chin. The information that has just been imparted has visibly rocked him.

"And you want Gleinheart to connect you with the spirit of Felicity for what purpose?"

"To ask her forgiveness. To find peace. To tell her that she's never been forgotten. That I loved her, and a part of me always will."

The room is spinning with emotion. Dragan's energy has shifted from one of excitement to one of caution and suspicion.

"I'm not sure about this, sir," Dragan says, taking to his feet. "I fear it's inviting something into this situation we shouldn't. What if she doesn't forgive you? What if this enables her to exact her own revenge? What if Gleinheart brings her forward and she refuses to go back, haunting you, the house, or Emeline? If her father was a mage, then that same magic ran through her—maybe still does."

Father shakes his head. "This is why I have waited so long. I wanted to make sure Gleinheart was secure in his knowledge and practice."

"And what of her father? We've ensured the wards created by the Luna Coven will protect Emeline from him as long as she remains in Havenwood Falls. The protection spells are secure, but nevertheless, messing with this kind of energy—we don't know what the consequences will be, and with all due respect, this feels too dark a magic."

"So are you refusing my request to bring her forward?" Father asks.

"I'm saying, I'd like some time to think about this," Dragan replies, "and to discuss the matter with Emeline, on our own. Does the Luna Coven know of your intentions with bringing Felicity back from the realm of the dead?"

My father shakes his head.

Dragan sighs heavily. "They should know. My brother should know."

"They may stop me."

"Perhaps with good cause," Dragan says. "And if they don't stop you, and this goes wrong—you may be exiled or . . . worse."

"I've thought carefully about all of that. I can't live the rest of my life with this not put to rest, always living in fear that our own magic might fade and Emeline returns to sleeping—or what if there's something in our blood now, and your own daughters suffer the same fate?"

Dragan glances at me. "Is that even a possibility? Surely that's all just supposition, sir. We're protected here in Havenwood Falls. We broke the enchantments on Emeline. I think you are acting out of unnecessary fear and putting us all in danger as a result."

"We don't have to pursue this avenue tonight. I'll give you time to think about it," my father says, heading toward the door of the library. Before he goes, he adds, "I honestly believe this is a way for us to make good the situation once and for all."

When he is gone, Dragan turns to me, his eyes wide with concern. "Your father has lost his mind!"

My eyes fall to my knees. I don't know what to say. The whole situation is wrong, and I really don't think Father's plan will bring us peace.

"You agree the Luna Coven must know of this, don't you, Emeline?" Dragan says gravely.

I nod, knowing I'm betraying my father. "You should speak with Rodavan," I say without conviction. "He will know what to do."

Tears spring to my eyes, and Dragan leans across the space between us, placing his hand on my knee. "I'll make it all right, Emeline. I promise."

CHAPTER 6

*T*he demonstration is a success, and those not invited to the supper afterward leave chattering excitedly. Electricity is still a new and magical thing. The members of the Luna Coven are clearly impressed with the potential this might hold, although they've had to hold it together in order to conceal their true nature from the humans who are also there.

I attempt to follow the men into the dining room, but the door is shut in my face with no attempt to protect my feelings. Father isn't even going to enter into discussion—especially not in front of the coven and members of the Court of the Sun and the Moon.

I'm expected to join Mother, but the thought of spending the evening contained in a room with her fills me with a mild dread. Instead, I head up the stairs toward my own room and hope I can get away with spending some time on my own. I have no other intention than indulging in daydreams about Dragan and working in my sketch book.

It's not long before there is a knock on the door. It is Harriet, our maid. She has been sent by Mother to discover where I am. I tell her I have a headache, the result of too much excitement from the demonstration. Harriet nods and retreats out the door backwards. She knows my mother is going to be displeased that she has failed in her task to extract me from my room; I give it half an hour before Mother comes to check on me herself.

I'm sitting in the window seat overlooking the street, sketching an image of Dragan that is carved into my memory. I'm trying to capture that look in his eye, the one that is both spellbinding and a little cruel. It's like trying to capture the latent energy of some big cat or predator. Pride, violence, justice, and natural order. Supremacy.

My room is above the dining room, where my father is hosting. Every now and then, I catch the faintest trace of words floating up, but they don't fully form, bursting like bubbles before they reach me. I can pick out Dragan's voice, and this only adds to my frustration. I put the sketch pad down and head out of my room, sneaking along the corridor to the small door at the end, which leads to the attic. It had originally been designed as the living quarters for staff, but given our magical status, Mother prefers the staff to live away from the home, with their own families. It makes them less curious about ours.

I often sneak up to the space at the top of the house, far away from the gilded opulence of the other floors; it is like playing in my very own playhouse. Over the years, I've snuck in pillows and other small items, and it is nice to have a space of my own. Soon I will be mistress of Dragan's house, and it will all be mine, a thought that is a little overwhelming.

The other reason I love this space is because it's the only place I can stretch out my wings, something Mother discourages, as they're no longer really necessary. They're a relic from our ancestors. I undo my buttons and slip my dress to a puddle on the floor, relishing the feeling of cool air washing over my skin.

I turn my face to the ceiling and close my eyes, bringing forth my wings. The feeling is one of immense release. I look at the vision of me captured in the reflection of the window and watch as I move them back and forth, seeing how the almost translucent colors flicker, more like a series of lights, glimmering.

I inhale and exhale, inhale and exhale, willing my wings the power to lift me off the floor. I've been trying for months, and I know it's only a matter of mind over matter—that if I believe I can do it, I will.

I open my eyes as my toes rise to the tips and I'm connected to the earth by just the smallest point. I flap my wings faster, knowing I need to get the air just right to lift. I close my eyes again, willing power from the depths of my solar plexus, and then I can feel the slightest shift of sensation in my feet. Light. Free. I open my eyes and dare to glance down to find myself hovering about five inches off the ground. The will breaks, and I thud back down to the floor, turning my ankle and ending up in a heap on the floor. I cuss the only word I know, learned from Harriet, but my concern is quickly replaced by the overwhelming sensation of accomplishment. I've done it. My wings were strong enough to carry me. I was able to fly.

I gather my dress and hold it over me, seeking warmth, still in shock. Already, I'm beginning to think maybe I imagined it. I think about trying again, but I'm too exhausted, and I don't want to fail and extinguish the elation I feel.

"Tomorrow," I say, standing and dressing before returning to my room.

I WAKE AT DAWN, when the house is quiet, and sneak back up to my attic sanctuary. I'm like a child on Christmas morning, surging with excited energy. I want to see how easy it is to bring forth my wings when I'm dressed—to see the extent of my fae magic. It's been building inside of me—I can feel it—and I'm sure it has something to do with my move toward adulthood, triggered by Dragan. I have this new kind of effervescent energy, a sense of endless possibility.

Suddenly, my wings erupt, not caring about the mortal inconvenience of human restrictions. I smile. Somehow this eruption felt more powerful and determined than last night's, as if I am starting to take ownership of them. I close my eyes, reach on my tiptoes, and the knowledge that I know I can fly is all it takes to make it happen. I'm laughing as I'm forced to reach out my hand to stop my head from bumping into the ceiling. Tears of pure joy are streaming down my face. I'm free. Truly free at last. The curse of entrapment is beginning to fall away. All those painful, terrible memories of being caught between the waking and the non-waking world—living in a world of shadows and endless corridors, always running to get back to the living world—are slowly fading with my new glory.

A cough from behind me causes me to drop to the floor, but unlike yesterday, I keep my balance. It's Mother.

"What exactly are you doing?" she asks.

I resist telling her that her question is a little ridiculous as she's clearly just witnessed *exactly what I am doing*. I'm still grinning, refusing to believe she'll be anything other than pleased and proud, but the look in her eye is thunderous.

"You must never do that again," she says in a voice so cold that it doesn't even sound like her.

"But—" I begin to protest.

"No," she says, cutting me off. "I mean it, Emeline. You need to stop that—today."

"Why?" I ask, genuinely not understanding.

We live in Havenwood Falls, a sanctuary, a place we are meant to be able to embrace our supernatural powers, and although we must be careful to conceal them from the humans who have found their way to our town, we are meant to live in a home where we do not need to be ashamed of them. So why do I feel so ashamed?

"I don't understand," I say, my emotions quickly sliding toward tears. "What's wrong with my wings? They're a part of me."

Her look softens, and I can see she's battling some internal conflict. She's approaching me with her hands extended in invitation, to connect, woman to woman. She shakes her head.

"Emeline, please, you have to trust me on this," she pleads.

"How can I trust what I don't know?"

She inhales deeply. "Your wings are traces of your ancient magic. Most fae have lost their wings—evolved, so to speak. Their magic has manifested in other ways. After all, what use are wings in a world where you can't use them?"

Her argument is strong and full of reason, but it feels so wrong, so against how my body and soul are telling me it should be.

"But the ability to fly, Mama—it's such a gift, and we've thrown it away for the sake of . . . what? For fear of persecution for what we really are? Shouldn't our kind have fought for the right to be accepted?"

My mother laughs, and it's both gentle and sharp as a knife edge. "The world isn't like that, Emeline. You were sleeping for so long that the world changed and you didn't."

I take a moment to let her words sink in and to study her. Finally, I pluck up enough courage to ask her, "Do you still have your wings?"

My mother's look turns steely. "I'm not prepared to discuss this any further, Emeline. My instruction is clear. You are to put all thoughts of this . . . situation from your mind."

"But what if I can't control—"

"Then learn to, like we all did," she snaps, turning on her heel and leaving the room.

I'm left with the feeling of having been doused in humiliation. How can I simply forget I have such beautiful wings, or the sensation of unbridled freedom when my feet leave the ground? She can't make me just ignore them.

I flop into the chair in the corner of the room and try to hold in the storm of emotions swirling inside. I'm so angry. No, more than that. I'm enraged. I'm so sick of being held in the bonds of other people's expectations and notions of what is right and proper. I want to be me. All me. I want to love the man I love, and stretch my wings without fear of shame and punishment. I am fae. I am magical. I am supernatural. I do not have to adhere to the rules and lore of the human world. This is our home. Our Havenwood Falls. Our sanctuary, and it's the place I should be free to be who I am.

CHAPTER 7

The next day, I sit again in our library with Dragan. We had planned to take tea in the garden, but it is raining. I'm so tired of our courting being restricted to the garden and the library. It feels like we are just passing time until our wedding. I can't wait to get out more, to have more adventure. I feel so bound, and I know Dragan feels the same.

"The weather is so dreary," he says, staring out the window.

"Finish our story," I say.

He looks at me and cocks his head, his eyes sparking with some new mischief.

"We have a score to settle first," he says, standing and taking my hand.

I'm trembling with anticipation as he walks me toward the windows and then suddenly pushes me forcefully against the wall behind the open door, so that we are concealed. I gasp. I'm not sure if I'm inflamed or afraid.

"What you did, yesterday," he says grabbing my hands and lifting them above my head, pinning me to the wall with one strong hand, "that little trick with your buttons . . ." His other hand is cupped around my breast, his breath hot on the nape of my neck. "Was cruel and insubordinate. I won't stand for such brazen behavior."

He squeezes my breast, his mouth slamming into mine, his tongue stabbing into my mouth, his thumb grazing back and forth over the fabric of my dress until I'm dissolving in a space between the hard wall and his hard body. His kiss is full of violent delights, and when he breaks away from it, I strain like a tethered animal, desperate for him not to stop. Every part of my body is responding with need and desire. The room is spinning. His thumb grazes over my swollen lips, and he slips it into my eager mouth. I look up at him under my lashes, challenging him to try and take control back, because I know all this is nothing more than a pantomime of his power, and it is I—in this young and strong, healthy body, full of fertile energy—who holds it all.

He lets out a soft moan, releasing me from his grip and removing his thumb, kissing me deeply again before suddenly leaving the room.

When he is gone, I lean back against the wall, my chest heaving up and down with the exhilaration. I listen to his footsteps receding down the corridor as he makes his way to the downstairs water closet. I giggle at the thought of what might happen if we were to be caught in such a manner. My finger brushes over my bruised and stinging lips, delighting in the sensation. I close my eyes and try to calm the beating of my heart.

Part of me wishes it could always be like this; full of tantalizing anticipation, stolen moments and rule-breaking. I worry that when he can have all of me, he'll either no longer want me or he'll want too much of me, and the thought of either both terrifies and excites me.

I'm standing by the French windows, looking out across the gardens, when I hear him return to the room and come to stand by my side. There is still a slight blush on his cheeks, but his usual composure has returned.

"Emeline," he whispers quietly. "Do you know how wild you make me?"

I don't look at him but nod with certainty and satisfaction. "You were going to tell me the next chapter of our story. You had just seen the painting of me for the first time."

He sniffs, and I glance at him before returning my eyes to the garden, ready to listen.

~

"YOUR MOTHER HAD CHOSEN to carry your painting with her above all her other worldly treasures—and from that first, quick glance, I understood why. It was a potently magical and wondrous thing.

"Before I could ask if I could look on it again, she had hurried away with it, and it was as if it had been nothing more than a figment of my imagination. When I asked about it later that evening, she changed the subject at every attempt, and in the end, it was clear the subject was closed.

"We had been traveling with the caravan for about a year. It had been a long year, full of trials and tribulations. We were all tired, and it was clear the group was beginning to crack. There were too many individuals used to being in charge of their own destiny and who were now forced into some collective; it was a struggle for most of us. The only ones who really seemed to thrive were the fae, for they had been more used to living a community-focused life.

"The tensions that had already started to emerge were not helped with the arrival of the Blackstone witch hunters, whom we met in Missouri late in the winter of 1851. I didn't like the energy they brought with them. Marie Blackstone was a hunter, sister to Dante Blackstone, who had made it his mission to eradicate all witches.

"It was clear from day one that Marie did not like us, the Bishop family, and the feeling was mutual. I was very set against them joining our group, although not as set as Rodavan. He was furious that the rest of the party were even giving them the time of day. Marie Blackstone had the ability to sniff out dark magic, and it was evident she perceived our craft to be in that category."

"But it's not . . . is it?" I ask, unable to hide the hitch in my voice.

Dragan flashes me a look that turns my blood cold and my cheeks hot. "Emeline," he says gravely, "you know our craft slightly differs from that of the other witches. You know how we believe in the universal balance, of the sacred dependency between the light and the dark, how neither can exist without the other, how with the absence of one is the absence of other. Winter and summer, night and day, heat and cold. I'm tired enough of having to constantly defend our systems to the Court; I don't want to have to do that with you—is that understood?"

I nod shamefully. "Of course. Sorry."

He nods sharply, accepting my apology. "And besides, do you honestly think that pernicious meddler, Marie Blackstone, would let the practice of dark magic go unpunished?" He sighs heavily. "Some days, I really wish Rodavan had made good his pledge to shove her off a ravine."

There's a pout on Dragan's lips that makes me smile. Marie Blackstone is a nuisance. Even Father, who is tolerant to the point of fault, finds her immensely tiresome.

I want to kiss him. I can feel the heat of his body. The scent of him clings to the air around us. Instead, I reach out my fingers, and when they touch his, he weaves them through mine and turns to smile at me.

"I love you, Emeline," he says. "I always will."

The rain finally stopped early this morning, and now the sun is burning up the gray. It's going to be a beautiful early summer day.

When I hear the doorbell ring, I run to the door and throw it open, knowing by the chime of the clock that it will be Dragan, who has come for his morning coffee and walk around the garden, a pattern that defines our entire courting ritual.

Father has been ridiculously strict about this because he does not entirely trust Dragan to guard my virtue, and Mother has been no support because she's convinced I'll happily assist Dragan ruining me. What woman wouldn't?

So, it is with surprise that I see Dragan smile at my mother and ask if he might take me out for a walk to see the alpine flowers that have sprung on the mountain rock in the last few weeks. The morning is beautiful, and the intent sounds harmless enough.

Father isn't in, which means Mother has to make this monumental decision herself, and I know part of the answer will be based on her calculations of the possibility of Dragan taking advantage of me, and whether or not getting pregnant at this stage might ruin the hang of my wedding dress. I sigh and roll my eyes.

"Mother, please, we're to be wed in just weeks," I say, helping her out with the math.

Reluctantly, she nods, and I feel a little pang of guilt for playing so innocently when I know Dragan and I have a habit of falling into scandalous behavior at every opportunity.

I'm already putting on my leather button-up boots and am out the door before she can change her mind, dragging Dragan by the elbow in an usual display of power reversal. He notes my exuberant mood and flicks an eyebrow at me in question.

"Everything all right?" he asks suspiciously. "You seem a little . . . excitable."

I laugh. "Yes, I'm fine. It's a beautiful morning, and we're free for a few hours."

We're walking along the street, and Dragan is doing his best to maintain his usual stately gait and pace, but I'm bounding around like a puppy, hardly able to contain my joy in this moment.

"People are starting to look, Emeline. Can you . . . just fall into line a little?" he asks, gently but firmly pushing his arm through my elbow and slowing me down.

"We're going to the mountains, so why are we walking like folks heading to church?" I ask.

"Because we are in town," he explains, "and town is different."

Yes, town *is* different. We'd almost slipped into the terrible mistake of making Havenwood Falls just another American settler town. It could have been different, but Dragan and my mother are right—what people think in a town like this is important, a matter of survival, of reputation and power.

I pull my back up straight and fix my social grin, waving demurely at Mrs. Augustine, who is out on her front porch, pruning roses in an impeccable new blue cotton dress. She always looks so perfectly put together, her light brown hair tied back in some chic French style.

The Augustines are founding elders of the Luna Coven. There are smaller covens in our community, who share religious and philosophical beliefs—covens such as the one Dragan runs, although he denies it is a coven. There is also church for the humans. The most influential church, the Havenwood Falls Church, has a minister who is very aware of the supernatural world and those who inhabit it. He had formerly spent a lifetime fighting the darker elements as an exorcist and, after being exiled from the Catholic Church, was drawn here.

"Where are we going?" I ask, suddenly falling out of my daydream to realize we are walking the wrong way for a mountain walk.

"Home?"

"But I thought . . ." I say, frowning. "Have I displeased you? Are we going back? I'm sorry if I've made you uncomfortable."

His mouth twists in an unfamiliar smile. "You misunderstand, Emeline," he says, lowering his voice. "We're going to our home."

We walk a few more blocks and turn down the road toward Dragan's mansion.

"Won't people see?"

"Not if you don't draw attention to us," he gently scolds.

I notice how he's picked up his pace a little.

"But what if . . ." I begin. My mind is flooding with the idea of Mother and Father finding out that we have been alone in Dragan's house, with no chaperone. The fear is quickly replaced by a heady excitement. I can't believe Dragan is being so bold.

"I need you alone for a while," he says.

I swallow, and it's like my breath is suddenly formed of rocks. "What for?" I ask.

We're already at the grand sweeping steps that lead up to his house and for one moment, I have the strange sensation it's going to swallow me up whole and I'll never see the light of day again. I'm shivering with nervous anticipation.

"I've given the staff the day off," he declares, as if reading my thoughts about our being discovered.

"Won't they think that strange?"

He shakes his head. "I often give them the day off. I don't like to have servants' eyes on me all the time—besides, they can't help but talk. Gossip spreads around this town like wildfire if you're not careful."

Which is why, I guess, Dragan is hurrying me up the steps,

shielding me from view with his body as he magically unseals his front door.

~

OUR FAMILY HAS BEEN to Dragan's house on several occasions since my waking, for suppers and other social events. It's a strange house, full of totems and charms, many of which are like a foreign language to me. It is going to take me many years of schooling before I fully understand that part of him. The house is as enigmatic as he is, but I can't wait to get my hands on it, throw open the shutters, and let some light into the gloomy, dark rooms.

Once inside, he falters for a moment, and I wonder what thoughts are running through his head. My blood is still pumping with adrenaline from the forbidden nature of what we are doing, and I know that after our moment in the library yesterday, without the fear of being discovered, there are no clear lines.

"Shall we tour the house?" he asks. "Let you start imagining all the changes you're sure to want to make to this old bachelor's nest." He winks.

I'm under no illusion that any changes to Dragan's empire will be easily won, but I smile and am pleased for a moment that we have something to occupy our time other than each other.

My previous visits have been limited to the salon, the dining room, and the library, and as we walk through the house, Dragan throwing open door after door to strange new spaces, I can barely contain the thrill. The house is full of beautiful and darkling things. Objects d'art, the finest crystal and porcelain, exotic rugs and animal skins, books, candles, and crystals. The walls are scattered with ecclesiastical relics, brass candelabras, and painted icons, which strike me as strange in a house belonging to a witch.

"They are all symbols of the mother goddess," he says over my shoulder as I'm admiring a naïve piece of highly decorative folk art depicting the Virgin Mary and baby Jesus. It's from a land I have no knowledge of.

"That's the strange thing about humans," he says. "They almost have an understanding of the universe, and yet they stop just at the threshold, as if afraid to step over the line, and so they neatly package what they know and leave the rest as some divine mystery placed just out of reach, like their tale of Tantalus; the waters always receding and the apple never reached." He shakes his head. "I can't think why they never think to . . . fly?"

The mention of flying jolts me, and it's then I realize my wings have emerged. The crazy, nervous energy having caused them to spring open.

"You see them!" I say with surprise.

He's looking at me with new eyes, filled with awe and wonder.

"I thought I couldn't love you more than I did, but . . ." He shakes his head, words lost.

I blush deeply. My mother's warning words are on a loop inside my head. I'm desperately trying to get control over them and retract them, but they're being stubborn.

"Don't put them away," he says, reaching out his fingers and stopping just short of their outline. "May I touch them?"

His question is almost as odd as the effect they've had on him. He has never asked permission before touching me, not even when he has crushed his lips against mine and run his hand daringly up the inside of my skirts—but somehow this is different.

I nod, letting them fall back open. His hand passes straight through them, and I can see he is trying to work out their mechanism and substance.

"They're . . . impossible. Fae haven't had wings in generations. Can you fly with them?" he asks.

I nod shyly. "Just about. I've only been able to emerge them in the last couple of months, and they're a little weak, but they're getting stronger every time I exercise them. Clearly, they're still a little unstable." I laugh shyly.

"A part of you wanted me to see them," he says sagely, moving in closer to examine them. "That's why they revealed themselves. They're like shimmering lights, moving—an energy source of some kind, like a form of electricity, maybe?"

I shrug. "I don't know how they work," I say, almost apologizing. "Do you know *anything* about them? Mother won't talk about it; she says I need to put them away and not think on them again."

"But they're beautiful," he says.

There's something in his tone that unsettles me, but I can't put my finger on it. I summon my wings to retract and smile, waiting for him to kiss me, knowing this invitation will start a chain of events I won't be able to stop once started, like a runaway train heading toward a ravine.

"I love you," I whisper, my words cracked with quiet fears.

I'm expecting him to say it back, but he doesn't. Instead he pulls me by the arms and kisses me. His lips are soft, his tongue exploratory, but they lack the usual desire, the usual loss of control. There is no transfer of his power to me. He remains entirely in control, and this, coupled with the tone in his words about my wings, is eliciting some fluttering of alarm. It's as if he has suddenly seen my latent power and doesn't like it. Some small, significant thing has changed between us. We move apart, and he's smiling, but his smile does not reach his eyes.

"Come on, let me show you the rest of the house," he says, taking me by the hand and walking me up the grand staircase, which, like ours, splits the house in two.

"Left or right?" he asks, and I feel like the decision is somehow weightier than it is on the surface.

"Left," I say, and the answer seems to please him.

"Left it is," he says, pulling me down the corridor and opening doors to reveal bedroom after bedroom. There are at least four, all perfectly dressed and ready for guests. The yellow room with the blue velvet accents is my favorite of them; it's so pretty.

As I turn, I jolt at the sight of the last two doors. One is painted black, the other red. I'm about to ask about them, but Dragan is already heading down the hallway in the opposite direction. He clearly has no intention of sharing them with me.

"What about those rooms?" I ask, looking back over my shoulder.

He turns briefly and sniffs. "Those are my private rooms. They're strictly out of bounds."

I laugh nervously. "Out of bounds? Even when we are married?"

"Especially when we are married," he says. "You are never to go in them; there's enough of the rest of the house for you to reign over."

I don't get a chance to ask any more, as Dragan has his arm crooked around me and is leading me away in the other direction.

"Here is my study and private library," he says, opening onto a room double the size of the other bedrooms, and then onto another room, which he tells me will be mine.

"You can decorate it how you wish," he says, pushing back one of the French blue silk drapes a little further.

It's already a very pretty room, and I can't think I should want to do much more with it.

"And here is the interconnecting door to my room," he says, opening it.

I stand on the threshold, my stomach constricting with excited anticipation. The room is a heavy contrast to the room that will be mine.

The room is large, and a bed twice as large as any bed I have ever seen squats in the middle of it. It is hewn from rough wood, as if pulled straight out of the forest, and dressed in heavy cottons and furs. It's incongruous with all the other rooms in the house, which have been decorated with European elegance.

This room is all forest and mountains; the half-paneled walls have been painted a heavy dark green, the color of pine needles. There are tables full of fern plants and shimmering crystals. Hanging on the wall above his bed is a large loop laced with cotton and decorated with precious stones, and from which hangs strands of feathers, threads, and leathers.

"What is that?" I ask, pointing to the strange object.

"It's a dream catcher," he says. "It was given to me by a friend."

"Whilst you were traveling through the native lands?" I ask. My skin is prickling at the sacred magic it holds.

"It's meant to stop my nightmares."

I look at him, raising my eyebrow in question, inviting him to share but not wanting to pry.

"Every night, I dreamt of my mother burning," he states.

I slip my hand into his, knitting his fingers with mine. "And does it help?"

"Mostly," he says, looking at me with his eyes that have grown dark with deep thoughts. "But what helps me the most is knowing that soon, you'll be sleeping by my side."

His serious face grows mischievous. His hand cups my cheek, and we're kissing in a world that is no longer my own. It's all his.

CHAPTER 9

I've spent the night awake in my own bed, plagued with frustrations, my body running on some strange force of energy, sparked by Dragan's kisses, his touches, his desire. As we stood in his room kissing, his hands explored new uncharted lands. Then he stopped, just as I dared to hope he would lie me down and make a woman of me. When he saw the look in my eye, begging him to give in, he smiled against my lips and told me how much he was looking forward to our wedding night, and that things waited for tasted sweeter.

And if Dragan teasing me to the point of delirium was not enough, something else was now pricking at my hungry curiosity—the house, and the two doors I would never be allowed to enter. Both of these frustrations somehow felt part of the same.

As I lie luxuriating in the feeling of starched heavy cottons, I go back in my mind through every room he shared with me, including the library and study, and I cannot fathom what other possible facility the rooms might serve, especially ones so full of secrets he feels he must keep them from me. An ill wind circles around me.

~

I RISE, dress, and head downstairs, hoping breakfast is still on the table. As we have staff, I know there is always someone who will bring me breakfast if not, but nevertheless, it makes me a little uncomfortable. I have never felt easy asking others to do things for me, although when I am mistress of Dragan's house, I know I am going to have to; otherwise, as Mama has warned, the staff will run rings around me.

I find Mother at the table with an open newspaper. She is gripped by something she is reading, and she hardly lifts her eyes to me. I sit down, taking a piece of toast from the silver rack, and try to read the front page. When she realizes what I'm doing, she quickly folds the paper and places it under her napkin.

"Morning, Emeline," she says, pouring more tea in a bid to distract me.

"Morning, Mama. What's in the news?" I ask, my eyes going to the poorly concealed paper.

"Oh—just the usual Havenwood Falls non-news. The churches are petitioning to have the brothels closed—again. There was a miner killed. The usual human scandals, nothing of interest."

"May I read it?" I ask. It's not an unusual question, as I often read the newspaper.

"Not today," she says, smiling tightly. "We have other things to discuss."

"Like what?" I ask, furrowing my brow. I'm starting to tire of the word no.

"Such as how your hike went with Dragan yesterday?" She drinks from her cup, but her eyes are firmly on me, and I wonder if our secret diversion to Dragan's house is no longer secret.

"Yes," I reply, trying to ignore the constriction in my voice. "It was very pleasant. The weather was clement, and the flowers were very pretty."

She nods and smiles. "And was he gentlemanly?"

Her question makes me blush deeper, and I know if she presses me too far in this matter, I'm going to blurt out things I shouldn't.

"I'm not sure what you mean, Mama?"

She reaches her hand across the table and places it over mine affectionately. "You're soon to be married, Emeline. There are things you must prepare yourself for. Things that might be quite frightening and strange at first, but which, I promise, will soon get to feel natural."

My insides are churning. I really don't want to be having this conversation, especially not right now, when I've had such a sleepless night and I'm hungry. She takes my silence for innocence and continues.

"Dragan is a worldly man, who, being older than you, has experienced a lot more of the adult world. You are barely a woman, and so innocent, Emeline. You must trust that Dragan will look after you—I know how much he loves you. Quite besotted. There will be things he expects of a wife, and you must do your best to be as compliant and accommodating as possible." She stops to study my face, which I am sure must be the color of a beet by now. "Do you know of what I'm talking, Emeline?"

I shake my head. For sure, I want the floor to just open up and swallow me whole.

"And you know what really goes between a man and his wife at night? You know how procreation happens? You've seen the studding of the horses?"

I can hardly breathe, the room is so hot, and inside, I'm cursing Mother for bringing such an image to my mind, as it jumbles up in my head so that all I can think about is muscle and action and movement and energy and Dragan covering my body.

"Mama, please . . ." I manage to utter.

"I know it might make you feel a little uncomfortable talking about it, but it would be a terrible thing for a mother to send her innocent daughter to her wedding day without preparing her for the wedding night."

I want to scream. I can't get the images of Dragan out of my head. I'm starting to sweat. I want to tell Mother exactly what I know of man and woman, and how my body is aching with desire every time I think of him, how I have tasted his lips, his tongue, his skin, and how my body now craves him. I am not afraid of my wedding night, I am afraid of the wait—the seemingly endless wait, and the insanity that might take hold beforehand.

I bite down on my toast, which is a stupid decision, because my throat is so tight I can hardly swallow, and I'm forced to chew and chew whilst Mother continues her kindly education.

"I know it has been difficult for you both to adjust to each other in such chaperoned circumstances, and so all you know of each other is chaste friendship. I have discussed this with your father, and we have agreed that as the wedding is in close approach, perhaps you need a little more freedom to get to know each other in preparation for your new life."

I'm having difficulty catching hold of the direction Mother's conversation is turning.

"We think it is a good thing for you and Dragan to do more things together as a couple, out of the house, in preparation for being on your own."

"Okay," I say slowly, still trying to work out exactly where these new boundaries fall.

"Take your hike yesterday for example, which was something wholesome and public, but just the two of you. So if you'd like to walk into town, or go for coffee at the coffee house, or go hiking again, then your father and I are in agreement with that."

I want to laugh, but I don't. Instead, I shake my head and press my lips together in some kind of smile. It's hardly a free rein, but at least it gives us an opportunity to be away from the house and out from under my parents' eyes.

"Thank you," I say as she taps me on top of the hand as if to say her job has been done.

She pushes back the chair and picks up the newspaper, but before she can pass through the door, I call to her, "May I have the paper now?"

She hesitates, looking down at it. She clearly doesn't want me to read it, but I play my trump card. "I'm to be mistress of my own home soon enough, Mama. It would help to know what's happening in town."

She nods and reluctantly steps over, holding the paper out to me. "I guess you're all grown now. Just don't get yourself distressed," she says, turning to leave.

When she's gone, I unfold the paper hungrily, keen to discover the story that would have made her act so strangely. The front page story is an article about the discovery of a young woman's body.

I read with sublime horror about how she was found near the falls, naked and bound before being placed in a shallow grave and then later, discovered by a hunter's dog. She'd not been there long, and if that wasn't horrific enough, the details of her murder and the state of her body were both compelling and horrifying. Her body had been marked with many occult symbols, and her death had occurred as a result of a sharp blade to her heart. The theory was that she had been ritually sacrificed and left at the falls as some kind of offering.

My hand is over my mouth, my eyes wide. Havenwood Falls is a town made up of both humans and supernaturals, but rarely do those worlds collide, to the extent that almost all of the humans who live in Havenwood Falls have no idea they are surrounded by supernatural species of many forms—fae, witches, vampires, werewolves, goddesses, and so many more variants of being, it's impossible to list them all.

The discovery of this body in such a manner is bound to have a ripple effect across both the community and the wider universe. It's going to start talk of the occult and the supernatural, and it won't be long before hysteria grips a small town like Havenwood Falls. It's happened before—like in Salem. And even though the Court of the Sun and the Moon have ensured that we are protected from the outside world with magic and wards, I don't know how far that stretches to the threats from within. Such thoughts elicit a terrible and overwhelming sense of dread in my heart. It could all so easily happen again.

I read the article on a loop, unable to stop myself poring over the gruesome details. The girl is yet to be identified, and if she is one of the soiled doves from the brothel on the edge of town, she may never be. Accompanying the article is a macabre illustration, showing her body riddled in the strange symbols and a quote already from the minister of the Free Church, telling Havenwood Falls to remain calm and not jump to conclusions.

No wonder mother hadn't wanted me to read the paper. She's clearly as worried as I am. I look at the clock and see that it is only ten in the morning. Dragan isn't due for another hour, and I'm frustrated I can't just turn to him and ask him more about this. I'm sure the Luna Coven and the Court of the Sun and the Moon will have some ideas about the situation; after all, they're meant to be the ones protecting us from the world. Although, what if it's the other way around, and it's the world that needs protecting from us? The thought jars me, and I glance back at the clock. I really want to see Dragan. I need him to tell me that everything is going to be all right, because I have the most terrible feeling it isn't.

CHAPTER 10

$\mathcal{T}$hanks to my parents' new leniency, Dragan and I are sitting in the coffee house in the town square. It's the only place where respectable folk can get something to eat and drink other than the small restaurant, Napoli's, across the square that is run by an Italian family. The town's saloon isn't a place for ladies, although sometimes, the gentlemen of the town will stop by to play cards or gather to talk man-talk. A lot of the town's unofficial business takes place there. The saloon is right across from the coffee house, where we are sat in the window, with a dainty tiered platter of sandwiches and cakes, English style, in front of us, but neither of us are eating much. The news of the body's discovery has us both distracted.

I'm watching a couple of brightly dressed young women sitting on the rocking chairs, on the porch of the saloon. They remind me of exotic birds, and it's clear they are nobody's wives—not with rouge like that on their cheeks and the way they are so brazenly chatting and laughing, as they sit with their knees apart. I glance at Dragan, who is stirring the pot of tea with far more diligence than it requires, and I wonder how many women he has taken to bed, what carnal delights he has already tasted. I return to looking at the girls, thinking on mother's words about being accommodating and compliant—they look accommodating but they don't look exactly compliant—and I wonder what will truly be expected of me on our wedding night. I roll my hips against the hard surface of the chair in an attempt to relieve some of the sensations these thoughts are stirring, but rather than quell them, it creates a strange indulgence that Dragan can instinctively sense. He looks at me with questioning eyes and bites down on his lip before turning his head with curiosity to see what I'm looking at. His eyes fall on the women. I feel the light touch of my cotton skirts and petticoat moving up my leg, then cooler air on my stockings. I daren't look at him. I'm rigid with anticipation as his hand sweeps my leg and my thigh, his scandalous behavior concealed by the heavy linen table cloth. I clear my throat and straighten my back, wiggling to move my legs slightly apart, worrying a little how wanton this makes me appear to him. I glance at him briefly and see how his face betrays nothing about the happenings under the table. I sigh heavily. The graze of his fingers on my soft skin, the sensation of the smooth round amethyst stone of his ring stroking and knocking my burning flesh.

"I want to make you happy," I say, my voice thick and quiet with desire. "But I'm not sure how to."

I gasp when his fingers move even more daringly upwards. His voice is low in my ear. "Emeline, I love you. You're forever mine. Your very existence is my happiness."

The waiter comes to the table to inquire if we would like our teapot refilled. Dragan's hand has gone, and in its wake, there is an aching emptiness. I brush my skirts down under the table and pick up my teacup, noting how my hand trembles. My eyes return to where the girls sit. One of them is now standing, talking to a man wearing a black cowboy hat. I don't need to hear their conversation to know some negotiation is taking place. A few moments later, she walks him through the door of the saloon, leaving her friend behind. The curtains in one of the upstairs windows closes. I wonder how much of a price she puts on herself or whether the saloon owner's wife determines that. They must be lonely, I think. So lonely.

"The article in the newspaper today?" I ask, turning my attention back to Dragan.

He nods his head slightly. "Yes?"

"Do you think she has family? Do you think someone misses her?"

He clears his throat and adjusts his cravat. "I'm not really sure you should be reading such things, Emeline. It's unsavory for a young lady."

"Do we know anything?" I ask, emphasizing the *we* to mean the supernaturals.

"I think we should change the subject," Dragan says sternly. "This isn't a conversation to have here." He smiles, but it's a warning.

"Then tell me more of your story," I say.

He reaches forward to take a slice of cake from the plate and nods, taking a moment to think where he had left the story and lowering his voice to barely more than a murmur. He doesn't want to risk any of the humans overhearing him.

"We were at the point Marie Blackstone and her people joined the caravan," I say, taking one of the sandwiches from the plate and picking at it.

Dragan settles himself back into his chair, dropping his voice to ensure we're not overheard. "Ah yes. Marie Blackstone. So there were some very heated discussions between the members of the Luna Coven. We—my brother and I—were adamant we did not want the Blackstones joining us. We believed they would only bring trouble. However, our thoughts on the matter were soon superseded when the Luna Coven became the target of another coven, who had heard of our combined powers and felt moved to put a stop to them before they grew further.

"Marie Blackstone was instrumental in both alerting us to the attack and in fighting for our side when the attack happened.

"We did our utmost to try to make it work, for the sake of the coven. But the tensions between us and the Blackstones were difficult to conceal. We were all sick of wandering like hobos, of always being uncomfortable and afraid of bandit attacks—or worse. There had been many times we had come across the grim discovery of scalps hanging from trees as a warning to the white man."

I gasp. "That's horrible."

"That's justice," Dragan says, without breaking his gaze from the square beyond the windows.

Neither Mother nor Father had spoken much about their journey to Havenwood Falls. Dragan's stories about his past were also about our own, and that's why they meant so much to me.

"We decided to leave."

"You were going to break up the Luna Coven?"

"We didn't get very far. It's hard to explain. The bond that had grown between us had become fixed, like a cord. With each mile we had traveled, our hearts had grown heavier, and our thoughts darker. We knew, although we didn't understand why, that our home was with the people we had tried to leave behind. For some reason, that day marked a turning point in our relationship with Marie Blackstone and her kin. Perhaps it was our shared faith that was ultimately stronger than our differences."

"But you never became friends, exactly," I tease.

He smiles and shrugs. "We rub along. We understand each other. She knows we all have our place in the community. We don't always have to like each other to respect one another."

I pour another cup of tea and wait for him to continue.

"Before we left on our not-so-big adventure, I had made one last attempt at begging your mother to allow me to see the painting. She surprised me when she agreed—but she was very firm that it was only I who could look on it, even though I was desperate for Rodavan to also cast his eyes on it. I had spoken of it many times to him, and I don't think he understood why it moved me so. I believe he thought I was quite mad! I followed her around the back of their wagon, and she pulled out the painting, leaning it against the wheel.

"When I asked her who you were, she told me you were her daughter. It was clear my question had brought forth a great sadness and I offered my condolences, assuming you were dead. Your mother shook her head and scolded me, telling me you weren't dead but cursed, placed under a spell by one of her husband's enemies. It was a very powerful spell, she informed me.

"I examined the painting closely. Although your eyes were exquisite and so real, they were flat and empty, as if you had already passed into the realm of the dead. Your mother, seeing the question in my eyes, nodded and sighed heavily before confirming my suspicion. You were in the painting. She went on to tell me your father had sought out another powerful mage to find a way to keep you safe whilst they traveled. It was impossible. Our own witchcraft and magic were strong, but to do that—to take a living person and put them inside a painting—was something else. The problem was the mage had died, and now your mother and father had no way of knowing how to liberate you.

"At that moment, I swear I saw you move—just slightly. With that your mother hurriedly covered you up and dismissed me as if I were a mad man, imagining things."

"It's an extraordinary story," I exclaim.

"Just one of many that happened along the way."

"It must have been so hard for you all."

"Yes." He nods. "And if traveling had been hard, establishing a town was harder. It was headache after headache. How we didn't all murder each other is a mystery," he says, chuckling. "Everyone had opposing ideas as to how the town should be built, both physically and on all the other levels that make up a town. The Court of the Sun and the Moon was established, placing the Luna Coven as guardians of the original wards and protections necessary to keep Havenwood Falls a sanctuary. Marie Blackstone was put in charge of ensuring the supernaturals did not indulge in any of the darker arts—a watch guard. And steadily a town sprang up."

"I can't imagine how hard that must have been," I say, looking out the window to the small square that makes up the heart of Havenwood Falls.

"The simple structures were put in first, based on need and necessity. Simple wooden buildings, erected with the help of magic and superhuman strength. The saloon was one of the first buildings to go up, then a general store and after the timber mill, growth was relatively rapid. After that . . . well, somehow, here we are today," he says, dabbing his mouth with his napkin and summoning over the waiter for the check.

"Yes," I say, still in wonderment. "Here we are today. I wonder what tomorrow will bring?"

CHAPTER 11

*D*ragan and I are walking back to Fairchild Mansion when he suddenly takes a right turn across the road.

"Where are we going?" I ask, surprised. "I mustn't be late. I've got an engagement."

"This won't take long," he says, pulling me along so that my toes are barely connecting to the ground. We pass Fairchild Mansion on our right and head toward the stone-walled cemetery, where we enter by the small side gate. I'm giggling with nerves, wondering what mischief Dragan is now up to.

He looks around and then, confident we're alone, takes me off the path, leading me to the space between the grave digger's hut and the wall.

"What are you doing?" I laugh.

"It's impossible to find any privacy in this wretched town," he says, not really answering my question.

I don't need to ask his intentions again as I'm pressed up against the stone wall, his lips hard on mine, his tongue deep in my mouth. With one hand over my shoulder bracing himself against the wall, his other hand is riding my skirts up over my knees and slides between my parted thighs.

I need him to stop, but I don't want him to. Instead, I cup the back of his head in my hand and pull him back toward my eager lips. I'm dizzy with sensation. My body melts under his touch, my breathing ragged from both the kiss and the speed of my heartbeat. Tears prick the corners of my eyes from the overwhelm, and then I'm gripped by the sensation of falling, even though he's holding me up. My cry is smothered by his mouth until I begin to laugh, and he pulls back, resting his head against mine as he smiles proudly.

"What just happened?" I ask, still barely able to breathe, tears trickling down my cheeks.

"Did you like it?" he asks, studying my reaction carefully.

I bite down on my lip and nod, suddenly afraid of words. He strokes my cheeks, using his thumb to wipe away the tears.

"You're crying?" he asks curiously.

I laugh with embarrassment. "I'm not sad."

"Are you sure?"

"I've never been so happy."

He laughs against my lips, and I think how lucky I am to love him.

I ENTER THE HOUSE, having said goodbye to Dragan outside, and am greeted by our housekeeper Harriet, who looks unusually flustered.

"Mistress Emeline, Mistress," she says breathlessly, "your mother was just about to send me in to town to come and get you. You're late for your appointment."

I glance at the grandfather clock and see it's almost an hour later than my own watch, which must have stopped.

"Oh dear, is Mother very cross?" I ask, stuffing my parasol into the metal umbrella stand and fixing my hair, trying to calm the heat on my cheeks.

Harriet doesn't answer, but she flashes me a look of sympathy, and I know I'm going to be in one hell of a lot of trouble. Mother has an abhorrence of tardiness. I take off for the morning room without stopping to remove my boots, and end up crashing through the door.

For the sake of appearances, my mother tries to hide the look of horror when she sees her daughter come bounding through the door, leaving a trail of muddy footprints across the pale Dutch carpet.

Sitting in one of the blue velvet chairs, doing his best to keep the impression he is still drinking his tea and not staring at the wayward bundle of female energy that has just fallen into the room, is a handsome, fair-haired gentleman.

"Emeline," my mother says in a voice clipped enough to give me a taste of the tongue-lashing I am sure to get later, "this is Mr. Henry Hudson, your new art master."

I look back to Henry and do my best to disguise my wry smile as he bundles to his feet, knocking the delicate china cup in the process so it is left spinning in the saucer.

"It's a pleasure to meet you, Mr. Hudson," I say in my most polite voice.

"Mistress Fairchild," he says, sort of bowing.

The warning glare from my mother stops my laughter.

"I have been explaining to Mr. Hudson in the last hour we've been waiting for you to grace us with your presence, that you are marrying Mr. Dragan Bishop in the summer, and it is your wish to complete a portrait of him as a wedding gift."

Mr. Hudson has the kind of cheeks that always carry a blush, and I know he is going to cause quite a stir around our little town of Havenwood Falls. There's something attractive about artisans, the way they continually battle a world too ugly for their creative souls.

"Yes, that's right," I confirm.

My mother cuts in before I can say any more. "I'm afraid you have your work cut out for you, Mr. Hudson. I do hope you like a challenge!"

I flash a look at my mother, surprised by how publicly critical she's being of me.

"Although," she continues, "there's no doubt Emeline's actually rather talented," my mother concedes, and I love how she's never been able to stay cross at me for very long.

"Why, thank you, Mother," I say, smiling sweetly, but I know I'm not out of the woods yet. "I'm so terribly sorry for being late. My watch stopped, and time just ran away from me."

Mr. Hudson smiles warmly. "Time has a habit of doing that, in my experience," he says, bowing his head again before returning his warm brown eyes to my face. There's something in the way he looks at me that ignites a lick of curiosity, and I find myself momentarily captivated. If he's not a supernatural, then he's one of the most curious humans I have ever come across.

"So shall we say that lessons begin tomorrow morning?" my mother asks, breaking whatever weird moment that just ran between us.

Mr. Hudson nods and proceeds to gather up his belongings in haste. "Yes, that will be perfect. I'll call around nine."

"Nine!" I begin to complain.

"That will be fine," my mother says, escorting him to the door. "Be sure to bring whatever materials you need, and we will settle the bill with you tomorrow, unless you require payment up front for the items."

"No, no," he says, shaking his head and sending his flop of light brown hair on its own little dance. "That's all quite fine. I have everything we need already," he says, casting a look in my direction.

Mother watches him leave, and when she has closed the door, she rounds on me.

"Emeline Fairchild!" she scolds. "Can you at least try not to be quite so . . ."

"So what?" I ask innocently.

"Alluring!" she says with exasperation, causing me to laugh.

"Mama, I don't quite know what you mean."

She walks past me, tutting. "Yes, you do, young lady. Yes, you do. The goddess help it when you and Dragan finally marry—from the blush already on your cheeks, you're going to set the world on fire."

I chase after her, skipping across the mosaic of pretty pastel tiles that Mother has just had installed in the hallway. Father says it looks like a unicorn has been sick in the hallway, but I rather like it, especially the little gold stars scattered throughout.

"About the wedding," I say, "is father happy?"

"Why do you ask?"

I shrug. "Just small things that he has said in passing."

She sighs and flops down into the blue nursing chair. "We've known Dragan a long time. A man gets to really know a man when he's traveled by his side. That journey from Mississippi to what is now Colorado was tough, Emeline. You'll never know the trials and tribulations we suffered, or the bloodshed that went with a journey through frontier lands. We were robbed numerous times, attacked, raided, there were strange animals with poisonous fangs, and if that wasn't enough, there was the often unending desert and rocks—not to mention the natives.

"In such conditions, there's no hiding the truth of who you are. That's what bonded the founding families, for better or worse. In a strange kind of way, we were all married to one another out there. In the wilderness, there isn't the veil of polite society we've since built up around ourselves over the last sixty years. Life was about survival. It came down to the simple balance between life and death. Things were simple, and there are many days that I long to go back to those days, riding the wagon with your father, sat around the campfire, not caring about etiquette and appearances. There was an element of freedom in that.

"Havenwood Falls was meant to be more of that—but somehow, along the way, we managed to fall a little back into the trap of building ourselves a gilded cage. The gold and silver mines made the Old Families so rich that they forgot the times we'd had to go several days without knowing where our next meal would come from, or when we had to pass the bodies of slain pioneers and natives, or see . . ." Her words fade with the horror. "Now we are fine people in fine clothes, drinking from fine china, and we have managed to seal ourselves back up in the version of ourselves that we want the world to see—but that doesn't change anything, Emeline. Underneath it all, we're just the same raw and flawed beings we always were."

"And Dragan?" I ask. "What flaws does he have?"

She smiles tightly. "Honestly, even if I told you, you wouldn't see them. You're so in love with the *him* you've conjured from your imagination that you're in danger of not being in love with the real man."

"That's not true!" I protest. "Dragan's told me all about his past."

Mother laughs. "How could he? You've been told the bits he wants you to hear and the bits you want to listen to. You don't really know him. But your heart is set, and you'll have a lifetime to discover the truth of who you both are."

"Do we ever really know anybody?" I snipe defensively. "Take Father for example."

She flinches. "Let's not talk about that."

"You know he wants to bring her back, don't you?"

From the way my mother's face constricts, I guess she didn't know. She's too proud to admit it, though, and so nods, emitting some sort of strangulated, "Yes."

"Do you think it's a good idea?"

"That's not for me to decide. This is your father's demon he's trying to put to rest."

"But it affects us all. What if she discovers I am awake? What if this all triggers some terrible series of events?"

"She's a ghost, Emeline. What harm can the dead do to us?"

"Dragan isn't happy."

"This isn't Dragan's business. Neither the Luna Coven nor the Court of the Sun and the Moon know about father's intentions, although Elsmed does, and he's not exactly happy about it. Not only because he doesn't like the sound of it, but because it puts him in a very difficult position with the Court. He feels that your father is testing loyalties." She shifts in her seat, increasingly uncomfortable.

"I think you should speak with him," I say. "I think you should ask him not to do it."

The doorbell rings, and my mother stands, smoothing down her skirts.

"Who can that be? Emeline, are you expecting a visitor?"

I shake my head.

Harriet comes bustling into the room to announce that Miss

Beaumont has called. Mother instructs her to send the visitor in, but not before casting me a glance that shows a shared curiosity. Miss Beaumont is a member of the Luna Coven. Anne-Marie Beaumont, her mother, was a founding member of the Luna Coven, and when she died in the 1876 massacre, Saundra Beaumont took over her mother's seat.

Mother had found the death of Anne-Marie Beaumont difficult; they had shared so much. Now, Saundra is one of the town's most powerful women and isn't given to casual calls—despite the connection between Mother and her.

Harriet shows her in, and the usual pleasantries are exchanged. Miss Beaumont is immaculate as usual, and still so pretty with her brunette hair plaited and coiled.

Today, she is wearing a green-and-black-striped raw silk dress with black French lace. A diamond spider is making its way across her chest. The Beaumonts' ancestry is French, and with that comes a natural flair for elegance and fashion.

"Emeline," she says, turning in my direction. "How are preparations for the wedding going?"

"Very well, thank you, Miss Beaumont."

She nods with a strange sense of satisfaction. "Good. It will be nice to see Mr. Bishop finally settle down with a good wife."

I blush at her compliment.

"If you'll excuse us, Emeline, I need to talk privately with your mother."

Mother glances at me and nods, and I smile politely before making my way out of the room, wondering what on earth could have caused such a situation. Could it be something to do with the murdered girl? Perhaps, but why would Miss Beaumont be coming to speak with mother about it? Although the day is sunny, a shiver runs over my skin. I stand in the hallway, looking at the red roses on the polished table, and think of blood and the red door in Dragan's house, and the woman they found by the falls, and the fact that my father killed his first love.

They're all a jumble of ideas and thoughts bouncing around in the wind, but I have the strangest belief that somehow they're all connected, and before I know what is happening, I'm stumbling forward, my hand reaching out for the table to stop my fall as the darkness swallows me up.

I spent the remainder of the day in bed, resting. I'd fainted, and Mother put it down to the stress of the wedding and that I had started my monthly cycle, which I was happy to also put it down to, rather than the horrible vision I'd had just before the world had gone black.

I had been falling—falling from a great height—and even though I had tried to stretch out my wings, they were gone.

Harriet has woken me early this morning on account of my art master, Mr. Hudson, arriving, and now I'm in the morning room with my easel prepared and my sketchbook open. It is full of sketches of Dragan, which I have done from memory, his face etched on my mind as if it were my own.

Mr. Hudson arrives promptly at nine, garnering him the seal of approval from Mother. She puts great store in people who can keep to time. He is shown in and asked if he'd like tea or coffee. When Harriet leaves to make tea, the door is left open.

He is nervous, but I think Mr. Hudson is always a little nervous.

"Good morning, Miss Fairchild," he says, laying out various items of art equipment, after having first covered the rug with a piece of calico spattered with dried paint. He removes his tweed jacket and rolls up the sleeves of his white cotton shirt, and I realize I'm brazenly staring at him, studying these small movements, which have inexplicably excited an emotion in me that, as yet, has only been promoted by Dragan.

I have never seen Dragan's arms, and so it strikes me as a little odd that within moments of meeting, I have seen a part of Mr. Hudson I have not yet seen of my own husband-to-be. My mind wanders back to Dragan as Mr. Hudson continues his preparations, and to the time Dragan was reclining on his sofa, his dressing gown open, exposing his chest, a landscape of hard muscle and soft skin. Desire stirs in me.

My eyes travel back to watch Mr. Hudson, and I wonder what he looks like under the fitted tweed waistcoat and pearl-buttoned shirt. These thoughts are making it a little tight to breathe—either that or Harriet has been especially merciless in her lacing of my corset this morning. Either way, I'm worried that after yesterday's fainting session, I might suddenly pass out and make a fool of myself. I force myself to focus on the matter at hand, and when Harriet comes in with the tea tray, I ask her to bring me a glass of water, which causes her a little pique of concern that she doesn't voice.

Mr. Hudson is talking to me about the various elements of the portrait I wish to paint, but it's a little hard to keep a hold on the threads of his words with all these new sensations swirling around my head.

"Yes, head and shoulders," I reply in response to his question on composition.

"May I look at your preliminary sketches, Miss Fairchild?"

I nod and smile. "Be my guest," I say, standing and handing him my sketchbook.

I'm nervous about what he'll think of them. I know I am not without some talent, but I'm also no master. He flicks through them, and I watch as his smile begins to widen.

"These are really rather good, Miss Fairchild. Your mother wasn't wrong in her compliments." I can see the slight tease in his smile. "I don't think you'll be any kind of challenge at all."

His smile is infectious, and I begin to feel calm descend over me like a blanket. "Why, thank you, Mr. Hudson."

He stares at me for a moment longer than is comfortable, and then, as if remembering himself, claps his hands together with boyish enthusiasm and invites me to stand at the canvas, instructing me to begin sketching out the faint outline of Dragan's face.

Tea arrives and is placed on the table, but before Harriet can begin pouring it out and fussing, Mr. Hudson has thanked her and informed her that he will take over the proceedings. I turn from my task to look at the pair of them. Like me, Harriet seems surprised that a man should be capable of pouring his own tea. She begins to protest, but Mr. Hudson is adamant and she's sent off, her head shaking slightly with bemusement.

Before he pours the tea, he nears my shoulder, close enough that I can smell warm sandalwood and the subtle scent of him, which smells of soap mixed with another fragrance I can't quite place.

"That's very good, Miss Fairchild. Perhaps you might want to bring the angle of the chin in here," he says, reaching over me and sketching in the faintest of lines, "and then bring it out here, so he's looking more directly at the observer."

I bite down on my lip and inhale deeply. This intimacy is unsettling me, but Mr. Hudson seems quite oblivious to my agitation, encouraging me to draw in the sketch placement lines of Dragan's eyes. Whilst I do that, he turns and pours the tea.

"When are you to be married?" he asks, taking up a position close behind me.

"June nineteenth."

"Have you known each other a while?"

I glance over my shoulder, surprised at the personal nature of his questions. Clearly, Mr. Hudson is not one to take much time in getting to the heart of the matter. I return my concentration to getting the spacing between Dragan's eyes just right. "Yes, a couple of years. He's an old friend of my parents."

Mr. Hudson is silent in response, but nevertheless, I can feel the weight of his thoughts. He's thinking about the age gap.

"Are you acquainted with Mr. Bishop?" I ask pointedly.

Mr. Hudson's teacup rattles in the saucer. "I can't say I've had the pleasure as yet. I've only been in Havenwood Falls for a couple of weeks."

"And how are you finding our strange little town?"

There's a hesitation again, and I'm quickly discovering that Mr. Hudson is a man who likes to choose his words carefully.

"It's very . . . pleasant," he finally says. "There's quite a sense of . . . nope, I can't quite put my finger on it. I've tried several times, but I can't quite articulate what I'm finding quite so attractive about the town."

"It's very pretty," I offer.

"It sure is. But you know, pretty is often a disguise."

I put my charcoal down and turn, and with perfect synchronicity, he bends over, retrieves a cup of tea, and places it in my hand.

"My, what a suspicious mind you have," I say, playfully. "So what do you think the pretty little town of Havenwood Falls is disguising?"

He shakes his head and tugs at his beard. "If I told you my theory, you'd think me quite deranged," he says with humor.

I laugh but stop when I see the way he's looking at me, as if he's really seeing me—fae and all. I cock my head, studying him, trying to work out what manner of human or supernatural he is. I can't place him.

"It's the artist in me. I can't help but see beyond the veil," he says cryptically.

His words skitter up over my skin, and I'm not sure what conversation we're actually having. How much does he see? How much does he know?

"Do you specialize in portraits?" I ask, diverting the conversation to safer territory.

He shakes his head. "No. I'm an illustrator by trade. Watercolors. I started off in New York, working for a publisher."

"How exciting, to have been in New York. What brings you to Colorado?"

"I have no idea," he says almost wistfully. "I guess it was the direction the wind was blowing."

"That's a terribly romantic answer," I say, smiling. "And evasive. Are you trying to make a mystery of yourself, Mr. Hudson?"

He laughs and places his teacup back down on the table before heading to my canvas to study the pencil lines.

"I think I should meet with Mr. Bishop and make some sketches of my own—so I can really understand the direction we need to take."

"But that would give away the surprise."

"Not if you were to simply say I was a friend of your father's staying in town for a while. People expect artists to always be sketching."

"I suppose it makes sense. Let me see what I can do."

The clock in the hallway strikes the hour, and I'm surprised to note how quickly time has passed.

"I think that's all for today," he says. "Like I said, I think I need to see the noble featured Mr. Bishop with my own eyes before we can move forward."

I drink my tea and watch as Henry rolls down his sleeves and pins them with cufflinks, and then replaces his jacket, transforming himself back into a gentleman.

"In the meantime, Miss Fairchild, be sure to spend as much time as you can studying the eyes of your fiancé. That's where you'll really come to know his soul."

Mr. Hudson efficiently gathers his possessions together and offers a civil goodbye accompanied by the small bow that is quickly becoming his trademark, before leaving me standing in the morning room, lost in daydreams.

CHAPTER 13

$\mathcal{W}$e are meant to be taking a civilized amble around town, and we did, but we ended back here, at Dragan's house, in the cool shade of the downstairs library, him lying on one of the large overstuffed sofas and me wrapped in his arms.

"Do you think we will always be like this?" I ask.

"Like what?" he asks, stroking my hair.

"So in love."

I feel his laughter under my back as well as hear it, and it's one of the sweetest feelings I've ever experienced.

"Why would getting married be any different—if anything, it will bring us closer together. We won't have to snatch moments and hide like outlaws."

I turn in his arms so I'm facing him, my hands pressed against his chest as I search out his eyes, which I stare into, trying to capture them in my artist's mind so I can get them just right on his portrait. They're full of shades.

"Mother gave me the wedding night talk the other day," I say more boldly than I feel.

Dragan's cheeks tinge pink, and a wicked smile travels over his lips. "Did she now? And what did she say?"

"She said I had to be 'compliant and accommodating,'" I say, testing for his reaction.

His laughter erupts under me once more. "Oh, gosh, I hope not— that would be . . . a little tiresome."

I frown. "Then how should I be?"

He strokes my cheek. "Exactly how you want to be, Emeline. Whatever curiosities or desires you have, you can explore them with me."

My hands toy with the buttons of his shirt. "Can I undo these? Can I touch you?"

He smirks. "You don't have to ask permission, Emeline. I'm all yours."

I bite down nervously on my lip, unknotting his grey silk cravat, trying to avoid the intensity of his eyes as he watches me with curiosity. I undo his waistcoat, each button a step toward adventure, and then before undoing the pearl buttons of his shirt, I stroke my hand over the cotton, reading the hidden landscape, taking my time to breathe him in.

I begin to undo the small delicate buttons, a task not made easy by the slight tremble in my fingers, and expose his torso, hard and defined. Muscle and strength. He's still watching me as I push my hands through the smattering of dark down and place my burning cheek to his cool skin, tracing the outlines of his tattoos. My heart quickens, beating twice to his single beat. So sure. So steady. So certain.

His hands tangle gently through my hair, lulling me into a half-sleeping state. This is what peace is: to be laid against the bare naked chest of your lover in the weak afternoon light, believing in forever.

I turn, inhaling him, before pressing my lips tentatively to his skin, tasting the delicate trace of salt and minerals before reaching up and seeking out his lips. I can feel the effect I'm having on him pressing through my skirts. The effect of this secret communication passing between us ignites me further. I want to feel his darkling energy collide with my light, taking me to the brink of wickedness. Our kiss is full of fire and promise.

We surface, breathless, almost delirious, and I flee from him, standing on shaking legs, fixing my hair and trying to calm my heartbeat.

"We should get back. Mother will start to grow suspicious," I say.

Dragan doesn't answer. He's too busy watching me, his tongue licking his lower lip and his eyes hungry.

"Undo your buttons," he says, his voice heavy with desire as he lies half dressed with no intention of moving.

"We haven't got time."

"I'm not moving until you do it."

I pick up the cushion from the sofa behind me and throw it toward him. Before it can impact, he's thrown out his hand, and the cushion suspends in midair.

"That's a nice parlor trick," I tease.

"Not as nice as this one."

I slide my eyes around the room, waiting to see what theatricals he's about to commit, but then I realize that half the buttons of my dress have been opened. I clasp at them, pressing my lips together and shaking my head. "Dragan Bishop!"

His eyes are laughing, but his mouth is still deadly serious.

"I command it!" he tries.

"You command it?" I ask, cocking my brow. "Well, in that case, if my master commands it . . ." I say, unclasping my hand and letting the fabric fall open before slowly undoing the last two buttons and sliding the blue silk off my shoulders, so I'm standing with my under corset exposed.

"And the laces," he says.

I shake my head coyly.

"You weren't so shy the other day!" he says.

"That was different."

"How so?"

"Because we weren't in a house alone."

"Don't you trust me?" he asks.

I shake my head. "Not entirely."

A wicked and delicious glint gleams in his eye, and he moves off the sofa, prowling toward me. "Good."

I step back, but there's nowhere to go, as the sofa is behind me. He swipes forward, catching the end of the ribbon lacing and begins to pull at the bow, loosening it. I can tell he's no novice. The ribbon slackens, and he's unwinding the satin from the hooks as my breath snags in my throat.

"Just one little look," he says, running his thumb over my breast and causing me to gasp.

"That's not just looking," I say, barely able to get the tumble of words out of my throat. His hand is round my neck, forcing it backwards, exposing the sensitive flesh where he delivers small butterfly kisses as his thumb continues to stroke circles, knotting my stomach and causing my toes to curl inside my boots.

"It's so many long weeks until our wedding night, Emeline," he says, pulling away and turning his attention to lacing my corsetry back up. "I think I might go mad," he laughs, turning to do his own buttons up.

Part of me is terrified. If this is the effect Dragan has on me with the slightest touch, then what will it be like when we go to bed together?

"Perhaps you should go to town, and get the wickedness out of your system with one of the whores," I say playfully, not really meaning it.

Before I know what's happening, there's the sound of a crack and a horrible stinging on my cheek. He's struck me. The world spins and flashes light and dark. He's standing in front of me, calmly winding his cravat around his neck as I nurse my cheek in the palm of my hand. My eyes are wide with shock.

"Dragan . . . ?" I whisper.

He reaches around for his jacket and puts it on, pulling at his cuffs as if nothing has happened between us.

"I'll be waiting in the hall. Put yourself back together." He strides out, leaving me whirling. My buttons are still undone, and whereas moments before they had represented something sweet and forbidden, now all I can feel is shame as I hurry to do them up, walking toward the mirror over the fireplace to fix my hair. There are tears on my cheek and a red mark where moments before there had only been blushes.

I take my handkerchief and using the carafe of water on the liquor tray, dampen it, pressing it to my hot skin. He struck me hard enough to cause a sting, but already the heat is fading out of it. I pinch the other side to make it look like I'm simply flushed.

I don't recognize the doe-eyed girl in the mirror. She's a stranger to me; a stranger Dragan has unleashed.

I step into the hallway, not wanting to look at him—wanting to be a million miles away from him—but he steps up to me, lifting my chin with his finger to inspect my cheek before kissing it softly and whispering in my ear.

"Forgive me, Emeline. My blood was hot, my emotions scattered. I shouldn't have done that—if only you know how you affect me."

Despite my horror, I find myself melting into him, his mouth on mine, kissing me gently, momentarily erasing the incident.

"Are you ready to go back?"

I nod, still not trusting myself to speak.

He picks up my parasol from the elephant-foot umbrella stand and throws open the door, escorting me out into the sun with a hand on the base of my back.

We are silent as we return to my parents' house, and I walk with the uneasy feeling that today I have learned another of the many facets to married life.

Mother is sitting on the porch sewing, with a large jug of iced tea by her side. She waves when she sees us approach, beckoning for us to sit and take refreshment with her. Dragan smiles politely and is as chivalrous and charming as usual, but I can't find the heart to play along—and it's noted. I can tell by the glance she casts me that there will be discussion on the matter later. My heart sinks a little further when Mother extends an invitation for Dragan to come to supper and meet our family friend Mr. Hudson, who she explains is a talented artist from New York and before that, Sussex in England, and who is new to Havenwood Falls.

Dragan accepts the invitation with much enthusiasm, always pleased to meet new and interesting people. He drinks down his iced tea, observing me closely over the top of the rim before standing and making his goodbyes, telling us he has some business to attend to in town. I'm still not entirely sure what Dragan's business is or how he has managed to amass and sustain such a fortune. Father tells me it's alchemy, and that Dragan and Rodavan are in possession of ancient knowledge. He always says this with a wry smile, designed to entertain rather than to explain.

When Dragan has gone, Mother turns to me and searches out my face, which I have dipped to the porch floor.

"Emeline? Is all well between you and Dragan?"

I stand, smoothing down my skirts. "Everything is absolutely fine. We had a small tiff over something silly. Wedding nerves."

She's still scrutinizing me, but she accepts my reason and nods.

I travel past my room and head up to the attic, where I curl myself up in the chair by the window and watch the light fade from afternoon to twilight with an unread book of poetry in my lap.

I spend the afternoon convincing myself it was all a moment of madness; passion and violence wrapped up into one indistinguishable mess of high emotions—and I deserved it. That's what Mother would tell me if I told her what happened and how it had come to be. Rising blood. Heartbeats and breathlessness. And yet, something changed in that moment and we can never go back—only forward.

My body burns for him, and I hate myself for it, silently fearing I'm cursed once more, to love him for all his shadows. With each recall of him hitting me comes other memories; they rise to the surface like bubbles in the lake. Memories of touches and the way he takes me to the edge of sweetness right up to the line of bitterness. I stand and rage in the empty room, growling deeply, forcing my wings out, stretching them until they're at their fullest. I breathe deeply and center myself, promise myself that if he ever raises a hand to me in anger again, I'll hit him back. It's in my power. It's all in my power—to resist him, to seduce him, to leave him, to love him. Dragan may think he's the one in control, but he's wrong.

CHAPTER 14

*M*r. Hudson arrives on time. Dragan is late. And when he enters, offering apologies that don't sound very substantial, it is clear he does not like the way the young and handsome Mr. Hudson is sitting in the chair next to me, our heads bowed conspiratorially as we laugh and make conversation.

"Dragan," I say, standing and offering him my chair, whilst I gather a glass of champagne from the tray.

"Is there anything stronger?" he asks, seeing the champagne bowl in my hand.

I falter and smile tightly. "Of course. Bourbon?"

He nods and holds out a hand to Mr. Hudson in order to shake it and make introductions. Mother returns to the room a moment too late.

"Oh, I see you have already introduced yourself, Mr. Bishop."

"Dragan," he says, turning to Mr. Hudson. "Please call me Dragan. We're amongst friends here." His eyes slide over to me, and he gives me a look I can't entirely read.

"Henry," Mr. Hudson offers, and I wonder how we will now navigate that awkward informality the next time we are alone and he is standing behind me, his body so hot that I can feel him.

I hand Dragan his bourbon, and Father goes on to continue his conversation about the problem he's having finding a reliable gardener. Dragan undoes the button on his jacket and flicks it open, leaning back in the chair, his legs spread wide, making himself at home and leaving no one in any doubt as to his dominant position in the pack.

It should annoy me, but it does something else to me; something so luxurious that it is all I can do not to purr under my breath. I stare at him across the room, defiance and invitation blended into one communication. He cocks his head slightly, his brow moving upwards ever so slightly.

Father is still prattling on, Mother is fussing, and Mr. Hudson is doing his very best to look interested—but not Dragan. Dragan is watching as I bite down on my lip and play with the long strand of pearls that rest on the breast of my dress. Slowly, I run my hands up and down them, ensuring he sees my fingers trace the outline of my breasts under my silks. He's so captivated that he misses his cue in the conversation and is left fishing for air. Henry glances over at me, sensing the electricity bouncing between Dragan and me, but there's nothing now to see except for me drinking deeply from my champagne bowl.

Harriet comes in to announce that supper will be served shortly, and Mother starts to lead us through to the dining room. Dragan holds back until last, and as I go through the door, his hand is on my waist, pulling me back. His lips are hot on my exposed neck, his teeth snatching at my pearl drop earring.

"I'm so sorry about earlier, Emeline. Please forgive me," he says.

I turn so my back is pressed against the door frame and flick my attention back to the rest of the party, who are already out of sight, in the dining room. From nowhere, my hand rises and strikes him hard across the cheek.

"Okay," he says, manipulating his jaw and smiling through the obvious pain I have inflicted. "I guess I deserved that."

My eyes are locked on his, and I pull him toward me by the lapels of his jacket, knowing we have only seconds. I kiss him hard, my hand cupping his cheek. I haven't forgiven him, but now I know the ground is even, and I can see the shift in his eyes.

We break away just before Mother comes to the door to see where we are. She clears her throat in declaration of disapproval. She doesn't need to have caught us kissing to know we were up to trouble. I head in to the dining room, the adrenaline still coursing through my body. Dragan and I have been placed next to each other, with Henry opposite me, and Mother next to him. Father is naturally at the head of the table.

I can feel Mr. Hudson's eyes on me as I settle at the table. He's studying Dragan, who is still stroking his cheek. Sensing the intense energy flowing between the two of us, Henry blushes in the soft candlelight.

"So how are you finding Havenwood Falls, Henry?" Dragan asks, unfolding his napkin on his knee.

"It's a very interesting little town. A lot of interesting characters."

The table laughs.

"Yes, it certainly has variety," Father says.

"Have you been out to the falls yet, Mr. Hudson?" I ask, unable to fully navigate the shift in name formality.

"No, not yet." He pauses as Harriet pours water into his glass. "I'm thinking I might go out for a hike at the weekend."

"Oh, you certainly must," Mother says. "The mountains are so pretty at this time of year."

Henry nods. I can tell he's slightly awkward in such formal surroundings.

"Perhaps Dragan could give you some guidance. He and Emeline were out hiking only a few days ago."

There's something in the way Mother says this that makes me think she's springing a trap, but Dragan doesn't falter. "Absolutely. I'll draw you a map after dinner. We had a really wonderful walk, didn't we, dear?" he says, turning to me.

I've never heard him call me "dear" before, and it's this that throws me rather than the lie I'm being asked to cooperate in.

I'm rescued by the arrival of supper, and the business of serving. By the time we are all plated up, the conversation has thankfully taken a turn. The rest of supper is taken up in small chat and the usual polite conversation, which is only made interesting by the intermittent feel of Dragan's hand on my thigh and the way I catch Henry looking at me, his eyes soft and whimsical, his hands delicate—the hands of an artist.

"I've often wondered what it must be like to see the world through the eyes of an artist," Dragan states.

I straighten my back. Henry is flushed to have such specific conversation turned on him.

"Well," he laughs awkwardly, "that's rather . . ." He shifts in his seat and fiddles with his napkin. For some reason, this fairly general question is making him very uncomfortable. "It's not much different to anybody else, I guess."

"Oh, come come," Dragan says, pouring himself another glass of claret from the jug before topping up Father's and Henry's glasses. "Isn't it the gift, and the curse, of the artist to see the world differently? Take that Spanish fellow Picasso, breaking apart the world and putting it back together, or Monet, reducing the world to dabs of light."

"You take an interest in art?" Henry says.

"I collect a little. I'm fascinated by the idea of multiple views on reality," Dragan says. "I'd love to see how you view the world. Perhaps I could come by your studio and take a look at some of your work."

"Oh, I don't have a studio, yet. I'm lodging at the saloon until I can find more suitable lodgings."

By this, I know he means until he can afford more suitable lodgings. Although he isn't poverty stricken, it is clear that Henry isn't wealthy.

"And besides," he says, toying with his glass. "I'm not really sure my art is going to be suitable for your collection. It's more of an illustrative nature. Whimsical. Monsters and other paranormal creations of the imagination, like witches and fairies."

As he says this last part, he glances at me, and the certainty hits me like a bullet that impossibly, he sees what I truly am—what we all truly are.

Dragan falters for a moment, too, clearly surprised.

"Do you believe in the supernatural?" Dragan asks, unable to hide the suspicion in his voice.

"When you're an artist, it's hard to know what you believe and what you know, for reality and dreams have no clear boundary."

Mother coughs and claps her hands together gleefully, breaking up the strange tension that has emerged around the table. "Everyone ready for dessert? Harriet has made peach cobbler. It perfumed the whole house. I have to confess, I nearly snuck down there and ate it all up."

A series of smiles and gentle laughter grows around the table. The rest of the evening goes by without any further discussion of magical matters. Dessert is a triumph as promised, and then sweet wine and cheese is eaten before Henry leaves whilst the faintest trace of light is still in the air.

I escort Dragan to the door shortly afterward, and seeing how clement a night it is, I ask if he'd like to sit on the porch for a while. He takes my hand and leads me over to the wicker settee, and when we sit down, he does not let go.

"It's been somewhat of a strange day," he says, staring out across the front lawns where fireflies are dancing. Our canyon is one of the few places in Colorado where the fireflies glow, and it's just another mystery linked to the ancient and sacred power of Whisper Falls.

"Yes. I'm not sure I want another like it," I say, alluding to the incident earlier in the day.

"Quite." He turns to look at me, and we stare into each other's eyes. Henry is right—the truth of a man's soul is right there; all you have to do is force yourself to look. And what do I see when I look into Dragan's eyes? Passion, pain, cruelty, obsession, love, desire, pride, knowledge, secrets, power—and all of that is intoxicating, like a drug. I am under no illusion as to what I am bonding myself to by marrying Dragan. Mother says it's a legacy of what happened to me, this dangerous attraction to the darkness.

"I think our artist friend Mr. Hudson has found a new muse," Dragan says, returning his eyes to the lawn.

"Really?" I say, laughing. "Well, you are irresistibly handsome; it's understandable," I tease.

"You know full well I'm not talking about me. I saw the way he looked at you."

"I think you're being a little sensitive."

Dragan shakes his head. "I don't think so."

We fall quiet for a minute before I ask, "Do you think there's something strange about him?"

Dragan glances at me and smirks. "We live in Havenwood Falls, Emeline—'strange' is a bit of a loose term."

"I know that. But he's human, right? He's not a supernatural?"

"No. He's definitely human."

"But there's something about him that is more than human—did you sense it?"

Dragan nods. "He's a human creative—they're difficult to read. They don't fit in the usual box."

"Did you get the feeling that he could see us? For what we really are—that he knows you're a witch and I'm fae?"

Dragan tugs at his beard. "No. Humans don't have that ability. He just has an overly rich imagination, which is why you should be careful. A man like that can soon become obsessive."

CHAPTER 15

*M*r. Hudson arrives at his usual nine o'clock and sets up our studio in the morning room whilst I am still being dressed for the day. Why Mother insists on such an early start is beyond me. My head is still heavy from the amount of wine we consumed at supper last night, and my stomach is still in knots from yesterday's incidents.

However, as soon as I enter the morning room, a sense of peace falls over me. When I have some tea and return to sketching out Dragan's features, the tensions slough away. Mr. Hudson is the kind of person who can fill a room comfortably with his silence, and in fact, there seems less awkwardness when he's being silent than when he's forced to make small talk. This sense of calm is added to by the way the light falls through the many windows of the morning room, casting everything in a soft haze.

"There. I think I'm finished," I say, stepping back from the canvas to assess the sketch lines I have put in. It's a good likeness to Dragan.

Henry comes up beside me, his chin resting on his knuckles, his elbow resting in the palm of his other hand. He's thinking deeply. He doesn't say anything for at least a couple of minutes and then says, "Almost. Something isn't quite right. May I?" he asks, reaching out his hand for the charcoal stick. "I think the chin needs to be slightly harder, and his cheek bone drawn in a little more and higher to emphasize his true nature."

Mr. Hudson is too lost in his creation to properly monitor his words, and I stand watching as the smallest change in placement of lines brings Dragan's face to life, as Henry's mind talks. "Dragan is the hard granite of the Balkan Mountains and dark brooding English moorlands; he's storm skies and standing stones; he's ancient energy and dark crimson blood. His eyes carry the spirit of the night owl and purging wild fires."

My heart skips at the mention of the owl. How could he have possibly known such a thing?

Henry stands back and briefly looks at me, breaking whatever trance we both fell under. From the canvas, the witch Dragan stares back at us, and my blood runs cold. It is the face of Dragan that only I have seen; the face of the man who struck me and felt no remorse. The face of the man who places his hands under my skirts and takes me to the brink of oblivion. The face of the man who burns my soul.

My hand is over my mouth, and a whimper comes out before I can stop it.

"What is it?" Mr. Hudson asks.

I can't say the words, even if I could find them and put them in order, and so instead, I run from the room, stifling my cries with the back of my hand as I head to my room, where I throw myself against the back of the door and turn the lock.

Mr. Hudson sees us all for exactly who we are, and I'm not sure I like it.

CHAPTER 16

ragan and I are walking through the town square, having decided to take lunch in the small Italian restaurant, Napoli's Ristorante Italiano. I've never eaten Italian food before, but Dragan assures me I'll like it.

When Dragan was younger, he and Rodavan spent a couple of years doing the European grand tour. Part of that journey involved returning to their childhood village in Serbia where they commissioned a stonemason to make a memorial to their mother, to be placed in the grounds of the now ruined majestic house that had once been their home.

The grand tour had taken them to all of Europe's main cities and had given the Bishop brothers a knowledge of the world that few others hold. It was whilst Dragan was in Italy that he had fallen in love with Italian food. It reminded him of the food he'd had in his childhood, and now he ate at Napoli's, one of Havenwood Falls' few restaurants, at least a couple of times a week.

In all the years my family have lived here, they have never once visited the restaurant, and I'm excited to share this exotic part of Dragan's life. When we arrive, Dragan is greeted like family, wrapped up in an enthusiastic hug and kissed on both cheeks. This effervescent display of affection is almost alarming, and I'm sure to stick out my arm swiftly so that my hand might be shaken and I can avoid the same boisterous greeting.

Dragan and the owner are speaking in Italian, and for a moment or two, I am excluded from the conversation until the owner, who is introduced to me as Pedro, turns to me with the widest of grins and hugs me before I get a chance to escape. I'm guessing from the grins and claps on Dragan's back that he has just told them I am the future Mrs. Bishop.

Pedro speaks perfectly good American, which is thankfully how the rest of the interactions go as we're taken to a table covered in a red-and-white-checked tablecloth with an old wine bottle sufficing for a candleholder. Even though it is midday, there are heavy shutters on the windows, and the room is dark enough to make the candlelight matter.

I sit wide-eyed. Other than taking afternoon tea or a light lunch at the coffee house, I have never been in a restaurant before. The whole experience is a little overwhelming. A piece of paper is placed in front of me, on which is typed a list of dishes, all of which are entirely alien to me. Pedro is keen to point out his own favorites, and Dragan reclines in his chair, smiling with amusement at my bafflement.

"What is pizza?" I ask.

Pedro and Dragan slip into Italian for a moment and exchange jokes that are clearly at my expense, so I kick Dragan under the table, and he takes my hand and smiles.

"I'm sorry, dear. Let's get a selection of dishes, and you can try them all."

I nod and look at Pedro, smiling. His good humor is infectious.

"I shall prepare a feast!" he says, kissing his fingers, before turning back toward the kitchen.

"He's a friendly fellow," I say once he's out of hearing.

"Yes, the Italians are much more open with their emotions than us Americans," he says, smirking. I note how he's still holding my hand across the table as if the usual rules of polite society don't quite exist in this space.

I glance around the room, noting that there are a couple of other couples and a table of men, but mostly, it's fairly empty.

"Do you miss home?" I ask.

Dragan shakes his head. "No, Havenwood Falls is home now."

I nod, still slightly awestruck by the surroundings, and in a bid to distract myself, I ask, "How did you get me out of the painting?"

The question comes as a surprise to him, and he lets go of my hand. He inhales deeply before looking around and seeing we are pretty much alone, lowers his voice, and replies, "It took many years. Our transitory nature meant that it had been very hard to really develop our craft to the level of our father. We needed a workshop and supplies. When we arrived at Havenwood Falls, our homes were modest, temporary cabins built on the squares of land where our fine mansions now sit.

"However, Rodavan and I would often travel out of Havenwood Falls for short periods of time to visit a shaman who had made a home for himself up in the mountains. He had refused to leave the sacred lands because of the settlers and had remained as guardian to one of the native spirit portals. It was from him that Rodavan and I learned the truly magical properties of the land and the gifts of the indigenous minerals and flora and fauna. This, coupled with our knowledge of both ancient English and Serbian magic, meant that Rodavan and I soon made up for lost time, our magical abilities and powers strengthening with each passing season.

"All this time, I held the image of you in my heart. I knew I had to find a way to unlock you from the painting. I knew that our destinies were entwined. As transportation and communication lines became more established between Havenwood Falls and the outside world, we were able to gather increasing supplies of materials attached to our own magical knowledge.

"For Rodavan, his passion grew for alchemy, although why, when the very land we sit on is full of gold, Rodavan should still strive to hold this power, is a mystery to me. My obsession became the mystery of transmogrification—magical transformations. Not dissimilar to alchemy in some ways, although more of the physical discipline than the chemical."

Our conversation is halted by the arrival of a large plate on which are laid strips of raw-looking meat, cheese, and green leaves. On a side platter are fresh sliced tomatoes and soft white cheese.

Pedro returns a moment later with a bottle that looks a little like champagne, declaring, "Prosecco for celebration."

"Oh—" I begin to protest, knowing it's not the proper thing for ladies to drink in the day, but Pedro is insistent, and Dragan seems enthusiastic about the idea.

After toasting, Pedro leaves us to attend to his other customers. I stare down at the thin slices of meat and look to Dragan for reassurance.

"Is it raw?" I ask.

"It's cured. In the sun. Pedro cures all his own meats. It's a kind of slow cooking using the sun's energy. It's delicious," he says, grabbing a slice with his fingers.

I'm slightly scandalized. I've only ever seen sandwiches eaten with the hands, but there's something in the way Dragan's fingers slip into his mouth and the look of satisfaction on his face that stirs my nerves.

"Try some," he urges. "It's amazing if you wrap it around the cheese."

Tentatively, I follow his lead, and to my surprise, my mouth bursts with strange delicious flavors. I let out a small moan of satisfaction.

"Good, yes?" he says, watching my reaction.

"Very," I say, reaching out for more.

"So where was I? Yes, transmogrification. It's not the easiest of crafts. Effectively you're trying to defy the laws of physics, but after years and years of failure, and much mocking by Rodavan, I finally managed to turn a field mouse into a statue, and I knew at that point, my quest to free you was within reaching distance."

"Did you manage to turn it back?" I ask playfully, forking the creamy velvet cheese and sharp tomato into my mouth.

Dragan laughs and sips his glass of prosecco. "That was the sticking point. It seemed that turning something animate into something inanimate was a lot easier than the other way around. However, I remember breaking the news to your mother, and how she cried tears of hope. Like me, she believed it was only a matter of time before we managed to break the curse. She has always believed in me."

"How long was it after that until you broke the curse?"

"I worked day and night—drove myself half-crazy with the idea of being so close, and of course, my craft had to be perfect; there was no room for error. However, transforming you back from the painting was only half of the curse; even if we got you back, you were still destined to sleep for eternity. To my surprise, Rodavan had been working quietly away on such strands of magic, especially on the removal of curses and hexes. The Luna Coven had made certain strands of our craft a priority in order to ensure Havenwood Falls was as safe a sanctuary as could be."

"I remember the day I woke," I say. "Yours was the first face I looked upon. Something happened in that moment."

Dragan smiles and for a moment, looks almost bashful. "We were meant to be, Emeline."

"My very own Prince Charming. My one true love," I whisper.

"Forever, Emeline."

We've cleared the plate, and Pedro is now filling the table with dish after dish of delicacies. Pâtés, breaded chicken, rabbit with lemon, fried carp, green salads, and something called spaghetti—long strands of poached dough, covered in oil, garlic, lemon, and grated cheese. It's the messiest and most delicious thing I've ever tasted.

"This is divine," I say, struggling to contain the spaghetti.

Dragan laughs and tutors me in how to use a spoon and a fork to wind the spaghetti around until it's been tamed. This moment is one of the sweetest moments of my life.

"Can we go to Italy?" I ask.

Dragan's eyes drop momentarily, and he shakes his head. "No, it's too far away. We can't leave Havenwood Falls for that long a period. The wards don't allow for it."

I sigh heavily. As much as I love Havenwood Falls, there's a whole world out there that I'm desperate to explore.

"But," he says, "that doesn't mean we can't find a little piece of Italy here." He tops up my glass. "And I can't wait to bring our children and have us all sat at a table, feasting and laughing as one big family."

"Children," I say, smiling.

He nods. "May the goddess bless us with many."

I raise my glass. "To the future."

I feel like we've eaten a week's worth of food in one sitting, but it was all delicious. The bubbles have gone a little to my head, and all the world is tinged with a soft and happy edge. Yesterday's storm is but a distant memory.

By the time Pedro has cleared the table, the restaurant is empty except for one couple huddled in the far corner. They look camped in for the afternoon. Pedro returns a few minutes later with a bottle and three shot glasses, taking a seat at the end of the table. From the familiarity of the gesture, I take it that a lot of Dragan's meals end this way.

"Have you heard they've identified the girl they found at the falls?" Pedro says, setting out the shot glasses and filling them to the brim.

"You can't take me back to my parents drunk," I whisper to Dragan.

His response is to take my glass and place it in front of me. "We'll drink plenty of coffee, and there's time to walk it off." He winks, then returns his attention back to Pedro. "Who was she?"

"One of the girls from Madam Gerard's place out on the exit road."

"A prostitute?" I ask for clarification.

Dragan nods. "Do they know anything else?"

"There are whispers of dark magic," Pedro says.

I stiffen and suddenly feel Dragan's hand on my knee, warning me not to give anything away. Pedro is human and all but a couple of the humans in Havenwood Falls have no idea about the supernatural community that walk amongst them.

"Demonology," Pedro adds, lowering his voice and crossing his chest as if he is afraid of the word. "This isn't the first," he says, tipping the rest of the liquor down his throat and refilling it. "Apparently, there was another girl found in the same manner at exactly the same time last year. It was covered up. A girl from the saloon. The town officials didn't want a scandal."

I cock my eyebrow at Dragan. This is news to me, and I'm curious to know if Dragan knew of it.

"And they're sure it's the same circumstance?" I ask.

Pedro nods, and I take a sip of the amber liquid. It's sweet and tastes of almonds, but that's purely a trick before it burns my chest.

"Her body was all marked up with ancient symbols. Looks like whoever did it is making some kind of annual sacrifice," Pedro says.

Dragan pinches the bridge of his nose between his fingers. "But Sheriff Kasun is on the case, yes? They're not going to keep covering this up?"

"Didn't get much chance to this time. News spread like fire through the saloon. All the grisly details, too."

Dragan hard-eyes Pedro and nods not too subtly in my direction, as if to remind Pedro that a lady is present.

The alcohol is making me bold. "Don't worry, I read all about it in the paper. They didn't spare the details."

"There were symbols etched all over her body," Pedro continues, relishing the license he's just been given.

"Well, I'm sure the appropriate people are looking into it," Dragan says, downing the rest of his drink and then checking his pocket watch. "My, is that the time. We'd better be getting back, Emeline." Dragan stands and takes out several notes from his wallet—far too many to cover the actual cost of the meal—and places them on the small bread plate. "As ever, Pedro, a gastronomic triumph. I'll see you Thursday evening."

Pedro stands and escorts us to the door, handing me my parasol and Dragan his hat.

"What time is it?" I ask when we're outside the restaurant.

"A little after two."

"But we don't need to be back until three," I say, frowning. "I really didn't mind what Pedro was saying. I mean, it's horrible, but it's not the kind of thing to directly impact on a woman of my standing, is it?"

The alcohol has made the ground just a little less certain, and I'm grateful for Dragan threading his arm through mine.

"I just didn't want to engage in salacious gossip, that's all. This town is complicated enough without adding layers to the drama. The humans have a habit of getting worked up about such things. It's important that the Luna Coven and the Court of the Sun and the Moon put a stop to this before it gets out of hand. I'll be sure to talk with Rodavan about it. I'm sure Marie Blackstone has it all under control—she usually does."

It's then I remember the unusual visit from Miss Beaumont the other day. I had meant to mention it to Dragan before, but with everything else going on, I had forgotten—and now, I'm not sure what the point would be anyway, so I store it away again, thinking to myself that I will ask Mother when I get back.

"Do you think it's some kind of sacrifice?" I ask, as we make our way through the town.

"I really don't want to discuss this any further," he says, swerving toward one of the town's stores that sells trinkets and curios. One of the windows has a tray of jewelry in it, and I pore over it like a child at the candy counter.

"Look at that fairy brooch. The enamel on her wings is so pretty," I say.

"It's a little overt, don't you think?" he says, smirking.

I shrug. "Only to those who already know."

Dragan is tugging me away from the window and leads me inside, where he asks the gentleman behind the counter about the fairy brooch. He tells him it's a new piece, but it's already had a lot of interest, and someone has already made a reservation payment on it. My heart sinks a little. It's so pretty. When I ask if he'll be getting any others, the man shrugs.

"I don't think so. This came with a traveling trader. He isn't from these parts."

"Is there anything else that takes your eye, Emeline?" Dragan asks, keen to smooth over my disappointment.

I shake my head, thanking the gentleman behind the counter and leading Dragan out.

"It's such a pity; she was so pretty."

"You wear your own wings, Emeline, and they're far more beautiful."

I laugh. I love it when Dragan is uncharacteristically romantic. "Shall we walk? I could do with the air."

"Only if we can go somewhere quiet, so that I can kiss you. I want to know what kissing you drunk tastes like."

I gasp with mock scandal and hit him on the arm. "You are an outrage," I say, putting my parasol up, which he takes from me, not to be gentlemanly, but because he fears for his eye.

CHAPTER 17

I'm putting the first blocks of color onto Dragan's face under Mr. Hudson's instruction. It's strange seeing Dragan blocked in blues and greens, but Mr. Hudson has assured me they won't remain so strange. He seems a little out of sorts today, his usual calm tinged with a different energy.

Although we have not known one another very long, our daily quiet time alone in the morning room has become something intimate and familiar. He brings with him a sense of peace, and I increasingly look forward to seeing him. It strikes me as funny how different men can be.

"Have you heard about the town murder?" I ask, glancing briefly behind me as I block more color in on Dragan's face.

"It's quite the topic of conversation," Henry replies.

"Oh, yes, what are folks saying?" I ask, knowing Mother would be having a fit if she heard me engaging in such salacious conversation.

"There are whispers of demon worship."

I scoff. "In Havenwood Falls. That's impossible."

"We all like to think we know our neighbor, but who knows what dark and evil thoughts lurk behind the visage? We never truly know anyone," Henry says.

I laugh. "Mr. Hudson, you really do have such a gloomy mind."

"Henry. Please call me Henry."

I blush. "Henry," I say, feeling the name in my mouth. "Then I guess you had better call me Emeline."

"I'm not sure that would be proper."

I shrug. "Maybe not—but we are friends, are we not?"

There's a jarring moment of silence, and my stomach sinks. Perhaps I have overstepped a mark.

"Yes, we are friends."

I step away from the canvas and beckon him over to inspect. "Do you think that the shading is deep enough?"

He reaches out to take the paintbrush still in my hand, and as his skin brushes mine, it sends an unexpected level of sensation through me. He senses it too, and our eyes meet for a brief moment before both of us look away bashfully, knowing we came close to something forbidden.

"I think here could be a little darker," he says. "Mr. Bishop's eyes are quite deep set."

I nod as I watch him darken the space. "There, I think that's us done for the day. We'll wait for this to dry, and then we can start the flesh tones tomorrow."

I nod again, unable to quite bring forth words. Something has shifted between us. Something so small, and yet it feels like a mountain has sprung up in my chest. I watch him as he busies himself around the room, gathering equipment, the sunlight falling in streams around him.

"What's it like staying at the saloon?" I ask out of nowhere. All I know is I'm not quite ready for him to leave and for the room to be empty.

"It's . . . interesting. There are a lot of characters. I spend most of my evenings in the bar, sketching. I've stayed in saloons and bars before, in different towns, but Havenwood Falls certainly has its share of curious individuals. I can't explain it exactly, but I feel so inspired here. The creative muse seems to have found a home. Everywhere I look, there is inspiration for new monsters and magical beings."

"How does that work? Does your mind transform people into something else?" I ask. My heart is now hammering in my chest.

He shrugs. "It's difficult to explain. Ever since I was a child, I didn't just see normal human beings; they sort of transformed in my mind's eye. I told my mother, and she said I had an overactive imagination and that I must keep it in check or else folks would think me mad."

He glances up from the wrap bag he's filling with brushes. It's rolled out on the sofa, meaning he is bending over, and I can't get the thought of summer-ripe peaches out of my mind. I wonder what he would say if he knew what thoughts were running through my head. He's not the only one with an overactive imagination.

"When you look at me, what do you see?" I ask, flirting dangerously with the truths of our universe.

He stands up and studies me. I feel his eyes burning through the veneer of polite society, and I wonder if, for a moment, he's imaging me naked. "Your delicate features, high cheekbones, sculpted nose, ears that have an almost indiscernible point to their tips, your elegant neck, just a few centimeters longer than average, your hands, which go right up to the boundary of the golden ratio, your nipped waist, the slope of your shoulders, your wings glimmering in the sunlight—"

I gasp.

"Why, you're fae, of course," he says, smiling.

All at once I want to confess that it's true. That he's not imagining me, but seeing me. All of me. The truth of me.

"What do my wings look like?" I ask, barely able to breathe out the words.

"Too beautiful for words. Perhaps one day I will paint them, but even then, to get their translucence and the way they are iridescent in the sunlight, would most likely prove hard to capture just right."

I laugh nervously, startled by his observations. "And Dragan? What do you see when you see Dragan?"

He dips his eyes, his Adam's apple moving down and then up as he swallows nervously. He makes himself busy trying to avoid the question, but in avoiding it, only makes it more pronounced.

"That bad, hey?" I ask.

He shakes his head. "It doesn't work with everyone. Some people just don't speak to me in that way, that's all."

Mother comes bustling in and thankfully provides a distraction. "So how is your student progressing, Henry?" she asks.

"Very well. She has a fine talent for both painting and instruction."

My mother looks to me and raises an eyebrow, then walks over to take in the progress of the painting.

"It's very . . . green," she says, smiling. "Is it to be one of those ghastly modernist pieces?"

"Mama," I gently scold. "This is just the undertones. It will look as fine as an old master when it's done," I joke.

"He does look very stern," she says.

"That's Dragan for you," I say, glancing back over at Henry, who is finishing his tidying.

Mother lets out a small harrumph as if there's more she'd like to say, but won't. Instead, she holds out a paper check to Henry and smiles. "To cover the cost of materials and your time so far."

Henry takes it, blushing. I can see that he doesn't feel comfortable with such a transaction, and I wonder why he should find it so humiliating. The man has to eat.

"Thank you, Mrs. Fairchild."

"No thanks needed. You are proving to be a most excellent teacher, Henry. Perhaps when you have finished this project with Emeline, you might be interested in doing some group classes for me and a few of the other ladies?"

"Why yes, that would be a pleasure, Mrs. Fairchild."

I note how despite the fact that Mother uses Henry's first name, he still calls her by her formal name. I guess that makes him more *staff* than friend. Sometimes, I hate the complexities of our social world. Henry is all packed and waiting awkwardly for some kind of cue to leave.

"So, I'll see you tomorrow," I say, walking him to the door.

We say our general goodbyes, and when he is gone, I sense mother sidling up behind me. "He really is a charming young man. Such a gentle way with him. I wonder that he does not have a wife already."

I blush. "I'm not sure he's felt settled before."

"Well, let's hope he settles here in Havenwood Falls."

I nod and make my escape toward my room, where I have a good book to get lost in whilst I wait for Dragan to pick me up to go on our "hike."

CHAPTER 18

e're "hiking" in Dragan's front parlor. We've become adept at sneaking away to his house and increasingly domesticated. Dragan has made us tea, and we've spent the last ten minutes trying our best to be self-disciplined, but it's hard when all I can think about is peeling back the layers of his clothes to look at him.

"Do you want to fool around?" I ask.

The question surprises and delights him. "What do you have in mind, Miss Fairchild?"

"Oh, I don't know . . . perhaps we could see what kissing feels like in each room?"

"I have a lot of rooms; that's a lot of kissing," he says playfully.

"Okay then, let's play hide and seek!"

"Hide and seek," he says, almost spitting out his tea. "Aren't we a little old for such games?"

I shake my head, then nod. "Not when you know what prizes are on offer," I say, putting my cup down on the table and springing to my feet. "You've got to the count of fifty," I say, already heading out the door.

"Emeline Fairchild, I LOVE you!" he calls after me.

"Start counting!" I call back as my foot hits the first step of the stairs. I know exactly where I'm going; to the yellow room, to the wardrobe, which I'm certain will be just big enough for me to enter. My feet are swift, and Dragan's loud counting starts to fade behind me.

The room is full of sunshine, and the wardrobe is unlocked. I throw it open and release the smell of warm cedar, but just as I'm about to step in, fear grips me. The thought of my father's first love dying trapped in a wooden box strikes me, and I turn on my heel, making for the drapes, which I tuck myself behind, sure to cover the toes of my boots.

I hear him ascending the stairs, calling out my name. My heart is pounding, goose bumps erupting on my skin. As his voice grows louder, I can barely contain my excited giggle. His footsteps sound across the wooden floor, and then he stops.

"Ha! I've found you, little mouse," he says. I hear him throw open the door of the wardrobe, certain he will find me. When he lets out a little noise of surprised disappointment, I can't stifle the giggle. The curtains swish back, and Dragan is grinning.

"Found you," he says, throwing his arms around me, stepping me back into the room, and pressing his lips to mine. The strength of his kiss surprises me, and already being out of rhythm from the adrenaline, I'm soon swooning. I push him away playfully and take flight again, this time with him chasing close behind.

I've foolishly turned left down the corridor and toward the dead end flanked by the red and black doors. He's just a hand stretch away as I crash into the wall and laugh. He pins me to the wall, his hands in mine above my head.

"Now, I've got you," he says.

I bite down on my lip as he stares right into my eyes. The wait is almost painful, and he knows it. He's toying with me. I lean forward, enticing him in, knowing how hard he finds it to resist my kiss. He pulls his head back, still panting from the chase, but steps his body forward, pressing hard to mine, letting me know how aroused he his, watching my face to see my reaction. I'm so curious to see all of him, and yet slightly terrified too.

Then we're kissing, and it's different from all the other times. It's full of heat and dominance, and I find myself melting under his touch.

He releases my hands to place his around my middle. His hands are so big that they can almost circle my corseted waist.

"A little bird tells me that a certain Mr. Hudson is making daily visits to your house," he says.

I tense. Of all the times to bring up such a conversation. But perhaps this is the perfect time, when my defenses are down and I'm little more than a small, fragile beast in his hand.

"Mother is having art lessons," I say, which isn't a lie. She is. She had her first sketching lesson yesterday.

"Your mother? I had no idea she was so inclined."

"She has many hidden talents."

"Like her daughter."

I lean forward, stopping his chatter by pulling his lip with my teeth, inviting him to kiss me again, but his hand has snaked its way around my neck and he's pulling my head back to plant kisses along it, making me wiggle underneath him. Everything is so intense, and I'm looking straight at the red door with its brass knob, believing almost for a moment that if I stare at it long enough, I'll be able to turn it with the power of my mind and open it.

"What's in the room?" I ask.

"I've told you—it's a secret. A man's allowed to have secrets."

"From his wife?"

"Especially from his wife."

"How about his lover?"

"Hmm," he says against my neck, the vibrations sending shivers over my skin. "But you're not my lover—yet."

Dragan's hands are under my skirt, his fingers slipping through the layers of fabric.

"No!" I say, suddenly coming out of my trance-like state. "Not today."

He pulls back, surprised. "No?"

I shake my head.

"But why? Did you not like it?"

"I liked it too much. It does something to me. Makes me agitated." I pull my brows together. "It leaves me wanting . . . I don't know, I can't explain it. It's like the world slips a little, and all my mind can think of is our wedding night, to the point I'm a little crazy."

He's smirking. "Am I that good?"

I slap him playfully. "I mean it, Dragan. I can't go much longer like this. I'm on the edge of something. It's making me . . . silly."

"Silly!" he repeats, half laughing.

"Perhaps we shouldn't spend so much time alone," I say.

Dragan's biting on the inside of his lip, and his eyes have darkened. "If that's truly what you want," he says, all playfulness gone.

I grab at his lapels and tether him to me. "It's not what I truly want. What I truly want is for you to take me to bed and make me your wife—right now."

His face softens, and he laughs. "We're so close, Emeline; we can wait."

"I'm really not sure I can."

"Or . . . we don't wait," he says, pouting seductively. "We go right now, and I take you as you wish, and should you get pregnant, then it will be our honeymoon baby. Who's to know?" He takes my hand and begins stepping backward down the hallway. "Is that what you'd like, to go to my bed right now?"

I know he's bluffing. I know he's trying to shock me out of my temporary insanity.

"Yes," I say, defiantly.

He cocks his eyebrow at me, surprised his tactic isn't working. My heart is hammering, and I'm burning. Terror is beginning to replace desire. We reach his door, and he turns the handle, all the time his eyes on me, watching me.

"I can't do it," I finally admit. "You win."

"I think most men would agree that I've just lost," he says, smiling and folding me up into a chaste and comforting cuddle. "Oh, Emeline. My wild child of meadows and streams, my free spirit. How I love you!"

CHAPTER 19

Dragan and I have returned to more public engagements over the last couple of weeks, agreeing that too much time alone isn't good for either of us, not that we would get much opportunity to be together anyway. Dragan and his brother are in the middle of some difficult negotiations, which, from what I gather, involves some kind of land purchase in Denver. Twice this week already, he has canceled our usual arrangements, although flowers have arrived on both occasions, so I know it's not cold feet, like Harriet unhelpfully joked.

In some ways, I've been glad of the space. It's allowed me to progress with Dragan's portrait with less distraction, and it will not take many more hours now before it is finished. Although admittedly, I have slowed my pace down considerably, not wanting my lessons with Henry to end.

Over the weeks we have been together, we have discovered an unlikely friendship, and he has turned from Mr. Hudson to Henry. He is a good counterbalance for the tempest that is Dragan. Without Henry, I honestly think I would have lost my mind.

There have been many times during our sessions that I have idly wondered what would have happened if I had not been engaged to Dragan when Henry walked into my life. Although he is not technically of similar status, my father likes him, and he would make a good and kind husband. I am certain it will not be long, with his talents, before he'll be making his own fortune in Havenwood Falls with his quirky supernatural portraits.

Like all our other days, we are in the morning room, but unlike the other days, when Henry is usually so blithe and full of sunshine, today he is low and the mood in the room reflects it.

"Are you well?" I ask, inviting him to share.

He smiles a little sadly. "Yes, I am quite well, thank you. I was up late last night working on the sketches for a very special portrait."

"You do not seem your usual self," I push.

He sighs. "This day is never easy," he says, concentrating too hard on wiping down the brushes. "It's the anniversary of my sister's death."

"Oh, I'm sorry," I say with genuine sadness. "How did she pass?"

"She was with child. Her husband beat her, and she went into childbirth early. Both she and the little boy died. "

I gasp. "That's terrible. What a brute!"

"We all knew he had a dark temper, but she was besotted—there was no telling her. She eloped and was married before my father could stop it."

"I'm so sorry, Henry," I say, placing my hand on his arm and sensing that small spark of electricity that often occurs with our brief touches.

"Love." He shrugs. "It so easily makes you blind."

He's staring right into my eyes, in a way he has never done before. I feel my cheeks begin to burn. We're a decision away from kissing. I can feel it, and so can he. Madness swirls around us.

"There was nothing you could do, Henry," I say, dipping my eyes from the intensity of his stare.

"I should have said more. I should have helped her see him for what he really was, before it was too late. She might have hated me, but she might be alive today."

"Do you honestly think she would have listened to you?"

"Would you?" he asks, still looking at me.

The room spins. There's a weight in this question that makes me uneasy. I swallow hard and try to orient myself in the conversation, which has suddenly swayed to a different meaning.

I inhale sharply. "Are you asking if I would listen if someone knew something about Dragan I was blind to?"

Henry nods.

"I guess that depends on what they were telling me and why."

"What if someone knew a secret about Dragan, a terrible secret, and they didn't tell you and you found out later. Would you wish they had?"

I close my eyes for a moment, trying to process what he's saying. He's doing a terrible job of speaking hypothetically.

"Is there something about Dragan I should know?" I ask, trying to give our conversation some direction.

Henry pauses. "I've come to think of you as a dear friend, Emeline. I want us always to remain friends, but . . . I fear things might change between us if I speak out."

"They already have, Henry." I'm getting increasingly frustrated. "What is it you think you know about Dragan that I should know?"

"There's a lot of talk that goes down in a bar. A lot of gossip and hearsay, and most of it's nonsense—the liquor speaking—but there's no smoke without fire, and just because it's gossip, doesn't mean it's not true."

I run my hand over my face, flipping back the strands of loose hair that have fallen, and let out an exasperated sigh. "What exactly have you heard, Henry?"

"There's some talk going around that Dragan Bishop runs a coven; that he's a witch and that he's made a pact with a demon, which is why he's so wealthy."

I laugh with relief. "Honestly? That's absurd!" I exclaim, smiling.

"There are whispers that the coven has something to do with the murdered girls."

"Okay," I say, pressing my lips together to hear the rest of Henry's ludicrous gossip. "And pray tell me where you gained such reliable information," I say with heavy sarcasm.

"There's talk amongst the girls at the saloon. A couple of them know Dragan . . ." Henry pauses, his blush almost crippling his ability to speak. "I'm sorry, I shouldn't be saying this to you. You're a lady, and his fiancée."

"And I'm not dim enough to imagine Dragan is a saint, Henry. He's middle-aged and traveled halfway across the world. Do you think me so naïve to believe he is a virgin?"

Henry's blush deepens at the word. "No, I guess not. I just wasn't sure how much of the world you knew about."

"Enough."

Henry nods.

"And so the prostitutes have been gossiping about my husband to be," I say, angry at the pitch in my voice that denotes more shame than it should. "Should I be worried? Do his tastes run to the immoral and depraved?" I tease.

I can see that Henry wishes the floor would open up and swallow him. I'm not sure how he thought this conversation would evolve, but clearly it's gotten a little more candid than he thought it would.

"If it wasn't for my sister," he says, "I would be holding my counsel, but I made a promise, Emeline, that I would never stand by and say nothing again. I believe Dragan is dangerous. There, I've said it. And what's more, I think you're too good for him. You're full of light and love and kindness, and Dragan, well, let's just say, one of the girls from the saloon was never seen again after spending a night with Dragan. Something happened to her."

"And how long ago was this? How come I didn't hear about it? This town is small, and people's mouths, and imaginations, run large," I say pointedly.

"About a year ago. Apparently, she went with him to his house, which wasn't unusual, as Dragan often asked for the girls to go to his house. They were sworn to secrecy and paid well to keep their silence. However, this one girl went and didn't come back. The girls are afraid of him; they said he's into strange things, although they won't say what exactly. Mrs. Harrison won't let the girls go off the premises with him anymore."

I fall into the sofa and rub my head with my cool fingers. As much as I want Henry to shut up, I want to know everything he thinks he knows.

"And there are honestly people in Havenwood Falls who believe Dragan is behind this murder?" I ask.

Henry sits down on the opposite sofa, his knees apart and his elbows resting on them. "Like I said, it's bar talk—but I think it's right you should know what folks are saying."

"I think you should leave now," I say, standing. "Right now. I'll pack your things and have them delivered to the saloon this afternoon."

Henry stands, his face falling as he runs his hand through his hair. "I just can't bear the thought of anything bad happening to you, Emeline," he says, approaching me as if I were a dangerous animal. "It would break my heart to think that you found yourself trapped. He's a monster, Emeline. He's not right for you."

"And I suppose you are?" I ask. The question shoots out of my mouth. I snort with disbelief. "You speak too freely."

He shakes his head. "I'd never be so presumptuous to think I could be worthy of being in love with you, Emeline. I'm a poor artist. You're a fine lady. But that doesn't stop me caring deeply about you."

"You should go," I repeat, feeling the world pull apart at the edges.

Henry shakes his head and moves toward the door. "I understand you don't want to believe any of this, and of course, it's hard with no proof. And, with a man like Dragan Bishop, there's never likely to be any proof. The rich have a way of creating their own reality. But I beg you, one last time before I leave, to search your heart, Emeline. And if the girls' references to a red and black door mean anything to you, then maybe search there, too."

I inhale sharply at the mention of the doors. Such a detail can't be explained away by coincidence. And although I don't believe much of what Henry has said, then at least part of it is true. Dragan has had whores back to his house.

"Goodbye, Mr. Hudson."

When Henry has gone, I fall back into the sofa and sob

uncontrollably. It's as if an explosion has gone off in the room. Emotions swirl. Everything is chaos.

I look toward the easel and study Dragan's face, staring back out at me. There's a flash of cruelty in his eyes, and I know that Henry saw it, clear as he saw my wings.

Even though I have calmed myself, tears continue to leak down my cheek, which makes me angry. I'm not the kind of young woman to cry so easily, and yet the overwhelm is intense. It's humiliating enough knowing your fiancé frequents a bawdy house, and that it's the talk of the town, but to think that there are people in Havenwood Falls who believe he is capable of murder—if any of this were true, then Marie Blackstone would have put an end to it months ago. As a witch hunter, she is built to sense evil and the dark arts. There's no way any of it can be true.

I walk around the room, slowly gathering Henry's things. His scent lingers in the air, and it's now tinged with sadness. He was my friend. One of the few friends I've ever had, and I know he felt compelled to tell me such things out of friendship and love, but I wish he hadn't. I wish I could rewind the clock and we could end that whole conversation before it even started. We can't be friends any longer. Not now I know the true extent of his feelings about my marriage to Dragan. I love Dragan.

But why then, as I pack away Henry's things, do I feel the most terrible sense of loss I've ever felt? As if with Henry leaving, the sun has gone down, and now all I'm facing is an endless night full of sweet pleasures and deep sorrows.

"Has Henry gone already?" Mother asks, coming into the morning room, surprised to find me alone.

"He had an urgent message and had to return to town."

"Really? I didn't hear the doorbell."

I shrug, not in the mood to invent more lies. "I said I'd have his things sent over this afternoon."

"Surely they can just stay here until the morning," she says with good nature.

"He won't be coming back, Mother," I say.

Mother's jaw slackens with surprise. "But surely the painting is not yet done," she says, walking over to inspect it.

"I can finish it alone from here."

"Emeline, what happened?"

"Nothing."

Mother's mouth opens and closes but no words come out. I can tell she's confused and can scent trouble as keenly as a blood hound.

"Was he inappropriate?" she finally asks.

I shake my head. "No. We just had a disagreement, and I told him it was best that he should leave."

"About what?"

I shake my head again. I really don't want to start that conversation, but Mother is at my side, her hand gripped firmly on my arm. It doesn't matter to her that I'm soon to be wed and a woman in my own right. To her, I'm still her child. "I'll ask you again, Emeline, what went on between you and Henry?"

"I think he has romantic feelings toward me," I say, blushing deeply.

"Did he tell you so?"

"No, not quite. He said he cared deeply for me but wasn't worthy enough to love me."

"Your father shall have a word with the young man. He has no right coming into our home and causing upset weeks before you are to be married; surely he understands you are unavailable. What possible hope could the silly feckless boy have had in having such a conversation with you?"

"I think he wanted to protect me," I mutter.

With that, Mother drops my arm and fixes me with a steely eye. "Protect you from what? From Dragan? What did he say?"

I turn from her. I'm desperate to tell her everything, but am afraid of the consequences. "It's nothing, just town gossip. You know how it is sometimes."

"Some people have nothing better to do than make up stories about fine folk to make themselves feel better, Emeline. You really shouldn't listen to gossip—and Mr. Hudson should have known better. I had high expectations of him."

I note how she's shifted back to the formal name and know that the door is now shut.

"Are you going to take the word of a presumptuous, jealous, lovesick artist, or are you going to trust what's in your heart?" Mother asks.

"But you said yourself that Dragan is a complicated man, that you worry about the shades in him. And we both know that Father is hardly pleased about the idea of Dragan and me marrying, even if he's not been so bold as to say it. There are whispers that he runs a coven that practices dark arts—could that be possible, Mama?"

Mother's face flickers with a series of expressions before finally settling on one. "Miss Beaumont, the Luna Coven, and the Court of the Sun and the Moon are all perfectly confident Dragan Bishop is a credit to this community. You know that if there was a hint he was dabbling in dark arts or anything else that wasn't entirely appropriate, then Marie Blackstone and the rest of the Court would be on the situation immediately."

"What if they didn't know it, or they couldn't prove it?"

"There are very powerful wards that protect the town of Havenwood Falls, and along with those, an awful lot of petty politics that all combine to ensure that everything runs as it should. Dragan Bishop wouldn't be able to operate any kind of wrongdoing without someone knowing about it."

I sit back down on the sofa and sigh. "I'm just overwrought," I say. "It's all a little emotionally intense at the moment."

"Then you won't like the fact that your father has invited Professor Gleinheart to do his experimentation this evening."

I groan. "I thought we had put that idea to bed. I thought we were all agreed that it was dangerous and foolish."

"We all have—except your father."

"Dragan is not going to be happy about this."

"Well, as it stands, it's your father's house and you're your father's daughter, so I guess he thinks Dragan doesn't have as much a say as Dragan would like."

"What if I refuse to attend this circus?"

"That's your choice, but it means the world to your father to have this all reconciled once and for all. He lives in constant fear that the curse will return."

"But Dragan has the knowledge to stop that happening; he'll protect me."

Mother just nods, but doesn't give her full agreement. "Professor Gleinheart will be here at seven. Would you please go over to Dragan's and invite him to join us? I'd send Harriet, but she's out on errands. Besides, I didn't think you'd object," she says, smiling and standing to make her exit. "Perhaps it will give you the chance to discuss all of these little nerves privately."

She leaves me sitting amongst the ruins of the painting session. I shouldn't have told Henry to go. He was only trying to look after me. With a heavy heart, I pack up the various artist's tools and pack them away in their wraps and bags.

A small voice whispers in my head, *It's not too late.*

I laugh into the empty room. The very thought of calling off the wedding is insane. I am utterly in love with Dragan. I can't imagine life without him.

I leave the house, pulling my shawl around my shoulders. There's a cool breeze and a storm coming. As I walk, I think about everything that has been said. I would be a fool to risk everything on idle gossip. Henry's words go round in my head like a carousel. His mention of the red and black doors will not leave my mind. Maybe that's how I can resolve this. I can give Dragan the ultimatum: either he shows me the rooms or the wedding is off. If he has nothing to hide, then surely . . . The thing is not to make rash decisions, to think things out properly and decide on a course of action. There are still a few weeks until the wedding, which will give me time to properly investigate.

When I arrive at Dragan's house, his butler opens the door and summons me in, telling me that Mr. Bishop is out meeting with a friend, but he should be back in an hour. He offers to make me tea and to make me comfortable in the library where I should find something to keep me occupied. The butler is studying me with a wily eye. He knows I will soon be mistress of the house, and him.

"I don't require tea, thank you," I say, taking off my shawl and heading toward the library with the air of someone who already owns the place.

He slinks off into the shadows of the cool house, not without casting a glance back in my direction.

I take a moment to indulge in being in Dragan's space alone. It smells of him. The light, softened by the leaded windows, causes the dust motes to shimmer slightly. The house has a presence of its own. It's as I'm walking around the room that my eyes catch sight of two keys in a metal bowl. Strangely, each key is attached by a metal hoop to a playing card. One the Queen of Hearts and the other is the King of Spades. They are the keys to the red and black doors; I don't know how I know this, but I do.

I stop in my tracks, my eyes unable to leave the sight of them. The house is so silent. It would be easy to take the keys and sneak upstairs to discover what was behind the doors. I know it's madness, but if I'm to marry Dragan, I need to be certain that . . . what? Do I honestly believe he's capable of such horrors? Do I seriously believe what the gossips in town are saying?

I don't like the answer that forms in my mind. There's doubt. I've seen the flash of darkness in his soul. Isn't that exactly, deep down, what I'm attracted to?

My hands wrap around the keys. If I'm going to do it, the quicker, the better. I look at the clock on the mantel piece. I've already been here almost ten minutes. I snatch them from the bowl, feel the weight of them in my hands. I glance toward the door. Before I can talk myself out of it, I'm creeping up the stairs and along the corridor, my heart pounding so hard it hurts.

I stand equidistant between the two doors, facing the dead end, my head turning from one door to another with indecision. I decide to let fate decide and select one of the keys without looking. It's the black door. With trembling fingers, I insert the key and turn it, hesitating once more as my hand turns the knob. Then the door is open, and I've made the decision to act on my quiet doubts. I sigh with relief. It's just an empty room. The windows have heavy shutters, meaning it's hard to see, but the light from the door is enough to see the chalk white outline of a large pentagram. On each point is a burnt down candle. I know Dragan is a witch, and so none of this surprises me. The room smells of rich incense; frankincense and sandalwood. It's a ritual room, and so maybe part of Henry's knowledge is true, but humans have a propensity to exaggerate based on their own fears, especially about things they don't understand.

I retreat from the room, sure to close the door softly, and turn the key. Flooded with relief, it's almost as if checking the red door is just a formality. My heart is calmed, and the only anxiety I now feel is when I hear the half chime of the grandfather clock downstairs. I put the key in the doorknob and turn it, expecting to find nothing more than another ritual room, or his private study, which must be hidden away from human visitors.

I push the door open and stop on the threshold, trying to translate the sight in front of me. The room is painted red, and the soft low light from a series of gas lamps makes the room look as if it is a living thing.

In the middle of the room is a stone altar, but it has a channel around it and there's no mistaking the bloodstains that have seeped into the stone. My chest tightens. Large candelabras stand at each end, which hold black candles burned down to stumps. I walk around the altar like a somnambulist, taking in the various other terrifying items. Strange masks hang on the wall, and a table hosts an array of ritual paraphernalia, including a selection of sharp knives and other instruments I can't fathom. A wooden book holder holds open a heavy tome, and it's all I can do not to scream when my eyes fall on the drawing of a woman, her body marked with various symbols of the occult, just like those on the girl they found. Just like those etched over Dragan's body.

Henry was right. The town was right.

I turn, desperate to leave, but my flight is halted by the sight of a large painting on the far wall. Framed in heavy gold, the canvas is now nothing but a pale blue background. Once it had contained me. I can barely breathe. The sight of it in this dark arts temple tells me everything I need to know: I exist in this realm because Dragan employed the dark arts to free me, and Mother was right—somehow I am now drawn to the darkness.

I rush from the room, barely able to lock the door for the shaking of my hands. In my desire to leave, I almost forget to return the keys to the library, and I have to turn back on myself, praying I can make everything right before Dragan returns. The keys hit the bowl just as I hear the front door open.

Dragan comes striding in, jumping when he sees me sitting on the sofa. I'm hoping I can hold myself together long enough to issue Mother's invite.

"Emeline!" he says, breaking into a grin. "What a pleasant surprise. What are you doing here?"

"Mother sent me."

He takes off his hat and places it on the end of the sofa and smooths his hair. "Your mother sent her innocent daughter to the lair of the big bad wolf?"

I smile tightly. I want to be sick. I can barely look at him. Standing and smoothing my skirts down, I decide to impart the invitation as quickly as I can and then leave, telling him I have other errands.

He reaches out and takes my hand. "So, what did my wonderful mother-in-law send you over for?"

"Father has decided to go ahead with the experiment with Professor Gleinheart. They're going to do it tonight. Father said you are welcome to come, and Mother extended the invite to supper."

"I can't believe your father is going ahead with this nonsense!" Dragan says, clearly displeased.

I shrug. I don't want to get into a conversation. I want to leave. I want to get as far away from here as possible. I want this all to be over, for Dragan to disappear and for me to never have to think on any of this again, but it's not going to be that easy. I have to tell someone. Who? Marie Blackstone? Would she believe me even if I did tell her?

117

"Emeline?"

I jolt back into the room and see Dragan has been trying to hold a conversation with me.

"Are you all right? You look pale and a little clammy. Are you coming down with something?"

I shake my hand free of his, and make toward the door. "I think I should get home and lie down. I suddenly don't feel too well."

"Shall I walk you back?" he calls after me, but I'm already halfway out of the door.

"No, I'll see you later."

I practically run from his house, glancing over my shoulder only once. I want to find Henry and tell him everything, but since he's a human, it would mean breaking every code of the Court of the Sun and the Moon.

When I arrive home, I fly past Mother, who is arranging a bowl of fresh red roses on the table at the foot of the stairs, with the intention of heading straight to my bedroom.

"Emeline?"

"Dragan will be over later," I call behind me. "I'm off to lie down. The humidity has got to my head," I say, rounding the corner. "A storm is coming."

"I'll call you when . . ." Her words fade as I close my door and lean against it for support. Suddenly, the world seems so fragile, as if it might just fall apart under my feet at any moment.

CHAPTER 20

The rest of the afternoon passes in a tumult of emotions. Several times, I go to my door thinking I will confide in my mother. But I think she would rather believe that I was mad than that Dragan was capable of such things—or that the Court was not able to detect such things. They all hold such faith and pride in the protection of the wards and the power of the magic that the very idea that evil might be within our circle is almost inconceivable.

As the afternoon borders evening and the soft sound of distant thunder fills the sky, I hear the faint background noises of Professor Gleinheart arriving, lugging his heavy equipment with him. Every aspect of the coming hours makes me physically sick to my stomach.

The previous demonstration by Professor Gleinheart had been testing enough, even if a little thrilling. The spirit of a Native child had come through. It had been weeping and speaking a language none of us other than Dragan and Rodavan could fully understand. It had caused a ripple of general distress and wonder. Then there had been the old woman, who was apparently a relation of Gleinheart; some aunt or other scolded him about messing with the afterlife. The whole episode had been so unintentionally comical that, rather sadly for Gleinheart, the audience had settled into the comfortable belief that he was nothing more than some illusionist entertainer and the whole experiment an artfully written show—once again proving that people are happy to believe what they want to believe. And to be fair, neither of the "spirits" had been particularly convincing. If I had been a human, I would have been looking for smoke and mirrors, too.

It's with the hope of it all being a charade that I steel myself for the evening's events. And even if Gleinheart is able to somehow bring forth spirits from beyond the grave, who's to say that he can bring forth Felicity on demand?

Harriet comes to let me know Dragan has arrived, and with him, Marie Blackstone, which surprises me. My stomach twists. I know why Dragan has brought her—he hopes to put a stop to it all with the idea she will view the experiment as dark arts and put an end to it before it begins. There are so many ironies at play that I almost laugh.

"I'll be down in a minute," I say to Harriet, who is hovering at the door. Mother will be displeased I have not changed from my day dress to more suitable evening attire, but my limbs and my soul are too heavy to think about such frivolous things.

When Harriet has left, I stand for a moment, thinking over the idea that maybe Marie Blackstone is here for another reason—the gifting of a universal sign. Maybe she has been put in this place and time so that I can confide my worries and discoveries.

A moment later, the door opens, startling me. It's Harriet again.

"Sorry, Miss Emeline," she says, blushing, "but I have something here for you that I promised I would pass on. It's from Mr. Hudson."

My heart flutters. "Mr. Hudson?"

"Yes. He was waiting at the bottom of our street; just sat on the wall he was, waiting for me to pass, so he says, and then he handed me this and asked if I could give it to you, in secret, like."

She holds out a thick cream envelope that bulges with the shape of a small box.

"Thank you, Harriet," I say, frowning as I take the offering from her hand.

She hesitates as if hoping I might open it in front of her. I wait for her to leave, seeing the slight drop of disappointment on her face.

I open it, removing the little brown paper box that is tied with a thin pink ribbon and hold it in the palm of my hand as I take out the piece of neatly folded paper. Henry has a beautiful hand, and the words flow across the page with elegance and grace.

Dear Emeline,

I am writing to you with so many regrets in my heart. In our short time together, I have come to cherish our friendship more than you can know.

I offer you the most sincere apologies for the route my conversation took earlier this morning. It was ill-judged and inappropriate. I wish you all the happiness in the world; you deserve a life filled with love and kindness.

I humbly request that you might see it in your heart one day to forgive my foolishness and that you accept my hand of friendship, which will always be extended to you.

Wishing you all the very best in your forthcoming marriage to Mr. Bishop, and may life be everything you wish it to be.

Please accept this little token of my affection. May it help you to remember our days fondly and to see the strength of the magic that you hold within you.

With kindest regards.

Henry.

I place the letter down on my dressing table, both relieved and a little disappointed at the reserved nature of his words, then pick open the small bow that holds the box together. With the lid removed, the enamel-winged fairy brooch is exposed, her wings glinting in the lamp of the gaslights. She's so beautiful. I pluck her from her velvet bed and attach her to my dress. Even the horrors of the day are unable to steal away the smile that the sight of her has caused or the meaning behind it. Henry had been the reason she hadn't been for sale. Even before our falling out, he had intended her as a gift for me.

For a moment or two, I'm lost in the idea of what could have been between Henry and me, how life might be playing out differently if I had just reached forward in one of those moments I knew he wanted to kiss me. Would we have become lovers? Would he have saved me? Henry's gift made it known he had seen my wings, my power, my goodness exactly for what it was.

What if it's all still possible? A good life with Henry, full of happiness and love and art? A free life. Maybe we have a future. Maybe love feels like sunshine rather than sweet agonies.

With this new understanding, with this hope, there is no way I can now either marry Dragan or let him get away with the dark arts rituals he's conducting, or else my soul will become as stained as his and I will be lost to the darkness.

Henry has shown me how strong and true I really am.

"Strong enough to also stop this farce with my father and his stupid obsession with a contraption to bring back the dead," I say to myself, as I head out my door with the intention of telling Father that I shall have no part in such an experiment.

Dragan and Marie Blackstone are already in the library, and Father and Professor Gleinheart are making final preparations to the equipment. It bursts into life, its crackling static electricity filling the room with its hideous noise, forcing everyone to either shout or be silent.

Dragan looks over to me and smiles, and then he sees the fairy brooch, cocking his brow in question. Not that I would tell him the truth, even if it wasn't made impossible by the noise.

"Father," I shout.

"Yes, Emeline! Isn't it amazing!" he says, scurrying toward me. "Gleinheart says the storm is good; it will make it stronger."

"Can I have a word?" I ask, nodding in the direction of the door.

He makes his excuses to Professor Gleinheart and follows me outside, closing the door behind him.

"Yes, child."

"I've come to tell you I'll have no part of this. It is against everyone's wishes but yours."

His face crumples with disappointment. "But it's for the best."

"You can't know that. I have a terrible feeling no good will come of that contraption being in this house. I have a terrible feeling about it. Like it's going to do me some harm. I'm going to go back to my room."

His hand flies out and grabs my arm. "I command you, Emeline. I am your father, and you will obey me."

"You don't have that power, Father," I say, shaking him off and heading toward the stairs. "I'll be down for supper," I say, "when you're done with it all."

Father is speechless. He's not used to not having his own way, and certainly not in his own house, but I don't care. This is about me and my life, and I'm tired of everyone thinking they know exactly what's best for me.

ABOUT FIVE MINUTES LATER, there's a knock on my bedroom door. I'm expecting it to be Mother with the threat of a sharp slap, my mother's usual threat when I'm disobedient, but it's not her. It's Dragan, and my blood runs cold.

"What are you doing here?" I ask, suddenly feeling vulnerable. Perhaps he has a way of knowing what my intentions are? Does he know about my secret wanderings through his house; that I opened the doors?

"Your father asked me to come and talk some sense into you—but to be honest, I'm on your side," he says, sitting down on the edge of the bed.

He goes to stroke my cheek, but I flinch, and he notices it.

"What is it?" he asks, his brows knitting together. "You've been cold toward me all day."

"It's nothing. I'm tired, and fed up of all this nonsense."

"What particular nonsense would that be?" he asks, and there's something in his tone that pricks my anxiety.

The question feels more loaded than it should be. I sigh and pinch the bridge of my nose with my fingers, breathing in deeply and steeling myself. I've already stood up to my father, it shouldn't be so hard . . .

"I want to delay the wedding," I finally say.

"What?" he says, jumping to his feet in agitation.

"Just for a couple of months. Everything has happened so quickly and . . . I'm not ready, Dragan. I'm confused."

"You're not ready?" he says through gritted teeth, his eyes darkening as he looms over me.

I stand, wanting to change the power dynamic, and step so that my back is to the door so I have an escape, should I need it.

"Everything has happened so fast. I've only been awake for just over a year, Dragan. It's different for you. You fell in love with me years before I even knew you existed. You've had more time, but for me, waking up in a strange new land, in a completely different time, falling so deeply in love with the man who rescued me from the years of darkness . . . it's all too overwhelming."

"Overwhelming! That's what true love feels like, Emeline."

I shake my head. "I don't even know who I am. I've not had a chance to grow and learn about the true nature of my heart yet. I need time. Time to explore this crazy new world and to explore myself."

Dragan's eyes fall to the fairy pinned to my green cotton dress.

"Would it have anything to do with this little trinket?" he asks, snatching it off and not caring that it's torn right through the fabric. "Does it have anything to do with a certain doe-eyed art tutor who has been calling daily at the house? Is it him you'd like to spend more time *exploring*? Is it, Emeline? I know how my touches have awakened something in you, something wild and uncontainable. Has it sent you wild with lust for all other pretty men?"

"No!" I protest, backing farther into the door and feeling the handle in the palm of my hand behind my back. "It's nothing to do with Hen—Mr. Hudson. Nothing at all. He's a friend, that's all."

Dragan grabs me by the neck, his hand just loose enough not to interfere with my breathing, but tight enough to let me know he could snuff out my life in a moment.

"A friend!" he sneers.

"He's not the reason," I say, staring defiantly into his black eyes.

"Then what is the reason, Emeline?" he says, his spit landing on my face.

"I just don't want to marry you," I say, strangely emboldened.

"You. Just. Don't. Want. To. Marry. Me?" he asks, incredulously. His laughter is cruel, and he punches the door above my shoulder. "After everything I have done for you? I spent decades of my life dedicated to breaking your curse, to bringing you back, and this is the thanks I get. And why, exactly? What's changed since last week, when I had my hand between your legs and you were begging me to make you my wife? Help me understand this madness, Emeline."

I refuse to cower, and as soon as he steps back, sweeping his hand through his hair with angry disbelief, I open the door behind me and step back out into the hallway, hoping they'll be able to hear me above the sound of the terrible cracking static noise that is now filling the house.

Dragan grabs me by the wrist, and from his inside pocket, he pulls out a thin piece of carved ornate wood, like a magician's wand, and points it in my direction, muttering under his breath as his eyes glower darkly. I continue to try to pull away, making small progress. Dark magic swirls around me. My limbs and soul grow heavy as he enchants me. I can feel him entering my thoughts, and no matter how hard I try to press him back, he advances.

"My, my," he says, his face morphed into someone I barely recognize. "You have been a busy little bee, haven't you? Exploring my home when I was not there. Going places I expressly forbid."

I swallow hard. "I-I don't know what you mean," I stammer.

"Yes, you do, Emeline. You opened the doors, and now I understand."

"You're not the only one who understands everything now," I say in barely a whisper. "I know you for what you really are. A murderer, a black arts witch. And what's more, I'm going to go downstairs and tell Marie Blackstone everything I have discovered."

"Do. Marie Blackstone has no power over me. My magic is greater than hers. I wouldn't have been able to do all I have otherwise."

We have been conducting a strange waltz whilst Dragan has been casting me under his spell, and now we are at the top of the stairs. I glance over the banister and thankfully see that the door to the library is open. I'm so close to safety, all I need to do is call out and they'll come.

The doorbell rings.

"I know you murdered that girl," I say, "and the one they found last year. I know you're a monster," I say, as tears roll down my cheeks. "I loved you—so much so that I could forgive you almost anything, but not this, Dragan, not this. I can't live in the shadows when I was born for the light," I say, opening my wings and feeling their power at my back. Magical energy surges through me.

The doorbell rings again, and Father, clearly impatient of waiting for Harriet, hurries across the hallway.

"When I tell Marie Blackstone," I say with a tightened jaw, "she'll tell the Court and they'll deliver justice—justice for those girls."

Dragan's hand tightens around my wrist, so much so that I'm afraid he might snap it. His rage is almost all-consuming, his eyes dark as the stormy night.

"Let me go," I growl under my breath. "Let me go before I start screaming."

I glance toward the door and see Henry standing on the doorstep, talking earnestly with Father.

"You wouldn't dare," Dragan whispers low in my ear. "I have the power to destroy everyone you love. My magic knows no boundaries. It's too powerful for their pathetic wards. How do you think I got away with it for so long?"

"Let me go!" I shout, loud enough for Father and Henry to turn in my direction.

"Emeline?" Father shouts as Henry forces his way forward, sensing the threat and seeing that Dragan is attacking me.

A strike of lightning cracks the sky and the contraption in the library is fired up to such a capacity that it has become a quieter whir, allowing the rest of the party to come out from the library and witness the commotion unfolding. The sight of Marie Blackstone's stony face causes the slightest break in Dragan's concentration, and I break free of his grip on my wrist, flying upward with the power of my wings.

A great wave of energy thumps me in the chest, and I'm tumbling backward, over the bannister and toward the oh, so pretty floor. Time slows as the realization hits me that Dragan has bound my wings. There's no way to . . .

EPILOGUE

I had known Professor Gleinheart's contraption was a bad thing. I had known it would bring me harm. And so it did. Whatever powerful dark energy the machine used to create a split between the worlds of the living and the dead, it caused my soul to be trapped forever in the rooms of the Fairchild Mansion. In the end, justice won, and I paid for my father's sins.

Years passed. The Old Families grew in power and wealth. Dragan was exiled, although my father didn't think that was punishment enough—he had petitioned the Court to have Dragan executed, not just for my death but for the murders of the human girls too. When the Court refused, Dragan's name was forbidden to ever be spoken in Father's presence again, and the Fairchilds and Bishops have been at war ever since.

Time doesn't heal all wounds.

Often, as I spent my hours looking out the windows of the Fairchild Mansion, I would see Henry Hudson break from his daily walks past the house and pause to look up, as if he could sense I was still there. How I longed to yell out to him, to touch him, to tell him what a fool I had been to not see what we might have been until it was too late. I wanted him to know that the biggest regret of my life was that I had died not knowing how his lips tasted or how his hands felt wrapped around my waist.

Every year on the anniversary of my death, he would come with a bouquet of roses and leave them on the bottom step. My mother would stop to read the card, and then she'd leave them there until they faded. For a few years, his bouquet would be joined by others. But time makes people forget.

Then, one year, Henry didn't come, and I learned he too had died. Influenza. I'd had a hope he would come back to me in ghost form and that we could finally be together, but Henry Hudson was too good for this Earth.

I mourned his death more than my own.

My parents died, and the beautiful house fell into disrepair. No one wanted to live in a murder house. I watched the town and its people change day by day, decade by decade. Unimaginable wonders—technology, fashion, politics—all played out on the small stage in front of the mansion. Then a family arrived, filling the house with life and noise and energy, breathing new life into it. And with them came their son, Harry—an artist.

We hope you enjoyed this story in the Legends of Havenwood Falls series featuring a variety of supernatural creatures. Want to know more about Emeline? Read more in *Forever Emeline* (A Havenwood Falls High Novella) by Katie M. John.

ABOUT THE AUTHOR

Katie M. John is the London based author of several bestselling and award-winning Young Adult titles. She is most well known for her internationally bestselling series, The Knight Trilogy.

Katie lives with a handsome giant, two mud-puddle fairies, and two cute kitties. She likes to eat Jaffa Cakes whilst writing and also is a complete Ghost Adventures fan.

You can discover more about Katie at her official website www.katiemjohn.com

RELEASED FROM A CURSE

BY BRYNN MYERS

~ A Legends of Havenwood Falls Novella ~

HAVENWOOD FALLS

LEGENDS

RELEASED FROM A
CURSE

BRYNN MYERS

ALSO BY BRYNN MYERS

The Prophecies of The Nine Series
Entasy Book 1
Redemption Book 2

The Jorja Graham Duology
The Life & Death of Jorja Graham
The Echoed Life of Jorja Graham

Falling Out of Focus

Captivated by Crimson

Fairytale Confessions—print only

One Last Con—e-book only

"They slipped briskly into an intimacy from which they never recovered."
—F. Scott Fitzgerald, *This Side of Paradise*

CHAPTER 1

EGYPT

Thoth checked on Khalida and found her sleeping soundly. She looked so innocent, but as he found out earlier, looks can be deceiving. Khalida had yet to calm since arriving here. At first, she'd been vicious, and he'd assumed it was a result of being contained within the Prison of Asria, a watcher's vessel used only by the elite guard. It had the finest accommodations and was more than adequate to house any djinn, most certainly a betrayer the likes of Khalida, but Thoth opted to try to earn her trust by offering her a choice—stay in the vessel or move to a home of her choosing. Khalida had of course picked the latter, but there was a catch Thoth had neglected to mention. The *home* would have invisible walls, allowing him to observe her every move. It was for his research. He needed to know everything he could about her. His frustration had been that he wouldn't be able to observe Amani too.

"I'm tired of living in this glass house. I'd rather be in the prison," Khalida raged, her fists banging the clear glass.

"The choice was made. You will live within the boundaries," Thoth replied coldly.

Khalida began to change, her skin paling as her eyes turned opaque. Silver hieroglyphs appeared on her arms and chest, and her raven locks turned stark white. Khalida was enraged, exactly as Thoth hoped she'd be, when he took a sample of her blood. He held his palm outstretched, and silver liquid began to flow from her to him, incensing her even more. The blood easily passed through the barrier between them and swirled in a tornadic twist, hovering just above Thoth's hand.

"That should be enough this time," he said as he willed the blood into a vial on the table behind him.

Khalida had not felt any pain—Thoth had made sure of it when he extracted her life force—but she raged on nonetheless. He quickly became annoyed with her tantrum and snapped his fingers. In an instant, Khalida returned to her human appearance and began to float midair. Thoth used his thoughts to move her through the air until she was hovering above her bed. Gently laying her down, he moved the blanket placed at the end of her bed to cover her.

"Sleep well, djinn."

Thoth thought back to when Khalida was a young girl, before the djinn in her matured and she became the force of destruction and chaos she was today. She was a quiet child, introspective and curious. Some called her aloof, but Thoth saw she was always thinking, always planning. Khaldun had been assigned to them as a watcher the day of their change—a mistake too late to remedy at this point, but a mistake nonetheless. A watcher is only there to observe and report. Action is only taken when commanded by one of the gods, himself included. Amani and Khalida had been different, though, and while the normal course of action was taken to keep guard over their upbringing, Thoth had wanted to observe the twins firsthand. He'd never wanted to appear as the god he was and only have them respond to him in reverence. Instead, he appeared as a servant working in the house. It gave him a chance to see them in a relaxed atmosphere, where they didn't feel as though they were being monitored. They were, after all, children growing up in a human world, no one ever suspecting what lay just beneath the surface.

Amani was warm and thoughtful, easy to approach, while Khalida was cool and cautious, wanting to understand people's intentions before she allowed them in. At one of Thoth's impromptu visits, he posed as a guard. He watched as the girls came down the hall, Amani carrying a doll and Khalida a familiar rectangular box filled with dice —Senet, a favorite game among children and adults. When one of the maids tripped and fell as she came down the stairs, Amani rushed to her side, asking what she could do to help, while Khalida stared at them, arms crossed and agitated.

"Will our breakfast be late now?"

"Khalida," Amani scolded. "Syrah has hurt her ankle. We can get our own meal."

Khalida glared at them for a moment before she turned and walked away. Thoth broke character as a guard and asked her what happened, even though he'd seen it all play out from across the room.

Khalida's response was swift. "She was clumsy, and now I have to suffer."

"How are you suffering?"

Khalida glared up at him. "What concern is it of yours?"

Thoth shook his head and went back to his stance as a guard as she walked away, not once turning back to see if Amani and Syrah were still seated on the floor. This was just one of many examples over the years of how they were two sides of the same coin— opposites in every way. Light and dark separated, but then again, they were born of an argument between Sekhmet and Shu. It could just be that the twins were elements of their makers' personalities, and the differences between them had nothing to do with one another at all. All Thoth knew was he had much to learn about them, and what he'd hoped would be easy had become a challenge, a riddle to solve.

Thoth made his way over to his lab and began to process Khalida's silver blood. He knew one of these times he'd find a unique marker that would show him the path to separating Amani and Khalida. He was just missing one piece, and once he had that, the process could begin. However, this missing link was elusive. How connected and linked were they? They were twins, yes, but they shared so much more. He needed to find out their secrets.

Khalida began to moan, and Thoth turned to understand why she would be awake. He'd put her to sleep, and she should be down until he chose to wake her. Khalida was writhing on the bed and tugging at her linen sheath. Thoth turned to grab a vial to extract more of her blood to try to identify the cause, but when he did, he noticed the blood he'd taken earlier was changing—reacting to something. Thoth took a closer look and noticed gold flecks shimmering within Khalida's mercurial blood. He turned back to Khalida and grinned when she called out Nathan's name. This was it, the moment he'd been waiting for.

Thoth held out his palm and summoned more of her blood as she continued to writhe in ecstasy. This time her blood swirled in his palm, not in a silver vortex but a twisted gold and silver ladder. Was Amani the same? He needed to know.

Khalida awoke in a spark of light and stood before Thoth. She was still trapped behind his invisible cage, but awake nonetheless.

"What have you done to me?"

"Nothing. You woke of your own accord," Thoth replied as he placed the blood he'd just received from her into a crystal container. "I have no idea how you've managed it, but I will uncover it soon enough."

"RELEASE ME!"

Thoth snapped his fingers, and Khalida's screams were silenced. She continued to rage, but at least he didn't have to hear it. Thoth moved back to his vials and the container holding Khalida's blood—correction, Amani and Khalida's blood—and went to work on finding the solution, now that he had the pieces to the puzzle.

CHAPTER 2

HAVENWOOD FALLS

$\mathcal{A}$s the morning light spilled into the cabin, Amani began to wake. She was in Nathan's arms, their bodies intertwined, naked and unabashed. The covers on the bed were tousled, and the cool mountain air was blowing in from the slightly open window.

"You are so beautiful in the morning," Nathan said as he twirled one of the curls near her face. "I mean, you're beautiful every morning, but now, here in my arms . . ."

"I thought the only way I could feel another person's emotions was to be in contact with their blood or life force, but with you," she paused, "I've never felt a connection so deeply."

"Amani, I've spent my entire life hiding my emotions. I assumed it was better than letting anyone in to see my pain. Losing my parents at an early age was hard. Yes, I had Lillian and I'm grateful for her, but I chose to bury myself in my work instead of experiencing life." He brushed back the hair from her face. "Then, in the process of trying to find closure, I found you."

Amani reached for Nathan's hand. "We found each other, it seems."

"You have stolen my heart."

"I didn't mean to steal anything," she protested innocently.

"Not in the actual sense." Nathan chuckled. "I mean, you've made it so I will never be able to be with another. I am yours and yours alone, Amani."

She leaned in closer, their lips inches apart. "I've been learning about what it means to love. A parent loves a child, and the child loves the parent. I thought I loved Khalida, but I was wrong about what her love meant. What does it mean to love someone other than your family?"

Nathan pulled her closer until their lips touched.

"It feels like this," he said as he kissed her. He deepened their kiss and held her gently in his arms.

Amani pulled back after a few moments. "I think I like love."

"I think I like love, too."

The two spent the next hour talking and making love. It was glorious to be in perfect communion with what had become the other half of their souls. They had an inexplicable connection, and if it wasn't love, then love surely didn't exist.

"In your eyes, Amani, I see the hope of a thousand futures, and my only wish is that I get to spend at least one of them with you."

Amani placed her hand on the side of Nathan's face. "It is I who hopes to spend more than that with you."

Nathan rose with a final peck to the tip of her nose. "And that we will, but first, it's time for me to meet Calla Lily."

Amani smiled, acknowledging his commitment, then watched as he sauntered to the bathroom. Upon hearing the water of the shower, she turned to gaze out the window as another deer passed in front of the cottage they'd been offered outside Whisper Falls Inn. It was small and quaint and served as the perfect place for the two of them to stay while Thoth and the goddesses figured out a solution to break the link between her and Khalida. The views of the mountains were amazing, and of all the places they could've ended up, they were lucky it was here. It had been a long time since Amani had seen animals roaming about or trees swaying when the wind blew before a summer rain. Everything about Havenwood Falls seemed like a dream.

The days following the incident in the square had been hectic to say the least. The supernatural residents were now aware of the powerful djinn they had living in their town and were reluctant to embrace Nathan and Amani as a result. Amani, however, wanted nothing more than to meet each and every one of them. She wanted to learn about what made them unique and if any of them were like her. Calla Lily explained that it might take time and them getting to know her before the tension would ease and they became welcoming.

"You simply need to show everyone the Amani we know, and not the djinn Roman has informed them about," Calla Lily had said.

"But I will not harm them," Amani had replied.

"They don't know that—yet," Calla Lily had insisted.

However, time was the one word Amani didn't want to hear. She'd lost too much of that and missed out on so many experiences when she was bound to the camera and the canopic jars. Now all she wanted to do was make up for it. She spent most days trying to be as normal as possible, which for her was hard. Amani couldn't turn off the immense power coursing through her veins, and yet all she wanted was to be like everyone else. She wanted to show not only the goddesses and Thoth, but Nathan, too, that she could make this work—that she could live in the human world and not hurt anyone—but not using her powers was a work in progress.

Nathan and Calla Lily were trying to help her to understand her powers and what it meant to be a djinn. Calla Lily had found some ancient family tombs, but they were of little to no help, considering Amani and Khalida were unlike others of their kind. The three of them thought if Amani could learn to control the energy surging through her, she'd be all right. However, whenever she used her powers, the Court of the Sun and the Moon, the supernatural leaders of this town, sensed the surges and insisted on boundaries until they could feel comfortable with her abilities. They'd convened a meeting and collectively decided to mark her with a magical brand to try to bind her powers, or at least subdue them. Their attempt ended in failure.

Amani's hieroglyphs began to glow, and it was clear the Court would have to find another way. She tried to explain she wasn't angry, that the symbols were a reaction to the intense magic they were wielding, but they weren't willing to risk it. Instead, they asked her to never use her magic without consulting one of the members of the Court. Mihail Petran, who owned the inn and was also on the Court, along with his wife Irina and sister-in-law Madame Luiza, had volunteered to keep a close eye on her—not that there was much to see.

Whenever Amani wasn't communing with nature, she was reading to learn about modern society.

For all the years she was bound to the canopic jars, she wasn't without education. Thoth had given them a library full of ancient texts and information about the beings who roamed the worlds, along with languages and customs for every culture. It was available to her and Khalida, but Khalida didn't care to learn about things she'd never experience. Learning about the outside world only made her acrimonious, so she refused to ever read them, but thankfully, Amani had, and now she had a wealth of knowledge.

Amani already knew something about every being living in Havenwood Falls, but only had snippets of information for some. Which was why she was so excited when she'd encounter one in person. She wanted to ask them questions and compare notes to what she already knew about their race. With that in mind, Amani caught sight of more movement outside the cottage and quickly dressed, running barefoot out the front door.

CHAPTER 3

*T*ilting his head from side to side, Nathan stretched the tight muscles as he continued to dry off. Spotting Amani outside, her golden curls glinting in the sun as she knelt next to a tree, he wondered what she was doing. However, if he'd learned anything during the past few weeks, it would be a waste to assume anything other than she was communing with nature and connecting to the energy within Havenwood Falls. At first, he had no clue what she was talking about, but after a few examples and some help from her and Calla Lily, he too could feel the electrical buzz. Calla Lily referred to it as "magic in the air," while Amani seemed to feel it from every living thing. Either way, Havenwood Falls had become a special place for them both.

Nathan took one last look at Amani before continuing to get dressed. He was set to meet with Calla Lily shortly. She'd left word that she received a letter and they needed to talk about it. He'd wondered what it could be about but quickly dismissed it, since no one other than Lillian knew he was still here. He'd called her a few days after the showdown in the town square to say he was going to be extending his stay a bit longer—that he was enjoying the tranquility of the mountains. Lillian had of course questioned him, but then told him to enjoy his much-needed vacation.

"I'll expect you in a week then," Lillian had quickly stated, then said she loved him and hung up. It was, after all, a long-distance call.

"Hi," Nathan said as Amani walked into the room.

"There was an angel outside, but when I went to talk to her, she vanished, so I talked to the trees instead."

Nathan kissed her cheek. "And did you learn anything today?"

"Only that the trees love being close to the pond and close to the aether."

"Aether?"

"Yes, it's a part of the universe—part of everything. The aether was put there many years ago by a witch—a Howe witch to be exact."

Nathan put on his waistcoat and buttoned the buttons. "That sounds interesting."

"It was. She was beautiful and powerful."

"More powerful than you?"

"I am uncertain. I could only feel her magic through the land, but based on that, it is possible," Amani said as she found a vase for the handful of wildflowers she was holding in her hand.

"You don't normally pick the flowers."

"No, they were a gift from the pixies."

"They're beautiful."

"You are ready to go?" she asked as Nathan sat to put on his shoes.

"Yes, I'm headed to see Calla Lily now. Would you like to come?"

"No, but I'd love to walk with you until you start to head past the inn. Madame Luiza offered to show me how to cook food. Maybe soon I can cook for us here." Amani beamed.

"I'd like that," Nathan said, reaching for his pocket watch. "Are you ready to go?"

"Yes," she said as she picked up the vase of wildflowers. "I want to give these to Irina."

"I think she'll love them," he replied, latching the door to the cottage.

Nathan dropped off Amani and made his way down the cobbled street until he reached Calla Lily's shop. He moved to open the door, but was halted when it swung toward him. Nathan stood face to face with Roman Bishop, who glared at him before walking past without a word.

"Good morning to you too, Roman," Nathan said as he shook his head and looked at Calla Lily standing in the doorway. "What's his problem today?"

"Well, despite that being his normal demeanor, he's especially agitated because I won't help him find out more about the djinn race and their abilities."

"Why does he want to know so badly?"

"Because he saw her strength. And Roman always wants to align himself with power. He was asking me about ancient texts, but unfortunately I'm fresh out," Calla Lily shrugged.

"Is he always like this with visitors to Havenwood Falls? I mean, does he always want to investigate the supernaturals who visit?" Nathan leaned in close and whispered.

"No, not necessarily investigate, but after what happened, I'm sure he sees Amani as a threat, and therefore the research he's doing on the djinn species is more intense. Amani and Khalida are unique, and I'm sure he just wants to know all he can about his foes."

Nathan's brow arched. "Amani is not his foe."

"I know that, but since she refuses to give him information regarding the Prison of Asria and why it can contain a djinn, he's taking it personally."

"Well, he needs to get over it," Nathan snapped. "We'll be gone soon enough."

Calla Lily frowned. "He's the only one who won't miss you two. Madame Luiza, Irina, and I were all talking to Saundra Beaumont about how much fun it is to watch Amani as she experiences the world. She's thousands of years old, but in many ways, she's just a young girl who has the wonder of youth in her favor."

"Yeah, she does. This morning she was talking to the trees."

Calla Lily laughed. "The aspens behind the cottage?"

Nathan nodded. "Apparently, some pixies gave her some flowers."

"Well, this is good news. They are comfortable with her, and we need others to feel the same."

Calla Lily walked to the back of the shop for a moment, returning with a package. It was postmarked to him c/o Calla Lily Mircea.

"What's this?"

"I'm not exactly sure," she said as she pointed to the return address, "but it's from New York."

He scrunched his face. "I sent her a letter after our call to explain everything—well, as much as I could explain, that is. I wonder what she has sent."

"Only one way to find out," Calla Lily said as she handed him a pair of scissors.

Nathan opened the box, and the edge of his lips turned upward into a grin. "She sent some of the parchments I'd been working on before I left."

A customer walked in, and Calla Lily moved out from behind the counter to go help her. It was then that he opened the handwritten letter and pulled his glasses from his vest pocket.

Dear Nathan,

I'm glad you're taking some time for yourself, but we both know all too well you'll be missing your work soon enough. I took the liberty to send you some pages still in need of translation. I hope the mountain air and peace and quiet will help clear your mind so you can return to New York fresh and inspired. This is the new start you've so desperately needed now that you have closure with Samuel's camera and journal. I miss you terribly and look forward to seeing you soon.

Love, Lillian

Nathan folded the letter and began to look through the parchments. He'd always wondered what some of the hieroglyphs meant, but now looking at them again, he recognized more of them. He'd seen them recently.

"Look at this. Recognize these?" he asked after Calla Lily said goodbye to her customer.

"Amani has these same markings," Calla Lily gasped.

"This one is fire." He adjusted his glasses. "This one means wind, and this one here is related to Sekhmet." He pointed.

"Could this be about her and Khalida then? About how they were created?"

"Possibly, but why would it be amongst the things I was working on? I had no idea about djinn before I came here."

Calla Lily's brow arched. "That's the thing about fate, Nathan— you can't hide from it. It finds you whether you want it to or not. You were always meant to be here. You and Amani were always meant to be together."

Nathan's eyes went wide. "I wish I understood things the way you do. Being human is a bit of an inconvenience," he laughed. Calla Lily chuckled and bade Nathan farewell, but as he walked back toward the inn, he thought about what she'd said in regards to fate.

With a clear picture of Amani in his mind, he felt as though his life had started with a single letter regarding his father's camera.

"Did you and Calla Lily have a good meeting?" Amani asked, taking notice of the items in his hands.

"Oh!" Nathan said as he jerked back, almost losing his grip on the parchments. "We did," he said, lifting them in his hand. "Lillian sent these."

"I didn't mean to startle you."

"It's all right. I was just thinking about you and then there you were."

"You were thinking about me?"

Nathan smiled. "I'm always thinking about you."

Amani's face lit up. "So, what are they?"

"Stories and mentions of you and Khalida, I think," he replied.

"About us? Why would you have parchments written about Khalida and me?"

"To be honest, I'm not certain, but these were ones sent by the other Egyptologists after my father's disappearance. They were apparently found near your vessel." He moved toward the parlor. "Do you remember me telling you about the jar sitting on a ledge with a barrier of red stones carved like scarabs and a shimmering liquid no one could identify?" Nathan asked, spreading out the parchment on the coffee table. "The one with the mysterious hieroglyphs?"

"Yes, I remember. The ones the night raiders came in and attempted to steal when they were badly burned."

"Yes." He pointed to a line of hieroglyphs. "This here, if I'm reading it correctly, talks of the protective magic surrounding the two jars."

"This references the scarabs. They're colored red to show they were made of carnelian." She pointed to the next. "And this references the mercury."

"That's mercury?"

Amani nodded. "What did you think it was?"

"I thought it represented Hathor, with the circle and half-moon here at the top."

"No, Hathor is here," Amani said, moving down the page a bit. "Oh my, this *is* a reference to Khalida and me."

"Why do you say that? I mean, I am happy to confirm my suspicions, but I'm too curious for you not to clarify it."

"All of these symbols and their descriptions. Sekhmet and Shu are here, along with Hathor and Ma'at. Then, there are the references to silver and gold, fire and ice, darkness and light. All of this here shows how we were made and how we ended up broken." Amani shook her head. "I don't understand. Why would they have our story documented? We were a disgrace and had to be hidden away."

Nathan sighed. "You are not a disgrace, Amani. I think it's more likely that they wrote it down to explain how you two came to be. It's been said many times that you and Khalida are special and nothing is more evidence of that than the power you two wield."

"I suppose so."

"I find it interesting and comforting in equal measure," Nathan said, rolling up the parchment and putting it into the leather sleeve.

"Why is that?" Amani asked as Nathan set the container on the settee.

"Calla Lily told me when we first met that sometimes the answers we seek don't always come the way we hope. Sometimes, we find something entirely different. She said that it was important to keep an open mind when it came to the possibilities beyond understanding."

"And how does that apply to Khalida and me being part of the parchment?" she questioned.

"Because if my father had never been in Egypt and been a part of your past, you would never be part of my present and hopefully my future," Nathan said, reaching for her hands and pulling them to his lips. "I think Calla Lily knew what was about to transpire all along, and those words were meant for me to keep an open mind."

Amani blushed. "I guess fate did bring us to this point, and I'll be forever grateful."

CHAPTER 4

*T*he next morning, Nathan was shaving when he heard the front door close. When he walked out of the bathroom with a towel around his neck, his suspenders hanging at his sides, and his undershirt exposed, Amani stared at him curiously.

"What is on your face?"

He laughed. "Shaving cream. You use it to get rid of facial hair you don't want."

"I like your facial hair. Do not use that cream to remove it."

Nathan used the towel to wipe it off and grinned. "Very well. I will keep the whiskers for you."

Amani rushed into his open arms. "I heard the wolves roaming the woods earlier and was up hoping to catch their attention. I would love to talk to one of them. I have so many questions." Amani beamed as Nathan held her close.

"I'm certain you do, but like Calla Lily said, the town is still trying to adjust to you being here. Give them time. I'm sure they'll be happy to talk to you soon," Nathan said as he kissed her forehead.

Amani looked up at him. "The pixies talk to me, but that angel is still elusive. Are you hungry? I made breakfast."

"You did?"

"Yes," she beamed. "I made oatmeal."

Nathan's brows furrowed. "How'd you learn to make oatmeal?"

"Madame Luiza showed me yesterday," she said as she took Nathan by the hand and led him into the kitchen. "Mine doesn't smell exactly like hers, but I think I did it right."

There on the stove was a large cast iron pot with steam rising. When Amani reached for the spoon to stir it, Nathan knew something was off.

"Amani, honey, what did you put in here?"

"Oats, water, cinnamon, and salt."

Nathan nodded his head. "And what else?"

"Garlic." Amani beamed.

"Ah yes, that's it." Nathan scrunched his nose.

Her face fell. "What is wrong with that? My mother often put garlic in with the breakfast grains."

"We don't really use garlic for breakfast," he said as he tugged his ear, "but I appreciate that you went to the trouble to make food for me. You know you don't have to, right?"

Amani's face fell and her shoulders slumped.

"No, no, no." Nathan said as he brushed the hair from her face and gently caressed her cheek.

"But I failed. Maybe I can't be a human after all."

"I don't think anyone ever expected you to. I know I certainly don't. You're perfect just the way you are."

A smile spread across her face. "Really?"

"Really," Nathan answered. "Besides, why would I ever want you to be a boring human like me when I've seen how amazing you are when you embrace your djinn?"

Amani's face fell again. "It is not good for me to embrace that side of me, Nathan. Not for you and not for those around me. I'm dangerous."

He reached for her hands and pulled them to his lips. "Beautiful and dangerous, yes, but you are good, and more importantly, you are not your sister."

"Khalida is only part of the story, and she wasn't all bad either. She

155

had a good side—a sort of loving side." Amani sighed. "She chose to let the bad rule her—to be different."

"That's what I'm saying. You choose good, and therefore the parts of you that scare you can be controlled."

Amani met Nathan's eyes. "I just hope Thoth finds a solution soon. Then I won't have to worry anymore."

"I'm sure he will. In the meantime, how about we get dressed and head over to the inn for some of Madame Luiza's blueberry jam and biscuits."

Amani nodded. "I do love that jam."

Nathan turned off the burner and used a towel to push the hot pan to the center of the stove. "Best to let that cool before we do anything with it."

Nathan and Amani left the cottage and walked over to the inn, hoping they hadn't missed breakfast. "Do you think there are still some biscuits left? I want a biscuit."

Nathan laughed. "I'm sure Madame Luiza will have extra."

When they rounded the corner and walked into the dining room, the scent of freshly cooked bacon wafted over to them. "Now that is breakfast."

"Nathan," Amani scolded.

"I'm sorry. Garlic and oatmeal are just not a good combination."

"What is this about oatmeal and garlic?" Madame Luiza asked as she headed out of the kitchen.

Amani's face fell, and Nathan scrambled to answer the question without upsetting her any further. "Well, ugh, yeah."

Madame Luiza crossed her arms in front of her chest. "What did you do, Nathan?"

Amani interjected before Nathan could respond. "I made the oatmeal just like you told me to, but I added garlic like my mother used to, and he didn't like it."

Madame Luiza bit back a smile. "Well, garlic is not exactly a good addition, Amani," she said as she put her arm around Amani. "How about we meet again tomorrow and learn something you can use garlic in."

Nathan mouthed, "Thank you."

"You're not off the hook, Nathan," Amani said as she walked toward one of the tables.

"Madame Luiza, you still have biscuits, right?" Nathan whispered.

Madame Luiza laughed. "I have blueberry jam as well, but I doubt that will save you from this, dear."

"Yeah, but a fella can try, right?"

"Flowers might help." She winked.

Nathan and Amani laughed as Madame Luiza brought out their breakfast. Conversation flowed smoothly as they talked to Irina and Madame Luiza about going into Montrose, but things turned somber again when they cautioned against Amani leaving, out of concern for any repercussions with the goddesses or even with Roman and the Court. They agreed it was best for her to stay put until Thoth, Hathor, and Ma'at returned.

Amani turned to face the lobby when the door opened and Roman walked into Whisper Falls Inn, his arrogance leading a few steps ahead of him. Amani caught his eye as she walked out of the dining room and into the parlor. The two glared at one another before Mihail interrupted the nonverbal exchange.

"What can I do for you, Roman?"

"Just stopping by to make sure things are going smoothly. You know, for the town and the Court's safety," he said, casting a glance in Amani's direction.

"Everything is going well. Nathan and Amani have settled in quite nicely. We see them every day."

"You do?" Roman questioned.

Irina came to stand next to her husband. "Yes, Roman. We do," she insisted.

The chime on the door drew all of their attention. There in the doorway stood a man in dungarees and a rugged worn shirt rolled up to mid-forearm.

"Oh good. You're here," Roman said as Sheriff Ric Kasun strode toward them.

"The question is why, Roman. Why did you ask me to join you here?"

Mihail offered his hand. "Good morning, Ric."

"Can I get you a cup of coffee?" Irina asked.

"That would be great. Thank you."

"Are you all done with niceties? I'd like to have a real conversation," Roman snapped.

"Of course, Roman, because the world exists for your needs only, it seems," Ric quipped.

Irina returned with a mug and handed it to Ric. "Madame Luiza said she has a plate waiting for you when you're finished here."

Ric nodded. "I appreciate that. Hopefully this won't take long," he said, taking a sip of the coffee and glaring at Roman over the rim of the mug.

Roman's lip curled into a snarl. "We need to have yet another discussion about our new residents and how they—or she—should be monitored. You may not have been in the square that night, Ric, but that djinn is more of a threat than she appears to be."

"What is your concern? From what I understand, she is doing well here and is no threat to the town or its residents. Unless *you* are feeling threatened, Roman."

The look on Roman's face spoke volumes, and everyone present knew Ric had struck a nerve. However, when Amani entered the room, Roman's tension seemed to amplify—hers too.

"Amani, we'd like to you to meet Ric Kasun," Mihail offered.

Her eyes lit up as he extended his hand in greeting. "You are one of them—one of the wolves I've seen in the woods. I've wanted to meet you. To say hello," she rambled on. "You're beautiful."

Ric cleared his throat. "Um. Thank you?"

"Yes. I've been watching you and the other wolves in the mornings. I've never met any human wolves. I mean, shifters," she said quickly as she glanced over at Irina. "I've been learning more about the people who live here in Havenwood Falls. I hope I haven't offended you."

Ric smiled. "No, not at all. It's nice to meet you as well. Welcome to our town. If you need anything, feel free to reach out to me or my wife, Gaby."

"Thank you. I will do that. I'd love to know more about you and your kind. I transform, too, but not like you."

Roman huffed, and Amani cast her eyes to him in disgust, a few of the hieroglyphs shimmering on her arms and neck. "Why is it that you are here, Roman? I have done nothing to warrant questioning. The little incident of magic was me helping one of the pixies in the forest this morning, nothing more."

"You are not allowed to use your powers within the boundaries of this town," Roman barked. "And it's clear you do not grasp what exactly that means."

"I'm no threat to you or anyone here."

"And how can we be certain of that when you refuse to talk about who and what you are?"

"Is that what this is all about, Roman?" Ric questioned. "Because if it is, Conall saw her this morning doing just as she said—helping. A rabbit became trapped in a briar patch, and she helped free it from the snarl."

Amani arched a brow, and Roman narrowed his eyes at Ric. "No magic means no magic."

Ric took another sip of his coffee and addressed Roman. "I think this is about something more than anyone breaking the rules or laws, and I'm hungry. I don't think we have an issue here." He turned to look at Amani. "Thank you for helping the rabbit. It was an act of mercy and kindness." Ric nodded at Mihail and Irina before walking past the group on his way toward the dining room. "Madame Luiza," he called out.

"Useless as usual," Roman grumbled.

"What is it that you hoped to accomplish, Roman?" Amani asked. "Why do you harbor resentment toward me? I've done nothing to deserve your angst."

"You have the power to destroy even your own kind. It makes you a liability," he said as he moved to leave. "I'm serious about no magic, and I will make certain your sanctuary is revoked if you continue to break the rules."

The moment Roman's hand touched the handle of the door, Amani moved in a blur to stand next to him. "I think you're afraid of me, but again, I am not a threat to you."

Roman glared at her. "You have no intention of listening, do you?" he said, then opened the door and walked out without another word.

Amani turned to Mihail and Irina. "What have I done to make him dislike me so much?"

Irina shook her head. "Don't take it personally. It's just a power trip. If he doesn't control said power, he'll continue to count it as a threat. It's just who he is."

The door chimed again, and Amani spun around, expecting it to be Roman again with another round of rules she was to follow, but instead Calla Lily walked in.

"What's wrong?" she asked, reaching for Amani's hand. "You look upset."

Amani shook her head, doing her level best to control her budding frustration.

Calla Lily's nose crinkled. "Roman was here. Never mind, that explains everything."

Calla Lily, Mihail, and Irina all chuckled as Amani walked back into Nathan's arms. Madame Luiza quickly changed the subject and offered to show Amani how to make chocolate cake. The distraction was just what they needed.

Nathan and Amani both spent the afternoon helping out at the inn, then cleaning up after the dinner service, finally heading back to the cottage once the last dish was put away.

"I think I'll take a bath before I change for bed," Amani said before she rose up on her toes to kiss Nathan on the cheek.

"How about I make us some hot cocoa? I found some sugar and cocoa powder in the cupboard."

"That sounds wonderful."

"Enjoy your bath," he said as he kissed her lips.

Amani didn't take long in the bath, but when she came out, she appeared calm and at ease. Nathan had started a fire, and the wood's crackling was the only sound in the room.

"Feel better?"

"Yes, thank you," she said as she took the mug from Nathan and sat down on the couch beside him.

Amani nodded and took a sip. "This is delicious."

"Nothing fixes things faster than a warm cup of hot cocoa," he said with a grin plastered on his face.

Amani laughed. "Can we give some of this to Roman then?"

"I'll see what I can do."

Amani took one last sip and curled into Nathan's lap. The two of them stayed like that, talking and laughing until the fire died out, then moved to tuck themselves into bed.

Nathan winked at her as he adjusted the covers. "Goodnight, beautiful."

"Goodnight, Nathan."

CHAPTER 5

athan woke to Amani crying out in the middle of the night and bolted out of bed. She wasn't awake, but she was talking in her native tongue. He recognized it from the fight between her and Khaldun. It was the bizarre language the watcher had spoken before he tried to trap Amani. Tears began to stream down her face, and Nathan wasn't sure what to do to help her. He took a step closer and reached for her leg.

"Amani, can you hear me? Wake up."

Hieroglyphs started to glow on her skin, and Nathan took a step back. *Oh no.*

"Sweetheart, you need to wake up," he said as calmly but as urgently as he could. Her djinn symbols cooled from a vibrant gold into a steely grey. "There you go. Can you open your eyes and talk to me?"

Nothing happened. Amani remained motionless. When she hadn't spoken or moved for several moments, Nathan decided the threat of her changing had passed. He moved back to his side of the bed and sat down beside her, placing a hand on her arm. A smile tipped her lips, and she turned toward him.

"I heard your voice. I didn't know where I was, but I heard you calling to me just like you did in the town square to bring my djinn side to heel."

"Where were you?"

"I'm not sure, but I could feel Khalida. I felt her rage and pain."

"Is Thoth hurting her?"

"No, she is free."

"Free?" Panic lit Nathan's eyes.

"Not in the literal sense, but in a cage of sorts—like our canopic jars. She has all she could ever want and need supplied for her."

"Then why the rage and pain?"

"That was for me and the loss of her love, Khaldun."

"You were speaking his language. Did you know that?"

Amani nodded. "She wanted me to know she is still with me despite her entrapment. That she will come for me and take all I care about as payment for my deeds."

Nathan reached for her hand. "But the goddesses and Thoth have her. She can't harm you."

"Not physically. But I will need to do a better job of blocking her."

"Maybe there is something Calla Lily can do to help."

Amani nodded. "Maybe."

"We'll figure out something. We're in this together," he said as he pulled her fingers to his lips and kissed them gently. "Try and get some rest. I'll be right in the other room, okay?"

She met his gaze. "Will you stay with me? I feel better when you're close."

Nathan nodded. "Of course."

Amani moved to lay back down, and Nathan slid in beside her. She shimmied backward until her body melded into his. Nathan smiled and put his arm around her, pulling her closer.

"Amani, you mean everything to me," Nathan whispered, kissing the nape of her neck. "I will go to the ends of the earth to keep you safe and happy."

She turned to look back at him, her eyes speaking all the words her lips refused to utter.

"I may only be human, but there is more than one way to care for you." Nathan pushed the strap of her nightgown over her shoulder and continued to kiss her bare skin. Amani arched her back and moaned as he let his hands roam, following the curves of her body.

Amani fit perfectly against him, and he loved how her skin felt against his. Nathan's body reacted to hers instinctively. He lifted the end of the satin gown up over her hips, exposing her bare bottom.

"I plan on taking my time with every inch of you," he said as he kissed his way up her neck. "Every inch," he crooned, wishing this would never end. He wanted to love her not only in this moment but for the rest of their lives. He never knew love could happen so fast. He'd seen his friends go from single to married in no time flat, but he never thought it would happen to him.

Amani writhed beneath him. She wanted him as much as he wanted her, and that only pushed him further over the edge. When she rolled over and tugged open his shirt, running her hands run up his chest, Nathan sucked in a breath at the feel of her hands on his skin.

"You have my heart," she whispered.

Nathan smiled at her and moved his hand over hers. A warm sensation tingled in her fingertips, and the golden liquid that initiated their whole journey together flowed from her directly into his heart. Nathan winced for a moment, then sighed at her as recollection dawned. He could now feel her emotions, hear her thoughts again, as their connection reignited with another drop of her djinn blood.

The two of them made love again and again, finishing, then starting as if they'd never started to begin with. They were insatiable for one another until they finally wore themselves out. However, a few short hours into their second round of sleep, there was a knock at the door. Nathan grabbed the blanket on the edge of the bed and tied it around his waist in a simple knot that hung at his hips. On the third knock, he opened the door.

Calla Lily sucked in a breath and pursed her lips. "Um okay . . . so it seems like I've intruded. Sorry about this, but we have a problem that needs immediate attention."

"Come in." Nathan stepped aside. "Sorry, I should've dressed," he stammered. "Is everything okay?" He reached for a shirt that happened to be hanging on the back of the chair to try to ease the awkwardness.

"We need to go to Montrose," Calla Lily said in a rush. "Now," she added as she stepped just inside the doorway.

"Of course. Is something wrong?"

"I got a call from a friend who works at the train station, and he said I need to get there as soon as possible."

"Why? Is someone hurt?" Nathan asked as he buttoned his shirt.

"No, but Lillian arrived and was inquiring where Havenwood Falls is, since it was not clear on her map or from the people she was asking."

"What?" Nathan's eyes went wide. "Give me fifteen minutes, and I can meet you at the shop."

Calla Lily nodded and reached for the door handle. "Sounds good."

"Calla Lily, hi," Amani said with a bright smile.

"Hi to you," she answered. "I'm very sorry I interrupted you both."

"Oh, it's nothing. We were sleeping."

Calla Lily stifled a grin. By the look of Amani's hair and Nathan's bruised lips, sleeping wasn't the only thing that had happened, if it happened at all.

Nathan rubbed the back of his neck and blushed. "A quick cleaning, and I'll be ready to go."

"Where are you going?" Amani asked.

"Calla Lily and I have to go to Montrose. It seems Lillian has decided to come for a visit," Nathan said, hoping to hide the panic in his voice, but Amani could sense his anxiety and looked over at Calla Lily for understanding.

"Everything is fine. We just need to pick her up, and we'll be back after a while," Calla Lily soothed.

Amani reached for Nathan's hands. "Then why are you so nervous?"

"Well, I, uh, haven't exactly told her about you and the secrets here in Havenwood Falls. I'm just not sure how she'll react."

"I'm going to go get the car ready," Calla Lily interjected. "Bye, Amani. I'll see you later."

"See you later. Please be safe on your journey."

"We will," Calla Lily called out just before closing the door.

Amani's face fell. "Will Lillian not like me? Is that why you are so nervous?"

He shook his head. "I don't think that will be the issue. I think she will love you, but now I just have to explain how we met and what you are."

In the moment he said that, two of the pixies Amani had befriended tapped on their window. Amani dragged the sheet behind her and opened the pane. She leaned down and picked them up, bringing them face to face with her. There was a bit of chatter between them, some of which Nathan understood, but he waited until Amani translated before he spoke.

"Hello to you too, Tierri," Nathan responded before he nodded at Ushka. "Where are Enya and Aeiri?" he asked, looking around for the mischievous ones of the bunch.

"Enya set a bush on fire, and Aeiri was fanning the flames," Tierri replied as Ushka simply nodded her head in agreement. "We have to go and help Madame Tahini with them, so we can't stay to work today. Maybe tomorrow we can come back to finish the garden."

Amani and the pixies exchanged blessings and gifts before the two sisters disappeared in a puff of shimmering light.

Nathan sighed. "See, things like this don't happen in New York. We don't have magical fairy gardens and pixies who work with djinns to create a special place for the rabbits to dine."

Amani laughed. "Well, I can explain to Tierri and Ushka that I will return to our work once your guest leaves. And I can promise you I will be on my best behavior. I won't embarrass you."

Nathan pulled her hands to his lips. "You never embarrass me, and Lillian is going to love you."

Amani blushed. "I hope so. I know how much she means to you."

Nathan checked his pocket watch. "I'm sorry. I have to go."

"I will go speak with Mihail and Irina and make sure a room is ready for her when she arrives."

He kissed her once and started to walk away, but went back to kiss her once more. "You're my heart," he said, before he headed off in the direction of Calla Lily's shop.

Nathan didn't know whether to be elated or terrified that Lillian had taken it upon herself to show up in Montrose. How was he going to explain this? Explain Amani? *I know I've intentionally avoided relationships to focus on work, but in the process of finding my father's camera, I've also found the love of my life. Yes, it may be sudden, but there is no one I'd rather spend the rest of my life with. Amani is perfect. Oh no, no, do not worry about her being a thousand or so years old and capable of annihilating cities; she's sweet, loving, and kind.*

"Are you going to continue mumbling or are you ready to go?" Calla Lily asked as she stood by her car.

Nathan laughed nervously. "No. I was just bantering to myself about how to explain Amani, Havenwood Falls, and my need to stay here a bit longer to Lillian. She's rather inquisitive and incredibly persistent."

"You don't have to worry about that. The wards and the Court already make certain the humans remain unaware. Lillian can be in town and not realize there is magic happening all around her, and once she leaves, passing the town's border, she won't remember her time here at all," she said with a grin.

Nathan's brow furrowed as he got into the car. "What do you mean? She won't remember anything?"

"No, she won't."

Nathan rode in silence, sucking in a nervous breath as they drove past the Havenwood Falls sign.

"Don't worry. The wards won't affect you, since you've been approved as a temporary resident," Calla Lily explained.

"For now," he said with an arched brow.

The two passed the rest of the long drive talking about the parchments Lillian had sent a few weeks prior and their connection to Amani and Khalida. They also talked about the glossed-over topic of Calla Lily's lineage. Nathan wanted to know more of what it meant to be a gypsy demon.

"Were you born like that or were you turned into a demon? I mean, can anyone be a supernatural being?"

"No, you cannot be turned, Nathan. I was born a Shuvani. It is similar to a high priestess in any pagan religion."

"I'm completely out of my element here. I've studied the gods of Egypt as a part of my studies, and I've read the old penny dreadfuls my father had packed away in the basement, but other than that, you and Amani are my first magical beings and certainly the only ones who've clued me in to their abilities. I'm still unsure of exactly what Mihail, Irina, and Madame Luiza are." He chuckled. "They're wonderful, but I wouldn't want to get on their bad side for sure."

"They are moroi vampires, and yes, crossing them would be a mistake for sure, but let me try to describe things in terms of what you do know," she said as they made the final curve out of the mountains. "My job as a Shuvani is to ensure the traditions of my kind are passed on to the future generations—for them to understand their abilities."

"What can you do? I mean, can you do things like Amani?"

She cast Nathan a glance. "No one can do what Amani does. At least not that I know of."

Nathan nodded. "Okay then, what are your special talents, beyond being able to see the past like you did with Amani?"

"Now, I can't go and give away all my secrets." She laughed.

"I'm sorry. I didn't mean to pry. My curious nature gets the best of me sometimes."

"I'm teasing you, but we will have to get into this later. We're almost there," Calla Lily said as she turned the Model T onto the main street in Montrose.

"Before we see Lilian, can I ask a favor?"

"Of course," Calla Lily replied.

"Do you have a way to read Lillian without her knowing it?"

"Yes, but may I ask why?"

Nathan ducked his head. "I want to know if she's happy. She's taken care of me ever since my father died, and before that, she filled in as a mother after my real mother died. All Lillian has ever wanted for me was to settle down and have a family of my own." He cast a glance at Calla Lily. "She wants to be a grandmother."

"And now you're worried she'll meet Amani and think she can have all she's ever wanted?"

Nathan nodded.

"But Amani and any children you two could have in the future will be unique, and you'll most likely not be able to be a family the way Lillian envisions."

"It would break her heart, and I can't bear the thought."

"I think we should cross that bridge when we come to it. Right now, we need to focus on the reason she's here to begin with."

As they parked, Nathan scanned the area for any sign of Lillian, while Calla Lily stepped out of the car and made a beeline to meet the man she knew in Montrose. He was the conductor who'd dismissed Nathan when he first arrived and was inquiring about Havenwood Falls. As Nathan watched Calla Lily hug the burly man, he wondered what kind of supernatural he was, if any. He made a note to himself to ask when they were in private as he made his way inside the train station.

There, with a book in one hand and a paper fan in the other, was Lillian with her tattered suitcase sat next to her feet and her black pocketbook tucked in neatly by her side. She must have been engrossed in the story, because she completely missed Nathan standing in front of her.

"I hope you haven't been here too long."

"Oh, Nathan," Lillian cooed as she closed her book and stood to hug him. "It's so good to see you. I've missed you terribly."

"I've missed you too," he said as he returned her embrace. "If I'd known you were coming, I would've been here waiting for you."

"Oh no, no. I wanted to surprise you. When you talked about this place and described how peaceful it was, I just had to see it for myself."

"I'm glad you're here. I'm excited to introduce you to the people I've met. They're wonderful."

"I can't wait." She beamed. "How did you get here?"

"Calla Lily drove me."

"Oh, Calla Lily is it?"

Nathan shook his head. "No. It's not like that. She's just a friend."

Calla Lily walked up behind Nathan and extended her hand in greeting. "You must be Lillian. It's nice to meet you."

The look on Lillian's face spoke volumes as she reluctantly shook Calla Lily's hand, while shoving her book into Nathan's.

"Nathan expected someone older as well." She smiled. "Are these your bags?"

"Yes," Lillian replied, reaching for her suitcase and handbag.

"I've got these, Lillian," Nathan said as he picked up her suitcase. "Good grief. How long do you intend to stay? This thing feels like it's filled with rocks."

"Oh, don't be silly. I packed a few of your things in there as well. You left without your suit and tie. How are you getting along in only your casual clothes?"

Nathan shrugged. "Havenwood Falls isn't like New York, Lillian."

"Well, nonetheless, I brought the navy tweed and your oxfords," she professed, before taking back the book she'd given him.

"What are you reading?" Calla Lily asked as Lillian smoothed the edges on the dust cover.

"This Side of Paradise by F. Scott Fitzgerald. It's a lovely story. Have you read it?"

Calla Lily shook her head.

"Well, you should. I can lend mine to you while I'm here."

"And how long will that be?"

"Nathan Allan Wade, why do you keep asking me that?"

"Just curious is all."

"The car is just out front here," Calla Lily said, hoping to distract them.

CHAPTER 6

*T*he drive back home to Havenwood Falls seemed longer than
the last time, but it had more to do with Lillian hammering
them both with questions than with the actual distance. She was
thoroughly convinced there was something brewing under the surface
between Nathan and Calla Lily, and no amount of talking seemed to
deflect her inquisition. All of it fell on deaf ears. Lillian had set her
sights on the prospect of marriage and children, and there was not
going to be anything to deter her—for now at least.

"Lillian, I promise you my relationship with Calla Lily is strictly
platonic."

Nathan hoped this declaration would squelch the conversation,
because he didn't want to mention Amani until they were all together
and he could make the proper introductions.

"Lillian, how was the train ride here? Good, I hope," Calla Lily
asked, hoping to change the subject . . . again.

"It was a bit rough at times, but I managed just fine. Thank you for
asking." Calla Lily gave Lillian a gentle smile when she turned in her
direction. "Colorado is quite a change from New York. This mountain
air is heavenly, but being this high up can surely take your breath
away."

"Yes, it can, but you'll adjust after a bit. The weather is different than in the city, too, Lillian. It's a different kind of cool—less smoggy." Nathan laughed.

"I can see why you like it here. It beats the heat in Egypt, too," Lillian said as she turned to look back at Nathan in the backseat.

"By far. I love Egypt, but there is something special about Colorado," Nathan replied.

Lillian fell silent as Calla Lily turned onto Main Street and headed toward the inn. She was taking in the town's quaint, inviting features as they slowly made their way over the cobblestone streets. Nathan watched her as she took in the tallest building. It was only three stories and small in comparison to what she was used to seeing. Lillian had been born and raised in New York, and only knew the steel and concrete of the city. She was not used to the tranquility of the country.

"That is quite a charming fountain. We have one in Central Park, but I don't get to enjoy it as often as I'd like," Lillian said as they drove past the town square.

When the car stopped in front of the inn, Nathan got out and opened the door for Lillian, offering his hand to help her out.

"This is lovely," she exclaimed. "What wonderful architecture," she continued as she surveyed the tower and turrets. "I haven't seen one of these since my grandmother Jane moved from Oneida."

"This is where you'll be staying," Nathan said, grabbing her bag and handing her her purse.

"Where I'll be staying? Where will you be?" Lillian inquired. "This is the exact place I made your reservation."

Nathan started to rub the back of his neck, trying to find the words to explain, when Amani walked out the front door of the inn. She took his breath away every time he saw her, but this time was different. She had her hair up in a style befitting the contemporary time period, and she was wearing a dress he could only assume she got from Calla Lily. Amani curtsied at the three of them, quickly moving aside.

Nathan cast a glance at Calla Lily and mouthed, "Was this your doing?"

Calla Lily grinned and walked up next to Lillian. "This way. I will introduce you to Mihail and Irina. They run the inn."

"Oh," she paused, "and is that their daughter?" she asked, tilting her head in Amani's direction as they passed.

"No," Calla Lily stated flatly.

"Madame Luiza has tea waiting for you in the parlor," Amani called out as they stepped onto the porch.

"Thank you, Amani. The dress fits you perfectly, I see," Calla Lily acknowledged.

Amani blushed. "With a little help, yes. Thank you for finding just the right one for me."

When Calla Lily hurried Lillian inside, Nathan made his way to the porch and stopped at the bottom step. "I've never seen you with your hair up. It looks nice."

"I wanted to look like a proper lady of the time and asked Madame Luiza to help me. I was going to use magic, but didn't want to cause any problems while Lillian was here," Amani said as she nervously fiddled with her hair.

Nathan stepped up and stood in front of her. "I don't know what I did to deserve a woman like you, but I do promise to treasure you."

"Oh, Nathan. It is a simple gesture."

"But it's not. It's you doing all you can to fit in to a world where you cannot be who you were made to be," he said as he pulled her close to his chest. "I appreciate it more than I can say." Nathan kissed her softly on the lips. "I'd be happy to show you how much, later, if you'd like," he teased.

"Nathan," Amani scolded, before wrapping her arms around his neck and kissing him again.

Breaking their kiss, Nathan held the door open for Amani, and she began to walk through, but stumbled. "Are you okay?"

"Yes. I just felt a little light-headed all of a sudden. I'll be fine," she said, as she steadied herself with Nathan's help.

"Maybe you should go back to the cottage and rest."

"No. I want to be here. I'd love nothing more than to talk to Lillian once you have introduced me."

Nathan nodded. "On one condition. If you don't feel well while we are visiting, just excuse yourself, and I'll bring you back home."

The smile Amani attempted didn't meet her eyes, but she reluctantly agreed to Nathan's request.

Nathan intertwined their fingers, and the two of them headed toward the parlor.

Laughter filled the room as Irina, Calla Lily, Madame Luiza, and Lillian all chatted and sipped tea. However, the moment the two of them walked into the room, you could have heard a pin drop. Nathan squeezed Amani's hand gently.

"Ladies," he nodded, acknowledging their presence but quickly moving on to address the one person in the room who did not know Amani. Nathan took a deep breath and said, "Lillian, now that you're settled, I'd like you to meet Amani."

The energy in the air seemed to freeze at his announcement. The only sound that could be heard was the nervous shake of Lillian's porcelain cup making contact with its matching saucer. Lillian looked at Calla Lily and then over to Amani beside Nathan.

"Oh. I seem to have . . ." Lillian stammered.

"It's wonderful to meet you, Lillian. I mean Mrs. Hartman," Amani said as she cast an awkward glance at Madame Luiza and Irina, who both smiled with faint nods of encouragement.

Nathan walked, with Amani still by his side, over to the couch where Lillian was sitting. "I didn't say anything on the ride back to town, because I wanted you to meet her in person."

Tears started to well in Lillian's eyes. "And is this young lady the reason you've delayed your return home?"

"Yes, she is," he replied without hesitation.

Lillian stood and pulled Amani into a crushing hug. "I know this is not proper, but I've waited so long for him to find happiness, and now it seems he has."

Relief washed over Nathan as the tension in the room eased, Lillian peppering Amani with questions—some she stammered to answer.

"And are you from here in Colorado, dear?"

"No. I am from . . ."

"She's from Egypt, originally, but has been here in Havenwood

Falls for several months," Calla Lily interjected.

Nathan's eyes went wide at the mention of Egypt and the mention of several months, considering it had only been a few weeks. He worried this would be a curiosity Lillian would not skim over—that she would instead home in on the connection—but was pleasantly surprised when Lillian exclaimed, "Egypt! No wonder Nathan was fascinated by you. Between your beauty and his love of all things Egyptian, this was destined."

The five women and Nathan visited in the parlor for a bit, until it was time for Madame Luiza to begin cooking dinner for the inn's guests. She told them that she'd made a pot roast with all the trimmings for Lillian's first meal with them. She thought it was only fitting to welcome her the same way she welcomed Nathan.

"You must try the biscuits with her blueberry jam. They're amazing." Amani beamed.

"Amani had never had blueberry jam before she came to Havenwood Falls. I'm sure if she had some elsewhere, she'd love theirs, too," Madame Luiza interjected.

"It sounds delicious. I make a cinnamon-spiced pear jam. We should exchange recipes," Lillian replied.

The bell rang at the front desk, and Irina rose from the couch. "Please excuse me. It's been a busy day of check-ins, and Mihail needs help escorting someone up to their room. I will find you when I'm finished."

"Anything I can help with?" Amani offered.

"No, you enjoy the company. I will come find you if we can't manage it," Irina answered.

Nathan pulled out chairs for Amani and then Lillian, before he moved to do the same for Calla Lily. It was just in time too, since Madame Luiza was bringing plates in to tempt their senses.

"Everything looks delicious, Madame Luiza. Thank you," Nathan said as he took a seat next to Amani.

"I hope you all enjoy. I'll check on you in a bit," Madame Luiza said, excusing herself to head back toward the kitchen.

As Madame Luiza left the room, Lillian looked at Calla Lily and

Amani. "I swear I must be the oldest person here. Everyone I've met so far is young. I look like a dowager compared to all of you."

Nathan started to fidget, but Calla Lily replied to settle his nerves. "We do have older residents. You just haven't had the pleasure of meeting them yet."

"Oh. Have you lived here in Havenwood Falls long, Calla Lily?" Lillian asked.

"I've been here a few years."

"And are you married? Children?"

"Lillian," Nathan scolded.

"I'm just curious. A beautiful young woman like yourself should've been scooped up by now."

Amani sat quietly, unsure of what to say. She wasn't familiar with this type of conversation. She almost felt embarrassed that she'd never thought to ask Calla Lily if she had someone special in her life. Amani cast a sorrowful glance at Calla Lily before looking at Nathan, who was visibly agitated by Lillian's line of questioning. The hair on Lillian's head started to float, as if she'd just been doused by a surge of electricity. Calla Lily and Nathan tried to remain composed, hoping Lillian didn't notice. Amani, however, was wringing her hands.

"What's wrong, dear?" Lillian asked.

"Nothing," Amani said with a quick shake of her head. "I . . . I . . ." Amani stood and rushed away from the table.

Calla Lily stood a moment later. "I'll go check on her." Nathan nodded, and she eased him with the touch of her hand on his. "There is nothing to worry about. I'm sure it's just nerves."

"Did I say something wrong?" Lillian questioned.

"No, but you may need to lessen the inquisition, Lillian. We're not in New York, and these people are less like the gossip circle of ladies you meet with on Thursdays," he said with a faint smile.

Lillian dipped her chin. "Of course. I meant no harm."

"I know, but I would appreciate it if you wouldn't put your nose in Calla Lily's business."

"She's lovely, you know," she said as she unfolded her napkin and placed it in her lap.

"Amani or Calla Lily?"

"Both, but I specifically meant Amani."

"Yes, she is," he said as he too placed his napkin in his lap. "If I am being honest, I can say without a doubt that I've fallen in love with her."

Lillian smiled a broad, proud smile. "Well, it is about time."

"I knew you were going to say that."

"Are you going to ask her to marry you?"

"I haven't gotten that far yet. The only thing I know is that I only ever want her."

"It is sudden, but I know well enough that when you know, you know. That is how I fell in love with Charles. Two hours at the garden party my aunt Edith had, and I was ready to go that evening to the minister and start our new life."

Nathan leaned forward. "And did you?"

"No, he needed to get my father's blessing first and then we had to wait for a few months after that for his parents to return from a family trip, but the moment everyone was back, we went the very next day." Lillian inhaled. "I loved him every day since that first moment."

"I don't think you've ever shared this story with me."

She patted his hand. "Never had the occasion, it seems, until now."

Madame Luiza arrived at the table with a tray of desserts, placing two of them in front of Nathan and Lillian.

"Where are Calla Lily and Amani?" Madame Luiza asked.

"They should be right back. I don't think Amani was feeling too well and excused herself," Nathan replied, his eyes speaking the words he could not in front of Lillian.

Madame Luiza got the message and patted Nathan on the shoulder. "I'll go check on them, but in the meantime, you two go ahead and enjoy the cobbler. I used fresh blueberries from the garden."

"Thank you, Madame Luiza."

When she left, Lillian took a bite of the cobbler and moaned. "These have to be the best blueberries I have ever put in my mouth. They're almost magical."

Nathan laughed nervously. "Yep, magical indeed."

CHAPTER 7

"*A*mani, are you okay?" Calla Lily asked when she found her in the corner down the hall.

"No. Something's wrong."

"What?" Calla Lily asked in a panic.

Amani turned her hands over and tried to hold them steady for Calla Lily to see. Gold hieroglyphs shimmered on the surface of her skin, while trails of silver flowed through them, creating sparks of energy that popped and shimmered. Calla Lily reached out to touch her, but Amani reeled back. "I don't want to hurt you."

Madame Luiza came around the corner and rushed to Calla Lily's side. "What's wrong? What can we do, Amani?"

Amani had slid down the wall and was curled into a ball, trying to contain the energy surging through her. She was pleading with herself to calm down. The problem was, she wasn't upset and couldn't for the life of her understand why this was happening.

"Help me. I don't want to change. I cannot allow my djinn to surface," Amani cried.

"I can help, Amani. I promise," Calla Lily soothed.

"Do you remember the tea you made with the lavender and valerian root?" Calla Lily asked Madame Luiza.

"Of course."

"Can you please add some passion flower and some lemon balm? I think that, with a bit of magic, will calm and soothe our girl," Calla Lily said in a calm clear voice.

Madame Luiza didn't hesitate. Instead she moved in a blur to do as Calla Lily asked. When she returned, Amani was sobbing and was paler than normal.

"Do you trust me?" Calla Lily asked as she took the mug from Madame Luiza.

"Of course," Amani replied, looking into Calla Lily's eyes. "I'll do anything to stop this."

"Good." Calla Lily inhaled slowly before chanting words Amani and Madame Luiza were unfamiliar with. As she continued to spell the tea with her gypsy magic, it began to boil and smoke before settling. When Calla Lily handed the mug to Amani, it was cold to the touch.

"Drink it all. It will make you sleepy, but don't worry. We'll take care of you and get you back to the cottage, okay?"

Amani nodded and drank the tea without hesitation. The gold and silver threads receded, and Amani's eyes grew heavy. Calla Lily moved next to her and steadied Amani, holding her in her arms until she was asleep.

"That was close," Calla Lily sighed.

"What was that? The stress of Lillian being here?" Madame Luiza asked.

"No, it came on suddenly, and there was true panic in her face as it was happening. Hopefully when she wakes, we can ask her more questions."

"Do you want me to go get Nathan?"

"No, I don't want to alert Lillian to it, and he won't be able to hide his emotion over something being wrong with Amani. Let's just get her back to the cottage."

With vampire strength, Madame Luiza carried Amani to the cottage and settled her on the couch while Calla Lily started a fire.

"Can you please let Nathan know, after Lillian is in her room, that I'm here with Amani and will stay until he can be with her?" Calla Lily asked.

"Of course. Are you sure you'll be okay?" Madame Luiza responded.

Calla Lily gave a faint smile. "That concoction will knock her out for at least nine hours, if not more."

"You're certain?" Madame Luiza insisted.

"One hundred percent. That spell has never failed me, supernatural or not."

"I'll bring you a plate in a few so you can eat while you wait."

"Thank you, Madame Luiza."

She gave a clipped nod and closed the door behind her.

"I don't know what happened tonight, Amani, but we'll find out. I promise," Calla Lily said as she laid a quilt over Amani's sleeping form.

Calla Lily wasn't sure how much time had passed, but it was enough that Madame Luiza had come and gone with dinner and long enough for her to tidy up the cottage to pass the time.

When Nathan walked in the door, he was concerned but not shaken. However, the moment he saw Amani lying motionless and Calla Lily holding her hand while she slept, he became alarmed. "What's wrong? Madame Luiza said she wanted to rest and that she sent her apologies. I didn't think anything was wrong other than that. If I'd have known—"

"There wouldn't have been anything for you do to anyway. You were better suited entertaining Lillian."

Nathan tugged off his jacket and laid it over the back of the chair. "Tell me what happened."

"She started to lose control. Energy started to surge through her, and she was afraid of her djinn side surfacing."

"Why? Was it all the questions Lillian was asking?"

"No, I think it's something else, or shall I say someone else."

"Who? Is Roman doing this?" Nathan snapped.

Calla Lily shook her head. "No. Actually, I think it's Khalida, but I cannot be certain. I've been trying to read her thoughts while she sleeps, but I can only get flashes of images. Nothing that makes any sense, but when Amani's hieroglyphs were surfacing, silver trails flowed through them, which as you know is indicative of Khalida's power, not Amani's."

Nathan sat in the chair opposite Calla Lily. "I didn't think Khalida could be a problem anymore. I guess I thought wrong."

"Maybe Amani will know more when she wakes, but that won't be until tomorrow sometime. I spelled her tea." Nathan's eyes went wide, causing Calla Lily to quickly add, "She knew and wanted me to do anything to stop the change. She'll be fine."

Nathan nodded. "You look exhausted. You should head home."

"I am tired," Calla Lily said as she stood. "I'll be by in the morning to check on her."

"I'm sorry I can't walk you home," Nathan said as they made their way to the door.

Calla Lily stifled her laugh. "I appreciate the sentiment, Nathan, but I can more than take care of myself."

Nathan chuckled in response. "Yeah, I assume so. See you in the morning then."

"Unless something with her changes, then send for me right away, okay?"

"Hopefully she'll get some rest and be better in the morning."

Calla Lily touched Nathan's forearm. "We'll figure this out," she said as she turned to leave. "And Nathan, make sure she knows you're near. You soothe her, and she needs that."

Nathan's lips turned upward. "I will. Thank you again."

"You're welcome," she replied as she walked onto the path next to the garden. "Goodnight, Nathan."

"Goodnight, Calla Lily."

CHAPTER 8

$\mathcal{N}$athan lifted Amani off the couch and carried her to the bed, where he could keep close watch over her. She slept through the night, but it was a fitful sleep. Amani cried out in pain several times when silver and gold hieroglyphs appeared and disappeared on her skin. Nathan tried to make them out, but they were gone before he could recognize any of them. When her hair started to change from blond to black, he really became worried. She didn't look well. She was pale and clammy to the touch, and even though her eyes were still closed, it appeared as though Amani was struggling against something or someone. When the morning light started to peek into the windows, Nathan went into the bathroom to splash some water on his face.

Nathan heard a knock on the door. Softly at first, but then again, a little more aggressively.

"Nathan? Amani? It's Calla Lily," he heard her call out from the other room. Nathan made his way to the door and opened it.

"You look awful," Calla Lily professed.

"Thanks. That's what no sleep gets you."

"Did she not sleep through the night?"

"She did and she didn't. She never once woke, but things were happening unbeknownst to her. I don't know," Nathan said, running his fingers through his already tousled hair.

"Is she still sleeping?"

He nodded.

"Go get cleaned up, and I will stay with her. I can't imagine she'll be asleep much longer."

"All right," Nathan relented, "I'll be quick."

"THOTH?" Amani questioned. "Am I dreaming?"

"Not exactly, child. You are still entranced, thanks to your friend, who I must say, is quite the skilled alchemist. But I've bypassed it to speak to you directly."

"I'm certain she will appreciate the compliment," Amani said as she sat up and stared up at Thoth. "How is this possible for me to be up and around and yet still out from her elixir?"

"I woke your subconscious. I need your help, and I didn't want to do anything without your consent."

Amani's brows furrowed. "Is Khalida consenting?"

"No. She's fighting me every step of the way."

Amani nodded. "What do you need from me?"

"Some of your blood and answers."

Amani extended both of her arms, wrists up, toward Thoth. "Whatever you need."

Thoth took her wrist in his hand and began to call forth her blood. It rose up like it had with Khalida and floated in a stream from her to the vial he was holding. Vibrant gold flecks with hints of copper shone as if lit by an unseen light.

"Interesting," he said aloud.

"Is something wrong?"

"I've never seen cooper in your blood, Amani. May I?" he asked as he closed the vial and began to move his hand to her forehead.

She replied by leaning in, her head slightly bowed in his direction.

Thoth's touch was gentle as he read her thoughts and her internal systems. The answer he was looking for was right there.

"You mated with Nathan?"

"Yes," Amani whispered, a blush pinking her cheeks.

"This explains a lot, but also offers an additional challenge."

"Why is that?" she asked as she stared up at him, her eyes pleading.

"Because, my dear one, you are with child."

Amani's face fell. "What?"

"You are well within the age of maturity for reproduction. It is the way of the djinn, and while it is preferred you mate with your own kind, as you know, you are unique, and therefore there is no one else like you."

The information swirled in Amani's brain as she asked, "But what about Khalida? I'm connected to her, but will she now be connected to my child?"

"I have a bit more work to do, and now with your blood, I may be even closer. I need one answer, though, before I can proceed." Amani nodded. "How many times have you sensed Khalida? Felt her as if you were connected?"

"I've always felt her. The first time you put us in the temple jars, I had to find ways to block her rage, to protect myself from it."

"And can she sense you the same way?"

"Yes, but I'm not sure if it's exactly the same."

"And why is that?"

"She always keeps a part of herself hidden. I think it's too dark even for her to embrace, until she wants to. I've felt her anger more and more since I killed Khaldun."

"I see," he said curiously, "and the blocking you are doing isn't helping?"

"It only lessens the intensity. Nothing more."

"Very good. I think I know what is happening and how this came to be," he affirmed. "I need a bit more time, and then we may proceed. In the meantime, I think you may need to inform Nathan that his life is about to change even further."

"Is everything going to be all right? Please be honest with me. I've never had anything to lose once my parents died, but now with Nathan and—" she looked down at her belly—"a baby to consider, I don't want to hope for too much and end up heartbroken."

"I still have a few things to sort, but after your answers here, I can say that one piece of the puzzle has been solved. You and Khalida are not twins, as originally thought, but instead, one and the same. Rather, you're the same person split in two. It explains everything."

"What?" Terror flashed over her features. "That can't be."

"Everyone has light and dark within them, and in your case, you and Khalida were split the moment of your creation. The details are what I need to work out, and I will. In the meantime, you should only concern yourself with Nathan and the child. Understand?"

"I'm scared. What if he is angry about becoming a father so soon? And what kind of mother will I be, knowing I am not a whole person and could lose control at any time?"

"That is an unlikely outcome on both fronts. I doubt he will feel anything other than elation at the thought. In regards to you losing control—" he shook his head and a grin tipped his lips—"you're a djinn whether you've been split or not. Anything could trigger the parts of you that are not human-like. This façade before me is not the whole of you. You are special. Stop hiding that and embrace the gifts it brings you."

"Thank you, Thoth, for all you've done for me."

"You are welcome, but it is I who should be thanking you. You had the answers to the riddle." Thoth tilted his head at Amani and disappeared via wisps of sand.

When Thoth left, Amani lay back and rejoined her body, lying peacefully for a few moments before sitting up in bed and laying her hand on her belly.

CHAPTER 9

halida woke the moment Thoth returned. She tried to act as though she were still asleep, but Thoth knew otherwise.

"Your games may work on others, but they are lost on me," he said as he put the vial of Amani's shimmering blood next to the one he'd taken from Khalida earlier.

"I'm not playing games. I'm not interested in being used as an experiment."

"I will need another bit of your blood to test a theory."

"You're actually asking this time?"

"I'll ask only once."

Khalida's eyes flashed a mixture of gold and blue, and went from clear to opaque as hieroglyphs erupted on her neck and arms.

"What have you done to me?" she cried out as she put her hand on her stomach.

"Nothing, but it seems your connection to Amani is just as I thought."

"What does that mean?" she snarled.

"It means you feel what she feels and vice versa."

Khalida stood and glared at Thoth. "Then why am I the one in here, and she is the one free to roam the earth?"

"Not the earth, just the small town you and Khaldun tried to conquer. Does that answer your question?"

"Let me out of here!" Khalida raged, slamming her fists against the invisible barrier.

"Do you know any other forms of communication besides rage and deception? I've grown tired of your childish tantrums."

Khalida transformed, releasing the djinn just below the surface. Inside her cage, she arced electrical currents from her fingertips, loving it when they bounced off the barrier and surged back into her. Her now white hair blustered, while silver-blue streaks danced over her skin. "If you will not release me, I will make it my mission to torture your pet."

Thoth crossed his arms in front of his chest and let her play her game. Until he heard Amani's pleas. Thoth turned to see where they were coming from when the blood in the vial began to swirl in a vortex, shattering the glass. The blood hovered midair and howled as Khalida continued to wreak havoc.

"STOP, KHALIDA! ENOUGH!" Amani's voice boomed in an echo inside the invisible prison, their connection stronger than ever.

When Khalida laughed, the blood above Thoth's head rushed to break the barrier of the cage, but when the attempt failed, the crimson liquid burst into flames. Thoth watched in amazement the power the two wielded. However, since Khalida was the only one contained, he snapped his fingers, silencing the two djinn. Khalida fell to the floor with a thud, and Thoth hoped Amani was somewhere where she hadn't hurt anyone, or herself.

"The merging must take place sooner rather than later, but I will not be able to do it alone," he said as he disappeared into thin air.

～

"NATHAN!" Calla Lily screamed from the bedroom.

Nathan tore back to Amani's side, only to find her hovering above the bed, her skin dusky grey and her hair ablaze.

"Amani, what's wrong? What's happening?" he pleaded.

"She can't hear us, Nathan. Khalida is doing something to her," Calla Lily said as they watched Amani talk to someone not seen or heard.

"What do we do?" Nathan pleaded.

Calla Lily began to chant. At first, nothing happened, but she continued as the air around them became dense.

"What is this? What are you doing?"

"Blocking her energy as best I can. The last thing we need is for Roman and the Court to show up and see her like this."

Calla Lily had yet to finish her chant when Amani screamed, "STOP, KHALIDA! ENOUGH!"

Amani's arms flew wide, her full djinn on display as white-hot energy blasted from her, knocking Nathan and Calla Lily to the floor. She collapsed back onto the bed, and within moments, changed back into her human self, passing out as she did. As the last bit of Amani's skin returned to its natural color, Roman, Mihail, Irina, Madame Luiza, Ric Kasun, Saundra Beaumont, Tierri, and Ushka all burst into the cottage.

"Everything is okay," Calla Lily announced, holding up her hands to stop the onslaught of questions as she and Nathan stood to regain their footing.

"Do you have any idea how much energy just surged through the town?" Roman snarled.

"Yes, Roman. I have an idea, since I watched it all happen from only a few feet away," Calla Lily remarked.

Roman glared at her, but it was Ric who spoke next. "What happened?"

Calla Lily looked to Amani, who was still unconscious, but now wrapped in Nathan's arms. "Honestly, we don't know. She was asleep and then all of a sudden her djinn side emerged and she started to scream at Khalida."

"Khalida was here?" Saundra exclaimed.

"No," Nathan replied, "she was talking to the air."

Madame Luiza, Tierri, and Ushka made their way past Roman and Ric and went over to Amani. Beads of sweat lay untouched on her forehead, and her breathing was labored. Tierri appeared to flit about, landing on the bed near Amani's shoulder. The pixies took one look at Amani and knew what to do. Ushka disappeared and reappeared in a flash with a pail of water and two African violet plants. She and Tierri hurriedly lay the petals over Amani's neck and used the water to cool her skin. Tierri whispered something to Madame Luiza, who then repeated the sentiment to the crowd. "The water from the falls and violets will work to soothe her."

"The danger has passed, but she shouldn't be agitated," Calla Lily added.

"Well, I don't want to be agitated either, and yet I am," Roman balked. "Why do you all continue to protect a woman capable of destroying this town? Why is she worth such loyalty?"

Tierri and Ushka gasped and were suddenly in Roman's face, scolding him for saying something so vicious. Ric tried to calm the pixies, but he was getting a kick out of the tongue-lashing they were giving Roman. Tierri was going on and on about how he was insufferable and inconsiderate of someone who has done nothing but be gracious and kind.

"Amani's my friend. And that I'll defend!" Tierri declared.

"Me too!" Ushka added.

Both pixies looked around, waiting for the "me three" and "me four" they were accustomed to hearing from their sisters.

Roman didn't reply, but the snarl on his face spoke volumes.

Ric clapped Roman on the shoulder. "It seems we should all get going. Tierri, Ushka, Calla Lily, and Nathan seem more than capable of taking care of Amani," he said before nodding at Madame Luiza, who was still sitting next to Amani. "I hope Amani feels better soon. If you need me for anything, let me know."

"Thank you, Ric." Madame Luiza nodded.

Everyone moved to leave, but Roman stood his ground.

"There is nothing left for us to uncover, Roman," Mihail said sternly. "I think it's time to leave. Now," he insisted.

Roman sneered and started to speak, but Saundra nudged him forward, and he finally made his way out the door of the cottage.

Saundra turned back before she walked out. "If she needs anything, Calla Lily, I'm happy to help. She doesn't look well."

"Thank you, Saundra."

"I'll bring some tea and towels back in few," Irina added as she waited for Mihail.

"I'll check in later as well," Mihail said, before pulling the door closed.

Tierri and Ushka continued to fuss over Amani, as Madame Luiza touched her forehead. "I think she has a fever, but then other times she feels cold as ice. What should we do?"

Calla Lily shrugged and turned to Nathan.

"I feel helpless," he answered.

"There's no need," a voice said behind them. They spun around, their mouths agape as they stared at Thoth. "I've got what she needs."

Calla Lily and Nathan stepped aside as Madame Luiza stood. Tierri and Ushka sailed to where Nathan was standing, resting on his shoulders, watching as the god made his way to Amani's side.

"I was here earlier, talking to her."

"What?" Calla Lily exclaimed. "When? She's been asleep this entire time."

"Yes, she has. You made an effective elixir, I might add."

"Thank you, but that doesn't answer the question." She crossed her arms.

"I was speaking to her through her subconscious. Not long before she lost control and released her djinn."

"How did you know?" Nathan interjected.

"Because Khalida intentionally set hers free and was agitating Amani to do the same. The blood she gave me earlier reacted and burst into flames. I knew then what was happening."

"The blood she gave you? When did Amani give you her blood?" Nathan asked.

"I was here earlier checking on her."

"Then what is wrong with her now? Why isn't she awake?" Madame Luiza added.

"I had to put them both in a trance, but between my power and the Shuvani's elixir, it seems to have had an adverse reaction."

"Oh dear, I never meant to . . ." Calla Lily stammered.

"You did nothing wrong," Thoth interrupted. "This was all Khalida's doing." He touched Amani's head and snapped his fingers, and Amani's eyes opened. "There you are, sweet one."

Amani's voice shook. "Please tell me I didn't hurt anyone. I didn't mean to lose control."

"I'm afraid that was Khalida's doing, but it was all worth it."

"Worth it?" Nathan exclaimed, forgetting for a moment whom he was yelling at.

Thoth nodded. "Yes, because now I know how to fix it."

"Really?" Amani questioned.

"They are not twins, as we all previously thought."

"Then what are they?" Calla Lily asked.

"They are one and the same. Two halves of a whole . . . light and dark split. It is my belief that when Sekhmet and Shu used their powers to attack one another, a different kind of being, not previously seen, was created. They were djinn, as others of their kind are because they are made of fiery wind. However, when Sekhmet and Shu continued to argue, the *whole* was split in two. It explains why they have elements of both, and yet those elements are housed in different beings. Amani is the empathetic one, while Khalida carries all the rage," Thoth finished.

"But . . ." Nathan muttered.

"If one dies, so will the other—that is true," Thoth continued. "Therefore, we must merge the two halves and make them whole again."

"What if I'm not strong enough? What if she takes over?" Amani said, her chin trembling. "I don't want to die."

"This is insane. Make them whole or she'll die or Khalida will die," Nathan stammered over his thoughts. "How can you even think about doing something like this?" he said, running his hands through his hair before reaching for Amani's hand.

"It will not be easy, but it can be done. They are the same person.

When one is balanced by the other, they will no longer need to fight for dominance."

"But through all of this, how can we be certain which half will emerge as the dominant personality?" Nathan asked, his voice unsteady.

Thoth turned to face him. "Amani. She is the stronger of the two. Khalida was only strong when Amani wasn't around to combat her. With the two of them connected, they feed off one another. Khalida is trying to use that to tip Amani over the edge and prove she is the dominant one, but I know the truth."

"And what will this mean in the end?" Calla Lily asked. "If they are *merged* as you say, where will that leave Amani?"

"She will be the djinn she was intended to be. The Amani we know will remain, but she will also have traits of Khalida. One will balance the other."

"I'm going to be like Khalida?" Amani said shakily. "I don't want to be anything like her. And what about . . ."

"Everything will be fine. You are stronger than you think you are. You always have been, and that is even without her influence. Soon you'll be a force to be reckoned with."

"Heavens, isn't she that now?" Madame Luiza joked, hoping to ease the tension in the room.

Everyone went silent, but when Tierri and Ushka giggled, the rest of them joined in.

CHAPTER 10

*T*hankful for the break in tension, Tierri and Ushka went about helping to clean up a bit. Tierri ordered Ushka to fetch some more water from the falls and bring it back posthaste, to help with the color in Amani's cheeks.

"She still looks flushed. The water will bring her back to good health," Tierri insisted.

When Ushka returned, Thoth was intrigued, as the water seemed to glisten the moment it touched Amani's skin.

"What is this? It's like no water I've ever seen . . ."

"It falls from the falls! The Great Falls falls," Ushka replied.

"May I?" Thoth asked, extending his hand.

"It's magic!" Ushka said, handing him a small bucket filled with the shimmering liquid.

Tierri piped in, "She means it's imbued with magic."

"Magic?" Thoth questioned, pouring a bit of it in his hand and dipping his fingers into it. "Interesting composition. How did it come to be filled with this 'magic'?"

"According to Ric and Gaby Kasun, centuries ago, a witch and her family were here in our canyon, and she left a gift for all of us," Madame Luiza answered.

"It's quite the gift," Thoth replied. "Do you know what gives it the special qualities?"

"Aether," she stated flatly. "We were blessed to have been given it, and it has been cherished. Why do you find it so intriguing, though?"

"Because I think it may hold the key to the merging. This, combined with the goddesses' magic and mine—" Thoth paused to look over at Calla Lily—"and your gifts, will keep Amani safe and the merge a success."

"You want my help?" Calla Lily questioned.

"You have the skill, and you are close to Amani. The combination will be welcome, if not necessary to ground her. Will you assist?"

"Absolutely. Without question."

"Very good," Thoth said as he stood. "Do you mind if I take some of this liquid aether? I want to do some tests to confirm my hypothesis."

"That is not much. Would you like me to take to you to the source?" Calla Lily offered.

Thoth nodded. "Yes, more would be helpful and would give us a chance to speak further."

"Very well," Calla Lily said, moving toward the door. "It's about a fifteen-minute walk."

Thoth moved toward her and held out his hand. "Care to travel another way?" he said with a tilted grin.

Calla Lily was taken aback at first, but then put her hand in his, an electrical charge surging through the two of them. In the blink of an eye, the two were gone in a vortex of sand.

"I don't know how it's possible that there is never a speck of sand left when he or Amani disappears," Madame Luiza said with a shake of her head.

~

THOTH AND CALLA Lily arrived near the waterfall, and Calla Lily took a moment to catch her breath.

"Wow, that is certainly a way to travel," she said as her hand lingered in Thoth's. The images flashing in her brain were rapid and vivid. Thoth stood before her in his ceremonial garb, decked out as any god of his stature, but the god she was seeing with her sight was far different—more relaxed.

Thoth grinned at the blush in Calla Lily's cheeks. "I apologize. I didn't mean to fluster you."

"I'm not flustered. I simply wasn't expecting to see so much of you in those visions."

"I'm not usually impressed by the skill set of ordinary witches, but then again, you are no ordinary anything, are you, Calla Lily?"

"No. Ordinary would not be a term used to describe me," she said as she continued to meet his gaze.

"I'd assume not."

Calla Lily cleared her throat and turned toward the water. "It's exquisite, isn't it? There is something soothing about the peacefulness of the water after it makes its trek down the thunderous fall," she said, walking to the water's edge and dipping her hand into the pond.

"Where is the aether? It looks like an ordinary body of water," Thoth asked.

"Right here," she answered, pulling up a handful of the shimmering, glittery liquid.

"It hides itself until it is touched?"

"Everything here in Havenwood Falls is not what it seems. I like to think of it as self-preservation." Calla Lily winked.

"This place is unique, I will admit that, but why the secrecy?"

"We are all special and have many qualities the human world would be frightened of. Their fear leads to their aptitude for violence. We merely want to live in peace. Here we can do that."

"And yet you have some among you who lack tolerance?"

"Roman can be difficult, but he does it to keep us all safe. Rules are in place for that to remain possible."

"Why does he feel Amani poses a risk to him?" He paused. "Yes, her djinn side can be intimidating, but the things that occurred when she first arrived were her attempt to protect. She never intended to harm innocents. Amani is not the one out to destroy."

"No, she's not, and most of us know that, but Roman sees things differently than most."

"This Roman only sees things in his own favor."

Calla Lily chuckled. "Well, I cannot argue with that."

"I have not spoken with Hathor and Ma'at, but I know they will agree once I explain my position."

Calla Lily's brows ticked upward. "Your position on what?"

"I feel the need to perform the merging here in Havenwood Falls, right here near the aether. Its power and energy will sustain Amani in the event Khalida tries to take over."

"I thought you said Amani would emerge the victor."

"And she will, but I'm afraid there is always a chance Khalida could weaken Amani to try to gain the advantage."

"What do we do if that happens? None of us will stand for losing Amani—especially not Nathan." Calla Lily sighed. "And he's hardly capable of protecting her, since he's human."

"All precautions and actions will be taken to make certain that does not happen."

"And what do we about Nathan and the Court? How are we to include them in this process?"

"Like you, Nathan is a necessity for Amani's sake. Your friend Roman and the rest of the 'court' as you call them, should be aware of the plan, but they must not interfere."

Calla Lily scoffed. "You're asking for quite a lot if you think Roman will agree to that. I am certain the others will come around, but him?" She blew out a breath. "I'll see what I can do to convince them."

"I'm hoping to wait until the new moon on the twelfth of September. I think with everything else planned, it yields the most favorable time to perform the merging. Do you agree?"

"You're asking my opinion?"

"Why not?" Thoth asked as he made her personal tarot deck appear in her hands. "I know Amani showed you the way with those when she first arrived. Care to try again?"

Calla Lily stared up at him in confusion. "How did you know that?"

"I know everything."

"Humble, I see."

"I mean simply that I'm aware." Thoth tilted his head in the direction of her hands. "If you look, you'll see what I mean."

Calla Lily knelt down and began to run her hands over the cards, connecting her energy to them. "What am I supposed to be looking for?"

"Nothing more than the evidence of what I believe will be our success."

She closed her eyes and used her Shuvani gifts, whispering enchantments and incantations before pulling the first card. "The High Priestess," she whispered. "The archetype within. The representation of us that descends to hell and back, but not without bestowing symbolic lessons to coincide with it."

"What else do you see?"

"11:11 gateway? The High Priestess is between the light and dark pillars." Calla Lily questioned, "It can't be?"

Thoth gave her an apathetic look, kneeling down beside her. "And yet it is. Khalida and Amani are represented here and here." He pointed. "With Hathor's depiction at the center of it all."

"That is not Hathor," she protested.

"Not exactly, but the horned diadem does represent her in a way, does it not?"

"I . . . I don't know what to say."

"Say you will speak to your Court and show them the proof of my hypothesis. The blue in the High Priestess's robes is a symbol of water, and all of the pieces of the puzzle come together and culminate to one place."

"Havenwood Falls," she answered.

"Yes, on the twelfth, here by the aether and while the new moon is overhead."

"It's not a lot of time to prepare. That is only a few days away."

"At the rate Khalida is surging, it could be several days of torment for Amani. I will do my best to control the phasing between them, but in the meantime, you need to make sure the Court is ready when we return."

Calla Lily nodded, but remained stoic until Thoth reached for her free hand and brought it to his lips.

"I know it's a lot to take in, but you are powerful, and I trust that your power of persuasion will turn this situation in our favor."

More images fluttered in her mind, and the corners of her mouth curved into a smile as she studied him. "I never imagined a god flirting to get what he wants."

"I'm not flirting to get what I want. I always get what I want. I'm simply showing you potential options."

"Oh," she said softly, a grin forming as she continued to watch the images playing in her vision.

"There is one more card amidst the deck that you need to take heed of," he said as he touched the deck in her left hand. "It will enlighten a thought you've yet to think of."

"All right?"

"Until we meet again, Calla Lily Mircea," Thoth said before vanishing into a vortex of sand.

"No ride home?" She sighed.

Calla Lily began to make her way back to the road by way of the forest path, but was stopped when the sound of twigs snapping caught her attention.

"That was quite the exit."

"Excuse me?" she demanded as Roman moved out of the shadows and into view. "Were you spying on us?"

"Didn't seem like much to spy on, but I do find the consistent presence of him annoying."

"Twice doesn't make it consistent," she huffed, walking past him.

"Why was he here again, and why were you both here by the aether?"

"If it wasn't so late and I wasn't so tired, I'd stop to explain, but you are just going to have to wait until I am good and ready to tell you. Until then, try a little patience, Roman. It might do you some good."

"I wonder if you have overextended your welcome here in Havenwood Falls, Miss Mircea," Roman shouted as she continued to walk on, putting some distance between them.

She stopped and turned back. "No, but do try your best to remove me. It might be fun to watch you fail," Calla Lily responded, her voice echoing.

Calla Lily gripped the cards in her hand, ignoring the rest of the ignorant, arrogant remarks Roman continued to call out. Thankful to finally be out of earshot of him, she could see the Whisper Falls Inn sign and was relieved to almost be back to the cottage. Roman's idle threat meant nothing, but it would make it harder to present Thoth's plan to the Court if he was going to constantly be interrupting with his venomous words.

Calla Lily made her way onto the path, but tripped on a loose rock. The cards in her hand flew into the air and landed in a scattered mess on the moss. All of the cards but one landed face down. The one card that shone in the moonlight was the Empress in all her glory, the bright yellow background a beacon declaring the card's meaning. The Empress sat on her throne, wearing a starry crown and holding a scepter in her right hand. *Stability, abundance, nurturing, and new opportunities.* Calla Lilly gathered all the cards, taking one last look at the Empress before flipping it over and pocketing the tarot deck in her skirt.

"Message received, Thoth," she whispered, turning the handle on the cottage door. "I'm back," Calla Lily announced.

"I thought you were only going to grab some of the aether. What took so long?" Madame Luiza asked. "Are you all right?"

Calla Lily nodded. "Yes, I'm fine. It took a little extra time. Thoth was explaining the plan for what's to come and the things we need to do."

"Nothing to be worried about, I hope?"

"I'll explain later," Calla Lily said in a low tone. "How's Amani?"

"Much better. She's resting. Nathan is in there with her now, and Tierri and Ushka said they'd return tomorrow with more violets and some poppy milk, just in case you need to make a stronger potion for Amani."

"They are too kind."

"Hey. Glad you're back. How was your visit with the God of Wisdom?" Nathan teased, as he walked out of the bedroom.

"I'd assume like any other conversation you'd have with a god."

Nathan laughed. "Human here. My chats with God are more like, 'bless this food' or 'can you heal the sick.' The stuff going on here is a bit epic. It's a lot to digest."

Calla Lily grinned. "And yet, you're doing a great job of it."

Nathan rubbed his forehead. "Do you two have any thoughts on what I should do with Lillian? Do I pretend like none of this is going on? Send her home early? I mean, you said it yourself—she won't remember any of this once she leaves."

"There is no denying her timing couldn't have been worse, but now that she's here and has seen you and met Amani, do you think she'll go back without a word?" Calla Lily asked.

Nathan shook his head. "Not likely. Not until she can spend some more time getting to know Amani."

"Well, then I say we take it day by day. I could make an elixir to wipe her thoughts daily, but I'm not sure that will be helpful," Calla Lily said with a shrug.

"I say you don't do a thing. Let her see and experience whatever she will experience and it won't matter. The wards will keep the magic of it all hidden from her sight, and the memories will be wiped anyway once she leaves. She could see Amani go full djinn, but she'll never take that back to New York," Madame Luiza added.

"That is true," Calla Lily interjected. "We'll just need to keep her safe. Beyond that, it will all go away."

Nathan frowned. "She'll never even remember meeting her here, will she?"

"No, but maybe that is for the best, Nathan," Madame Luiza sympathized.

"She's right. This way we can get past Amani's transition and Lillian will be better off meeting the Amani we all know and love, and not the one currently being manipulated by Khalida," Calla Lily added.

Nathan sighed, but agreed.

"Nathan, dear, would you mind running up to the inn and getting some firewood?" Madame Luiza asked. "You know where Mihail stacks it."

"Of course. I didn't realize we were running low," Nathan replied.

"I don't want the two of you to get a chill in the middle of the night," she added.

"I'll be back in a bit," Nathan said, heading for the door. "Do we need anything else?"

"I think that should do it for now."

Nathan nodded and closed the door behind him.

Calla Lily gave Madame Luiza a sideways glance. "It's not supposed to be too cold tonight."

"No, but I needed him to go so we could talk freely."

"About?"

"Do you hear anything unusual?'

Calla Lily furrowed her brows. "No. What should I be hearing?"

"There are three of us, and yet I hear four distinct heartbeats."

"What?" Calla Lily exclaimed as she tapped into her inner sight and used her Shuvani powers. "I thought I heard something earlier when I was near Amani, but I assumed it had something to do with Khalida influencing her."

"Do we dare ask?"

"I think after what we just found out from Thoth about the merging, we need to ask. I mean is it possible it's already begun? Maybe part of Khalida is already here with Amani."

"Well, there is only one way to find out," Madame Luiza said with a sigh.

The two of them walked in to where Amani was resting. The sound became clearer and more distinct. It was rapid and had a specific cadence.

"How are you feeling?" Calla Lily asked.

Amani gave a faint smile. "Better, but I'm still so sorry to have frightened everyone."

"I can't lie and say it wasn't unnerving. I thought if things continued, Mihail was going to have to build a whole new cottage," Calla Lily teased.

"Thankfully it didn't come to that," Amani said with a slight laugh that shifted into something more somber. "I would have wanted to die if I had hurt anyone here."

"We know, and it didn't come to that, so we're all free to move on," Calla Lily said, moving to sit on the edge of the bed next to Amani. "Can we ask you something now that it is just us?"

Amani nodded. "Absolutely. You can ask me anything."

Calla Lily looked at Madame Luiza and then back to Amani. "We can hear another heartbeat, and its rhythm is not your usual tempo. Madame Luiza and I wanted to ask if maybe some of Khalida transferred into you when you changed, and that is what we are hearing."

Amani's gaze dropped to her hands. "No, my sister—or whatever she is—has nothing to do with it." She met their curious stare. "I'm with child."

Madame Luiza and Calla Lily gasped and then burst into joyous praise.

"This is wonderful news," Calla Lily cooed.

"Yes, wonderful indeed. Have you told Nathan?"

Amani shook her head. "I just found out amidst all this chaos. Thoth told me. I guess I'm not doing a good job so far at being a mother, if you two were able to hear the heartbeat and I could not."

"Don't you dare say that. You've had quite a lot to contend with," Calla Lily insisted. "Would you mind if I read you? Madame Luiza can hear the little one much better than I, but I can sense it better through my sight."

"Thoth only said I was with child, nothing more. I hadn't had the chance to tell Nathan because, well, with everything—I don't know exactly how to tell him. What with Lillian here and all. What will she say at Nathan being a father before he is married? Isn't it the custom of humans to marry before they are in the family way?"

Madame Luiza scoffed. "Maybe, but you are not human, Amani. Nothing about you and Nathan will ever fall into the normal confines of the world."

Amani's face fell. "I want so much to fit in."

"Why, though, dear? You are unique, not only because of your djinn powers, but because you are a lovely, kind woman. You will be a wonderful mother. Motherhood is a blessing to be cherished," Madame Luiza lamented as she moved to sit on the other side of Amani.

Amani placed her hands on Madame Luiza's and Calla Lily's, connecting the three of them. Together they went on a journey, watching as the energy from the baby drew their attention. The heart was fully formed and beating in a melodic rhythm, a radiating glow of pink and red, with casts of orange surrounding the little bundle. As they grew closer to the child through their mental connection, the baby turned to look at them. Peace and love radiated from her. Yes, she made herself known and smiled at them all. The moment slipped, and the three of them were suddenly back on the bed, staring at one another.

"Did you see that?" Amani beamed.

"It's a girl," Calla Lily cooed.

"I can't believe it. How wonderful was that? It's as if she knew we were there. Oh, I've never experienced anything like that," Madame Luiza raved.

"She's bigger than I assumed she would be. Doesn't it take longer for babies to grow in their mother's womb?" Amani asked.

"Well, that depends on when she was conceived," Calla Lily answered. "But, I think it's safe to say that your little girl is part djinn, and we may need to consult Thoth or Hathor about this. She's growing fast, which means you need to tell Nathan as soon as possible," Calla Lily said with a faint smile.

"I'm back," Nathan's voice boomed from the other room.

"Speak of the devil."

Amani's brows furrowed. "Oh no, Nathan is no devil. He's my angel."

Calla Lily and Madame Luiza chuckled.

"It's a saying, nothing more. People say it when they're talking about someone and then they show up," Madame Luiza explained.

"We should be going. We'll check in on you in the morning," Calla Lily said as she stood.

"You ladies okay?" Nathan asked as he popped his head into the bedroom. When Madame Luiza and Calla Lily moved to leave, Nathan frowned. "Don't leave on my account. I'm going to start a fire to warm the living room."

When they walked out of the room, a chill hit them, sending a shiver through them both. "Yes, it seems you do need to warm up this room."

"I don't get it. The temperature is at least ten degrees cooler in here than outside. I'll get it warmed up, though," Nathan said as he tossed a few logs into the stone fireplace.

"That is odd," Madame Luiza said, casting a curious glance at Calla Lily.

"Sleep well, Nathan," Calla Lily said as she and Madame Luiza made their way to the door.

"You as well. I will be up to the inn first thing to check on Lillian. She's an early riser, and I don't want you all to have to bother with her inquisition." He winked.

"She's no trouble, but I'm sure she'd rather see you than us at breakfast," Madame Luiza replied.

"I don't know. She seemed right at home with you ladies. It was like watching her with her knitting circle back home."

"Now, Nathan, we may seem like that, but you know we are so much more than *knitting circle* ladies," Madame Luiza said, something flashing over her grey-green eyes.

Nathan laughed out loud. "Please excuse my confusion. You are definitely not like her normal friends—I think you're more fun, though. Does that count?"

"For now," she teased, closing the door behind her.

As Calla Lily and Madame Luiza walked away from the cottage, the chill they felt in their bones eased with each step they took.

"What is that? Do you think Roman put a hex on the area?" Calla Lily asked, casting a glance back at the cottage. "I don't see anything, but there is definitely something lingering, and with Roman's remarks earlier about Amani, and then him seeing Thoth and me at the falls . . ." She trailed off.

"What comments, and why on earth would he hex the cottage? To what end?" Madame Luiza speculated.

"Why does Roman do anything?"

"I can have Mihail check with him. Or could it be Thoth's doing?" Madame Luiza asked.

Calla Lily shrugged. "At this point anything is possible."

"Do you want me to walk you home?" Madame Luiza offered.

"No, I'm fine. I'll stop by and see you tomorrow. Thank you for the offer, though."

Madame Luiza turned and headed toward the inn. "Until tomorrow then."

"Until tomorrow." Calla Lily waved before putting her hands in her pockets to warm them. Her fingers tingled when they made contact with her tarot cards. She pulled them out and there on top was the Empress card, face up, even though she remembered flipping it back over. "Everything is going to be just fine, Amani. You'll get your happily ever after in the end," she said under her breath, rounding the corner on her way home.

CHAPTER 12

hen Khalida woke, Thoth was gone, but she could sense where he was—had felt it through Amani. Rage coursed through her veins at the thought of her sister.

"Why do I feel you now more than ever before?" she snarled. Amani did not respond, of course, but there was no doubt their connection had strengthened lately.

Ice crystals began to form on the hair of her arms almost in concert with the cold hatred she felt for Amani. Khalida watched as icicles continued to spread to every surface around her, wondering how it was possible and why she didn't feel the cold herself. When the process stopped, Khalida found her cage to be completely frozen. Khalida looked at the ice shards and smirked, thinking they could be useful in battle. The ice was different than her usual power. Typically, energy surged through her, until the intensity arced out of her and into whatever she chose as a target, but this—she twisted her hands and arms, admiring the icy crystals as they glistened—was intriguing. As she continued to admire the clear stalagmites, an odd sensation fluttered in Khalida's stomach, shifting her attention. She could feel movement and hear a faint thrumming rhythm. Shock resonated through her. It was a heartbeat. Amani was with child.

"NO!" Khalida screamed. "You do not get to have everything you want while I am here, trapped in Thoth's prison."

The rage and pain continued to surge. Amani had killed Khaldun and was now living her dream of being a wife and mother—it was all coming to fruition while Khalida's dreams were shattered as she awaited punishment. Waves of energy pulsed under Khalida's skin, building until the crystal shards covering her and the space around her exploded. The frozen cage was now filled with powdery bits, falling and floating from every direction while the walls remained intact. A fine snow blustered around her, hiding Khalida from view to anyone who would attempt to look in. It was the perfect camouflage as tears started to stream down her face.

"Tears?" Khalida cried out. "I refuse to feel your weakness, Amani. REFUSE!"

Ever since she was a young girl, she never understood why Amani would stop to help people who were suffering. Why she'd cry when they cried or laugh when they laughed. Khalida never felt any of those emotions. Even with Khaldun, it wasn't love she felt. Lust, passion, a shared desire to elicit pain in others—that was what drove them, bound them together. However, now she was feeling sentiment. Sorrow was now intermingled with joy, fear, and love for whatever was connected to the tiny movements within her. The sound of the heartbeat became a beacon for her to home in on. Then realization dawned and snapped her back to the truth of the situation. The child may not be hers, but with a *shift* or a *change*, it could be. She could be the one to emerge—no, she *would* be the one to emerge—as the dominant personality.

The air around Khalida warmed, clearing her vision and thawing everything around her. She wondered what other things she could *feel* or *manipulate* to her advantage. They were connected earlier, and that led to feeling more of Amani's emotions.

"Guess it's time to find out," she whispered, looking around to make sure there was no evidence of her glacial explosion. When she was certain there were no remnants to alert Thoth, she lay down in her bed and closed her eyes, dreaming of the life she'd take from Amani.

"How are you feeling?" Nathan asked as he brought a cup of hot tea in to Amani.

"Much better. I just can't seem to shake this chill," she said, shivering.

"Here," he said, handing her the tea. "Let me get you an extra blanket."

Amani took a sip of the tea and moaned. "Oh, this so delicious. I can taste vanilla and the raspberries along with a tiny hint of mint."

"Well, that is rather specific. You can taste each one?" Nathan said as he brought the blanket over to Amani and covered her with it. "Why are your teeth chattering? Is the tea not warming you?"

"I can't shake the cold because it is not anything here in the cottage. It's Khalida's doing."

"How? What can we do to stop this?"

"There's nothing anyone can do until we merge. She's angry that I'm free and she is not," Amani said before she drank the last bit of tea. The cup was still warm, so she gripped it with both hands, hoping to steady the shaking. "The link between us is becoming more fluid."

"Can't you counteract her power by using your own?"

"I can, but I'm worried it may strengthen her, and I don't need her stronger. Besides, I don't want to anger the Court by using more of my magic."

Nathan shook his head. "No, we definitely don't need that," he said, sitting on the edge of the bed next to her and wrapping his hands around hers.

Amani gave him a somber smile. "I'm sorry I've become such a burden. I should've known better than to believe she'd allow me a moment of peace." Her eyes lowered to his hands on hers. "Especially after I killed Khaldun. I'm here with you, happy and moving on with life, and that is what she'll fight to destroy."

"You didn't have a choice. You did what you needed to do to save yourself and all of us."

"I know, but Khalida has never seen herself as others have. She's always believed that my goodness was my flaw . . . my weakness. She sees me as the one who needs to be removed, not her."

Nathan rubbed their hands together to create more warmth. "Well, that is not going to happen. I will not lose you now that I have finally found true happiness."

Amani's eyes lit up. "Nathan, I need to tell you something," she said softly. "I'm—"

Amani was unable to finish that sentence, however, because the mug she and Nathan were still gripping exploded. Shards went everywhere as the two of them were blown backwards by a massive blast. When Amani came to, she saw Nathan lying a distance away on the floor of the living room, motionless.

"Nathan," Amani screamed as she scrambled to him, lifting him into her arms. There was blood on his shirt, and he was unresponsive. "Please don't leave me. I love you and we're going to have a baby. Please, Nathan, please come back to me," she cried.

When Nathan remained silent, Amani's heart sank. She felt something wet on her fingers and lifted them up to see crimson coating her hand. Nathan was hurt worse than she knew. Amani cried out for Thoth, Hathor, Ma'at, and Calla Lily, anyone she could think of to help, but for the first time since this day started, they were alone. Amani closed her eyes and embraced her djinn. Using her power had brought the Court and others running every other time. She could only hope this would not be the exception. Amani's eyes were ablaze, but not the rest of her. She was managing to contain the surge, but knew Khalida would use this as a way to gain control. Maybe that was her plan all along. However, in this moment, nothing else mattered except saving Nathan.

Mihail, Irina, and Madame Luiza came through the cottage door in a blur and stopped the second they saw Nathan in Amani's arms.

"What happened?" Mihail asked, kneeling beside Amani.

"Khalida exploded the mug we were holding, and when I came to, he was like this," she said, showing him the blood on her hands.

Mihail inhaled deeply, pinpointing Nathan's head wound, then again moved in a blur. He'd grabbed a blade and drug it across his palm, quickly pouring his pooled blood down Nathan's throat. Silence filled the cottage as seconds turned to minutes, the others from the Court filtering in, until Nathan gasped and opened his eyes.

Nathan's eyes were wide and his skin pale. "Where's Amani? Is she okay?" Nathan croaked, his voice raspy and on edge.

Mihail, Irina, Madame Luiza, and Calla Lily were all speaking to him, telling him to lie still, that he'd need a minute and that he was okay, but Amani stood motionless, staring at him. Nathan propped himself up on his elbow and peered at her.

"What's wrong with her?" Nathan asked.

They all turned to look at Amani, Mihail moving to instantly shield Nathan. They stared as her hair turned black, with long white strands flowing down past her arms. Her skin was pale, almost blue, and her now opaque eyes were staring blankly at Nathan.

"You were supposed to have died. Too bad. I'll get you eventually." Her voice was harsh and not her own.

"That's not Amani," Saundra offered before tossing a spell bottle at Amani's feet.

Amani's head twisted toward Saundra. "You have no power or dominion over me, witch."

"No, but I do," a baritone voice said from the bedroom doorway.

Everyone turned their attention to Thoth. With a snap of his fingers, Amani fell to the floor, and Calla Lily rushed to her side. As she held Amani in her arms, she changed back to the woman they knew, but she didn't wake. Calla Lily fixed her gaze on the God of Wisdom. "Care to explain what the hell that was and why Nathan almost died tonight?"

"The simple answer is, we are not going to be able to wait until the new moon to merge Amani and Khalida." He turned to Nathan. "What happened in there tonight?" he asked, pointing to the bedroom.

Nathan quickly recounted everything up to the mug exploding. "I don't remember anything else after that."

"Amani opened herself up to embrace her djinn to try to save Nathan," Mihail interjected. "After feeling her magic, we all arrived, and I used my blood to save Nathan, but have no idea how much time passed before Khalida took over Amani's body."

"Their connection has become stronger lately, and they're feeding off of one another," Thoth replied.

"Amani said she wouldn't use her djinn power to fight Khalida's link because she thought it may strengthen her," Nathan said, sitting up with Mihail's help.

"Nathan, was anything happening to Amani before all this transpired?" Thoth asked.

"She was freezing. I just thought she was cold until she said it was Khalida's doing."

"It's been cold here in the house, too," Madame Luiza said. "Calla Lily and I noticed it before we left earlier."

"I can feel a presence too," Saundra offered. "It's gone now, though." She turned to Roman. "Are you getting anything?"

"No, but there's no denying the power behind what we just saw," Roman answered with narrowed eyes and a flexing jaw.

Thoth nodded. "She plans to divide you all and make you hurt one another. She's using Amani to achieve her goals."

"And why should we believe that Amani is not a part of it?" Roman snapped.

Thoth turned to face him. "Your need to make Amani the villain is acknowledged, but not verified. I've explained that they are not twins but two halves of a whole. Once the two parts are reunited, you will see the truth."

"And if you're wrong?"

"I'm never wrong."

Calla Lily bit back a grin but focused on Amani. "What can we do for Amani in the meantime?"

"The best choice is for her to return with me, but I know that won't be acceptable to you. I'll return tomorrow," Thoth replied, then flicked his wrist, causing Amani to float up and out of Calla Lily's arms, hovering midair. "She'll need to rest and not be agitated in any way. That's what gives Khalida the opening she needs to take over. Don't give it to her." Thoth cast a quick glance at Roman. With another flick of his wrist, Thoth led a still hovering, still unconscious, Amani to the bedroom and laid her down gently before returning to the kitchen where everyone was still standing.

"I've never seen anything like that," Nathan said with a quick shake of his head. "I know Roman has reservations about Amani being here, Thoth, but I'm telling you, she has no ill intentions toward anyone. Just tell us what is needed to get her back to herself, and we will make it happen . . . all of us," he said confidently, looking to the others.

Roman sneered while the rest nodded in agreement.

"The task will be more difficult now, but we can manage it. I've informed Hathor and Ma'at of the situation, and they are already preparing what Amani will need," Thoth said, looking at Calla Lily.

"What are you two not telling us?" Roman questioned. "You both were at the falls having a private discussion, and now there is something unspoken in your exchange. If you expect my cooperation, you'll divulge your plan—now."

"I don't expect your cooperation. I expect your compliance." Thoth glared at Roman. "I will not answer for anything. You will help to save yourself. And you'll help to save Havenwood Falls. Otherwise Khalida will take over a weakened Amani, and she'll kill you all." Thoth turned his attention back to the rest of the group. "I'm not asking for your help. I'm demanding it for the sake of us all. We can stop a tragedy by joining together and working as one. Are the rest of you willing?"

Nods and collective yeses followed, and Roman reluctantly included his agreement with a huff.

"When the sun begins to set, the goddesses and I will be by the water's edge near the falls. Bring what is needed, and we will finally be rid of this once and for all." Thoth nodded at Calla Lily, another unspoken conversation between the two of them, but one Calla Lily acknowledged with a nod of her own.

"We will be ready," she said, just before Thoth vanished in a wisp of sand.

"You never cease to amaze me with your ability to anger people, Roman. You decide to go toe to toe with a god?" Calla Lily said, shaking her head. "Saundra, should you go talk to the rest of the Court?"

"It's the middle of the night."

"I know, but it seems we have a clock ticking and much to be done." Irina grabbed a piece of paper and fountain pen out of the drawer and handed it to Calla Lily. "Make us a list of what we need."

Calla Lily scribbled on the page. "Madame Luiza and I will take care of Amani. Irina and Mihail can keep an eye on Nathan, and soon this will all be over and we can get back to our normal, boring everyday lives."

"What about Lillian?" Nathan interjected.

Calla Lily blew out an exhausted breath. "In all this chaos, I completely forgot she was here."

"The wards will keep the magic from her, but the Luna Coven will make certain she stays safe but unaware," Saundra offered.

"Thank you, Saundra."

"So, we have a plan?" Mihail asked, looking at the group.

"So it seems," Roman quipped.

"We'll meet tomorrow morning at nine at the inn to make sure we are all ready," Mihail said, taking Irina's hand in his. "Nathan, take it easy tonight. My blood healed you, but you almost died, and we're going to have a lot to do tomorrow to prepare."

"Yes, sir," Nathan replied. "And thank you. Thank you for saving me and for allowing Amani and me to stay here. We never meant to cause any harm."

"We know, Nathan. We're fond of you both, and like Calla Lily said, this will be over soon." Mihail extended his hand to Nathan.

Nathan shook his hand, then watched as everyone but Calla Lily and Madame Luiza left.

Calla Lily turned to Nathan. "Go be with her. I'm going to sleep at the inn tonight just in case anything else should happen. That way we're all close. We don't know what tomorrow night will bring, so talk to her and then get some sleep."

Nathan complied, leaving Madame Luiza and Calla Lily alone in the kitchen.

"Amani didn't get the chance to tell him about the baby, that's what was unspoken between you and Thoth, wasn't it?" Madame Luiza asked as she picked up the list and started to move toward the door.

"Yes, the baby adds a wrinkle, but with a binding, we can save them both. I'd like for Amani to be the one to tell him and not have him find out he's going to be a father while everything is happening."

"Oh, dear. This is an impossible situation, it seems. I adore them, but life has been a little too exciting for my taste since they arrived," Madame Luiza said as she and Calla Lily walked out of the cottage.

"We'll be begging for some excitement after they're gone, I'm sure," Calla Lily joked.

*a*mani sat up and stared down at her tattered and torn dress. Tears welled in her eyes as she looked at the blood—Nathan's blood. She almost lost him tonight and knew Khalida would stop at nothing to make her as miserable as she was. Amani remembered the threat she'd made over the centuries, that she'd kill them both to save the ones she loved. However, now it was Khalida making the threats and turning them into actions. The problem Amani faced, though, was that she couldn't follow through with her threat, because it would kill her child, and that was something she would never do.

"How am I going to fix this?" Amani said under her breath as she undressed.

As she stood in her slip, she ran her hands over her belly and promised to keep her baby safe at all cost. Amani bent down and picked up the clothes and folded them neatly. She pulled the comb out of her hair and let her blond curls spill over her shoulders.

"If you'd only stayed locked away, then none of this would've happened," Amani said aloud.

Just then, Nathan walked into the bedroom. "If you'd only stayed locked away, then I would never know what love felt like," he answered as the door clicked closed.

"Oh, you startled me."

Nathan walked over to her, but stopped short. "You are so beautiful," he said, stepping closer and taking her hand in his, "even with soot on your cheeks."

Amani shook her head. "I'd assume beautiful would be the last word to describe me tonight."

"What's wrong?" he said, pulling a handkerchief out of his pocket and using it to wipe her face. "I know Khalida is causing you trouble, but I feel like there is something else bothering you."

Her eyes flashed to his. "There is something I've been wanting to tell you, but all these things keep happening and . . ."

He kissed her forehead gently and then her lips. "Want to tell me now? It's just us."

Amani rose up on the balls of her feet, her hands on his cheeks, and captured his lips. The kiss spoke a thousand words, but not the ones she most needed to say. When she broke their kiss, Nathan was dazed as he stared at her.

"I cannot believe I almost lost you," she whispered.

"But you didn't. I'm right here."

Amani met his eyes. "I love you, Nathan."

He smiled down at her. "I love you, too."

Amani glanced down, but then finally blurted, "I was going to tell you earlier . . . before the . . . but then everything—"

"What is it?" Nathan said softly, sensing her nervousness.

"I think I'd rather show you."

"Okay." A grin played at his lips as he looked down at the nude silk slip she was wearing.

Amani reached for his hand. "Do you remember when we first connected?" Nathan nodded, and she continued, "It's been unintentional, but I've been blocking our link. I've had to disconnect myself so Khalida couldn't get to you, but what I need you to know is too important."

"I thought something felt off with us, but assumed it was because of all you were having to deal with. I can still feel our connection, though. It's just faint."

"From now on it will only become stronger."

He cocked his head and reached for a lock of her hair. "Okay."

Amani linked their fingers and let all she needed, no, *wanted* him to know flow from her to him with ease. Gold tendrils wound down her hands and made their way into his. They coiled and snaked up his arms and headed straight for his heart.

Nathan sucked in a harsh breath at the sensation.

"It's okay, just breathe. I'm here."

The tendrils changed and formed into hieroglyphs, then returned to lines flowing through his veins. Amani was sending him her every thought, every joy, every passion, and every pain she'd ever endured. Nathan stared down at her, feeling every emotion, every bit of her essence until they came to a single moment—the first time they made love. He pulled her closer as they watched themselves intertwined and full of passion.

Nathan lifted Amani and carried her over to the bed, their fingers still linked, their bond surging. He laid her down gently, hovering above her as the images of them making love continued to replay. The way he let his fingers roam over the soft contours of her skin. The way she arched her back when he felt her warmth on his fingers for the first time. Every second was tingling on his skin until it felt as if they were actually doing it right then.

Amani moaned, and Nathan pressed his lips to hers, pausing only a moment to whisper, "I loved our first time together, but we don't have to relive it in a dream. I'd be happy to show you just how much I love you right now if you want."

"But you needed to see this first time to know what I needed to show you," she replied between his kisses.

Nathan stopped when something ignited between them. Gold and crimson merging in a tornadic swirl, changing and shifting—exploding, until the soft sound of a heartbeat clicked. Nathan watched as a glow he'd not seen until now radiated from her. Nathan continued to watch the spark turn into a bundle and then move to face them, her soft features coming into focus.

"A baby? Ours?" Nathan stammered.

Amani nodded, and Nathan kissed her again.

"Is she a djinn like you?"

"She's a bit of both of us, and I honestly don't know what she will be."

"Well, just like with you, I will take her as she is and be grateful for the gift. Oh Amani, I'm so happy."

"I wanted you to see how we created life. How the love we share made something special and unique."

"Well, you did more than that," he teased, "but I don't know what to say other than I love you."

"I didn't know if you'd be upset. We're not married, and I know how much it means for human couples to be bound in such a way."

"Amani, all I care about is that you love me and you're mine. The rest, we can figure out later. Your life, your health—" he slid his hand over her belly—"and this baby are all that matter to me. We'll have plenty of time later to figure out titles and social mores."

Amani ran her hand up Nathan's chest and caressed his cheek. "Make love to me," she breathed. "I don't know what tomorrow will bring, but I refuse to lose any more time with you, Nathan."

Nathan didn't think about a response; instead, he acted. Neither of them needed to think about tomorrow in this moment. All they needed was to embrace their desire for one another, making love until they were both spent.

THE FIRE WAS NOW a slow crackle in the room, the amber glow flickering on the ceiling as Amani lay draped over Nathan's chest. She ran her fingers over his heart, her thoughts a steady flow from her to him.

"I know you're nervous about tomorrow, but I will not let anything happen to you—you or the baby," Nathan reassured.

"I know, but Khalida knows about her too now, and she wants to be the one to surface and raise our child." Amani sighed.

"And from all I gathered from the group and Thoth, all

contingencies have been accounted for. You're going to be fine—we all are."

Amani sat up, wrapping the sheet around her chest.

"Are you getting cold? I can add more wood to the fire."

"Would you mind?"

"Not at all," Nathan said, slipping into his trousers before he headed into the main room.

When he returned, he tossed two logs into the hearth, then used the iron poker to stoke the fire. When the new logs began to burn, he walked back over to their bed and sat on the edge next to Amani.

"Can I get you anything? Water? Something to eat?"

She shook her head and blurted, "Can I ask you something?"

"Of course."

"I know that no matter what, I will always be yours. I want to bind us with more than just our thoughts. I want to make certain that Khalida cannot corrupt our love. Will you help me ask Hathor for her blessing to bind our union?"

"Yes." Nathan reached for her hand. "How do we ask her?"

Amani took Nathan's other hand in hers and turned them both until they were palms up. "In a reverent prayer," she answered, adding her hands to the top of his. "Goddess, I know I've asked for so much, and now I am asking again. You've blessed Nathan and me with a gift of the highest honor, and we humbly ask for one more wish to be granted. Release me from this curse and show Nathan and me how to bond together to defeat Khalida, so we can raise our daughter in peace."

They sat in silence, waiting, until a white feather appeared above their heads, then floated down to land softly in their outstretched hands. The feather burst into flames but was still cool against their palms. What remained was a golden feather on a matching chain.

"Isn't that your mother's necklace, the one you used to summon Hathor in the town square?"

"It is," she said, trying to choke back her emotions.

A voice, soft and gentle, spoke as if it were part of the air around them. "You have my blessing. You will need the union to ground yourselves tomorrow. I am pleased. You two are well suited."

Amani stared at Nathan as she offered her gratitude for this blessing. "Thank you, Goddess."

Nathan stammered, unsure of what to say or do, but he followed suit by thanking Hathor as well. "I promise to love her until the day we can both walk the duat together," he said out loud, his eyes never leaving Amani's.

"Very well."

The gold necklace twisted and coiled like Amani's blood until it knotted itself around both of their wrists. A searing pain burned where the golden cord was bound. "Forever until the end, you two shall be one."

The two of them watched as the necklace melded into their skin. The only visible evidence that it even existed was the faint markings on them both. Moments passed and the two just sat there, transfixed. Their thoughts had become one—they were in perfect harmony. Amani and Nathan went to release their hands but stopped when they felt something underneath their forearms. They watched as hieroglyphs appeared in a single row. It began at their wrists and moved toward their elbows—an ankh, the Eye of Horus, an image of Ma'at with her wings colorful and outstretched, followed by Hathor and Thoth's hieroglyphs. The final image to appear was a blue water lily. Nathan had seen these many times and nodded appreciatively. It was an important symbol in ancient Egypt, representing creation and rebirth—an homage to their child and Amani's merging. They had Hathor's blessing, and were now forever marked for all who dared to question the union between them.

"Thank you," Nathan said appreciatively. "I will not disappoint you. I will care for them both. Always."

Amani leaned forward and kissed Nathan. "Thank you for choosing me. I am the one who is honored."

The baby moved, and Nathan and Amani both laughed. They now felt everything together and would forever feel each other's thoughts and emotions, pain and joy.

"I think she wants to be included," Nathan chuckled. "Not even here and already demanding to be heard."

Nathan lay down, and Amani curled into him, laying her head on his chest. Her eyes grew heavy, and she once again thanked the goddesses and Thoth for their blessings before falling asleep. Nathan closed his eyes and listened to the sound of his daughter's and Amani's heartbeats until he too fell asleep. The three of them would be a family forever, bound through love.

CHAPTER 14

$\mathcal{N}$athan was up early and got ready before Amani woke. He leaned down and kissed her forehead before he left to go meet with Calla Lily, Mihail, Irina, and Madame Luiza at the inn. With everything that happened last night, Nathan knew he didn't need to leave her a note, because she'd already know where he was when she thought of him. He left the cottage quietly and made his way to the inn's backdoor. He grabbed a handful of the firewood he chopped a few days ago and was headed for the parlor, but ran into Madame Luiza in the kitchen.

"You're up early," Madame Luiza said when she saw Nathan. "Are you hungry, dear?"

"Starving."

"Almost dying can do that to you," she teased. "How's Amani?"

"Still sleeping," he said as he lifted the wood in his arms. "I thought I'd bring in some wood for the hearth and meet with you all before bothering her. She's exhausted."

Madame Luiza focused on the eggs she was cracking. "When we're finished here this morning, I will send you home with a plate for her. Calla Lily said she'd be downstairs by eight."

"Did someone say my name?"

Madame Luiza laughed. "Good morning. Did you sleep well?"

"As best as I could," Calla Lily said, moving toward the tea kettle. "Do you mind?"

"Not at all. Help yourself," Madame Luiza responded. "Saundra and the rest of the Court aren't due here for another hour or so. That should be enough time to feed the guests, clean up, and gather the items we need."

"I'm happy to help with anything. Amani too, once she wakes," Nathan offered as he added the wood to the pile next to the stove. "What can I do in the meantime?"

When Nathan moved to shift the wood on the rack, his new hieroglyphs peeked out from under his sleeve, catching Calla Lily's eye.

"Did you and Amani have a chance to speak last night?" she said, gesturing to Madame Luiza to look at Nathan's arm as he rearranged the wood so it wouldn't fall.

"Yes, we spoke," Nathan said nonchalantly as he continued to stack. "And yes, I know you both know."

A grin tipped Madame Luiza's lips as she whisked the eggs. "Then it's safe to offer our congratulations."

The tea kettle whistled, and Calla Lily pulled it off of the fire to let it cool while she put two pinches of fresh lavender over the top of some green tea leaves. She grabbed an orange from the basket on the butcher block and begun to peel it as Nathan rolled up his sleeves and showed her and Madame Luiza the markings.

"Amani and I have the same hieroglyphs. We connected our lifelines to one another with Hathor's blessing. We are one."

"We're happy for you both," Calla Lily said as she looked over at Madame Luiza.

"I don't know what those mean, Nathan, but a blessing from Egyptian gods is a wonder in and of itself," Madame Luiza stated.

"It will serve us all tonight that you are linked to her," Calla Lily said, placing the peel in the bottom of her cup before reaching for the kettle. The scent of orange and lavender filled the kitchen as the hot water hit the ingredients, overriding the smell of the biscuits cooking in the oven. "Anyone else want a cup?"

Madame Luiza went to answer, but the bell chimed, and she turned toward the sound. "Duty calls. I will have to get one later."

"I can check on that, Madame Luiza, and you can finish the eggs and enjoy a cup of tea," Nathan offered.

"That would be great. Can you check with Irina, too, and see how many guests we'll be having down for breakfast?"

"Sure thing," Nathan said, grabbing the notepad Madame Luiza used to write down the food orders. "Amani is awake, by the way, if you needed to speak with her."

"How do you . . ." Calla Lily asked.

"She just said good morning, and that she'll be over to help us soon." Nathan winked.

Madame Luiza stirred the eggs on the stove and shrugged. "Seems you have some supernatural abilities of your own now, Nathan. Now go and get those orders for me. These eggs will be finished in a minute, and so will the biscuits."

Nathan gave her a quick nod and headed out of the kitchen. When he rounded the corner, he stopped short.

"Nathan, where have you been? I thought I was having breakfast with you and Amani this morning," Lillian said, moving to hug him. "You're not dressed for a meal."

"I'm sorry, Lillian," he replied as he embraced her. "I completely forgot, and Amani is still resting. How about just the two of us?" he offered, leading her into the dining room. "I am helping Madame Luiza with the breakfast, but as soon as I'm finished, I'll be all yours."

"You've always been a helper. I'll be here." She lifted her book. "I have a few more pages, and I'll be finished."

Nathan pulled the chair out for her. "Would you like coffee or tea this morning?"

"Coffee would be wonderful."

"Breakfast will be ready in a bit."

An older couple and their daughter walked into the dining room, and Nathan made sure to mark down what they'd like to drink before heading to the lobby to check in with Irina. "Good morning."

"Good morning to you. You look well rested. How is Amani?"

"Amani and I slept well, thank you."

"Is she feeling better? Mihail and I have been worried about you both."

"She's feeling much better and is looking forward to getting tonight over with so we can move on with our lives."

"And the baby?" Irina beamed.

"You knew?"

"Mihail and I heard the heartbeat, and then Madame Luiza and Calla Lily confirmed it. We're happy for you both."

Nathan nodded. "Thank you. I'm a blessed man to have them both."

Irina gestured toward Lillian. "And don't worry. We'll keep the secret. No one else need know until you and Amani are ready to tell it."

"Good morning, Nathan. It is nice to see you up and around. Can you tell Madame Luiza we'll be having six guests for breakfast?" Mihail called out, putting him back on task.

"I can do that," Nathan said before he turned to leave. He stopped short, though, and turned back to face Mihail and Irina. "I don't know how I will ever be able to thank you for saving my life last night. I'll forever be indebted to you." He ducked his head. "All of you."

"No need to thank me. I've grown to like you, Nathan." Mihail smiled. "Can't imagine the world without you a part of it."

Words caught in Nathan's throat, and he gave Mihail and Irina a quick nod before heading back into the kitchen.

The next hour flew by, and all the guests were taken care of and had moved on with their day. All except Lillian. Nathan had stopped by her table several times to offer apologies and more coffee, but he could tell she was growing tired of him coming and going. Amani had sensed his agitation and came to help in the kitchen so he could finally entertain Lillian, though it quickly became obvious he was failing in his duty.

"Nathan, did you even hear a word I said?"

"What?" he stammered. "I'm sorry, Lillian. I was distracted."

"By what?" she said, before following his sightline and realizing why in an instant.

There in the doorway was Amani. Her blond hair fell over her shoulders in soft curls, and the pale gray dress she was wearing made her look ethereal. Lillian watched as Amani and Nathan stared at one another as if they'd known each other for a lifetime. Love and peace radiated from them both, and Lillian's heart swelled. The boy she'd taken care of for so long, the young man who'd endured years of suffering, had finally found joy. Nathan stood and walked over to Amani.

He intertwined their fingers and tucked her arm under his. "You look beautiful."

Amani blushed and leaned in closer to Nathan. "You say that all the time. Soon I will start to believe it."

Nathan kissed her cheek and led her over to the couch where Lillian was now sitting.

"I'd like to apologize for last night. I wasn't feeling well and needed to go rest. I hope you enjoyed your evening, Lillian."

"Nothing to worry about, dear. I know how to amuse myself when company is absent," she insisted. "It gave me a chance to read my book, and for that, I am grateful."

"Did you enjoy it?" Amani asked.

"Very much. Would you care to read it? I can give it to you, and you can read it at your leisure," Lillian offered.

Amani glanced at Nathan before she smiled at Lillian. "That would be lovely. Thank you."

Calla Lily came into the parlor with a tray in her hand. It had a floral teapot, several matching cups, and a pile of cookies on a plate.

"Anyone for tea?" she asked. "Madame Luiza sent out some homemade oatmeal cookies, too."

"I love oatmeal cookies," Lillian responded.

"Lillian, I'd like you to meet Saundra Beaumont. She lives here in Havenwood Falls," Nathan said, standing when Saundra walked in a few steps behind Calla Lily.

Saundra regarded Nathan and Amani as she moved to sit next to

Lillian. "Calla Lily was asking for the two of you to assist with some tasks in the kitchen. I'll be more than happy to entertain Lillian for a few minutes."

"Very well," Nathan said, leaning over to kiss Lillian on the cheek. "I'll find you when we're done."

"No rush," she answered. "I can't wait to pick Miss Beaumont's brain about this wonderful town. I overheard some of the other guests talking about the Great Falls and how majestic they were. It sounded wonderful."

"They are. We'll see you soon, then," Amani added before she and Nathan walked out of the room.

Gathered in the dining room were Mihail, Irina, Madame Luiza, Ric, and the remaining members of the Court. Calla Lily walked in a second later, followed by the pixies of the Spring Fae Court: Aeiri, Ushka, Tierri, and Enya. Amani squeezed Nathan's hand.

"It's all going to be all right," he said into her mind.

Ric turned to Calla Lily. "Where do we start? Gaby and Conall are awaiting word, and everyone in support of Nathan and Amani is ready to help with what we need to gather."

Calla Lily fiddled with the bracelets at her wrist. "Saundra has reinforced the wards and is taking care of watching Lillian and the other guests to keep everyone safe, so I think we're ready to get started."

Amani stepped away from Nathan and moved closer to the group. "I'd like to say something first." Everyone turned to look at her. "When I addressed you all last time, I said I would honor you and that I was at your service. Since then, I've done everything in my power to keep my word. I never meant to bring any harm to Havenwood Falls, but I'm once again needing your help." She bent her head and sighed. "As it was before, I will not let Khalida hurt anyone and will sacrifice myself if it comes to that. All I ask is that you take care of Nathan, if the need arises."

Mihail spoke first. "We will not be losing any of you."

"No, not one," Irina added.

Amani turned to face Roman. "I know we have conflict, but I need not be your enemy," she stated.

"I wouldn't consider you one if you didn't feel the need to keep secrets."

"Even you have your secrets, Roman. I am no different. However, the question you are dying to know the answer to is small in comparison to what we are about to face. I promise you that I am not a concern, but if you don't look at the bigger picture, Khalida most certainly will be." She extended her hand to him. "Peace for now?"

Roman narrowed his eyes and reluctantly extended his hand to meet hers. "For now."

With the pleasantries out of the way, the group went about making a plan. Each person had a task, and with the hours dwindling until sunset, there was no time to waste.

"Gather everything and meet at the water's edge at seven thirty," Calla Lily finished. "Be well until then."

CHAPTER 15

*A*t times the day seemed to drag on, while other times it seemed to speed up. Either way, everyone had been working diligently to gather all that was needed. As the sun began to dip in the sky, Amani changed into the dress she wore when she first arrived in Havenwood Falls. Thoth had requested that everyone be dressed in white to perform the merging because it symbolized power, purity, and simplicity—all traits important to their success.

The sky was changing from azure blue to varying shades of coral and magenta. The sun was setting, and the time was drawing near. Amani walked out into the garden and ran her hands delicately over the heather, watching as the season's last white and purple blooms swayed in the breeze.

"You should pick some and put it in your pocket," Calla Lily said softly.

Amani turned and gave her a half smile. "I hate picking them. I can feel their sadness at the loss of not being connected to the earth."

"I understand, but I think under the circumstances, they'd want to be with you."

"Why is that?"

"Heather is used to cleanse and protect. It also is used for good luck," Calla Lily said as she knelt beside the plant. "Will you offer your gifts to us this day?" The shrub bent forward, as if it were acknowledging Calla Lily's request. "Thank you," she answered as she snipped just what she would need for Amani.

She wrapped it with a piece of white muslin and handed it to Amani.

"I'm scared," Amani admitted as she took the floral bundle. "I can feel something stirring, and it reeks of ambiguity."

"Everything is going to be fine."

Amani took Calla Lily's hand. "I need you to promise me something."

"Of course. Anything."

"Protect Nathan and the baby no matter what happens," Amani pleaded.

Calla Lily's features hardened, and her eyes started to well with emotion. "I promise."

"I'm connected to Nathan. He knows and feels all that I do now that our lifelines are linked, but the baby is still too small and too vulnerable. Khalida will try to use her to break me."

"We won't let her," Calla Lily insisted.

"I've asked too much of you already, but there is no one other than Nathan that I trust more, and since he is human and you are Shuvani, I must ask one more thing," Amani said, her voice unwavering. "Will you link your bloodline to hers, so in the event something happens to me, she will have a tether to this world?"

"Oh, Amani. Have you talked to Nathan about this?"

"He knows it now that I've said it to you, and while he refuses to accept any outcome other than all of us together, he also understands he'd be powerless against Khalida. You and Thoth could save her."

Calla Lily lifted her chin and steadied her resolve as she took Amani's hands in hers. "I will do whatever you ask. I know we've only known one another a short time, but you are like a sister to me, and I will protect you and your daughter with all the power in my bloodline."

The two women embraced one another and sobbed, a golden white light surrounding them until they were of one mind. Like Nathan and

Amani, Calla Lily and Amani were linked through a magical bond—part djinn, part Shuvani.

"That little girl has one strong heartbeat, and if she is anything like her parents, she will be a force to be reckoned with," Calla Lily whispered.

"I agree," Nathan said from behind them.

Amani and Calla Lily broke their hug, and the three of them linked hands.

"Love and truth will rise above the darkness threatening to consume us," Amani avowed.

"Love and truth will rise," Nathan and Calla Lily repeated.

"Are you two ready to go?" Nathan asked. "It's time for us to head over."

The three of them made their way down the long path and onto the lane toward the Great Falls. When they arrived, Roman, Ric, Gaby, Conall, Mihail, Irina, Madame Luiza, and Saundra all stood in a pure white circle of light.

"We're waiting for Elsmed and the rest of the Court to join us. Then we will be ready," Saundra stated.

Tierri and Ushka skittered near Amani and moved to hug her before rushing away when the others suddenly appeared. Everyone was here. It was time.

Thunder cracked, and lightning burst open the sky as the distinctive aroma of frankincense filled the air. Another flash went from sky to ground, and Thoth appeared where the bolt was struck. Next to him were two rectangular stone sarcophagi, ruddy in color and etched in hieroglyphs. Thoth looked in the direction of the group and tilted his head in acknowledgement.

"You all look well this night," he announced.

The group offered welcoming greetings of their own as they stepped closer.

"What are these for?" Roman asked.

"These are for Amani and Khalida. Identical in every way except for the symbols etched into the surfaces."

"Why the difference?" Ric asked.

"Each is represented by their traits, and yet Amani's is unique because hers features Havenwood Falls and a symbol for each of you here to support her," Thoth said as he walked to the water's edge. "May I?"

Elsmed nodded. "Of course."

Thoth scooped up a handful of water and walked it over to Amani's sarcophagus. He let the aether-filled water spill onto the surface, and everyone watched as it lit up in vibrant colors. The sides and the top were covered in symbols and markings, each telling a story.

Nathan knelt down and studied the writing. "This is unbelievable. It's coming to life as the water reaches the symbols."

"And it will continue to change and evolve as Amani changes and evolves into the true nature of who she was meant to be."

Amani bowed her head to Thoth. "What do I need to do?"

"I will need you to lie here," he pointed. "Nathan, you will be by her feet to ground her, and Calla Lily, I will need you to stand by her head, to *guide* her."

"And the rest of us?" Mihail asked.

"The wolves would be best suited on the outer perimeter," Thoth suggested. "And the pixies will be helpful here by the water's edge, in case we need anything."

Ric, Gaby, and Conall wished everyone well and took off toward the forest, while the pixie sisters found a spot away from the stone monuments but close enough to be of service.

"And us?" Roman asked.

Thoth moved his hands in the air, and an ankh emblazoned itself in the sky above them. "A barrier that includes this would be most useful."

Saundra, Roman, and the rest of the Court made their way into their positions, the witches drawing on the others' magical energies to enchant the area surrounding the water. Another thunderous clap and a forked bolt of lightning struck near the water's edge. Hathor and Ma'at towered over everyone, until they noticed Thoth and transformed into a human stature that was much less intimidating.

The jackal guards who'd arrived just after the goddesses maintained their towering height.

"Goddesses," Amani said, bowing in reverence as they made their way over to where the sarcophagi were positioned.

"Amani." Hathor smiled. "You and Nathan look well."

"Thank you again. Your blessing was more than either of us could ever have asked for," she replied.

Ma'at looked at them both curiously, but when she saw the markings on Nathan and Amani's arms, she plucked a single blue feather from her ceremonial cloak and motioned for the two of them to come closer.

"When the day comes and we meet again in the Hall of Two Truths, remind me of this moment by returning this to me," Ma'at declared. "You have my blessing in this union."

The blue feather flew into the air and transformed into a million sparkling lights that shimmered like magical birds before landing softly on Nathan and Amani's forearms, joining their other markings. Nathan took Amani's hand, and they both knelt before the three gods.

Nathan pulled his father's pocket watch out, the chain jingling as he held it out for Thoth. "I know it is customary to offer a gift, and I am woefully unprepared, but this is my most treasured possession. I give it to you freely in gratitude for giving me something far more precious."

Thoth took the watch from Nathan. "Exquisite piece," he said, looking at it more closely. "A pillar verge fuse, and in perfect working condition, I might add." He looked back to Nathan. "Why is this your most treasured possession?"

"It was my father's."

"I see. The same father who made meeting Amani possible, yes?"

"Yes."

"Samuel honored my forty-two laws, and when his time came to be judged, his heart was lighter than a feather. He walks in peace. I thought you should know," Ma'at interjected.

A small gasp came from Nathan before he closed his eyes, struggling to compose himself. Thoth shook the watch to regain his attention. "You know, if you listen closely, this sounds exactly like the rhythm of your daughter's heartbeat," Thoth suggested.

Nathan nodded. "I know. It's almost as if one is connected to the other," he replied.

"Maybe they are," Thoth insinuated, "but for now, you keep this and let's get on with what we came here to do. Khalida is growing restless now that she is so close to Amani." Thoth handed the watch back to Nathan.

"Where is she?" Amani asked.

Thoth swirled his hands in the air and materialized a glass bottle with a brass neck, spout, and base. They all stared as the bottle seemed to pulse and shimmer with a pale blue light, as if an enchanted liquid were churning within.

"She's here," he said as he held the decanter in his hand.

"In the Prison of Asria?" Amani asked in a whisper. "But . . ."

Thoth gestured for Amani to lie down. "Is everyone ready?" Resounding yeses came from various parts of the space they were all occupying. "Then let's begin."

Amani lay down with her head closest to Calla Lily, while Nathan stood by her feet. Thoth stood next to her, between the two sarcophagi, and the goddesses stood at either end of the place where Khalida was to be laid out. Amani cast a glance at the stone slab next to her and wondered why Thoth had not used the water to activate the hieroglyphs on it. Was hers supposed to be dark and etched in black?

As if he reading her thoughts, he leaned down and whispered, "Light and dark, remember? You are the one we want to come forth, while she is to merge into the shadows." Amani nodded. "Now close your eyes and let me free you both."

Amani did as she was asked, but sent loving messages to both Nathan and Calla Lily before she closed her eyes.

"Out of the darkness there will be light," Thoth began.

"Be true of heart and weigh the cost of your actions against your love and truth," Ma'at added.

"This night, we right a wrong and bring peace to a lost soul," Hathor finished.

Amani could hear chanting and then the sound of something wet spilling onto rock. She didn't open her eyes for fear she'd disrupt the process, but the sound of thunder booming overhead startled her. Nathan sent images into her mind to help soothe her agitation. Khalida was now lying motionless next to her. Thoth was doing something Nathan didn't understand but assumed was part of the progression needed to perform the merging.

"Amani, it is time to embrace your djinn," Thoth commanded. "Release who you are and allow all of you to be seen." Amani shivered at his words. "Don't worry. The fire that burns within you will not harm Calla Lily or Nathan. You must do this to allow the merge."

Amani did as instructed and embraced the side of her she had so desperately tried to keep hidden. Within a moment, her skin turned a dusky grey and her hair was ablaze. The sound that followed was gruesome. Khalida was awake, but bound and enraged. Amani could feel her trying to enter her thoughts, and when that didn't work, she tried other ways to take hold. First it was Amani's connection to Nathan, but Thoth had thwarted that. She then tried Calla Lily, but her Shuvani power sent Khalida searching for another link. She screamed again, a ghastly wail, but Amani held steady—that is, until Khalida went for the baby. Amani wrapped her arms around herself and curled into a ball. Thoth, Hathor, and Ma'at instantly reacted.

"Nathan," Thoth shouted, "your watch—give it to me."

Nathan fumbled in his pocket and handed it to Thoth. Nathan watched as the inner workings of the watch sprang to life in a far different way than he thought possible. First it stopped altogether, and he panicked, but then the watch whirred and clicked to life, beating faster than a hummingbird's wings.

Amani began to cry, and her body was turning cold. Her legs felt like ice, and Nathan held on for dear life as she continued to writhe in pain. Calla Lily's face turned pale, and he wondered why she was so shaken. Voices began to whisper and call to him. Nathan had been so focused on Amani's physical well-being that he stopped listening to her talk to him in his mind, but it seemed Calla Lily had heard every word.

"*Calla Lily, please. I beg you. Help the baby. Khalida is taking her from me. I cannot bear to lose her. Please, please help my child.*"

Nathan stared at Calla Lily and then addressed Thoth. "Khalida is trying to kill the baby."

"No," Thoth snarled, moving back toward Khalida, but stopped when Calla Lily held her arms out wide. Tapping into the magic of her bloodline, and also that of the Court, power surged through her, and she used her thoughts to create her actions. The palm of her hand began to slice open, blood pooling where the cuts were visible. Calla Lily's hair blew wildly in the wind as she started to speak Romani. No one understood her except Nathan, thanks to their link with Amani, who heard her words clearly.

Blood to blood, bound to thee,
Guardian to child, accepted by three
Link us now, and forever remain
Protected by the Shuvani vein

When the last word was spoken, Calla Lily took her blood-soaked hands and laid them across Amani's womb. Amani gasped, and her body went slack.

"What's happened?" Thoth demanded.

Calla Lily's eyes opened in a rush. "I've protected the baby, but her heartbeat is dangerously weak. Khalida is now going for Amani. Save her!"

"No, save my baby," Amani pleaded, reaching for Thoth.

"I can only do one thing. I either save you, or I save the baby."

"The baby," Amani breathed. "I willingly give my life for hers. I will not let Khalida have her."

Thoth stood frozen for a moment, their lives in his hands. "Then again, perhaps there may be a way I can do both." His eyes snapped to Amani. "In order to succeed, I have to give the baby your power and you will end up human."

Tears spilled from Amani's eyes as she looked at Thoth and then Nathan, nodding as they silently made their decision. "The baby is our choice. Nathan and I will raise her until it is our time to answer to

Ma'at. Beyond that, Calla Lily and those in her line will guide our girl until we once again meet in the afterlife."

Calla Lily wiped Amani's forehead as beads of sweat pooled. "I promised you I would, and I will keep my promise."

Ma'at stepped over to Amani and touched her hand, reaching out for Nathan's as well. "It is my will that your lifelines will be bound. You are not only linked in life but so shall you be in death. Whomever dies first, the other will follow, so you may walk the duat side by side. This is my blessing to you both."

The air sizzled, and Thoth shot a look over at Khalida. Hathor and Ma'at could feel it too, and reached for Nathan while Thoth grabbed Calla Lily. The two djinn had risen and were hovering above their sarcophagi. Electrical charges sparked from Khalida's fingers, while Amani's hair lit up the moonlit sky and flickered in the water's reflection.

"I'm finished with you doing everything you can to destroy me and the ones I love. You want everyone to see who I am? Then let's finish this, Khalida."

Amani didn't wait for Khalida to respond, but instead cast the first blow. A streak of fire flew from Amani's fingers, hitting Khalida square in the chest, knocking her backwards. Unfortunately, the flames did not affect her in the slightest.

Khalida smirked, regaining her footing on the rocks. "You're pathetic. I thought you had more to give than that. This will be easier than I thought," she said as she used her power to lift the boulders scattered about and tossed them toward the Court members. "Stop that incessant chatting!" she shrieked.

Thoth managed to deflect them away from the group and snapped his fingers, hoping to bring the djinn to heel. It didn't work. "There is nothing I can do. I am disconnected from them right now." Confusion laced his every feature.

"Amani can do this," Calla Lily offered.

Overhead, the two djinn raged. Their powers met each other equally as they blasted one another with fire and sand, electrical bolts and Khalida's new gift of ice. Their gold and silver hieroglyphs glowed brighter than the sun and moon combined. They stopped only for a moment, and in that brief flash, Khalida sent a shard of ice at Amani —striking her in the chest. Amani flew backwards, her hands gripping the frozen rod within her. She splashed into the pond, falling under its surface as Calla Lily and Nathan cried out. Thoth, Hathor, and Ma'at were huddled together, trying to figure out what to do next, when suddenly, the air became blisteringly cold. The goddesses and Thoth shielded themselves within a barrier, along with the jackals, Calla Lily and Nathan, but could only stand by and watch as Khalida turned the pond to solid ice.

"I can feel Amani beneath, but she isn't responding," Nathan cried out.

"And the baby?" Thoth asked Calla Lily.

"Her heartbeat is weak, but I can still feel her."

Seconds ticked away, and the chill in the air had frozen everything around them. Even the waterfall had been silenced by Khalida.

"This is only the beginning. When Amani's power is merged with mine, I will be unstoppable," Khalida taunted.

She had no sooner spat those words out of her mouth than her skin started to burn. The ice coating the ground beneath her melted into puddles. Khalida cried out, unsure of what was happening to her. Tiny fissures of gold began to replace the silver streaks beneath her skin. She was splitting open from the inside out. Khalida's body was hovering in midair, her white locks changing to black as everything that was ice was now becoming fire. The waterfall had once again begun to thunder and crash below, and Khalida was powerless to stop it as Amani burst from the pond to hover in midair.

"I said enough!" Amani raged, the silvery hue of the pond's water coating her skin. Her hair was not ablaze but there was fire within— something different. Amani was changed. Her skin was no longer dusky, but tawny. Her hair no longer golden and shimmering, but a mix of light and dark. Khalida tried to speak, but Amani clenched her fist, silencing her instantly. Amani was in control once again, allowing Thoth and the goddesses a chance to let down the protective barrier.

"You did well," Thoth said to Amani. "For a moment, it appeared as though Khalida was going kill you."

Amani did not reply, keeping her eyes on Khalida, but instead spoke into Calla Lily's mind.

Calla Lily touched Thoth's arm. "She did. The ice pierced her heart, but the aether in the water healed her. Strengthened her. She is changed, but unless you finish this, she and the baby cannot maintain control."

"Understood," he replied.

Hathor called out for her jackal guards, and they appeared instantly beside her. "Restrain that beast," she snarled.

The guards plucked Khalida from the air and placed her back on her sarcophagus. Thoth, Hathor, and Ma'at, all using a series of hand gestures, bound Khalida in place.

Once she was immobilized, Amani walked out of the water and lay back on the stone surface. "Please end this. For not only my child's sake, but everyone else's as well."

"I could never have predicted the strength of your union. I'm sorry the merging did not go as planned."

"Do not apologize. I never relished my power to begin with. It will be better suited for the goodness that lies within me."

"Very well," he relented, before looking over at Calla Lily. "When the power leaves Amani and Khalida, you should feel a surge within the child. Bind her. The age at which a djinn reaches maturity is twenty-five. It is not until then that we will know just what she will become," Thoth admitted.

Thoth lifted his hand, the watch Nathan had given him earlier appearing out of thin air, its internal mechanism in perfect syncopation with the baby's heartbeat.

"This belongs to the child. It is now part of her—connected to her through space and time. It will keep her safe and linked to all who love her," he proclaimed as he transformed it from a pocket watch into a locket. The chain of the watch had become a chain for a necklace instead, Thoth placing it on Amani and turning toward the goddesses.

Thunder and lightning roiled overhead as the three gods pooled their power to end the djinn who'd done so much damage over the centuries. The jackals held Khalida in place, and one by one they struck. First was Thoth, removing her Ren (name) and her Sheut (shadow). Second was Hathor, leaving Khalida without her Ba and Ka, her personality and vital spark. Lastly, Ma'at took her Jb (heart) and sent it to Ammit to devour. Khalida's body lay motionless before it dissipated into dust. Amani gasped, but when she opened her eyes, she felt the same as she always had in her heart and her mind. Nathan took his first real breath for the first time in minutes, and Calla Lily sighed in relief. The tension she had been feeling was now gone, and the baby's heartbeat was no longer erratic. They'd all survived—except Khalida.

Amani turned to Ma'at and Hathor. "What will our daughter be like?"

"That is unknown. She too is unique—part djinn, part human, and as of now, a bit of gypsy demon," Hathor answered.

"May I?" Thoth asked, reaching for Amani's arm. "I'd like to confirm a theory."

Amani nodded and watched as Thoth once again summoned her blood. This time, though, when it swirled in his palm, it was a trio of silver and gold mixed with copper. The copper shone and shimmered as the twisted ladder continued to levitate in his hand.

"Just as I thought. The baby's blood is the copper I couldn't identify before. Now it is clear."

"She is a mixture then of Khalida and me, as well as Nathan?"

"And Calla Lily. She is one of a kind for sure." He paused. "Remember you and Khalida were one and the same, split. Now you are reunited, and the other elements are from them," he said as he turned to Nathan and Calla Lily.

The ankh hovering in the sky above dissolved, and the Court all emerged from the ritual circle to look over at the group by the water. A lot had happened while they were protecting the perimeter, but they were clueless as to what exactly transpired except for the disarray of the area. They'd been too focused on their own task to know the specifics.

"Amani, Amani, Not Amani, Yet Amani," Tierri said in a singsong voice as the other pixie sisters joined her in the chant.

Amani gave them a confused look, reaching for her hair. "How is it that I look different? Is this the human side?"

Thoth shook his head. "There are no more sides, Amani. The parts of Khalida you were denied are now merged. You overpowered her and took back what was yours all along. Your djinn powers now reside within your child, making you fully human."

Roman and Mihail made their way over to the pond where everyone was now standing.

"Is everything okay?" Mihail asked as he took in Amani's new appearance. "You look well and healthy, and I hear the . . ." he paused, stalling his words.

"Why does everyone keep making cryptic comments? Hear the what? What are you not saying?" Roman demanded.

Amani eyed Roman. "I'm pregnant, and we didn't say anything until now because we wanted to be past the worst before sharing the good news."

Roman scoffed. "Another djinn?"

"Actually, only one now—her. I am no longer a threat, but neither is our daughter."

"Daughter! How could you possibly know the sex of the child? The baby couldn't be more than . . ."

Thoth interrupted to answer Roman's inquiry. "Because the baby's part djinn. That is why, and *she*," he emphasized, "will be none of your concern. We will be in charge of her well-being."

"And when can we expect you to be leaving Havenwood Falls?" Roman pushed.

"Seriously, Roman? It's been minutes, and you're already kicking them out?" Calla Lily snapped.

Saundra and Elsmed walked up to the group, with Irina and Madame Luiza only a step or two behind.

"They are welcome to stay as long as they wish," Saundra stated without hesitation. "Roman, you cannot decide alone who stays and who goes. We will convene a meeting and discuss this, but in the meantime, they may stay. Especially after what we have witnessed."

"And what exactly have you witnessed? We all saw the same thing.

Us working magic, and this one," he pointed to Amani, "changing into something else. How do we know she's even pregnant, or that they didn't just merge one evil into another?"

Thoth and the goddesses started to speak, but Amani spoke first.

"How dare you," she seethed. "We will end this once and for all, Roman. That is, if you truly care to know the truth and not a made-up version of things."

"And how do you propose to show it to me, if you're changed as you say?"

Amani cast a glance at Thoth, who gave her an approving nod. "Give me your hands, and I'll show you."

Roman snatched her hands, gripping them in his own. "I don't trust you. Try anything, and you will pay."

Amani looked at Calla Lily and then over to Nathan before looking at Hathor, Ma'at, and Thoth.

"Watch closely," Thoth answered for her, "and she'll show you the way. Amani is human now, but for as long as the child remains within her, djinn power still surges through her veins."

Amani closed her eyes and splayed her arms out wide, letting the light within her build. The wolves came to stand by the shore, the pixies fluttered over the glistening water, and the Court all watched as a bright golden light radiated out of every pore in Amani's body. Everyone stared at her in awe as Amani's life—from birth to now—played out in a vision for all to see. When the last image appeared, they all could see the little bundle curled up and looking at them all. Nothing but peace radiated from her. She was perfect. She was strong, and she would be a formidable djinn when the time came, but for now, she was no more than the size of an apricot, and the proof everyone needed was finished being on display. The light dimmed, and everything went back to normal.

Amani sighed, and Nathan reached to hold her steady. He could feel how drained she was, and he stood by her side.

"I think you all have seen the truth. We are not here to hurt anyone, and I will tell you that it is not my or Amani's intention to stay in Havenwood Falls permanently. We believe we have other things to accomplish in this life, but until she is well enough to travel, we're asking for your blessing to remain," Nathan said, his voice unwavering.

"You have our blessing, Nathan. You and Amani are welcome to stay," Elsmed answered.

"Very good," Thoth said as he addressed the crowd. "It is time for us to return. Our work here is finished, but we couldn't have done it without your cooperation. If you're ever in need, you may reach out to me via Calla Lily. We now have a common interest to care for," he acknowledged.

Calla Lily nodded, and Thoth turned toward Ma'at and Hathor. "Shall we clean up?"

The two jackals lifted their burly arms and smashed the sarcophagi into dust before nodding at the goddesses and disappearing into wisps of sand. Thoth and the goddesses cleansed the area with a golden-hued smoke. As the air cleared, two flames emerged and Hathor and Ma'at stepped into the vermilion glow, disappearing into thin air.

Thoth walked over to Calla Lily and took her hand in his. "Another day?"

"Another day," she replied, a moment before Thoth vanished in his usual manner.

"Let's go home, everyone," Mihail spoke to the collective.

The group gathered their things and moved to head back into town. Calla Lily, however, stopped to pick up something she saw glinting in the moonlight.

"What do you have there?" Roman asked.

Calla Lily used her power to transform the blue glass bottle into solid brass before she turned around to face him. "Nothing but a simple decanter. They used it to hold some water to pour on the sarcophagus."

"Hmm."

"Can we go now?" She moved to leave.

"Of course."

"Still distrusting after all you've seen?" she needled.

"No, not at all," Roman said with a sly smirk as he stepped aside. "After you."

CHAPTER 16

*I*t had been a long night, and it was going to be another long day as everyone prepared for the "proper" wedding ceremony that would make things official between Amani and Nathan. Lillian was preparing to leave soon, and even though she wouldn't remember it, it was important to Nathan that she be a part of it, which spurred the urgency.

Ric served as the officiant, while Calla Lily, Irina, and Madame Luiza stood beside Amani in support. Everything was perfect. Everything was as it should be—as it was fated to be.

Lillian stayed a few more days, and then she took the train back to New York, carrying with her Nathan's letter to resign his teaching position. He and Amani would be staying in Havenwood Falls until after the baby was born. Then they would decide the best time to move on. They'd discussed perhaps visiting and even living in New York for a time, but eventually knew they'd most likely end up in Egypt, closer to Amani's roots.

As the days turned into weeks, Amani's pregnancy became impossible to conceal as the magically enhanced pregnancy continued to stun them all. The residents who had come to know her were all excited and joyous about the upcoming arrival. Amani, Tierri, and Ushka had used their gardening talents to spruce up the town square and every other available space where chrysanthemums would bloom. It was their way of adding some color to the world, and short of Roman, everyone loved the additions.

The air and the season shifted into fall, and Amani was glowing. Their daughter was anxious to arrive, as evidenced by the exaggerated kicks and movements. The cottage had become their home, and Nathan a welcome addition at the inn. He helped Mihail, Irina, and Madame Luiza with whatever was needed. He also worked at the library. He'd sent away for books and other miscellaneous items that might help the Court and the town.

Calla Lily, Nathan, and Amani had all agreed the day after the merging that the Prison of Asria needed to remain hidden. Amani could still recognize it, because the watcher's vessel always seemed to call to her. Now, though, Amani assumed it was not her the vessel was calling to, but the baby's djinn traits. The night Calla Lily picked it up by the falls, she read its intent, and without knowing the details of the images she saw, all she could do was hide it to keep it out of the wrong person's hands. The watcher's vessel now sat inconspicuously on a shelf in her house, alongside other decanters. Like the locket Amani wore around her neck that was linked to the baby, it was spelled with Shuvani blood and could not be broken or changed unless she was aware.

It was a crisp fall morning, and Amani was walking toward Callie's Trinkets and What Nots with a handful of blue water lilies—Calla Lily's new favorite flower—to meet her friend for lunch when her water broke. Amani gripped the flowers and her belly.

"All right. It seems you're hoping for a grand entrance," Amani said to the baby.

Nathan replied in her mind, *"I'm on my way."*

After a few hours in the privacy of their cabin, Qadira Nymphaea Caerulea Wade was born on November 22, 1920. She was healthy, happy, and above all, where she belonged. Nathan and Amani wanted to give her soul the same blessings Neema had given Amani on the day she was born—a name befitting her, a name to enhance the life she'd been given. Qadira meant powerful and capable, while Nymphaea

Caerulea, the scientific name for blue water lily, was an homage to the strong women in Nathan and Amani's lives—Lillian Hartman and Calla Lily Mircea. It was also to honor Thoth, Ma'at, and Hathor for all they'd done to make this moment possible.

Amani held Qadira in her arms and whispered, "You are my life, little one, and I will cherish every second I am given with you."

The floor of the cottage was instantly filled with a dozen or so bright blue lotus blooms—Egyptian water lilies—along with a papyrus of a woman holding a child to the sky. It was a gift from the heavens. A message that even when it seemed impossible, we could all rise up, find the sun, and be released from a curse.

EPILOGUE

$\mathcal{N}$athan and Amani loved Havenwood Falls and hated leaving the peace and tranquility of it, but the time had come for them to move on. Qadira was now two and more curious than they ever could've imagined. She loved connecting to the magic of the Great Falls and playing with the pixies. Even the wolves and the angel took interest in the little djinn. However, the one person whose fascination she could never seem to thwart was Roman. To him, Qadira was something to study and watch. Amani always kept her close, but without powers of her own anymore, Amani was unable to know what his intentions truly were. Calla Lily suggested that the time was right for them to go to New York. Nathan had secured a new job offer, and they'd be in Egypt after the New Year arrived.

It was hard to leave the place they'd met, fell in love, changed, and had their daughter in, but it was for the best. Amani, while still pregnant with Qadira, had worked with Calla Lily and Saundra to create a way for the town to stay safe from outsiders, but retain their memories after leaving. They'd created a marking system inspired by the marks Amani and Nathan received from their binding that would allow the Court to track and monitor the visitors to the town. From that time forward, all who entered Havenwood Falls would be welcomed, with conditions for the supes—a mark specific to each that linked to the town's protection wards. And now that Amani was human, she and Nathan had no need to receive the marks, but the Court insisted on marking them as a way of keeping track of them— an insurance policy of sorts. Amani was a lovely person, but no one yet knew what powers she still held while pregnant, nor what the child would become. The tattoos would serve as the Court's hidden tracking.

Their tattoos mirrored each other, in the form of two ankhs wrapped lovingly in a pair of golden wings, but were also infused with a spell that would allow Nathan, Amani, and Calla Lily to maintain the communication link they had opened with their blood. For as long as Nathan and Amani lived, they'd be connected mentally with Calla Lily and Qadira at all times—no matter where they were. It was a failsafe Thoth and Calla Lily added during the merging. It, along with the locket, kept them all safe and in sync, should something arise with Amani or Qadira.

Calla Lily had blessed the locket around Qadira's neck and kissed her gently on the cheek. "Call to me whenever you need me, little one. I will always be here," Calla Lily whispered as they all said goodbye at the Montrose train station. Hugs and tears spilled as they bade each other farewell.

"I'll see you all when you get settled in Egypt," she said into their minds as the train pulled away from the station.

"Love you, Aunty Calla," Qadira replied sweetly.

When Calla Lily arrived back in Havenwood Falls, the town seemed quieter, emptier, but that was because everyone knew they'd never forget how a human, a djinn, and a very special baby girl had changed their lives forever.

~

ABOUT THE AUTHOR

Brynn Myers is an adult paranormal romance author. After considering writing a hobby for years, she finally turned her passion and talent into a career. She came into the paranormal genre later than most, but has always loved fairy tales and all things magical. Using that love, she creates charmed worlds by writing stories involving passionate, strong-willed characters with something to discover.

You can find out more about Brynn and her all titles by visiting www.brynnmyers.com and subscribing to her newsletter at www.brynnmyers.com/subscribe.

ACKNOWLEDGMENTS

I'd like to thank Ang'dora Productions for letting me be a part of the Havenwood Falls crew again for part two of Nathan and Amani's story. I'm so grateful to be among the amazing authors in this shared world. I'd also like to give a special thanks to Kristie Cook for allowing me to use Madame Luiza, Mihail, Irina, and Saundra in some of my scenes. Randi Cooley Wilson, THANK YOU times a million for letting me tap into Calla Lily Mircea and bring her to life in these two stories. Amani is asking I keep the kudos for Roman to a minimum, though. LOL! Also a special thank you to T.V. Hahn's pixies, Kallie Ross's Ric Kasun, and E.J. Fechenda's Elsmed.

To Liz Ferry, I'm so grateful you're a part of the Havenwood Falls and Ang'dora Productions team. You're invaluable! Thank you for all your hard work and support.

Amber Leaf Publishing, thank you for your love and support in all my work. I will never be able to thank you enough.

To my readers and anyone new to www.brynnmyers.com—much love and gratitude!! Every time you pick up one of my stories and give my characters a chance to warm your hearts or royally tick you off, I am honored to be on your reading lists.

A PACK OF LIES

KALLIE ROSS

~ A Legends of Havenwood Falls Novella ~

HAVENWOOD FALLS

LEGENDS

A PACK OF LIES

KALLIE ROSS

ALSO BY KALLIE ROSS

Defying Gravity: A Havenwood Falls Novella
Written in the Stars: A Havenwood Falls High Novella

Descent: A Lost Tribe (Book 1)
Defend: A Lost Tribe (Book 2)

Evelyn: A Cupid Chronicles Novella
Unbreakable: The Cupid Chronicles

This story is for Gaby.
You are loving, generous, brilliant, and beautiful.

PROLOGUE

1860

"Momma!" Conall cried from his bedroom.

Ric and I looked at each other, me hoping he would offer to go check on our son. He shrugged. My mate stood in the kitchen over the sink, his hands covered in suds. We had fallen into a routine in the evenings. After tucking Conall into bed, I sat in the living room reading while Ric washed pots and pans.

"We'll have to teach Conall to do the dishes soon," I said with a smile, and tucked a ribbon between the pages of my book to mark where I'd stopped.

"I like that idea, and not only because it means I won't have to do them. My attention would be better spent on you after a long day of keeping the peace," Ric said, his voice low and flirtatious.

He winked at me and chuckled.

After he turned his attention back to his work, I tiptoed over to him and slid my arms around his waist from behind. He had changed clothes when he arrived home after work, but he still had dirt smudged across the back of his neck.

"If a traveler saw you right now, they might mistake you for a miner. It's been a long time since you've worked with a pickaxe, but you get just as dirty as sheriff. You need a bath as badly as that skillet," I teased, nestling my face between his shoulder blades.

"How about you go check on Conall, and I'll fill the tub?" Ric asked.

"Okay, but it's late, and chilly outside," I reasoned, knowing the trough we had in the back of the cabin would be private enough, day or night, but the temperatures grew downright freezing after sunset in the canyon.

Ric turned and held his hands out, so as not to get me wet. "I'm sure I could find a way to stay warm if you'd join me." He growled playfully and leaned down to kiss me.

His lips were full and warm to the touch, and gone again before I could explore them. I tried to pull him closer, but his frame was too wide and too strong. In a blink, he'd turned and started scrubbing the pans again.

My mouth fell open. "Wha—"

Ric interrupted, "You'd better go check on Conall before—"

"Momma?" Conall called innocently. He had gotten out of bed and was standing behind us.

"Oh, cuddle bug, let's get you back in bed." I turned to pick up our solid five-year-old. He was growing up too fast. His round face was becoming more square, like his father's, and his childlike faith was becoming more skeptical. I hated to admit it, but his cynicism had been inherited from me.

"Will you tell me a story?" he asked, with widened eyes and a pouty bottom lip.

I couldn't help myself. "Of course. Which one do you want me to tell you?"

"Don't be too long," Ric said, insinuating more than Conall knew, glancing over his shoulder and smiling at us both.

I giggled, and Conall waved a hand in the air, half delirious from exhaustion. Our boy had been at school most of the day, then ran errands with me in our growing community. Before six years ago, it had only been our wolf pack in the forest surrounding the falls. But in that short time, with the arrival of a party of supernaturals drawn to the magical water, the settlement had tripled in size.

Conall's room was small, but he spent very little time there. He preferred to be outside. His patchwork quilt hung haphazardly off the foot of his bed. When I sat him on his mattress, he laid his head on his pillow and waited for me to spread his blanket over him. He sighed thoughtfully as I sat down at the end of his bed.

"Momma, will you tell me about the time you went to the big city with Daddy?" Conall asked, and a yawn escaped him just before he finished the question.

"Um, sure, but why that story?" I wondered out loud and tucked his covers under his feet. Ric must have told him about our trip to St. Louis, because I had spent the last twenty years trying to forget it.

"Because I wanna go there someday and be just like Daddy. I wanna ride a steamboat, and be a gunfighter, and go to a ball," Conall rambled with a second wind of excitement. "And drink at a saloon, and play poker with cardsharps, and have a shootout, and save you from the bad guys, and—"

"Wait just one second," I told Conall, and held a hand up to keep him quiet until I could get Ric in the room. "Ulrich Kasun. You had better get yourself in here to explain exactly what you've been telling our son about St. Louis." I had intended to sound disparaging, but a chuckle escaped me.

I didn't have to yell, because like me, Ric had enhanced hearing. He heard me use his given name, and I expected him to enter the room with his tail between his legs. Ric and I had been on many adventures over the years, but there were certain things you didn't explain to a child, like shootouts.

"Yes, dear." Ric shuffled into the room with his eyes on the hardwood floors, wiping his hands with a small towel.

I cleared my throat, and he looked up. "What's this you've been telling Conall about our trip to the big city?"

"I merely told him the truth," Ric said, looking at Conall and avoiding eye contact with me.

"The truth, huh?" I asked with a little sass.

Ric shrugged.

"Sounds more like a pack of lies," I accused, and straightened my skirt.

Ric walked around Conall's bed and sat opposite me. "Well, then, I'd love to hear your version."

His challenge was accepted.

"This is what really happened . . ."

CHAPTER 1

1820

The October sun had set the sky ablaze, bright orange and red at the plateau's horizon. Another dry, unseasonably warm day. I'd felt a tug at my chest, and knew Ric was close. Our connection alerted me to his return and provided an excuse to leave our dusty, loud settlement. The quiet place reminded me of a time when our pack wasn't concerned with progress. I had diligently watched for the scouting party Ric was in to return, hoping they would have new supplies in tow to help us through the winter.

As alpha, I could have assigned anyone to the task, but members of the pack had been bickering for weeks about how to deal with our shortages. Coming up with a plan to replenish our supplies before the first snowfall had been my number one priority. I explained we would have everything we needed. The land would provide. But, because of the drought, some argued we needed more. More food, more cabins, more blankets, more tools to mine for gold—their list went on and on, and I had grown weary trying to convince them to see reason. We had to keep our discovery quiet, or greedy settlers would flood the mountains.

At the top of the ridge, near our people's settlement in the forest, peace and tranquility had embraced me. We'd built half a dozen cabins, scattered safely in the forest, and learned to store supplies in natural caves along the canyon walls. From a distance, no one would have suspected a group of people lived in the area.

I lifted my canteen to my lips, and took a long drink. The sound of the falls in the distance had always reminded me that it would provide us with the water we needed, but I wondered if I could provide the leadership my people needed to carry them through to spring. Our forest was like a protective barricade from the outside world, but from inside, with dangerous amounts of snow and ice, it felt more like we were being held hostage.

Ric's mother, our last alpha, would have known what to do.

I closed my eyes and took a deep breath. The smell of burnt grass still overpowered the scent of new growth pushing up through the ash in spots across the plateau. The drought had ruined our crops, but nearby natives had set fires as a warning around the canyon to keep us away from their camps.

"There is nothing left for us here," Nina had said sharply. I'd heard her approach, and turned to find her wearing a long cotton dress and a frown. I thought she should have looked happier. Nina Novak and her husband, Peter, had convinced the pack to abandon our guise as a native tribe and build a proper settlement. The change in appearance had probably been the reason the Ute felt threatened. Our pack's progress made us look more like the people attacking them from the east.

"That's not for you to decide," I told her with conviction, and folded my arms over my chest.

I may have given in when it came to modern conveniences, but we'd held our ground on guarding the falls, even after the Ute tribe rode through and lit the plateau on fire. The neighboring natives had never attempted to invade our land before, but they were being driven off their lands because of war, and what the British, French, and Spanish called progress.

Nina placed a hand on my shoulder and said, "Adele might have chosen you for Ulrich, but she's gone. No one would blame you if you gave up your role as alpha to someone more qualified." She sounded haughty, and her nose tilted up in the air.

"You're right." I shrugged out of her grip. "*Ric's* mother picked me. But the magic in our blood chose to bring us together as mates. Adele understood and made her decision. You're just jealous because you weren't chosen to be either."

Nina hated my nickname for my husband. As Ric's distant cousin, Nina had been born with Kasun blood, alpha blood, but her tactics reminded me of the life we had left in Croatia over a hundred years ago. The Blood Lake Pack had become savage, and Adele's own brother made an attempt on her life.

Some died to get us to the New World, including Adele, but not before naming me as her successor. Our people had lived as humans, with the ability to shift into wolves, for thousands of years. The magic that ran through our blood also called us to our mates.

"Adele forced her will on us all, but without a daughter, your legacy will die," Nina mumbled bitterly and turned to walk away.

"Even without Adele's decision, Ric and I would have mated. You never had a chance with him, and your selfish motives would have us all dead if you were alpha." I bit the inside of my cheek to stop all of my anger from spilling out. The taste of blood filled my mouth.

Nina had been a thorn in my side since we were children. Her ability to hit a nerve and scurry off without apology reminded me of the vermin that threatened our food stores. The rats ate, gorging themselves, and left disease behind.

The hint of a vibration in the ground caught my attention. I turned and tilted my head, tucking my hair behind my ear to listen. My wolf's heightened hearing alerted me to the approach of two horses, with riders, and a wolf.

Something was wrong.

There should have been two horses and two wolves returning from the scouting trip. Nina must have noticed, too, because she froze. Her mate, Peter, had been a part of the group with Stephen Horvat, Boris Greg, and Ric. The four men had been best friends growing up, but the journey to the New World had tested their bond. After the fire, the men put all of their differences aside to find a way for us to trade for supplies.

Along the horizon, the silhouettes of two riders and a wolf had become more distinct. One man was draped over a horse's back in front of its rider. In a matter of seconds, I was able to make out Ric, a black wolf running at full speed ahead of the horses, and Boris and Peter in human form on horseback. It was Stephen lying limp over Boris's horse.

"Go!" I shouted over my shoulder at Nina. "Get Maria and the others. Meet us at our cabin."

Nina would want to check on Peter, but my alpha orders had a way of overriding any pack member's personal inclinations. I hated having so much power over the others, and rarely asserted it. Nina flinched. And without question, she nodded and proceeded to shift into her wolf form. Her dress, shredded, fell to the ground as she darted toward our settlement.

$\sim$

THE NEXT FEW hours were spent trying to stop Stephen's bleeding. He'd stepped into a fur trader's trap, and the iron contraption had nearly taken his leg. The men had been scouring the area for possible connections to trade. For several days, no one had appeared along any of the paths occasionally used by travelers.

Then Ric explained who'd shown up the previous night, and why Stephen had been so careless in their rush back.

With a low rumble, my mate's voice carried across the room. "A messenger on horseback appeared to have been riding for his life, probably scared of the natives. We waited in the tree line to follow him, but then he stopped and called out for you, Gabriele." Ric reached out and took my hand.

"He knew my name?" I asked, shaking my head in confusion. There were only a handful of people I'd revealed myself to in the New

World, and Ric had always stood by my side when we encountered outsiders. "Did you recognize him?"

"No, I'd never seen the man before, but he clearly inspected the area before calling your name out. Like he'd been told exactly where to go and what to say. We all smelled blood, and knew he had to be injured." Ric looked over my shoulder to Peter and Boris. They nodded in agreement, and went back to tending to Stephen, who'd been placed on our bed. "After a few minutes, the stranger climbed down from his saddle. He was in bad shape, and stumbled to the ground, pulling his saddlebag with him."

I squeezed Ric's hand. "What did you do?"

"We waited for him to pass out. It seemed cruel, but it was the only way to make sure he would not ask questions or follow us." Ric slipped his hand out of mine and ran his fingers through his recently cut hair. "He was no trader, because there was no sign of a wagon or furs. Even though we'd taken measures to look like those traveling west, we had to protect the pack and the falls."

"I understand." I nodded, and placed a hand on Ric's arm. He shook his head slowly, struggling to say whatever it was he needed to tell me.

Peter Novak moved across the room to join us. "It is not your fault, Ulrich." Peter patted him on the back. "He could not be saved."

Ric shrugged out of Peter's grip. "We don't know that, because we waited too long," he gritted out, sounding irritated.

"He'd been attacked on his journey to us. What would we have done if he had lived, Ulrich? Send him back to St. Louis, knowing of our settlement? He would have sent others back to take what's ours," Peter claimed with an air of authority.

Since arriving in the New World, we'd encountered natives, explorers, pioneers, settlers, and once, time-traveling witches. The existence of supernaturals was no secret to a pack of wolf shifters, but protecting our secret was the only way we knew to protect our lives.

"Peter, I appreciate your reasoning, and agree with most of it, but do not be mistaken that we have any claim over these falls. In fact, the oath Ric and I took to protect them puts us in servitude, not ownership," I clarified, speaking across the room so the others would hear as well. I hated how Peter and the other men could manipulate Ric.

The Novak, Horvat, and Greg families had grown up with Ric and me in Croatia. We'd chosen to follow Adele Jezero, our alpha, to the New World when war divided our pack and led to the Ottoman Empire taking over our homeland. Through the years, the other couples had begun having children while I struggled to learn how to lead our pack.

I was still learning.

"Of course," Peter said, with a hint of hesitation, and nodded. "You'll want to read the letter we found in the man's saddlebag."

Peter reached into the chest pocket of his coat and handed it to me. I glanced from Peter to Ric.

Ric shrugged.

"Thank you." I took the worn piece of parchment from him and recognized my name written across the front. The black wax seal had been broken at its edge. "Who's read its contents?" I asked curtly, annoyed that any of them would be so bold as to read their alpha's correspondence.

Ric glanced at Peter, then he looked over at Boris, who looked up from Stephen's limp form. I knew they could all read English, because I had taught them. For the first time, I regretted it. They all knew I could use my power as alpha to force it out of them, but instead I left the question open.

Silence.

I looked down at my feet and gritted my teeth together. The sound of boots shuffling on the hardwood floor let out a loud creak. I looked up to meet Ric's gaze.

"We wanted to protect the pack," Ric answered slowly, unsure of himself. I was convinced the others persuaded him to read the letter.

"Outside," I barked at Ric with anger. "The rest of you—" I exhaled, taking in the room. The four walls suffocated me. Our friends called it an advancement from the tepees we'd found shelter in in the past, but I found the cabin more like a cage.

I pushed past Peter and Boris, then turned to face them. "Make sure we don't lose Stephen."

The brisk cool night invited me with a crescent moon peeking through a canopy of trees. If I were not alpha, I'd have shifted and run through the forest surrounding our settlement. The thought reminded me of a time when I could do whatever I wanted without the responsibility of the pack.

My life in Croatia had been spent watching my parents and older brothers fight in support of Adele, the Blood Lake Pack alpha. She'd trusted her wolf pack, not using her magic to bend others to her will, but some took advantage of her trust. There were pack members who had believed Adele was soft. Our battle, fighting for freedom from those who were willing to expose our abilities in exchange for power, was only one in a war that took all my family. Adele had been quick to invite me, a devastated ten-year-old, into her home. Her husband, Matthias, had become a father figure, and their daughter, Nikola, was a best friend. It was her son, Ulrich, whom I struggled to connect with, and it was not until ten years later, on our journey to find a place in the New World, that I understood why.

Ulrich had always been stubborn and quiet. He consistently fell in line with what his friends wanted to do. I relished the days he kept his distance. He infuriated me whenever he called me black sheep, because he said I was too kind to be a wolf.

Somehow, after a few months of traveling through rough terrain and missing home, I realized he had become my home.

My heart had grown to love him, and the magic running through my blood called to him. As is our custom, Ric took my surname when we married. He revealed that he'd been in love with me since the day his mother introduced us and explained I would be a part of their family. Only, Adele had not known at the time it would be as Ric's wife, and not as his adopted sister.

I paced.

Sensing Ric, I didn't want to be mad at him, but his constant attempts to protect me made me feel weak. He hadn't meant to undermine me, but I wasn't sure if Peter had the same good intentions.

Ric leaned one of his broad shoulders against a nearby trunk and crossed his arms over his chest.

"What do you want me to say?" Ric asked, wanting to fix the problem before he even knew what the problem was. "I'm not sorry we read it. Otherwise, we wouldn't have rushed back so quickly."

"*We*," I growled. "*We* is you and me. I am insulted you included Peter, Boris, and Stephen, before I was able to determine if they needed to know my business."

I huffed and turned my back to Ric. Looking at his handsome face would only make me more conflicted, even if he wasn't remorseful. I carefully unfolded the paper in my hands and slowly read the words scribbled on the page.

June 12, 1820

Dear Gabriele Kasun,

I hope my personal messenger has found you well. He has been ordered to protect my message with his life. Since our last encounter in New Spain, my trade business has brought much fortune. It would never have come to fruition if it were not for your daring rescue.

I traveled safely back to Louisiana Territory, now known as Missouri Territory, without any altercations with natives or bandits. My family has settled in a town along the Mississippi River called St. Louis. In fact, delegates have approved a proposed state constitution to establish a state of Missouri in the near future.

Your hospitality and generosity have not been forgotten, and it would be my pleasure to host you as my esteemed guests at my estate. My wife, Marie, hopes to show you her appreciation for saving my life in person. Our children are also eager to meet the brave woman who fought off a pack of wolves and mended my injured arm without a hint of a scar. Sometimes I think they don't believe me, so you must visit and prove them wrong.

Your beautiful furs and precious metals would be welcome for trade, and are handsomely sought after in our parts. It would be my pleasure to broker for any supplies you may need to endure the coming winter. The

*name Chouteau has grown more well-known since we last met. So follow
the map below, and when you arrive in St. Louis find the nearest trading
post and ask for me.*

I look forward to repaying your kindness,
Auguste Chouteau

I LOOKED up from the thick, creased parchment, and Ric searched my
face. My eyes widened at the prospect of providing for our pack, but I
knew why Ric was defensive about reading the letter.

"This might be the only way we all survive through the winter," I
said, waving the letter in front of Ric.

"*Might?* It is the first week of October," Ric said with raised
eyebrows, and took a step closer to me. "You won't have time to get
there and back before the first snowfall. The falls must be protected.
What if you're kidnapped, or someone discovers your magic? What if
you don't return at all? I won't let you go." His jaw flexed, and he
propped his hands on his hips, making him look more like one of the
walls of the cabin.

I glared at Ric until a man's throat cleared.

"You have no authority over her decision," Peter said.

Peter pushed a tree limb to the side and planted himself next to
me. The move was uncharacteristic of Peter. I made a mental note, but
took advantage of his support.

"What he said." I folded my arms over my chest and nodded in
Peter's direction. "Besides, Chouteau will be close to sixty by now. He
will pose no threat."

"Why is he reaching out to you now?" Ric asked with suspicion.
"Why wait so long? He must have an ulterior motive."

"I'm sure he does," I agreed, remembering his ability to sweet talk
me into helping with his fur trade so many years ago.

Auguste Chouteau had been a young fur trader when we first met,
and he had happened into our territory late at night. Out of supplies
himself, and desperate for food, he spotted smoke from our fires. A
wolf patrolling our borders, Stephen Horvat, attacked him without
provocation.

As a wolf pack, we've always been connected, and when in our wolf form, we have the ability to communicate thoughts to each other. Stephen had mentally pushed a call of distress out to the rest of us, and by the time I'd arrived, Chouteau had been in danger of losing his arm.

The irony of Stephen lying on my bed with a similar leg injury was not lost on me.

After ordering the pack to retreat, I approached Chouteau in my human form. In disguise as a native tribal woman, I wore animal skins with my hair tied back in long braids. Chouteau had as much reason to fear me as he had the wolves, but calmly pulled out a bag of gold coins and begged for assistance.

After I had nursed him back to health with medicinal herbs, Chouteau and I agreed to trade furs for supplies. He returned to the region annually for eight years. Eventually, I shared news of our settlement discovering some precious metals—small nuggets of gold, and a rare red gold. I sent him back with some of the metal and he returned with more supplies than we could have needed in two years combined.

After those eight years, I had to cut ties. He'd innocently complimented me. Chouteau remarked on how young I still looked, and I knew any future trade would result in more questions than I could honestly answer.

But thirty years later, we needed supplies for winter, and fast. We had mined more gold over the years, and even discovered another vein of the red gold Chouteau liked so much. I had a feeling it would trade better than furs.

Facing Ric, I mirrored the stern look on his face. I knew what I had to do. My word as alpha would be final. Magic would bind my orders to the pack. I had to make sure my words would also protect them.

Ric suddenly placed a hand on my cheek, stopping me, and whispered, "I'm going with you."

CHAPTER 2

1820

$\mathcal{A}$ week later, as we'd sprinted across a prairie in the autumn sun, I second-guessed my decision. I hadn't wasted any time. I'd packed a small bag of provisions and gave orders for the others to protect the falls. Stephen's leg wasn't doing much better when we left, so I added medical supplies to the lengthy list of provisions we needed. According to Chouteau's calculations, I could make the journey to St. Louis in two weeks on horseback. What the fur trader hadn't known was that I could shave two days off that trip if I traveled in wolf form.

I wore a leather parcel strapped to my back. The bag contained a pair of trousers, a shirt, dried buffalo, and a few pounds of gold rocks. Ric wore a matching parcel as he ran beside me.

My mate had insisted he join me, and I didn't bother arguing. In over a century of marriage, Ulrich Kasun was still the most stubborn man I'd known. His heart had been in the right place, but I hated to leave anyone else as acting alpha. Any time in the past when I'd met with a trader, or simply needed to get away to breathe, I'd handed my title and responsibility to him.

Before we left the settlement, I gave Nina Novak my

responsibilities. There was a glimmer in her eyes after I made the announcement to the pack, and it reminded me of the power-hungry wolves we left in Croatia. Nina usually let her mate, Peter, do all the talking, but we all knew she had the dominant, more conniving personality. I had been tempted to leave Helena Greg in charge, but Nina would have manipulated Helena to do her bidding anyway. Instead, I gave Helena the responsibility of being my eyes and ears while I was gone. She hadn't liked the idea of snitching on her friend, but I quickly reminded her that if Nina acted as alpha with the pack's best interests in mind, then she wouldn't have anything negative to report.

Ric and I were careful to run through the protection and shade of forests for the first few days, but when we reached the plains, the sun beat down on our backs for three days. It was the first time I'd considered shifting back into human form. In the mountains, my thick, black fur had always brought me warmth, comfort, and disguise. But out in the open, I'd never felt so exposed.

The only guidance Chouteau had given us in his map had been in reference to distances and landmarks. He hadn't described the landscapes.

Over the horizon, I recognized the shape of two trees standing alone in a field. The thought of sitting in the cool shade for a while had made me giddy. I increased my speed, and goaded Ric.

"*I'll race you.*" I pushed the thought to my mate.

Ric increased his pace to keep up with me. "*What's the prize?*" he asked.

"*A foot massage?*" I bargained, and looked over at him. In his wolf form, Ric was larger than me, and while my coat was solid black, his black coat was peppered with silver fur.

He countered, "*A foot massage and a back rub.*"

"*Deal. See you at the tree!*"

I pressed my paws to the hard, dry ground, and propelled myself forward as fast as I could. Ric, with more weight to carry, fell behind. The tall grass tickled as it whipped around my legs, and when I reached the edge of the trees' shade, I felt a nip at my hind leg. The pinch had startled me, and I toppled forward in a clumsy somersault. In addition to being bumped and bruised, I felt the hint of a sting on my backside. Ric sauntered past me and touched his nose to the closest trunk.

"*Cheater!*" I accused, shaking off a layer of dirt and grass.

Ric howled and proceeded to shift into his human form. His laughter rumbled in his tanned chest as he reached full height. "I did not cheat. You merely tripped."

I curled my lip, revealing my canine teeth, and let out a growl. Ric quickly unpacked his leather bag and slipped on his trousers, covering his most vulnerable parts.

"How about we call it a draw, and I'll massage your feet if you rub my back?" Ric bargained with a grin. He had probably planned to get a back rub out of our wager all along.

Only, Ric hadn't counted on me using one of his greatest weaknesses against him.

Me.

I shifted into my human skin, magic swirling around me as my muscles stretched and my joints popped. The transformation didn't hurt like it had the first few times I shifted, but felt more like getting out of bed the morning after having worked a long day. I appeared as naked as Ric had been, but I didn't rush to clothe myself. With Ric's full attention, I smirked at him as I circled the trees.

"Are you telling me you don't wish to give me a back rub?" I placed a finger on his chest and drew small circles over one collar bone to the other while I waited for his answer.

"You know, now that I think about it, I may have—"

The sound of a horse neighing in the distance startled us both. I quickly swept up my bag and pulled out my clothes to dress myself. A few gold nuggets tumbled to the ground, and I picked them up, shoving them back inside the leather pouch. Ric moved to block the traveler from seeing me while buttoning up his shirt. As I tucked my shirt into my trousers, I peeked around Ric's shoulder and sighted a wagon being pulled by two horses. A man with copper-colored hair sat perched on a spring seat, wearing an animal-skin coat with fringe and an old brown hat. I could hear him whistling a happy tune. The barrel of his rifle leaned against him like a tired wife. Behind him, in tow, was a pile of crates and barrels.

"This may be the answer to all of our problems," Ric said with a lilt of excitement. He stepped out from the cover of the tree and flattened his hand over his brows to get a better look. "Do you see that wagon? It's at least half full."

"It may be close to full, but even if it carried what we needed, it's only half of what we would require for the winter," I said calmly, trying to be realistic. "Our pack has grown in number since we arrived from Croatia, and I have just heard that Helena and Boris are expecting another baby in the spring."

Ric turned to face me. The wagon was still at least a mile out. The corners of his mouth lifted, and small wrinkles creased the corners of his blue eyes. I couldn't wait to grow old with Ric, no matter how many more wrinkles appeared over time.

"Do you think we'll be able to share the same kind of news soon?" Ric whispered as he leaned closer. His fingertips brushed over my hips.

The idea of raising children on top of my responsibilities as alpha had been overwhelming. I didn't know how Adele had managed it. The pack was my family, and while I dealt mainly with adults, they didn't always act mature. I felt the pressures of making sure everyone was healthy and provided for, in addition to being a wife. It was difficult to discern whether I had any real friends, other than Ric, because most of the women in our pack "confided" in me with an ulterior motive.

"I think what I've always thought. We'll have children after the settlement actually feels settled," I said with an exasperated sigh, fighting the urge to roll my eyes. "If we constantly have to trade for supplies outside our territory, then there is no guarantee our children will grow up with both parents. I don't want to subject our son or daughter to a life anything like mine. Don't get me wrong—" I rubbed Ric's neck and pulled him closer for a hug. "I loved your family, and I'm grateful they took me in. And I'm thankful to have been raised by my family as long as I was, but being a teenager without my mother and father to help me through my transition was more difficult than I can communicate." I spoke gently.

"I know." Ric wrapped his arms around me and nestled his face in my hair. He didn't argue, because we had already had the argument too many times to count.

Under the trees, standing on flat terrain, over a week's journey from our settlement, I felt at home in Ric's arms. But something, a gut feeling, cautioned me. I didn't know if my unease was over the approaching stranger, the idea of going to a big city, or what we would return to after leaving Nina Novak in charge of the pack.

Ric and I could handle the traveler, or at least outrun him. We had already decided what we would do about Chouteau. The St. Louis fur trader would not only be thirty years older, but he would expect me to have aged. The problem was being a wolf shifter, and living near the magic-filled falls, I had only aged five years at most. I would have to lie and say the Gabriele who saved his life was my mother. As far as the pack, I would have to put them out of my mind until I took care of the first two problems.

"Hey, y'all!" the stranger called, and waved his hat in the air.

Ric lifted his own hand and waved. I lifted the leather straps of my bag over my head and across one shoulder. Glancing at my feet, I regretted not packing shoes. I had chosen to pack the red gold instead.

"Y'all all right over there?" The man slowed his horses down and yelled out. He pulled his wagon to a stop a prudent distance away from us. I didn't blame him. "Did someone up and rob y'all?"

Ric nodded hesitantly, and I answered, "Yes, if you could offer us some help or direction we would appreciate it."

The man's eyes squinted as he took me and Ric in from head to toe. We didn't carry any weapons, but Ric was an intimidating sight, even barefoot and empty-handed.

"I'm Jacob Martin, but y'all can call me Jake." He nestled his hat back over his head and jumped down to the ground. A cloud of dust bloomed around his boots. "I guess it would be mighty unkind of me to leave y'all on the side of the trail. Especially since whoever held y'all up stole your shoes. That's just downright poor manners, if you ask me, even for a low-life thief," Jake said, sounding exasperated.

He was a head shorter than Ric, closer to my height. He wore a pair of brown trousers secured with suspenders. A pistol hung from his side under a jacket. Jake examined the trees behind us, then turned and rummaged in the back of his wagon for a few seconds. He revealed a small loaf of bread.

Jake moved in my direction, and Ric stepped over to stand between me and the stranger. Jake's eyes widened, obviously threatened.

"I was thinking ladies first, but if you'd rather have the first helping —" Jake said with a shrug.

Ric took the bread and lifted it to his nose. After taking a whiff of the golden brown crust, he handed the loaf over his shoulder to me. I immediately ripped the bread in half, happy to find a fluffy center.

"Thank you," I said to Jake.

Both men mumbled, "Welcome."

They glared at each other for a moment, and I burst into laughter. I shoved an elbow into Ric's side and handed him one half of the loaf as I took a bite of the other.

"Talk about manners," I said around my mouthful. "You will have to excuse my husband. Jake, I'm Gaby, and this is Ric."

Jake tipped his hat, then waved his hand in the air, swatting the matter away like it was a fly, and returned to shifting boxes in his wagon. We didn't need his help, but it was nice to have it. I never could pass up fresh bread. By the chewiness of the loaf's center, I figured the bread had been baked less than a day ago. Chouteau's directions hadn't mentioned a trading post in this area, but maybe Jake knew where we could trade for boots and horses nearby. I would feel better using our gold in a place where there were fewer people to ask questions.

"This is delicious." I smiled at Jake as he turned around with a pair of old boots in his hands. He dangled them out in front of himself, in my direction. "Oh, I couldn't accept those. If you will point us in the direction of the closest town, we'll find help without having to encroach on your supplies."

Jake's nose wrinkled up in confusion. "I'm sure I don't know what encroach means, but I figured you'd wanna wear these so's ya don't step on a roach, or any other critter for that matter."

"Oh," I said in a higher pitch than intended, trying to hold back a giggle. "Why, thank you, again." I nodded and took the boots.

I situated myself on the ground to slip them on. The leather was worn and soft, and the soles were thin. I pulled the laced strings and began tying them together.

"I'm sorry I don't have another pair," Jake said to Ric. "It's a shame someone would go so far as to steal a pretty lady's dress. It's a good thing your man had some extra trousers you could wear, but if you don't mind me sayin', they look mighty odd on a girl." His face scrunched up like he'd smelled something horrible.

I held my hand up in the air, and Ric took it and pulled me up to my feet. "Is there any chance the town where you bought this bread is close?" I asked.

The sun would only be out a couple more hours, and we would need to find water and make camp if the journey was more than a half day's walk. I had a feeling we would need more than horses and boots in the big city. Jake's reaction to me wearing trousers had been frustrating, but if I didn't want to stand out in St. Louis, I would need to buy a skirt.

"That there bread was baked on a farm a day's ride back east." Jake pointed his thumb over his shoulder. "The family and I do business regularly, so I'm not sure they'll take kindly to you two walkin' up without having been introduced or having anything to barter with."

Ric and I traded a glance.

"We only have what you see," Ric said with a tight-lipped smile. "But I'm a hard worker."

"Oh, yeah, well that might be worth somethin' to 'em." Jake nodded. "Where y'all headed anyways?"

"We are meant to meet with Auguste Chouteau in St. Louis," I answered, hoping Jake might recognize the name.

He did.

Jake's eyebrows lifted, and his chin fell. "Well, I'll be! Mr. Chouteau is one of my employers. He'll be horrified to find out about your predicament. You have quite the trip ahead. I wish I could turn around, but I'm on urgent business for one of his partners, Mr. Trudeau." Jake said the name with an air of reverence.

"We couldn't ask you to turn around," I said, and placed a hand on his bicep. "But if you could help us understand what to expect in St. Louis, I would greatly appreciate it."

Jake looked at Ric first, then me.

"Well, then, for starters," Jake said, pointing at Ric, "to make some of the men more amenable to your cause, you might consider introducing yourself as Gaby's brother."

Out of the corner of my eye, I noticed Ric's face contort in anger. His hand opened and closed like he was preparing to punch Jake, so I did the only thing I knew would keep us in his good graces. My hand whipped through the air and connected with Jake's cheek.

~

1860

"Momma, did you really hit him?" Conall looked up at me from his bed with wide eyes and tugged on my sleeve.

The point of telling him a bedtime story was to help him get to sleep, but it was having the opposite effect. Ric scooted closer to me on the bed and chuckled. His knowing blue eyes met mine, and he smiled.

"I did. But I don't want you getting any ideas. It's not all right to go hitting people. Me slapping Jake was only to keep your daddy from hitting him harder. Jake's notion that we'd be better off lying was as unwarranted as the people in St. Louis. But I'm getting ahead of myself," I said with an exasperated sigh.

Conall's head tilted to the side in curiosity. "What's unwarranted mean?"

I pressed my lips together, trying to figure the right words to explain. "When something or someone is unwarranted, it's not right or not reasonable. You know, maybe we should finish this story tomorrow?"

Conall's shoulders immediately pulled up to his ears, and the corners of his mouth turned down. "Aw, Momma, please finish the story. I promise I won't ask any more questions."

"Yeah, Momma," Ric said, imitating Conall's whine. "I like the way you're telling it. I'd forgotten about that slap." He raised his eyebrows and grinned, goading me.

"Fine, but you're not going to like the next part," I said and poked Ric in the chest with my pointer finger.

"Why's that?" he asked. Ric rubbed his chest and feigned being hurt. "The next part is when we—"

"Don't go telling my story," I interrupted. Ric's smile let on that he hadn't been trying to annoy me, but was only trying to get me to continue. "Both of you have to button your lips if you want me to tell the true story."

They glanced at each other, then made the motion of securing their mouths shut.

Like father, like son.

I knew it wouldn't last.

CHAPTER 3

1820

The black horse beneath me galloped at a steady pace. I'd named her Wilhelmina. She liked me better than Ric, and there could have been a number of reasons for that, but she kept positioning herself between us when we stopped to rest. Wilhelmina came across as a protective, nagging grandmother. She wanted her way, and wasn't easily intimidated.

Ric and I had traded riding each day, so I could stretch my legs. Wilhelmina hadn't given us any grief this particular morning, probably because I was in the saddle. We'd been on the trail five days since we'd crossed paths with Jake. Meaning we'd arrive in St. Louis later in the day.

I'd admired the clear skies and light breeze as we kept a steady pace.

Ric, in his wolf form, ran toward me. Wilhelmina's gait stuttered.

Three men are coming. I don't know how I missed them, but I don't have time to shift and get dressed. They're just over the hill. Ric's thoughts pressed into my mind.

I pulled on the reins and tucked my heels under Wilhelmina's belly. "You take cover," I said to Ric, pointing to a tree line in the distance. "I'll get past them."

As I steadied my heart rate, I thought back on how far we'd come. We'd left Jake on good terms. His cheek wore a red tint, but it was better than the broken nose I imagined Ric would have left behind. Ric's and my connection as mates made our bond unbreakable, and it wasn't often he came across as a jealous man.

After Jake apologized, and I apologized, we built a fire and hunkered down for the night. He lent us a blanket and cooked up some beans in an old crusty iron pan. He told us stories of St. Louis. I had to pinch Ric three times, because Jake would say something suggestive and I could feel Ric tense up beside me.

Sleep that night had come easy. The next morning, Ric and I decided to leave before Jake woke. I folded his blanket and placed it on the spring seat of his wagon with a small gold nugget. With a little adjusting, I managed to tuck one boot Jake had given me in my leather pouch and the other in Ric's bag.

We shifted into wolves and ran.

It didn't take us a full day to locate the farm Jake had mentioned. We scouted the livestock, barn, and house for at least an hour and decided it would be best if we didn't introduce ourselves. The more people who knew us, the more likely someone could find us or our settlement. So we waited until nightfall to make our move.

Dresses, shirts, trousers, and sheets billowed in the breeze on a clothesline at the side of the house. They looked like a family of ghosts waiting to greet us. Ric and I agreed we would only take what we needed to blend in when we arrived in St. Louis.

We nabbed something for each of us to wear, a horse and saddle from the barn, and a pair of boots from the front porch for Ric. I left a large gold nugget for the family where the boots had been kicked off, hoping it would more than make up for everything we took.

From that night, at least one of us had to stay in human form, dressed in the clothes we'd taken, to ride the horse and carry the rest of our things. The last five days had grown tedious. Ric and I had taken turns riding and running ahead in wolf form to scout, explore, and hunt. We'd been able to avoid every traveling party we might have crossed paths with so far.

I reached the hilltop, and the three men Ric mentioned were a few hundred feet away. Each one was dressed in black and rode his own horse. Their long coats hid any guns they might have carried. My surprise at seeing the men was not because they didn't look like they belonged on the road, but because we should have sensed them long before Ric saw them.

The only explanation was magic.

The closer Wilhelmina sauntered toward the three men, the more sure I was that they were using supernatural power to cloak themselves. At first, I could have sworn the men were brothers, each with fair skin and blue eyes shaded by the rims of their black cattleman's hats. They stopped about fifty feet in front of me, and one of the men tipped his hat in my direction. Getting a closer look, with my heightened wolf vision, I could tell the one who tipped his hat was significantly younger than the other two.

I kept what I believed to be a safe distance between us, and stopped my horse.

"Good morning," the younger man greeted with the hint of an accent. "You're up early." He smiled, and there was something dazzling about him. He was supernaturally beautiful for a man, not unlike Ric, but something more mysterious, a dark magic, shrouded him.

"Good morning, gentlemen," I replied, plastering the most sincere smile I could muster on my face. "Have you ridden from town? St. Louis?"

"We have," one of the older men answered with a gravelly voice, like he'd just woken up. His eyes roved over me, but I also felt magic caress my cheek. "It's no place for a young lady to be riding into without an escort." His ominous tone verged on threatening.

"I have friends I'm meeting, first thing," I said through a clenched jaw.

The man who had remained silent sat up on his saddle a little straighter and said, "You will have to excuse my brother, Leo." He waved a hand out to make the introduction more official. "This is my son, Julius, and I am Andrew Parris."

"It's nice to make your acquaintance," I said with a hesitant nod. "I'm Gabriele."

"Do you wish for an escort into town? We would be happy to oblige," Julius, the younger man, offered with a flirtatious grin.

The grumpiest of the three, Leo, furrowed his brow and frowned at the idea, but did not argue. Andrew chuckled, and looked from his son to me, then back to his son. Julius's mouth twisted in confusion at his father's reaction.

"I believe Miss Gabriele is capable of handling St. Louis without Le Cercle de Lune escorting her," Andrew said and winked at me. "Of course, we wouldn't dare impose on whatever business it is you have in town."

I frowned.

"Wha—" I started, and noticed the three men turn their attention to something past me, in the distance.

I looked over my shoulder, and at the tree line, a black wolf had shown himself.

When I turned back to the three men, they had already nudged their horses forward to ride past me. Leo made a clicking sound with his tongue and passed me first. Andrew moseyed by with a kind nod. But Julius slowed his horse to pause at my side. His knee was less than a foot away from mine.

Julius removed his hat, and his deep blue eyes searched me. "You can never be too careful. There are men in St. Louis who would take advantage of an outsider like you." He looked like his father, but up close I noticed a small scar over his right eyebrow. "Until we meet again," he said with a wink. His hand reached out to stroke Wilhelmina, and he missed, hitting my saddlebag. I heard a clattering sound, but ignored it, thinking the golden nuggets had been shaken loose inside.

Wilhelmina neighed, and I loosened my grip on the reins, allowing her to move on.

~

We arrived in St. Louis after lunch. Ric and I had noticed the smell of rot and waste before we could see the main street. A tent city stretched a mile downriver from where the more permanent structures stood. We decided it would be best if Ric shifted and we walked into town together. I held Wilhelmina's reins, and she hesitantly followed us through the crowded street.

The sights were as overwhelming as the scents, only in a good way. Buildings stood three stories tall. Steamboats pushed up the Mississippi River like salmon up a stream. And all the people were fascinating to watch. I had never seen so many people in one place. They swarmed like bees at the general store and docks, carrying boxes and baskets. One mention of our being friends of Auguste Chouteau led us to the center of town.

Several wagons and carriages were already traveling in the same direction. We took our time on foot, watching as men and women of means passed us. The passengers of the coaches and open carriages wore their best attire. Ruffles and bright colors stood out from the monotone shades of brown we witnessed coming and going in town. My own faded blue dress seemed to draw attention, but lacked the luster and embellishments worn by the town's higher class.

"This must be it," I said, breathless at the sight of Chouteau's estate. The house—no, mansion—was grandiose and made up an entire block of the city. A wooden porch with carved railings wrapped around the house on the first and second floors. Shutters framed each window. Auguste really had done well for himself. I smiled at the thought of our lost tradesman covered in animal furs wearing a suit instead and posing next to one of the tall white columns at the top of the staircase leading to his front door.

Carriages were lined up in a semicircle at the bottom of the stairs, and a footman guided guests to the porch. As they made their way, the men and women strapped elaborate masks over their faces. They were having a masquerade party.

We'd reached the end of the lane, and Ric took my hand in his and squeezed it. He looked torn, and I knew what he was going to say. So I stopped him with a kiss. Ric quickly pulled away with a frown and turned his head, checking if anyone had seen us.

I wished someone had seen us. It felt like someone kicked me in the chest to see Ric react the way he did.

"You know you can't be doing that," he said, half worried and half apologetic. He took a step back, creating more space between us. "We agreed we would introduce ourselves as siblings, like Jake suggested."

"You mean you decided," I gritted through my teeth. I folded my arms over my chest and lifted my chin. "This is ridiculous. You hated the notion at first, and we don't have time to make friends. We've almost been gone two weeks, and it will take twice that long to get back with supplies in tow. Not to mention, I have a bad feeling about all this." I waved my hands out in front of me at the partygoers.

Ric shook his head. "Your feelings come and go, but Jake made a point I can't ignore," he said softly, and leaned closer, cautious. "You're beautiful. Every man you passed in town made eyes at you, and as your husband, I'm a threat. As a brother, I can be considered an ally."

He nodded to the house. For every one woman in a silk gown, there were ten men in black d'Orsay hats.

"Ugh." I huffed, aggravated. He had a point, but I didn't want to admit it.

I shoved Wilhelmina's reins at him and grabbed the saddlebag. Then I made my way up the grassy lawn to the Chouteaus' front porch. Ric tied Wilhelmina off at a hitching post, then followed me. His posture changed as we marched closer. His squared shoulders hunched forward, and his eyes didn't quite meet mine when I motioned to a line of people making their way around to the back of the house.

"Where could they be going?" I asked.

He shrugged.

The footman greeted me with a smile and a bow, then looked to Ric for an introduction. Having lived my life in a matriarchal society, it was easy to forget that some cultures merely placed a monetary value on women, like they were different breeds of horses. These so-called civilized men made my blood boil, and the intrigue of St. Louis and its progress dwindled.

"Pardon us, I'm Ric Kasun, and this is my sister Gaby Kasun. We're here at the request of Mr. Auguste Chouteau, but it seems we've come at an inconvenient time," Ric said with a congenial ease, and tucked one hand in his jacket pocket.

"If you'll give me a few minutes, I will return with Mr. Chouteau," the footman said to Ric, and his jacket tails floated behind him as he made his way swiftly up the staircase and into the house.

I gritted my teeth, and resolved to find out what was happening behind the house. If the men in St. Louis treated women as an amusement, then I figured I'd best be amusing. Before Ric could stop me, I walked around to the back of the house. Ric glanced from me to the front door, and I knew he wouldn't follow. He had to wait for Mr. Chouteau.

Listening to the rambling guests on the wraparound porch, I overheard a few men discussing steamboat shipments from New Orleans. They mentioned it being the last week of October, and something about celebrating Halloween in style. There were too many guests talking over each other for me to make out any details. I'd slowed as I approached the back of the house, fidgeting with the buckle on my leather bag, and peeked around the corner. Everyone was walking down a marked path through the yard and across the next street, toward the river.

"Why, hello there, darling," a deep voice purred from behind me.

I jumped, and turned to face a broad, tall man with piercing blue eyes and a cigar in hand.

"Hello," I answered, feeling a little startled.

The man tipped his hat and stepped closer to me. He lazily lifted his cigar to his lips. He took a long, sultry drag and exhaled the smoke in small circles above my head. The patience he exhibited while drawing out his introduction contradicted an underlying eagerness I saw in his eyes as he looked me over.

"I'm Benedicte Trudeau, of the Louisiana Trudeaus," he said with a unique accent, and winked. He wore a midnight blue suit, with a matching vest. Like most of the men in attendance, he wore a less ornate mask and had a pistol strapped to his side.

I had no idea who the Trudeau family was, but I recognized his French accent. It reminded me of Auguste's accent when we first met. My face must have looked bewildered. Trudeau dropped his cigar and used the heel of his black boot to put it out.

He held his arm out for me to take.

"You must be new in town. Allow me," he said with a roguish smile, and took my hand, wrapping it around the crook of his arm. As his hand covered mine, the hair on my arm stood up. "So whom do I have the pleasure of escorting this evening?"

CHAPTER 4

1820

"Her name is Gaby Kasun," Ric gritted out as he walked around Mr. Trudeau. "And I'm Ric Kasun, her—"

Ric paused. His eyes darted to meet mine, and his lips flattened into a straight line. My heart held out hope he'd choose to introduce me as his wife.

"Brother," Ric mumbled, like he had to force the word out of his mouth.

Trudeau looked Ric up and down, taking in his brown, worn suit. Ric stood an inch taller than Trudeau, and while Ric's hair was dark and wavy, the hair peeking out from under Trudeau's hat was blonde and straight. The only thing the two men looked to have in common was their muscular build.

A slow smile spread across Trudeau's face like honey. "Why, I must insist that you accompany me this evening to the party." He patted my hand. "And your brother is welcome to join us," Trudeau said nonchalantly to Ric.

I tugged my arm back, but Trudeau held tight. "I'm not dressed for a party, Mr. Trudeau. You'll have to excuse me and my *brother*. We are here to meet with Mr. Chouteau, and then we'll be on our way back home."

"I beg to differ. It doesn't matter what a beautiful woman like yourself is wearing, or not wearing," Trudeau said, sounding slimy, and his smile slid into a deliberate smirk.

The man, if you could call him that, infuriated and disgusted me at the same time. A darkness emanating from Trudeau made me wary of him, similar to the men we'd passed on the road to St. Louis. I decided slapping his clean-shaven face wouldn't change his contemptible behavior, so I had to use his womanizing against him. Ric wouldn't like the idea I'd come up with, but his decision to introduce us as siblings had gotten us into the situation.

"I do appreciate your hospitality," I said coyly and squeezed his arm affectionately. "But we would hate to make Mr. Chouteau unhappy by showing up at his party unwelcome."

"Oh, don't you worry about that, sweet thing. You could never be unwelcome anywhere." Trudeau's reference to me being a thing made my neck burn with anger. "In fact," Trudeau continued, pulling me forward with him into the crowd, "we're all heading to one of my steamboats. There will be dinner, dancing, and I'll introduce you to the Creole Elite."

Trudeau caressed my arm softly, as if he were attempting to coax me forward. His hand left a trail of dark magic I could feel trying to permeate my skin. For some reason I recognized his power, but it couldn't bend my will. I figured if I weren't a wolf shifter, there was no telling what the man could have convinced me to do. In order to keep up Ric's ruse, I went along with Trudeau, and Ric followed close behind.

As we moved with the crowd across the street and toward the river, Trudeau rambled on about his connections in the city. He intermittently complimented me, and I heard Ric growl once or twice behind us. The people walking with us wore frilly silk ball gowns and formal dark suits. Ric and I resembled brown wilting buds in a field of wildflowers.

The closer we came to the river, the louder the crowd grew. It wasn't until I saw the steamboat we approached that I understood the reason for the commotion. The white water vessel looked more like a floating mansion with giant wheels attached to its back. The boat stood three stories tall. A group of men playing stringed instruments sat on a balcony. A railing around the flat roof protected several couples already dancing.

"You must be hungry," Trudeau said as we approached the ramp propped up between the dock and the first floor of the steamboat.

"I am, but we really must find Mr. Chouteau." I glanced over my shoulder at Ric.

"He'll be joining us as soon as all of his guests arrive, and until then I'll make you—" Trudeau winked at me, and caught me checking on Ric. His mouth turned down. "I mean, the both of you, more comfortable."

"Thank you, but—" I started to pull away, but Trudeau had a supernatural hold on me.

"I insist." His mouth tightened impatiently, and he waved me onto the ramp. "I have a private room on the second floor, and we will get you fed and in a new dress."

Mr. Trudeau's kindness felt overbearing, divisive. He led Ric and me up to his room, and while the narrow staircase made me feel claustrophobic, it led to a spacious room with red carpet and velvet-covered seats. A wardrobe, dressing screen, and chest of drawers, each made of walnut, lined a white wall at the center of the ship, and the other three walls were made up of windows.

The sun was setting over the edge of a grassy hill in the distance, and the sky had turned pink and orange. Lit lanterns hung from decorative iron rods making up the railing on the floor above us. Below us, on the first level of the boat, people mingled and drank from crystal glasses. All of their masks concealed their identities, and a sense of mischief lingered.

Mr. Trudeau opened the door of his polished wardrobe, and a rainbow of colors hung inside. He pulled out an ice-blue gown with cap sleeves and a full skirt, and hung it over the top of the screen. My lips twisted, trying to work out whether it would benefit us or land me indebted to Trudeau if I accepted his gift. Before I could decide, Trudeau retrieved a black jacket and white shirt from the wardrobe and a pair of black pants from the chest of drawers.

"I'll have one of my men bring up a tray of hors d'oeuvres and wait for you on the roof," Trudeau said seductively, taking my hand and kissing it. He looked from me to the dress. "You'll look ravishing in this gown."

He exited the room, pulling the door closed behind him. I hadn't had the chance to refuse. And whatever magic lingered on top of my hand, where he'd kissed me, had been meant to silence me. The scary thing was, I was unsure if it had been my own indecision or the magic that kept me from reacting. As a wolf shifter, our magic had always protected us against other supernatural powers. Our exposure to other supernaturals was limited, though, so I couldn't rule out Trudeau's darkness having an effect on me.

I shook my hand, as if the magic would fall off like water. "I don't like this one bit," I said a little too loudly, angry.

"You can't believe I do either," Ric reasoned, taking a step closer.

I took a step back, bumping into a settee.

"Gaby, please," Ric begged in a soft whisper. "I almost shifted in that staircase, wanting to rip that man's arm off for touching you." He leaned closer and lifted his hand to my neck. He slid his thumb along my jaw, gently guiding me toward him. "I hate this as much as you, but look where it's gotten us. We might meet someone here who can help us trade our gold for supplies."

He smiled enthusiastically, and the moment was gone.

I pushed him aside and disappeared behind the dressing screen. A small table with a bowl, pitcher of water, and towel was hidden discreetly for washing, and I made quick work of removing the grime and sweat from my face, neck, and arms. The dress I'd been wearing was simple, and easy enough to take off by myself. When I pulled the blue silk dress over the screen, I realized I would need help to button up the back. It irked me to have to ask Ric for help. Once I'd fastened as many of the buttons as I could, I bent down to my bag and emptied it of the gold nuggets tucked away. A few red gold nuggets were mixed with the others, and a small black stone rolled out. The rock was polished smooth, and it wasn't any larger than a coin. It looked, and even felt, like a stone I might find along the edge of the falls. Thinking back to the three men I crossed paths with before arriving in St. Louis, I remembered the clattering sound I'd heard when Julius passed me. He must have slipped the stone inside.

I scooped up all of the rocks and stepped out to the middle of the room to find Ric in his suit.

He was incredibly handsome in black. As my eyes drifted from his black hair to his crystal-blue eyes, I thought there couldn't be a better-looking man in St. Louis. Then my eyes reached his trousers. The cuffs of his pants revealed an inch of bare ankle on each leg.

I busted out laughing. After unloading our treasure onto the dresser, I quickly covered my mouth with my hand.

"Maybe we can let out the hem," I suggested between chuckles.

Ric squinted at me, and bent over to tug on one of his pant legs. "I already thought of that. You should have seen them a moment ago."

"Well, then, they'll have to do," I said matter-of-factly, and turned my back to Ric.

There were at least ten silk-covered buttons left to fasten on my dress. I lifted my hair, and looked over my shoulder at Ric expectantly. He quit fidgeting with his trousers and smiled.

"Let me," he said as his fingers grazed one of my shoulder blades.

"That is not *brotherly* behavior," I quipped, and fought a smile because I would remain frustrated with Ric.

"Then it's a good thing I'm not your brother." Ric leaned in and kissed the top of my shoulder.

"Stop it," I said and swatted at him.

Knock, knock.

I flinched in a panic, and said, "You are my brother here. Now, hurry."

Ric had a way of making me feel flustered, most of the time in a good way, but pretending to be his sister muddied my feelings.

After Ric tucked each tiny button into its hole, I scooped up the gold and called out for our visitor to come in. Ric took a seat, crossed his legs and got comfortable. A young man entered with a silver tray. He set it down on the top of the dresser and bowed before exiting.

Fruits, cheeses, bread, and two glasses of water were splayed out on the tray. The urge to tuck all the food in a cloth and save it lost out to my growling stomach. I quickly searched the drawers for a small beaded handbag and placed our gold and my rock inside, then tied it around my wrist.

I ate two bunches of grapes and half a loaf of bread. The cheese wasn't like the kind we made at our settlement. It was pungent and had to be cut with a knife, but Ric seemed to enjoy it.

"Are you ready to go find Trudeau?" Ric asked hesitantly.

I nodded, but as we made our way to the door, I grabbed his arm. "You need to know, every time he touches me I feel something."

Ric's jaw tightened.

"Not like that," I said quickly. "There's a darkness about him, and it feels like he's trying to persuade me with magic."

Ric faced me and slipped his hands around my waist. "Why didn't you tell me sooner?" he asked, his bottom lip pouting out, sad I would keep anything from him.

"Because I'm not here for me. I have to think about our pack. You had to know introducing us as siblings would lead to someone flirting with me. It just happens to be this creep, Trudeau. The goal is to find Chouteau and get the supplies we came for. Agreed?"

Ric frowned, regretting his decision, but nodded his agreement.

When we finally made our way to the gathering downstairs, the attendees weren't shy about whispering their thoughts of us to each other. I utilized my heightened hearing to eavesdrop. Some of the women admired my dress, but most of them admired my escort more. When one woman giggled about his pants being too short, my canine teeth pressed against the inside of my top lip. She whispered to her friend that if he wasn't wearing any pants he wouldn't have a problem.

Ric's chest rumbled in a chuckle at the same time, so I knew he'd also picked up on the conversation. At least the women were more discreet about their interest. The men's comments to each other bordered on crude as we made our way up to the roof of the steamboat. I didn't know how Ric stayed calm.

I was still so angry at him, I thought he deserved having to hear it all.

"Well, if it isn't my special guests," Trudeau called from across the rooftop.

The top of the steamboat was surrounded by an iron railing about three feet tall, creating a third story. Men and women appeared to be dressed even more ornately than the people below. Their jackets were embellished with silk to match their partners' dresses, which were decorated with jewels. That's when I noticed Trudeau's jacket lapel had been lined in the same blue silk as my dress. I plastered a convincing smile on my face, and pulled Ric with me over to them.

"It was fate that we met," I said with as much priss as I could muster, and held a hand out to Trudeau. "I cannot tell you how much my brother and I appreciate your kindness."

Trudeau took my hand and kissed it again, but lingered a moment too long. A throb of pain, darkness, crept its way up my arm and down into the pit of my stomach. I fought the urge to pull away and waited for Trudeau to begin the introductions. He was surrounded by a group of men, all older than himself, who looked distinguished and serious. Everyone wore masks except Ric and me, but the accessories didn't hide much. If wrinkles and white hairs measured wisdom, these men would have been the wisest guests at the party.

One of the men's mouths fell open at the sight of me, in awe. I recognized him as Auguste Chouteau immediately, but I couldn't let on that I knew him, since I was supposed to be my daughter. Luckily, Chouteau hadn't seen any of the other pack members in their human forms while he recovered near our settlement. I made sure to protect the others by being the only person he encountered when he returned to trade. If anyone else found out about the prosperity we'd found near the falls, they would try to take it away.

Trudeau pulled me forward, leaving Ric outside the circle of men, and placed my hand in Chouteau's. "This is the man you've been in search of, Auguste Chouteau. Mr. Chouteau, meet Gaby Kasun."

"I cannot believe my eyes," Mr. Chouteau said, stunned. He searched me from head to toe, taking in what must have seemed impossible. I watched as his features scrunched together in question, unbelieving.

"It is a pleasure to meet you, sir," I said warmly, truly happy to see him, and squeezed his hand in mine. "You know my mother, Gabriele. And when we received your letter, we knew we had to visit. She's told us so much about you." I motioned behind me to Ric.

"Is this—" Auguste started to ask and held his hand out to Ric.

"Her brother," Trudeau interjected with a proud smile.

Ric leaned forward and shook Chouteau's hand. "Nice to meet you," he said. Ric's smile was less than genuine.

I shuffled closer to Trudeau to make room for Ric, and Trudeau took advantage of the opportunity, slipping his arm around my waist. With his other hand, he pointed out each of the men surrounding us. Mr. Lane had frizzy brown hair, and was introduced as a doctor. Mr. Clark, the Missouri Territory governor, stood tall and lean, with silver hair. Mr. McNair, a businessman of some sort, had a long face with even longer sideburns growing in parallel to his ears. And Mr. Bates, the secretary of the Missouri Territory, stared at me with dark blue eyes, brown hair falling haphazardly over his forehead. They were all gentlemen, greeting me with a soft squeeze of the hand I offered and shaking Ric's hand firmly.

"You, my dear, have the pleasure of keeping company with some of St. Louis's Creole Elite this evening," Trudeau said and winked at Mr. McNair. "These men, along with a few others, are making Missouri a proper state, and we're building a booming city. It will take dedication and hard work, but with these men on our board of trustees, St. Louis will be the capital of this territory one day." His voice boomed with pride, catching the attention of the men and women mingling around us.

Mr. Clark shook his head, and chuckled humbly. "I'm not sure I can be included in your *elite* group. If it weren't for Auguste here, I wouldn't have had the supplies to explore this magnificent land with

Meriwether. God rest his soul." Mr. Clark frowned down at the floor beneath his feet.

Some of the others looked at each other, not sure how to change the subject. Mr. Chouteau pulled out his pocket watch and glanced at the time. Mr. Bates's eyes remained focused on me. And Mr. McNair fidgeted with the fit of his vest under his jacket.

I caught Auguste Chouteau's eye as he looked up from his gold timepiece, and couldn't think of anything to say. Auguste smiled at me the way a father smiled at his daughter, sweet and thoughtful. Trudeau's hand twitched at my waist. Auguste's eyes wandered to the place Trudeau touched me, and his smile melted into a disapproving glower.

"We've actually made the trip here from the West for supplies to take back with us," Ric interjected, startling me out of my thoughts. "Am I right, Mr. Clark, to recall you handling Indian affairs for a time?" he inquired with his eyebrows raised, interested to meet one of the few men on the continent who had the natives' best interests in mind.

I hoped Ric's question would take his mind off the untimely death of his partner, Meriwether Lewis. The rumors of his gunshot wounds being self-inflicted were unkind. It had been years since Mr. Lewis's death, but it was widely known that the two explorers had become the best of friends on their expedition.

"Why, yes," Mr. Clark answered and looked up at Ric expectantly. "Have you encountered natives?"

"Yes, sir," Ric answered with a smile. I could tell he was trying to tone down his enthusiasm.

Mr. Clark stepped to the side, pulling Ric into a conversation. I could feel my mate's eye on me, but knew he'd left me with the others to discuss the reason for our journey. Our pack may have been posing as settlers, but when we first arrived in the New World, it had been easier to blend in as natives. Most of the pack had dark hair, and with time our skin grew tan. While a few of the natives, like the Ute, were violent, most were hospitable. The Cheyenne taught us how to survive off the land. And we did, until some of the pack got it in their heads we needed to jump on the bandwagon of progress.

"Mr. Chouteau, your letter mentioned an opportunity to trade?" I asked, stepping forward out of Trudeau's grasp. "Maybe we can—"

"Now, you don't want to mix business with pleasure," Trudeau lured, moving in to close the distance I'd created.

Mr. Chouteau narrowed his eyes, searching me for a sign. I lifted my hair off my neck and gathered it to drape it over one shoulder, feigning being warm. Auguste Chouteau had been a good trader all those years ago because he could read a person. He took the cue.

"Mr. Trudeau, how about you find Miss Kasun a cool drink and inform the captain we are ready to leave port." Auguste nodded to the staircase leading downstairs and held his arm out to me. "Miss Kasun and I can conduct a little business until you return."

Trudeau's face gave him away for a split second. His smile twitched in annoyance, and if it weren't for my heightened abilities, I might have missed it.

With a sly smirk, Trudeau said, "I shall return soon."

"Not soon enough, I'm sure," I replied, pretending to be a little bashful, and curtsied.

After Trudeau reached the stairs, I shook my head, not believing what had come out of my mouth. Playing the part had come too easily, and it bothered me. I glanced at Ric, and his clenched jaw and balled-up fists let on that it bothered him too.

"Be careful, Miss Kasun," Auguste Chouteau warned in a low voice, and tucked my arm around his. "Getting entangled with Benedicte Trudeau would be like getting caught in that iron trap your mother found me in all those years ago."

1860

"Daddy!" Conall exclaimed and sat up in bed. "You never told me you pretended Momma was your sister." He clenched his teeth together and glared at Ric.

"Well, son, I was just taking the advice we'd been given," Ric reasoned.

Conall took my hand in his protectively. "I think you should say sorry," he suggested firmly.

"Believe me, I've been saying sorry for the last forty years," Ric grumbled and shifted on the bed.

"What's that supposed to mean?" I asked, a tad vexed, and turned to face him. My head tilted with burning curiosity at his meaning.

Ric rubbed the stubble along his chin, choosing his words carefully. He watched as Conall relaxed back under his covers and I tucked his quilt around him. I could see Ric's mental wheels turning. He was running his answer through every scenario he could think of to make sure he said the right thing.

"I *am* sorry," he said softly, and with a hint of sadness, he took one of my hands, raised it to his lips, and kissed it. "The only reason I hadn't ever told Conall was because I've been ashamed. And I'll be sorry about it for as long as I live."

I leaned closer to Ric, and he scooted to sit across from me. I laid my head on his shoulder. "I forgive you," I said with a smile and closed my eyes, relishing the moment with my boys.

Ric wrapped his arm around my waist, and I rested against him for a moment.

"Momma," Conall whispered. "Are you gonna finish now?"

CHAPTER 5

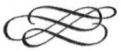

1820

"We have to get out of this godforsaken town," Ric barked at me as he paced in front of my bed.

After the party, the Chouteau family insisted Ric and I stay at their home while we were in St. Louis. We had been escorted up to bedrooms adjacent to each other, and since Ric had introduced us as siblings, no one remarked on my brother being in my room. The mansion had high ceilings, and the front hallway was decorated with tapestries two stories tall. It had been so late when the steamboat arrived back at the docks that we were able to watch the sunrise from the Chouteaus' back porch.

"I have a meeting with Mr. McNair tomorrow," I said in a whisper, and continued to brush my hair with a soft-bristled brush I'd found lying on the dresser. "He'll have an idea of what our gold can buy. He mentioned the closure of the bank last year made the value of gold fall in these parts, but it's on its way back up."

"And what of Benedicte Trudeau?" Ric asked and rolled his eyes.

I turned from my reflection in the mirror and took Ric's hand to stop him. "He invited us to dinner tonight, and I plan to make clear our desire to head home sooner rather than later."

"You watch," Ric growled, pulling his hand out of mine. "He'll find a way to get rid of me, and get you alone."

"Even if he did get me alone, I can take care of myself," I argued and stood to face Ric. "You're the one who wanted to save your own skin and call me your sister. You'll have to deal with the consequences."

"Believe me, I'm dealing," Ric gritted out, brushing past me as he headed for the door.

Ignoring his pouting, I reminded him, "Besides, with Mr. Chouteau's gift of supplies, the pack will have everything they need for winter. I just think we need to know what our gold is worth. Plus, I brought some of the red gold. I want to know more about its value, too."

"Gaby," Ric sighed and leaned his forehead against the door. "I wish you wouldn't show that stuff to anyone. We've got enough trouble with Trudeau drooling all over you."

"He's definitely trouble, but I'll let him down easy," I said, walking over to the door. I placed a hand on Ric's back, and his shoulders relaxed a little. "Maybe you could give me a few tips. If I remember correctly, you had to have a similar talk with Nina before we were married."

Nina Novak never stood a chance with Ric, but that didn't make talking to the obsessive, conniving woman any easier. She'd mated with someone else, but knowing she had feelings for Ric had always made my insides boil. Jealousy was like an iron skillet. When on the fire, it could be useful, but if you tried to handle it without caution, you'd get burned.

"There is a big difference between this situation with Trudeau and what we went through with Nina," Ric said in a low rumble.

"What's that?" I propped both hands on my hips.

"You never had to sit back and watch your mate flirt with another woman. I never gave Nina hope, and Trudeau is basking in it after tonight." Ric didn't look back at me. The muscles at his neck flexed as he twisted the doorknob and exited.

When Ric closed the door behind him, it felt like he sealed off the air from my room. I couldn't breathe. As mad as I was at him, he'd been right about one thing. Benedicte Trudeau had become more than hopeful, almost possessive. And the darkness I felt oozing from him over the guests at the party was proof that he was used to getting what he wanted.

~

TYPICALLY, I'd never sleep through the day, but after our travels and the party, my body collapsed onto my bed, and I fell into a deep slumber. Dreams of swimming in the cool water of the falls filled my mind. I thought I'd just fallen asleep when there was a knock on my door. Barely any light filtered through the quilt I'd used to cover myself from head to toe.

"Come in," I called out roughly. It felt like my eyelids had been lined with honey, heavy and sticky.

Someone entered my room without a word. I peeked out from under the corner of my blanket and saw a young woman tiptoe to the wardrobe across the room. The chambermaid carried a red silk gown, fancy shoes, and a black cowboy hat with red embellishments. She worked to hang them up quietly. Before she left, she bent over to check the chamber pot at the end of the bed.

Gross.

She hadn't left a message for me, but the dress she'd brought was beautiful. It had puffed sleeves and a broad neckline with black lace trim. The silk had been embroidered with a black floral design at the bottom of the skirt.

After the door closed, I rolled over on my back and stretched. A loud yawn escaped me, and as my limbs curled up, I tucked the quilt back under me. I longed to return to my dream, but realized the sun was no longer high in the sky, but setting outside my window.

I would have to meet Trudeau before long.

I scurried out from under the covers and held the new dress up to my body. I looked in the mirror and admired the sash, knowing it would be flattering on my figure. My hair had tangled up into knots, and would take some time to brush, so I washed up and dressed myself quickly. The shoes were too much, so I opted to wear my old, worn boots. Not everything I wore tonight would belong to Trudeau.

Knock, knock.

I opened the drawer I'd stowed our gold in and folded the rocks into the pleats in the sash tied around my waist.

"Come in," I called out, expecting the chambermaid's return to help me get ready.

My dress hung open at the back, where I couldn't reach the buttons. I glanced toward the door, and found Ric looking sheepish. The irony was that with a thought or emotion, he could magically shift into a wolf at any time.

I waved him in and said, "Hurry and shut the door, before someone sees me."

"Sorry," Ric offered softly. When he stepped into the fading light, I noticed the dark circles under his eyes and the stoop of his shoulders.

"Did you not sleep?" I asked, already knowing the answer. I turned my back to him and pointed to the buttons over my shoulder.

He started to fasten them, and whispered, "I've been trying to figure out what to say to you. I'm sorry doesn't seem enough."

Ric's fingers grazed the neckline of my dress as he finished.

"There's no reason to apologize," I said, because I couldn't deal with fixing things and then going off to dinner with Trudeau. "I had a dream we were back at the falls, and it made me wish we were there so I didn't have to go out with that Creole creep tonight."

Ric finished buttoning my dress, and I glanced in the mirror. The connection Ric and I shared could never be severed, not as long as we lived. I could feel how close he stood, and his presence usually brought me peace. But I was still angry at him.

Even if Ric couldn't hold my hand or take me into his arms in public, I knew he would be with me at dinner tonight.

The sound of a horse-drawn carriage clattering up to the front drive of the house disrupted my thoughts of Ric. He jumped, walked over to the window, and reported Trudeau's arrival.

I finished primping and preening while Ric and the Chouteau family entertained our guest. I did my best to pin my hair quickly, and decided to carry my new hat until we stepped outside. Expecting the others to accommodate a man none of them cared for seemed cruel. I had been the one to accept his invitation.

Trudeau's attention had not waned the night before, and because he owned a fleet of steamboats, I knew he had knowledge of the supplies being shipped to and from St. Louis. Benedicte Trudeau was a potential resource I couldn't ignore, even if his intentions weren't transparent.

Ric would have argued he could see right through Trudeau's motives, clearly, but the darkness I felt emanating from him at the party reminded me of a dense morning fog. You can know a path, and might have walked it a hundred times, but fog had a way of disorienting you and making you feel lost.

The saying "Know your enemies" had popped into my mind when Trudeau invited me to dinner. Only, he wanted to know me in all the wrong ways, keeping me close at his side quite literally. I'd decided I would use the time we spent together, chaperoned by Ric, to get information and be as disagreeable and unpleasant as possible.

As I made my way downstairs, I noticed Auguste Chouteau and Ric in deep conversation at the front door. Trudeau looked up at me from the bottom step. He had leaned against the banister, but as I descended, he snatched up his gold pocket watch and stood straight.

One of the hardwood steps creaked under my foot, and Ric's jaw twitched, but he continued to whisper to Auguste. I'd wanted Ric to be the one looking up at me from the entryway. I had desired to see his eyes sparkling with passion. It was my mate's smile I'd longed to find greeting me.

Instead, I'd found Trudeau with a smug look on his face and his chest puffed up with air. His blond hair had been slicked back, and he wore a light gray suit with red trim that matched the color of my gown.

"Why, I'll be," Trudeau said, his Creole accent thick. "You are a vision."

He held his hand out for me to take, and I did. With a tight smile, I said, "Thank you, sir, you're too kind."

"Benedicte," he said, captivated, and nodded without taking his eyes off me. "I insist you call me by my given name."

He took my hand and turned it over, palm facing up. Bending at the waist, he watched for my reaction as he brushed his lips over my skin. I tried to tug my hand away, but he was too quick. It was as if he'd anticipated how I'd react.

He tsked and shook his head ever so slightly, smirking. "So skittish, yet so alluring. I can't help myself. Your naivete is rare in a city like St. Louis, and oh so enticing."

"Mr. Trudeau," Auguste interrupted with a frown. "I hope you'll take special care of my guests, and be on your best behavior."

Trudeau's smirk morphed into a sneer, then quickly went blank. He clicked his boot heel loudly on the floor as he moved to shake hands with Auguste. The moment their hands connected, Auguste mellowed. A slow smile spread over his face, and he appeared to let go of whatever grievance he bore.

Trudeau had used his power over Auguste. The night before, I'd wondered if he had a dark side and was blackmailing Auguste. But after that display, I was sure it was magic. Trudeau hadn't used one drop of magic on me in the entryway, but I'd had a feeling he tried. His manners, or lack thereof, had gotten under all of our skin in a matter of minutes.

"I plan to show these two the best this town has to offer." Trudeau opened the front door with a flourish and waved Ric outside. I followed, and on the front porch Trudeau took my hand and slipped my arm around his. "Don't wait up!" He hollered over his shoulder with the return of his toothy grin. I had a sick feeling Trudeau thought he *was* the best St. Louis had to offer.

Trudeau's open carriage had been painted red, and was operated by a coachman dressed in black. The driver pulled out a horse whip, and it snapped in the air above two black horses. I placed the cowboy hat on my head, if anything to keep my hair manageable, and it fit like a glove.

Because the Chouteau family lived in the city, it didn't take long for us to arrive at our destination. We'd barely discussed the pleasant weather when the carriage pulled up in front of a brick building with a rowdy crowd gathering out front. The sound of music echoed out of a pair of swinging doors. Loud guffaws of laughter spilled over small glasses filled with amber liquid. Small clouds of white smoke escaped from men's pipes and cigars. A few of the women wore feathers in their hair, but the embellishments paled in comparison to the amount of cleavage most of them showed.

"What kind of place is this?" I asked in shock.

Trudeau stood up and jumped to the ground, laughing. "The kind of place I think you'll like."

My mouth dropped open, and I gasped. Obviously, we'd rolled up to a saloon.

The problem was, no gentleman would bring a respectable woman to a saloon. Either Trudeau had somehow discovered I wasn't always a *woman* or he was up to no good. Ric stepped down from the carriage and winked at me. The gesture was meant to keep me calm. As much as he hadn't wanted me to go out with Trudeau, I caught a glimmer of curiosity in his eyes.

Trudeau reached up and put his hands at my waist to help me down. I flinched, worried he'd feel the gold and the little black stone bunched in my sash. "You said you wanted to talk business, and this is a place of my business."

My feet came down softly on the packed dirt road. I searched the sign above. It read *Saloon* clearly. The few signs I could read along the boardwalk read *Barber*, *Mercantile*, and *Post Office*. Nothing had Trudeau's name on it or mentioned steamboats.

"Do you mean to say you're a bartender or postman?" I asked, confused and still looking for anything with his name. People, dressed in every shade of brown, crossed the street and conducted their business. Some of them stopped to watch us.

"You met me yesterday, but I think you know better." Trudeau straightened his jacket and frowned. "No, I own all of these establishments."

"Good for you," Ric said in a grumble from behind him.

"I'm not sure I understand where you're going with this," I admitted with hesitation. I wasn't sure I wanted to know.

Trudeau rubbed his chin, and one corner of his mouth crept up. "Don't play the fool, Gaby," he said slyly. "I overheard you discussing supplies with Chouteau last night, and then you wanted to meet with McNair about gold prices. I'm in."

I glanced from Ric to Trudeau and felt my eyebrows draw together. "In on what?" I asked.

"The town you're building out west," Trudeau said quietly, as if he had been revealing a secret. He crossed his arms over his chest and leaned back against a post, proud of himself.

"We aren't interested," Ric said flatly, and folded his arms across his chest.

Ric's passive-aggressive behavior would eventually blow our cover if I didn't find a way to keep Trudeau at a platonic distance. Showing off his acquisitions had proved his highest priority was money. I deduced that playing into his desire for more wealth would distract him from flirting with me and making Ric even more indignant.

I placed a hand gently over Trudeau's elbow and said, "Don't mind Ric."

I stepped up on the boardwalk and made to look like I was inspecting Trudeau's barber shop window. He followed close behind, and in the corner of my eye I saw him reach a hand out toward me. Playing hard to get would only tease a man like Trudeau into pursuing me more decidedly. Instead of walking ahead, I allowed him to wrap his arm around my waist.

"Benedicte," I cooed. "Our little settlement isn't much, and the kind of progress we've seen in St. Louis seems as many years away as it is miles. The land is wild and beautiful, and maybe by the time *we*, I mean, *I* have a dozen children, there will be a mercantile. I can't wait to start a family and fill the territory with boys as wild as the terrain and girls as beautiful as the scenery." Grinning up at him, I caught a flicker of reluctance when I said *dozen*.

Trudeau's hand loosened for a moment, then he squeezed me close.

"I wouldn't need beautiful scenery if you stayed in St. Louis," he said flirtatiously, and winked.

He was impossible.

When I glanced back at Ric, he was shaking his head. My attempt to direct his attentions somewhere else had failed, but I wouldn't give up. The direct approach would have to do, and not only to set Trudeau straight, but Ric and I needed to start our journey back to the falls in the next few days. If we waited much longer, the weather could turn on us.

Trudeau must have sensed my uneasiness, but mistook it for concern. He said, "Don't worry, I'd send a man or two along with Ric to help transport your supplies. We could get—"

"Stop right there, Benedicte," I said curtly. Trudeau's face blanched, and I realized how harshly I'd reacted. I softened my tone and continued, "Please don't say another word. We barely know each other, and Ric and I came here for the sole purpose of helping our family. I'm afraid anything more must be ignored."

"What if I can't ignore my feelings?" Trudeau said gruffly.

"You must," I answered and turned my head away. Ric's fists were balled up at his sides. "I have a meeting with Mr. McNair tomorrow, and he promises to give us a fair trade for our gold. He might even trade us for the red gold, and then we'll be making our way back to the mountains."

"Red gold?" Trudeau asked. His demeanor shifted from hurt to curious. He took a step back and slipped his hands into his pockets. His eyes roamed over me, and he asked, "Do you have it with you? I'd like to see it, if I may."

"It's back at the house," Ric interjected.

Pulling his pocket watch out, Trudeau opened it with a press of a button. He glanced at the time and pressed his lips together in a tight smile.

"Well, it looks like I'm running late for my next appointment. Would you mind if we called it a night?" he asked, distracted and blatantly rude.

"No," Ric answered too quickly.

Trudeau started for his carriage, and I looked from him to Ric. "What Ric means to say is, we'll walk back to the Chouteaus'. You go ahead," I said with a sigh of relief.

Something clicked in Trudeau. He nodded and leapt onto the first carriage step. I'd wanted him to realize I didn't have any intention of staying in St. Louis, and we wouldn't be doing business with him. But that would have been too easy.

"I hope you have a nice evening," he said with a cordial bow. "It has been a pleasure. Until we meet again."

Trudeau moved to his seat and tapped the side of the carriage. The driver whipped the horses into motion, and they merged into the bustling traffic. I didn't wonder if Trudeau would look back at us, so I turned to face Ric. We both understood his farewell was a promise.

CHAPTER 6

1820

*R*ic held out his arm for me to take, and I did. The busy streets were filled with townspeople, but not one of them rode in a fancy carriage or wore a silk dress. I had almost felt like I could be myself, except for the red dress. It felt like Ric and I could be a couple.

That had been my first mistake.

"How about a sarsaparilla?" Ric nodded to the saloon with a grin.

"Don't tell me you think this is the kind of place I'd like, too?" I asked with a frown.

A man flew out onto the boardwalk, leaving two doors swinging violently behind him. The crowd inside cheered, and an unseen female hollered, "I don't want to see the likes of you in here ever again!"

Everyone hollered in support, then settled into a steady stream of chatter and glasses clinking together. The place smelled musty. But something about it felt familiar. I'd never traveled to St. Louis or been near a saloon before, but there was an entity inside the swinging doors calling to me.

After the stranger picked himself up off the ground and wiped the dirt from his pants, he gave Ric and me a dirty look and walked past us. I barely heard the low growl that had rumbled in the man's chest. Ric, by instinct, postured himself between me and the stranger, but he'd kept walking.

Turning back to me, Ric said, "You may not like the place, but I know you'll like the company." Ric's eyebrows bounced up and down, and he gave me a lopsided grin.

"You're probably right," I admitted, and pulled him with me to the swinging doors. "There's something distinctly different about this place."

Ric's grin turned into a grimace. I'd hurt his feelings by not flirting back, but I couldn't ignore the desire to see what was inside. From what I'd heard, saloons were full of drunk men and half-dressed women. It didn't sound like a place I could see myself mingling. But what if this place called to me for a reason? It definitely felt familiar, supernatural. The same way the magical falls had always fostered our pack with energy.

Ric reached forward to open the door for me, and I froze. The main room was two stories tall, with three lit chandeliers hanging from the high ceiling. A bar had been strategically placed across from the front doors, and to the left a set of stairs led to a balcony that wrapped the room on three sides. Light yellow striped wallpaper made the space feel bigger. A wooden railing had been decorated with pretty girls in their undergarments, and behind them dark, wooden doors lined the walls. There had to have been ten of each.

"We don't have to go inside," Ric offered, and started to step backward.

"No, I'm simply taking it all in," I said dryly. My mouth felt like I'd eaten cotton. "Someone in here has something supernatural or is supernatural," I whispered.

"I can feel it too, but faintly," Ric said softly.

The room was filled with a sea of brown. Every table was mahogany with matching chairs, almost all of them occupied. The glasses were filled with golden liquid. Many of the men's faces were sun-kissed bronze. And the men's drab hats, shirts, and trousers were dingy and filthy.

"Can I get y'all something, sweetie?" a woman said cheerfully, navigating between two tables from our right. She wore a pair of brown, wide-legged trousers with fringe at the sides, and a brown hat. Her shirt was tailored like a man's, but made out of a floral print in shades of pink.

When my eyes met hers, I knew. She had magic.

There wasn't much power in her, but I had a feeling that wasn't always the case. Her blond wavy hair had been tied with a piece of leather over her shoulder. She held a tray over her head, and it was covered in glasses filled to the brim. Suds sloshed over the sides when a man pushed his chair back without warning. The blonde pivoted and saved the drinks like she had heightened reflexes, but pressed her hand to Ric's chest to brace herself.

"Two sarsaparillas, please," I said, stepping in her direction so she wouldn't miss that we were together.

"Coming right up," she said as she glanced at me. She patted Ric's chest before pushing off toward the bar. "If y'all will follow me, I'll set you up at a table. You mind sharing?"

"A table?" I asked, clarifying she wasn't referring to Ric.

"That's fine," Ric said. "My *wife* and I don't mind sharing, but we'd prefer more quiet company."

"You got it, sweetie," she said, and sat her tray down at the table next to her. The men each grabbed a glass. In a few seconds, she lifted the tray back up, and we followed her to the far back left corner of the room. The shadow of the staircase and balcony had concealed the table and its lone occupant.

His green hat was dusty and tilted downward so we couldn't see his face. An olive green coat with leather trim hung on his broad shoulders, and white shirt cuffs peeked out at his wrists from under his coat sleeves. His hands were tan and muscular, and they made his empty glass look small as he tapped it lightly on the wooden table.

"Have a seat here," the woman said and dropped her tray in a loud smack. The sound startled the man, and he looked up, clearly irritated. "Two sarsaparillas?" she asked.

She snatched the man's glass and set it on her tray.

"Yes, for us," Ric answered and held a chair out for me to sit down. "Sir, can we buy you a drink?" he asked the stranger.

The man looked from the barmaid to Ric and twisted his mustache-covered lips in thought. He nodded consent, and reached for a silver watch tucked in the pocket of his gray vest.

"I'm Della Rucker, if y'all need anything else," the woman introduced herself as she lifted her tray over her head. "And this is Anson, Anson Corey. I'll be right back with those drinks."

"Mr. Corey, I'm Gaby," I greeted, and pointed to my mate. "This is Ric."

Anson tipped his hat and tucked his watch away. "Please, call me Anson," he said, and his mustache, peppered with silver hairs, spread wide. I knew he was smiling. He reached across the table and held his hand out to me.

I leaned forward and felt Anson's power before our palms met. It hadn't only been familiar, but I'd felt an identical power over a hundred years ago, when I met a family of witches stuck in a time loop.

As my hand slipped into Anson's, he squinted at me and tilted his head to the side. The brown hair on his chin bristled, and he said, "You're not from around here." His voice was raspy, and his words were spoken carefully, like they had more than one meaning.

"No, we've traveled from the mountains in the Missouri Territory to trade for supplies before the winter winds come," I'd said matter-of-factly. I'm not sure why I'd been so forthcoming, but Ric's foot nudged mine under the table in concern.

"You wouldn't be needing much if it's just the two of you," Anson said, leading for more information. "I'm in the business of helping folks who come through town and want to go unnoticed."

"I'm afraid we've already been noticed," Ric grumbled and smiled tightly at me. "Gaby is hard to miss, and in the first few hours of our arrival, the Creole Elite were fighting for her attention."

I swatted the back of my hand at Ric's arm. Whatever had gotten into me was making Ric more loose-lipped than our pack's gossip, Helena Greg. Before placing my hand back in my lap, I felt the remnants of magic brush over my fingertips. Anson Corey was some kind of witch.

"Those men run this town, and you'd best be careful not to get caught up with their sort," Anson said with a frown. "Each one of 'em is heartless, and I should know. I used to work for the worst of 'em, Trudeau."

Ric and I glanced at each other nervously. We'd introduced ourselves as husband and wife. If Trudeau found out, I didn't know how he'd respond. He seemed a proud man, and in my experience, pride never sat well with deceit.

"Maybe you could help us," I said, leaning forward and lowering my voice. "If you've done business with Trudeau, you'll know how I should best cut ties with him."

I gritted my teeth, forcing myself to stop talking. For some reason, I had the urge to tell Anson about our red gold and the rest of our pack waiting at the falls for us. Something nudged the back my mind, not a thought or memory, but something magical. It took all of my mental strength not to succumb to the pull I felt. I met Anson's clear blue eyes, and after another mental nudge, his brows and mouth relaxed, and the magic disintegrated.

Anson cleared his throat. He glanced past my shoulder.

"Here are y'all's drinks," Della chimed in cheerfully. "If there's anything else ya need, just call my name." She winked at Anson and handed him a tall glass filled with amber liquid. Della grabbed the other two glasses by their handles together, and they landed on the table with a thud.

"Thank you," I said kindly, and lifted the sarsaparilla to my lips. The liquid was cold in my mouth, and the notes of vanilla and licorice were comforting and warm.

Anson took a long swig of his own drink, and then casually swirled what liquid remained in his glass, waiting. He was patient, and he acted as though he had all the time in the world.

The crowd in the saloon grew louder the later it got. Men rallied around poker players at multiple tables dotted around the room. A group cheered on two men at the bar chugging beer. All the while, Anson acted as if the place, and his present company, were invisible. While we were trying to save a few dozen people, it felt like Anson was contemplating how to save the world.

"I don't know how, but you're hiding who you really are," Anson finally said, his voice clear but his words still elusive. "I don't think I can work with folks I can't trust."

"I know who you really are, but only because I've met someone like you before," I said. "*They* could be trusted."

Anson waved his hand in the air like he was swatting a fly away, and a current of power passed over us. "*I* can be trusted. You folks are the ones working with Trudeau. So why can't I pick up on your power? I felt you withstand mine. Are you a shifter like him?"

I looked around the room, scared someone would overhear us, but the throng of drinkers and gamblers continued without paying us any attention. I asked, "How are you doing that?"

Anson lifted one corner of his mouth and answered, "My dear, if you know who I really am, you know that staving off prying ears is merely child's play for someone like me. Now, who are you? And how in tarnation did you get involved with Trudeau?"

Ric took my hand protectively, his way of slowing me down. When I'd become alpha, I hadn't realized the importance of taking my time. If someone came to me with a problem, I wanted to fix it as fast as I could. But I was learning that reacting and responding were two different ways to handle a situation.

"Trudeau is trying to get *involved* with Gaby, not the other way around," Ric defended me, and set his jaw.

Anson looked to me and said, "You are a beautiful young woman, but the same way you've shielded certain gifts from me, you must have cloaked yourself from Trudeau. Otherwise, you two wouldn't be sitting here now. You, my dear, would be paraded around town on his arm as a trophy."

Confused, and a little frightened at his claim, I wondered at how I'd been able to pick up on supernatural activity with Trudeau and Anson, but Trudeau hadn't let on that he knew we had power of our own. I'd even picked up on magic being used by others, like the barmaid, in the saloon.

"I think keeping Gaby as a trophy is his intention, whether he finds out we're wolf shifters or not," Ric said to me, concern etched in the lines around his mouth.

Anson's mouth fell open in wonder. "*Wolf* shifters," he repeated. He rubbed at the back of his neck, thinking, then asked, "What kind of talisman are you using to disguise yourselves?"

"Talisman?" I asked a little too loudly, worried someone would hear me, and shrugged in embarrassment. I'd heard the term before, but from natives. "I wouldn't know the first thing about that kind of magic."

"Well, you've got to be carrying something around with you, even if you don't know it's charmed," Anson said with concern, and looked from me to Ric like he was inspecting us. "Yep, you're definitely the one carrying it, darlin'."

I huffed, and asked, "What kind of object are we talking about? Could it be something as simple as a rock?"

Anson rubbed his chin and thought about it. I reached for the polished stone tucked into the sash at my waist and turned it over in my hand. Finally understanding Julius's purpose for placing the rock in my saddlebag, I couldn't help but wonder what he got out of keeping the truth about us being shifters a secret. I swallowed down the realization that I'd probably find out one day.

"Yes, a powerful witch or warlock could use a stone to hold that kind of magic, but it works better when the object is personal," Anson said thoughtfully. And when I held the black stone up, his eyes widened in curiosity. "May I?" he asked, and held out his hand.

Unsure if I could trust Anson, I looked to Ric. He pressed his lips into a straight line, just as distrustful as me. As alpha, it was my responsibility to make the call. So why had Ric decided to introduce us as siblings with Trudeau, but appeared indifferent with Anson? His passivity in one moment contrasted with his control in another lit an angry fire in my belly.

I leaned forward, ready to pass the stone to Anson, but fisted it at the last second. "How can I be confident you won't take this stone and use it against us?" I narrowed my eyes at him, watching for any signs of betrayal.

"Let me answer you with a question. Could you trust the magic wielder, the one who felt like me, the person you met before?" he asked, sure of himself, and crossed his arms over his chest.

"Yes, but what do they have to do with you?" I asked, exasperated.

"Magic is similar to dialects. And if my magic feels like that of a witch you've encountered before, then they most likely are from Salem, like my ancestors. Our people suffered a great deal during the trials, and I was the only one in my family to escape. I wandered from town to town until I made a home here in St. Louis. I accepted a job working for Trudeau, because I thought he was like me. Over time, I started a family of my own. It wasn't long before I started to understand Trudeau's intention to brainwash the community and build an empire where everyone does everything he demands. Most aren't powerful enough to fight his magic," Anson said ominously, and nodded at me. "I'm sure that talisman helped, but you must be one powerful shifter."

"Alpha," Ric said clearly, with a determined look in his eyes. He looked from me to Anson, and waited. Ric must have been getting the same vibe I had been since we sat down. Anson could be trusted, but I wasn't sure I wanted to tangle him up in the web we'd woven. He'd mentioned a family.

I set the stone on the table and slid it across the wood. Anson quickly scooped it up and held it up to the lantern light. His inspection was made with a frown, and ended with a grunt. He slid it back.

"It's solid spell work, but dark," Anson explained with caution. "Probably why it went undetected by Trudeau. I'd suggest you keep this with you at all times, while you're in town, that is."

Tucking the rock back under my sash, I admitted, "There are more of us, a growing wolf pack, back in the mountains. We just want to trade our gold for supplies, but we're waiting to find out what we can get for it, and if the red gold we have is as valuable as the regular gold. Could you help us negotiate a fair trade?"

My question was met with a smile from Anson. Ric took my hand in his and kissed the top of it, showing his support. Anson leaned forward and propped his elbows on the table. He linked his fingers together and nodded.

"Red gold, you say? Any chance your gold mine has been exposed to magic?" he asked, and his smile spread into a toothy grin. "If so, I think we can do business."

As Anson reached across the table to shake on it, the saloon doors swung open forcefully, with no regard for the men they pushed to the side. Benedicte Trudeau stepped inside, and his eyes landed on our table.

CHAPTER 7

1820

$\mathcal{A}$ ll at once, Anson's fingers twitched in the air, I ripped my hand from Ric's, and across the room, Della swept in front of Trudeau with a flirtatious giggle. Our magical encasement flickered and disappeared. I stood up and walked over to the bar, watching the reflection of the room in the large mirror behind the bottles of alcohol. Della led Trudeau teasingly by his necktie to a poker table.

I noticed Trudeau looking back to where Anson and Ric sat sipping on their drinks. He shook his head and grabbed a shot glass from the table, then swallowed all of its contents. Della ran a finger along Trudeau's jawline, and he smiled. She murmured something in his ear, but the saloon's patrons had grown so loud even my heightened hearing couldn't catch what she said. Whatever it had been, Trudeau sat down, pulled a wad of currency from his jacket pocket, and laid it on the table.

"Can I buy you a drink?" a man asked in a thick Irish accent. He sat on a wooden stool, and his suit was nice, not Creole-Elite formal, but clean and fashionable. "I'm Gabriel Doyle, and this is Viktor Azimov."

Viktor tipped his hat in my direction from his stool on the opposite side of Gabriel.

My mouth formed a tight smile, and I nodded.

I needed a distraction, so I said, "It's nice to meet you. I'm Gaby."

Gabriel knocked on the dark wooden bartop and held up two fingers. The bartender poured two drinks and slid them to Gabriel's hand. He set a glass in front of me and held his up in the air, waiting for me.

"A chara," he toasted with a grin.

I had no idea what he'd said, and I felt one of my eyebrows raise in response. I pressed my glass down on the bar. I wasn't about to raise it and mislead the man. I'd already given Trudeau, a member of the Creole Elite, the wrong idea. I wasn't about to do the same with an unknown, and possibly drunk, Irishman.

"Friend," Gabriel clarified in a lower voice, a little less enthusiastic, but not put off by my hesitation.

I lifted my glass timidly and repeated, "Friend."

I had tried to sound good-natured, but I think it came across more heavy-hearted. I downed my drink, hoping to hide my worry. The liquid left a trail of fire down my throat. My eyes darted from Gabriel to the mirror, searching for Ric and Trudeau.

"Are you looking for or avoiding someone?" Gabriel asked in a whisper, his brows lowered as he concentrated on the mirror's reflection. "Maybe Viktor and I could help, seeing as we are now friends."

"Oh, thank you very much, but—" I had started, but Gabriel placed his hand over mine, stopping me mid-thought.

"I'm also a friend to Anson and Della." Gabriel winked slyly.

"Oh," I exhaled, relieved.

Gabriel stood up and maneuvered himself to block Trudeau's view. He lowered his voice and said, "I'll escort you to the back hallway, under the stairs, where you can meet your man. Make sure to walk in front of me so we don't elicit any unwanted attention."

I fought the urge to look back, but still managed to catch Viktor shift on his stool to my right.

"What about you?" I asked him. It felt like we were leaving one of our own behind in battle.

Leaving without Ric, Anson, Della, or Viktor felt wrong. The wolf pack always stuck together, and had always strived for peace. From time to time, we were dragged into other tribes' squabbles, but we lived by a code that supported the pack, not the individual.

"I will create a diversion if needed," Viktor answered in a Russian accent, a devious smile tilting his lips. Just before I turned to walk away, I noticed a set of sharp canine teeth peeking over his bottom lip.

I had sensed they were supernatural, but they didn't smell like wolves. The magic I'd felt in the air around Viktor and Gabriel wasn't like Anson or Della either. They were vampires. I'd never met one before, and in a matter of seconds, I'd become friends with two. They hadn't seemed like any of the rumors I'd heard, natural enemies, and that made leaving with Gabriel less tense. I'd sensed there was no reason to distrust them.

"After you," Gabriel whispered and waved a hand out in front of him.

I walked along the staircase, under the shadow it cast, trying to stay unnoticed. A small doorway was disguised by the mahogany paneling. Gabriel reached his arm around me and pulled a lever hidden within the woodwork. The door opened, and I ducked inside. Gabriel didn't follow me, so I didn't get the chance to thank him.

"Hello," I called out in a whisper, squinting to see down the dimly lit hallway. My heightened ability to see in the dark kicked in, and I found myself alone. The low ceiling had me hunched over, and the wood-paneled walls made the space feel closed in, like I was confined inside a box.

It didn't take long before a sliver of light appeared across the floorboards as someone opened the door behind me. My body reacted instinctively, pressing against the wall. My muscles tensed, and I held my breath.

"Gaby," Ric said in a whisper, after the light disappeared. "Anson told me he'd meet us around back in a few minutes."

I stepped into the middle of the small hallway and nodded at Ric, knowing his eyes had had enough time to adjust. As I turned toward the exit, I felt Ric reach for me. His hand grazed my hip before latching onto my wrist and pulling me back to him. He enveloped me in an embrace, wrapping his muscular arms around my shoulders.

"I wanted to rush to you when I realized those men were vampires," he said into my hair as he leaned into me. "If it weren't for Anson's magic holding me in place, I might have attacked them and given us all away to Trudeau."

"Gabriel and Viktor were very helpful," I said, pulling back to face Ric. He'd wanted to protect me, but Ric needed to know our assumptions about vampires weren't accurate. "In any other situation, I think they'd be a handful, but they're friends with Anson. So I trusted them."

Ric searched my face. He slid his hands up to my neck, and his eyes stopped on my mouth. He leaned in, and his forehead pressed against mine. He waited for me. As annoyed as I was, I couldn't withhold my affection any longer.

I pushed up on my toes and gave in to my desire. I kissed him. His lips accepted my attention, then began to beg for more. I could taste the sarsaparilla on his breath. He kissed my bottom lip and left a trail of soft kisses across my jawline as he nestled his face into my hair. Ric's hands slowly traveled down my arms and lingered at my waist, pulling me closer. We fit together. He belonged in my arms, and I belonged in his.

Lost in the moment, triggered by extreme circumstances, I'd been distracted when the secret door leading to the hallway lurched open. It wasn't until the light revealed us that I realized we'd been found out.

1860

"Eww," Conall exclaimed, his face contorting as if he'd bitten into a lemon. "Momma! I don't wanna hear a story about kissing!"

"I'm sorry, sweetheart," I said trying to calm him. "But your daddy and I love each other, so sometimes we kiss. Is that enough storytelling for the night?"

Conall frowned as he took in my words. He hadn't wanted the story to end, but maybe I could convince him to let us finish it the next day. He took my hand in his and looked at Ric.

"I want you to love each other, but can you not talk about the kissing?" Conall's eyebrow lifted in question, the same way his father's did. Both too cute to say no to. "Please, tell me it was Trudeau at the door," he said mischievously.

"What?" I asked in a reprimanding tone. "How could you *want* it to be Trudeau? You have to know it would make him mad."

Conall's enthusiasm faded, and he fiddled with the edge of his blanket. "I just figured this is the part when Daddy has a shootout and beats the bad guy."

I looked at Ric, and my brows furrowed. I couldn't believe his nerve. Ric had been telling the story completely wrong. He'd been lying to our boy. I felt my teeth grate together.

Ric slipped his hand over mine, and said, "Conall, I may have stretched the truth a little when I told you the story before."

I squeezed Ric's hand.

"In fact, I might have told you the story the way I wished it would have gone," Ric added uncomfortably.

I squeezed his hand harder.

Ric glanced at me, then tried again, "Conall, I lied."

I released his hand.

"But why would you lie to me Daddy?" Conall asked with round, curious eyes.

Ric rubbed his chin, thinking through his answer, then he said, "You know how you think shootouts are cool?"

Conall nodded.

"Well, I do too. And, honestly, I've never been in one," Ric said, his voice soft and full of remorse. "I've always wanted to be in a faceoff, like your mommy."

Conall's wide eyes moved from Ric to me. I couldn't tell if Conall believed what Ric told him, but he seemed impressed by the idea. As a mother, the last thing I wanted was for my son to think of me as a murderer. I'd never heard Ric tell his version of the story.

"Momma, will you *please* finish telling me the story?" Conall said sweetly. "I want to be just like you when I grow up."

Conall had always wanted to be like his daddy. I'd never considered he'd ever want to be like me. The notion was more intimidating to me than facing off with Trudeau ever had been.

CHAPTER 8

1820

*B*enedicte Trudeau snarled at us. He barged into the hallway and took Ric by the shirt. Each of us had been startled. Ric and I were frozen in shock at being discovered, and Trudeau was enraged at the realization that we were not brother and sister. Before Ric could find his strength, Trudeau pulled him out into the open.

"Look at what I've found," Trudeau's voice was rough. He pushed Ric away from him, into a table. "This *dog* was taking advantage of a lady."

Most of the men in the room laughed. I recognized Anson and Della, still sitting at the table near the stairs. The vampires were nowhere to be seen, but I felt dark magic centered around Trudeau and growing stronger. I hadn't felt that much power in one place since meeting the Howe family, but their magic felt pure and light. Whether the power came from one source, Trudeau, or if it emanated from more than one supernatural in the room was something I'd have to figure out quickly.

"I say we put this *dog* down," Trudeau spat out loudly.

I shoved a few men to the side and stood between Ric and

Trudeau. I declared, "If anyone's going to be put down tonight, it's you."

A few people snickered, but Trudeau glared at the crowd forming, and they fell in line. Ric regained his footing, but still appeared to be shaken. He took my hand, and two things happened. Trudeau's head tilted, confused by something. And Ric's skin rippled as he fought the urge to shift.

"What are you?" Trudeau addressed me with a sneer, looking disgusted.

I recalled the stone tucked into my sash, and realized Trudeau couldn't see or feel that I was a wolf shifter. He clearly knew Ric was a wolf, considering all the dog jokes, but the talisman had protected my identity. I'd wondered if by holding Ric's hand the stone's power guarded him too.

So to test my theory, I let Ric's hand go.

"I am someone you can't control," I answered him with boldness.

Trudeau's face lightened, almost amused, and he looked from me to Ric. His maniacal laugh echoed through the room, and Ric crumpled to the floor. Everyone in the saloon joined Trudeau's laughter, but I noticed a few people, supernaturals, slip out of the room scared, including Anson and Della.

I scrambled to where Ric lay on the floor and kneeled down beside him. I placed a hand on his shoulder, and within the span of a second or two, I noticed him recovering from whatever dark magic Trudeau had used to hurt him.

"I'm not sure how you're doing it," Trudeau said gruffly, not much louder than a whisper, and his eyes shifted to Ric. "There's more than one way to rid this town of a backwoods liar like you."

Trudeau tucked the front of his jacket behind his sidearm and hooked his thumb in a belt loop. The gesture was relaxed, but he meant it as a threat. He may not be able to use his power to hurt Ric while in my reach, but I couldn't stop a bullet.

"Trudeau, you can put that away," I warned with a scowl. "We'll get out of St. Louis. We'll leave."

I turned and helped Ric to his feet. The movement made a few men flinch around us. They all kept eyes on Trudeau, either out of fear or for permission to act. Some had sidearms, and I sensed more dark paranormal power emanating from others.

"Oh, I expect you both to walk out those doors, but the only way your *brother* will be leaving St. Louis is in a coffin," Trudeau said with an ugly grin and a New Orleans drawl.

"I'd like to see you try to tame the likes of me," Ric provoked. He squared his shoulders and broadened his chest.

Trudeau ignored the attempt at intimidation, and his eyes examined my red dress from its hem to the lace at my shoulders, then moved to the hat I wore. It all belonged to him, and he saw me the same way—a possession.

He looked at Ric, who was smiling defiantly.

"I plan on shooting that smirk right off your face," Trudeau said and nodded to the swinging front doors. "Why don't you meet me outside?"

The crowd around us cheered their consent with awe and a few rowdy hoorahs.

When I looked back at Ric, the eagerness in his wide eyes surprised me. And the determination in his clenched jaw angered me. Then he had the audacity to take a step forward, between Trudeau and me, like he was planning to take the gunslinger on. The only problem was, Trudeau could use his magic to control Ric, making it easier for him to shoot his target.

My hidden talisman would give me an advantage, and the idea of facing off with me might be enough to distract Trudeau. I hated to use my magical influence as alpha to order any of the pack members around, especially Ric, but in this case, it would be the only way to save my mate's life.

"I'll meet you outside, Trudeau," I teased with a wink and nodded behind him.

The room exploded with laughter.

Trudeau chuckled, and when I started for the swinging doors, he waved his hands at the crowd to calm them. After the noise settled into a low hum, he said, "Darlin', you can't be serious. A lady like yourself?"

"I never introduced myself as a lady. You decided to dress me up like one." I picked up my skirt to reveal my boots under the beautiful gown he'd insisted I wear. "Who wants to lend me their gun?" I asked over my shoulder as I stepped onto the boardwalk.

Ric followed behind me, and by the time I'd walked out into the street, a few dozen men and women had filed out of the saloon. I inspected the street and saw Della and Anson in between two buildings, watching the events unfold from a distance. Trudeau flung the saloon doors open, and the bystanders stepped out of the way as if guided by an invisible force. A dark green flicker of magic danced across Trudeau's fingers at his side. I quickly turned to Ric and found him buckling at the waist.

Trudeau was taking his frustration out on Ric.

"Get out of here," I ordered through gritted teeth, and I pushed him in the direction of Della and Anson. "Go! Get the supplies from Chouteau and take them to our family."

Ric cringed.

The words I'd spoken were emphasized with alpha magic. I'd known forcing Ric to leave would hurt him emotionally, not physically. But then he tried to fight against my instructions, and I saw a different kind of pain ripple across his face. A loud cry of agony erupted from him, and I shuddered. There was no way for me to know if it was Trudeau's magic or my own causing him such discomfort.

"Go!" I yelled, and Ric turned and ran.

A thud at my feet startled me. I looked down to find a black leather gun belt. The holster contained a wooden-handled pistol with a silver barrel. I hoped it was loaded, because I'd never handled a gun before. Slowly, I knelt down and picked it up, then buckled the belt around my waist while watching Trudeau stroll to the middle of the dirt road.

"It would seem you need a real man to show you what it means to act like a lady," Trudeau said, and he pulled a cigar out of his coat pocket and tucked it in the corner of his mouth.

The people around us buzzed with curiosity. I, myself, didn't know what Trudeau was up to. He pulled out a match and struck it with a snap of his fingers. After lighting his cigar, he discarded the flame, and pulled out his pistol.

I knew then, he still planned to use his gun.

"Since you're no man and I have no plans to pursue being a lady, how about you tell me the rules to this little game," I challenged and took the pistol out of my holster, turning it over in my hands.

A few people snickered from the sidewalk, but the street grew quiet waiting for Trudeau to reply. He puffed his cigar and carefully released the smoke from his mouth in small circles. He had enjoyed dragging the encounter out. He was as entertained as any of the onlookers.

"The fast draw could be fun, but if you want to stand a chance, a duel would be a better choice," he said, sliding his gun back into its holster.

I mirrored his actions, and secured my sidearm. I created a little more distance between us, sliding back two paces, then asked, "Will you hurry up and decide?"

Some of the people watching shouted out their preference, most eager for the drama of a duel. Trudeau tilted his head up to face the starry night sky, but closed his eyes. His lips tightened and spread thin in deliberation. At first, I figured he'd call the whole thing off. It wasn't until I heard the click of his thumb pulling back the hammer of his pistol that I understood he meant to follow through with his production.

My boots kicked up a small cloud of dirt as I shuffled another step back. My hand shook as it hovered over my sidearm. I grazed my thumb over the hammer and struggled to pull it back. My hesitation hadn't been about the act of killing. I'd defended myself and our pack, and killed men in the process. The difference was that in hand-to-hand combat, I knew I had control. With a gun, the power of the weapon was too easily mistaken for control.

Trudeau had made a similar mistake using his power to control.

His mind made up, Trudeau shook his head madly and met my gaze. His mouth spread into a maniacal smile, and he said, "I don't think I've had this much fun since I left New Orleans. Everyone here is so easy." He flung a hand out and gestured to the crowd. A glittering spray of dark green magic fell over the townspeople, and they were dazzled.

I could feel Trudeau's evil intentions at work, manipulating everyone around him. Even the supernaturals had become pliable under his spell. I quickly surveyed my surroundings, hoping to find an opening. Running might be my only option, but I wouldn't take the chance unless I could find an escape leading away from the direction Ric had left. In the corner of my eye, I recognized Anson now leaning against a post on the opposite side of the street. I couldn't fathom how he'd moved there without me noticing.

"Don't get me wrong," Trudeau said, breaking my train of thought. "Not having others like us vying for position in town has made my plans proceed effortlessly. You would have made an excellent queen in my kingdom."

"That's where you've gotten me all wrong," I said, seeing the real Trudeau and the lengths he would go to prove himself, and keep his position. I cocked the hammer of my pistol back without wavering. "I'm no queen, nor sidearm for that matter. I'm a leader. And people don't follow me because I force them, but because I wouldn't ask them to go anywhere or do anything I wouldn't do first."

I didn't wait for Trudeau to make the first move, but I tugged the handle of my gun. The barrel slid out of its leather holster, and my finger found its way onto the trigger. I squeezed one eye shut, utilizing my heightened eyesight. I pointed the pistol at Trudeau's chest and pulled the trigger. The shot rang out loudly and was quickly followed by another. I hadn't seen Trudeau retrieve his weapon, but within a moment I felt its blow.

A sharp sting throbbed at the top of my arm. My body jerked, and the black hat I'd worn fell to the dirt.

I reacted before I could think too much about it, and I ran to where I'd last spotted Anson. When I reached the post, the man was gone. I glanced over my shoulder to find Trudeau grinning at me, untouched by the bullet I'd shot at him. He must have used his powers to avoid being hurt. There's no way my aim could have been that off.

"It seems you don't have much of a following anymore," he

taunted. "But I promise to find you, and eventually you'll see things my way." Trudeau straightened his jacket and made for his carriage.

"Psst." I heard someone behind me.

Anson stood behind the building in an alleyway. He waved me forward, and I didn't hesitate. Ignoring the pain, I ran as fast and hard as I could. My speed in human form didn't come close to how fast I sprinted as a wolf, but it was still impressive, considering the red gown I wore. It added fifteen pounds. Anson's eyes widened as I approached, and one corner of his mouth turned up.

"Follow me," he whispered.

CHAPTER 9

1820

$\mathcal{I}$ woke up on a hardwood floor. A sharp pain shot up into my shoulder from my gunshot wound. It had almost finished healing. I tried to turn toward the warmth an iron stove provided beside me and the muscles in my body spasmed. My hand moved to cover the wound and found it wrapped in a bandage.

"Ugh," I mumbled in a low, dry voice, willing my body to relax.

"Stay still," a female voice ordered sternly from a few feet away. The sound of clanking metal and sloshing water were followed by footsteps. "Here, drink this." Della came into view and knelt beside me.

Her long blond hair fell over her shoulder as she bent down to press a cool tin cup to my lips. She lifted the back of my head with her other hand and smiled when I took a sip. A stubborn wrinkle of worry remained between her eyebrows. I barely knew the woman, and couldn't tell if her concern was for me or herself.

I vaguely remembered following Anson through a maze of back streets and pathways, and meeting Della at a leaning shack near the river's edge. Her eyes had stared at my arm as I approached. A few feet away from the door, I paused, glanced down at my arm, and collapsed. I'd needed to shift to elicit my shifter magic and heal completely.

There was no way to be sure how long ago I'd passed out. Slender lines of light shone between the boards making up one wall and stretched across the floor. The air around us was crisp and chilly. I'd either woken up with the sun or slept through the day again. I didn't like the idea of either. Losing time meant Trudeau would have had the chance to make good on his promise to seek revenge.

The sound of someone entering the shack caught both Della's and my attention. Della's head snapped up. Her soft features had suddenly turned stony and cold. At the angle I faced, all I could see was brown, wooden walls and a black round stove with a pipe reaching up to the ceiling.

"It's me," Anson said, out of breath. "I found him."

Della released me and stood. Her eyes widened, and I heard someone clamber inside. She asked, "What were you thinking, bringing him here?"

At first, I feared they'd brought Trudeau to finish me off. But I hadn't felt the eerie darkness constantly surrounding him anywhere close. I did, on the other hand, sense something familiar.

My mate.

"Ric?" I asked, and my chest filled with hope. A tear welled up at the corner of my eye, and I bit my bottom lip waiting for his reply.

"I'm here," he said. He rushed to my side and pulled me into his lap. I noticed the gun belt I'd been wearing had been removed, when Ric wrapped his arms around me tightly.

"How?" I asked.

Ric shook his head, taking in the sight of my injury. "I'm not sure," he said solemnly. His eyes were sad and glassy. "One minute I was halfway out of town, unable to refuse your command. And the next minute, your power over me vanished. It was the worst feeling I'd ever experienced, worse than leaving you. It was like you were gone. Dead."

Ric closed his eyes and swallowed down his unease. I couldn't remember what happened after I'd fainted, but it must have been intense. Around us, I could sense Della and Anson moving around the room, avoiding us. The thud of piling items on the table and clank of pans being stacked made it clear they'd busied themselves, but I perceived they were listening in on our conversation.

"Did I die?" I asked loudly, and everyone came to a halt.

"Well," Anson said with some hesitation. "You may have gone a few moments without a heartbeat, but I worked a little of my healing magic. You're lucky it's my specialty." A chuckle lightened his voice as he moved closer to where I lay.

"After a few moments, you were back," Ric explained, sounding relieved. "You were, *are*, in my heart. Your authority as alpha is as strong as ever, but the magic behind the orders you gave me evaporated. They'd been like a wall I couldn't get around, and then I found myself turning and desperately searching for you."

"He was wandering around the Chouteaus' estate when I found him," Anson said sharply. "Foolish, since the whole family's under that voodoo priest's spell. Heck, the whole town's been manipulated by that scoundrel."

"How is it then that we haven't been taken in by him?" I asked, confused, and tried to sit up. Ric wrapped an arm around me and pulled me to lean against his body.

Anson answered, "Well, my magic protects me and my family. After we brought you here, I sent them to make camp with the pioneers along the outskirts of town. We all carry similar talismans to yours." He nodded to me, referring to the stone I had tucked into the fabric gathered at my waist. "Della fell under Trudeau's spell when she first arrived, but—"

"But," Della interrupted, "I came into my own powers recently, and somehow Trudeau can't get inside my head."

"Somehow?" Ric asked with suspicion. His brows furrowed, and he tightened his hold on me protectively.

Della moved across the room and sat on the floor next to us. She was young. Her bright green eyes and flawless skin weren't only perks of being a supernatural—she couldn't have been more than twenty years old. I flexed my own heightened abilities to find something familiar about her, but she didn't smell, look, or sound like anyone I'd ever met before. Her scent was earthy with a hint of floral. It was fresh. She didn't have sharp, elongated canines. And there wasn't a missing heartbeat, or an extra one, for that matter.

"I'm a sylph, a tree faerie," Della explained, and her hard exterior began to fall away. "When I turned eighteen, a few months ago, my supernatural hormones kicked in. See, most people think of fairies as little flying creatures who buzz around the forest. Sylphs are life givers and protectors. When we reach a certain age, we are called to root ourselves. It's kind of like settling down, but instead of building a house or starting a trade, I share my life force with a tree. Once I've chosen, I must unite with that tree every New Moon. I believe Trudeau's magic can't penetrate my mind because I have so much magic inside me. When I share my power with a chosen tree, he may have room to manipulate me. I've fought the urge for some time, but only because I'm afraid of what Trudeau could do to me or make me do. As long as the tree I choose lives, I will live. And the power I'll wield over nature could be used by Trudeau to exploit the river's flow or reshape the city's landscape."

"You're saying you have the power to make the water flow whatever direction you want?" I asked in awe.

"If the water saturates the roots of the tree I join my life force with, then yes." Della's eyes widened, amazed with the idea herself. "There are forests with trees connected by roots that span hundreds of miles, and my purpose would be to protect them. But being linked to them, I could just as easily destroy them under Trudeau's influence."

Being over a couple hundred years old myself, I'd been under the impression that I'd heard of everything. The only things that surprised me anymore were related to progress, not supernaturals. Della's abilities were like none I'd ever encountered. I was glad she wanted to use her magic for good.

Anson moved to stand behind Della, and said, "Trudeau doesn't know what Della is, and I intend to keep it that way." Anson's fatherly tone was protective, yet gentle.

"Why don't you come with us?" I asked Della, and looked up at

Anson for support. "We've settled in a remote canyon, and you could choose any tree in our forest. I have a feeling you'd flourish there, considering our water source."

"I don't want to leave Anson and his family," Della said sadly, and reached up for his hand. "They've helped me so much. If I disappear, I know Trudeau will suspect him."

"Nah—" Anson started, and attempted to wave her worry away.

"Yes, Trudeau would accuse you and use your wife and children against you. You know as well as I do, Trudeau wants power, and if he knew how much we all possessed, we'd be dead," Della said through clenched teeth. "I won't leave without you and your family."

I looked at Ric and realized he'd been watching me. Our connection as mates didn't mean we always agreed, and I could see the concern in Ric's eyes at what he knew I was about to do. My invitation to Della was one more mouth to feed, but Anson's family would be hard to explain to the pack. Especially since we didn't have any supplies to take back with us.

I couldn't, in good conscience, leave any of them behind.

I took a deep breath, mentally pushed through all the doubt that flooded my mind, and said, "You should all come with us."

Ric consented with a tight smile. I could tell he was worried, but I also knew in my heart he supported my decision. I examined Anson's face, and wondered why he hadn't met my proposal with a resounding yes. He twisted his mustache between his thumb and finger instead.

Della's eyes drifted from Anson to Ric and me. With a melancholy voice she said, "Maybe we should all split up. It would create better odds for each of us to escape St. Louis and lessen Trudeau's chances of catching us all."

She had a point.

"He wants me," I admitted, "or at least to figure me out and get his hands on our red gold. We all split up, but I'll set up a distraction and lead him in the opposite direction."

"No," both Ric and Anson said at the same time.

"Why not?" I argued, and pulled away from Ric. The movement sent a sharp pain down my arm, and I froze. "I can't go back to our pack without provisions, and the first snowfall will be soon. Maybe you'll cross paths with that trader, Jake, and he can give you something to take back."

Ric shook his head from side to side stubbornly. Anson's ornery expression, on the other hand, melted into acknowledgement. His mind had been processing all of the possibilities, and he'd come up with a plan.

"We will need to split up," he concurred, "but you won't be the distraction. I will. It's your red gold he wants. Just promise me you'll get my family as far away from Trudeau as you can."

Ric nodded, but something inside me rejected the notion and turned my stomach, like milk turning sour. Anson and I were alike in the sense that we would rather suffer the consequences on behalf of all our family members than have one go through pain. I wouldn't allow him to take on this burden.

"Other than the red gold, what makes you think Trudeau would follow you and not me?" I reasoned with them, hoping we could all agree on something soon. "He's been pursuing me since the moment he laid eyes on me. Until he catches me, I don't think there's anything—"

"Oh, there's something he wants more," Anson said with a grin. "He simply hasn't let on about it. That red gold you carry—it's called copper, and he knows that I can use its power to heal. In the past, I've refused to use my magic for his personal gain, but if he thinks I'll do whatever he wants, he may let the rest of you go."

I'd been so consumed with the building tension between Trudeau and myself that I hadn't considered why Anson consistently avoided the tyrant. I'd been counting on Anson and Della to help us out of St. Louis, but maybe they'd been depending on me, too. If my aim had been truer, and Trudeau's magic weaker, we could have all escaped. As hard as I'd tried, I couldn't think of a way to help them, help ourselves out of town, or solve our pack's dilemma.

Trudeau had each of us right where he wanted us. We couldn't escape this town or him without giving him exactly what he wanted. A low rumble of frustration vibrated in my chest.

I balled up my fist and rammed it into the hardwood floor. I was so mad at myself for not having the answers. The board splintered at my attack, and Ric snatched my hand up to check for an injury. As alpha, I should have been able to come up with solutions.

"Why'd you go and do that?" Ric asked, and he gently kissed my knuckles. "I know I've done my share of idiotic things since we left the settlement, but I think you'll be pleased to know that before Della found me, I collected all of our things from the Chouteau estate, even Wilhelmina, and hid them."

"Where?" I asked, careful not to get my hopes up.

One of the corners of Ric's mouth curved upward playfully, and he admitted, "On that doggone steamboat."

"What in tarnation were you thinkin', son?" Anson exclaimed, and he walloped Ric on the back of the head.

A low growl rumbled in Ric's chest. He barked, "I was thinking it'd be the last place that no-good reprobate would go lookin'."

"He's right," Della said, placing a hand on Anson's shoulder. "Trudeau will be turning this city inside out, but he wouldn't even consider searching his own property."

I leaned into Ric and kissed his cheek. He looked down at me and smiled, proud of himself. As I moved to stand, Ric hopped up and helped me to my feet carefully. We'd been going about everything separately since we left the falls, and the results were disheartening. When we depended on each other and did things together, our circumstances had a way of turning out more favorably. It was then that I realized my mate was my partner and everything in my life would only be better when I included him.

"I have an idea," I said with excitement. "We won't be splitting up, and Trudeau won't be getting his hands on our red gold. In fact, our best chance of us all getting out of St. Louis in one piece will be to stick together. Anson, can you get word to your family and have them meet us at the steamboat?"

CHAPTER 10

1820

*W*alking across town in broad daylight, without being recognized by one of Trudeau's informants, would have been impossible if it weren't for Anson's magic. Ric and I even considered shifting into our wolf forms, but Anson explained the transformation would have been registered by Trudeau. The only way Anson's magic hadn't been detected was because of talismans he and each of his family members wore, similar to the one I'd been carrying. He told us Trudeau was a voodoo priest, and he had a way of sensing supernatural activity within the city's borders.

We darted from one building to the next. When crossing the street, Anson mumbled enchantments to disguise us. The trek had been less than a mile, but the amount of magic Anson used to conceal us physically, as well as cloak our whereabouts from Trudeau, drained him. Ric had to carry Anson up the stairs when we made it to the steamboat. I concocted an explanation to the ship's crew for being on board, but convinced them Trudeau would be along any minute.

When I joined the others in the sitting room, Ric had placed Anson on the settee. I poured everyone a glass of water to stay busy, while Della kept watch for Anson's family. I raised the water glass to Anson's lips with a shaky hand. If we were going to escape St. Louis, we had to make our move quickly.

Magic had been used to communicate our meeting place with Anson's wife. I'd never met her, and I wondered if she was like Anson—supernatural. With his magic nearly drained, we could use another supernatural's help. But if I was being honest, the amount of power being used made me nervous.

"How are you feeling?" I asked Anson, but I knew his answer. Sweat beaded along his forehead, and his skin had grown pale.

"Weak," he croaked. "My family will be here soon. Please don't leave them."

"We wouldn't," I said and squeezed his hand.

Anson closed his eyes. Before I could panic, he squeezed my hand back.

I looked from Della to Ric and knew the next step in my plan was up to me. Della would work to get Anson's family settled, Ric would watch over Anson and be ready to defend us if anyone realized what we were up to, and I would figure out how to convince the pilot to take us down the Mississippi River. I had a feeling Trudeau would eventually discover we'd taken his boat, but I hoped he'd follow it all the way to New Orleans.

My plan was to abandon ship and travel back to our settlement through the Arkansas Territory. We could stop at Fort Smith for whatever supplies we could scrounge up before traveling through the area inhabited by the Choctaw people. Ric and I were familiar with how to camouflage ourselves among the natives. Once we reached the falls, their magic would protect us, and Trudeau wouldn't stand a chance of finding us.

"I'll need you to signal me when everyone is on board," I said to Ric.

He nodded, and I rushed up the stairs to the pilot house. The crew recognized me from the party, and they were willing to hear me out. But being accompanied by Della and Anson made them wary of my instructions to head south.

The small room perched at the top of the steamboat was made up of windows. We could see in every direction. A large wheel with spokes was mounted at one side for steering, tubes connecting the engine room protruded up through the floor with holes for communicating back and forth, and pedals were rigged to ring the ship's bell and activate the steam whistle.

The pilot paused when, in the distance, we saw a woman and four children running down the dock toward us. Their fast, panicked pace led me to two conclusions. First, someone must have been chasing Anson's family. Second, the pilot wouldn't be agreeing to do anything for me without a little extra enticement.

"I have gold," I said, not bothering with the niceties. "There's enough for you and your men to get out from under Trudeau's thumb and make something of your own."

The man, tall and lanky, looked down at me and narrowed his beady eyes. If he didn't accept my bribe, we'd have to devise a Plan D. There wasn't much time for him to decide or for us to run. Three seconds felt like an eternity.

Thundering footsteps pounded on the stairs, and Ric appeared in the doorway. He looked from me to the pilot, then growled, "We're ready."

I lifted a hand to stop Ric, and the pilot took a step back. Pivoting to turn to the pedals, the pilot pressed one and a loud whistle blew. Ric lunged for him, and I jumped between them. The whistle had been identical to the sharp sound I'd heard at the party before we took off.

And, as I'd predicted, the giant wheel at the back of the boat began to churn. The steamboat lurched forward, and white clouds exited the smokestacks. Before I could sigh with relief, a group of men came into view, all carrying guns. At least ten men filed out from around the Chouteau estate and marched across the street to the river bank. Behind them, I recognized Trudeau yelling orders with hands raised in the air. Sparks of green swirled around him, like a storm.

I could sense his anger.

There was no way to know if his power could reach us, so I ordered the pilot to keep moving. Gunshots were fired, and the sound of shattering glass echoed from below us. We all ducked down and headed for the cover of the staircase. It wasn't long before the men on shore ran out of ammo. Once the fear of being shot again was removed, I noticed the steamboat had stopped moving.

The engines sounded as if they were working at full strength, but to no advantage. I rushed to the top of the stairs and peeked out of a window to find Trudeau's green sparks of dark magic surrounding the boat. The river below us flowed naturally, but the current wasn't carrying us away. We had to do something to keep Trudeau from using his magic.

"Ric, we need to stop him," I said, unnerved.

The problem was, the only thing I'd come into contact with that could block his power was a stone the size of a silver dollar. I rubbed my hand along my sash, and my fingers felt the bump where I'd hidden the smooth black stone. When I'd carried the talisman, Trudeau's magic couldn't take hold. I wondered what would happen to Trudeau if it were to have been on his person or even touched his skin. Would he have been able to project his magic past himself?

I had the craziest notion, and raced to get to Anson and ask what he thought. Ric followed close behind me, and when we reached the sitting room, Anson was surrounded by his family. His wife sat at his side, holding his hand. His daughter had curled up in his lap. And three boys, all the spitting image of Anson, stood around him protectively.

The idea of having so many to love, and love me, warmed my soul. It also ripped my heart out, knowing I was the reason they were in danger.

"Anson, I hate to interrupt, but are you still wearing your gun belt?" I asked from the doorway. I glanced out of the broken windows to the river's edge where Trudeau stood. Della was keeping a close eye on him as well.

Anson nodded, and lifted his daughter to sit in her mother's lap. "You remember what happened the last time you tried to shoot him?"

"I do," I answered, "but I don't think his magic will work on the bullet I'm planning to shoot him with." I fidgeted with the fabric at my waist.

Anson's head tilted to the side.

Della moved from the window to join us, and looked at me knowingly. She said, "It's a brilliant idea, but I think we'll need a shotgun." She left the room and headed down the stairs.

Anson still looked confused, along with his family.

"What are you getting at?" Ric asked from behind me.

I turned to face my mate, and revealed the stone tucked away in the folds of my sash. "This." I held the talisman up in the air.

"Oh," Anson began with realization. "That is brilliant, and it just might work."

"Do you really think it could stop him?" Ric asked, and he reached out to take the stone. He turned it over in his hand carefully, then gave it back to me.

I squeezed it tight, and wished it would destroy Trudeau, but deep down, I knew it would take more to rid him and St. Louis of dark magic. Trudeau's magic was strong and ancient. No matter how many people he had power over, the darkness controlled him. He was merely a vessel.

I admitted, "I think it could give us enough time to get away. And Della's right. We need a shotgun, but we also need the perfect shot."

"I believe I can help with both," Della said as she entered the room with confidence and a rifle propped up over her shoulder.

My chin fell. I gawked at her as she moved to the window and knocked the jagged glass away. Della got down on one knee and braced the stock against her leg while she used the hinge to open the two barrels. I walked over and handed her the stone.

"It's not like a bullet," Anson said. "How are you going to get it to fire?"

"I have an idea for that," Della answered, and pulled a brass shotgun shell out of her pocket. She picked at one end of the cartridge and poured the shots into her hand, then replaced them with the stone. After loading the shotgun, she closed the break, and it clicked. She braced the stock against her shoulder as she took aim.

"What part of him are you planning to hit?" Anson asked, and stood to get a better look outside. Men were running to the dock with belts of ammo.

We didn't have much time before Trudeau's lackeys would reload and start shooting at us again. I didn't care where Della shot him, but the stone needed to make contact if we wanted to limit his power. If she could hit him, embedding the stone inside him, the talisman might block his magic entirely.

"I'm gonna aim for his chest," Della answered. "That way if I'm slightly off, there's a better chance of him still being hit. It won't be lethal, because he can probably heal himself to some extent, but it'll hurt like hell."

Della hunched over and pressed her cheek to the stock. She cocked the hammer and took aim. We were over a hundred yards away.

I inhaled and waited.

The noise around us fell away.

Ric reached over and took my hand.

Della pulled the trigger, and the sound of her shot rang in my ears.

In the distance, Trudeau reached for his upper thigh. The dark magic surrounding the steamboat seemed to dissolve, and I felt the ship moving with the current immediately. Trudeau cursed at us, and the men around him looked around like they'd woken up from a bad dream. They scattered, leaving Trudeau to wallow in his failure to stop us.

If my theory was correct, Trudeau wouldn't be able to use magic until he removed the stone from his leg. He'd also walk with a limp for the rest of his days, thanks to Della hitting her target.

"How'd you learn to shoot like that?" I asked.

"A girl's gotta know how to protect herself," Della teased and smiled up at me.

CHAPTER 11

1820

*W*e spent two days on the river. The crew took their compensation and continued toward New Orleans, and we had to travel by foot to Fort Smith. My first course of action when we reached land was to change into my trousers. Luckily, Ric had not only gathered our belongings, but enough provisions for the three-week trip home. Considering it would take at least a week to make it to Fort Smith, and we'd added seven people to our party, our rations would get us to the trading post. Then, we'd need to restock.

Traveling with the others was uncomfortable at first. Ric and I had wanted to scout ahead in our wolf form, but we hadn't ever shifted in front of anyone but our pack. We all took turns carrying supplies, except Anson's youngest. She skipped ahead and hummed a tune.

It wasn't until our fourth day on the trail that I heard a wild animal in the distance. To ensure everyone's safety, Ric offered to shift and travel ahead. He opted to undress and make the transition in private. Then he bounded off the trail, and I walked with the others until he came back that night. We'd made camp, and I heard Ric's thoughts reach mine.

We don't have to worry about an animal attack.

I was tempted to shift into my wolf form, but I'd volunteered to be on the lookout while the others rested. Ric could communicate his thoughts to me, but being in my human form meant I had to speak out loud to him.

"You didn't find anything?" I whispered out into the woods behind me.

Ric stepped out from behind a tree and inspected the area. Everyone appeared to be asleep, but the last thing we needed was for one of the children to be scared of wolf-Ric. I nodded for him to come join me, and he cautiously crept around the sleeping family. He curled up next to me, radiating a welcome heat.

I found an old friend. The fur trader we met on our way to St. Louis, Jacob Martin. He took care of the mountain lion we heard earlier.

My eyes widened in surprise.

"Is he hauling supplies?" I asked with a lilt of optimism, and quickly covered my mouth with my hand. I didn't want to wake anyone up.

He is, and if we get going early enough, we can catch up to him in the morning and travel together to Fort Smith. There should be room in the wagon for the children.

The news was a relief. My body relaxed into the tree I leaned against, and my eyelids became heavy. The scent of our campfire lulled me to sleep. It wasn't until the sun peeked over the horizon, filling the sky with hues of pink and orange, that I woke up. Ric was gone, and everyone was stirring.

"Good morning," Della greeted in a sing-song voice as she secured her bedroll with a leather tie. "Ric said something about getting an early start, so we're going to eat dried meat for breakfast while we walk. You'd better get going."

Della nodded down at my bag. The contents had been strewn over the ground, but I noticed Ric's clothes missing. He must have shifted back into his human form. As I finished stuffing everything back inside, Ric stepped out from behind the tree I'd slept against, dressed. He took the bag from me and smiled. After everything we'd been through, he didn't look fazed. His blue eyes were bright, his shirt clean, and even the scruff lining his jaw looked good.

When I stretched, my joints popped and my muscles ached. Coffee would have been welcome. I could feel the bags under my eyes, and my hair was tangled. I frowned and asked Ric, "What?"

"Here, let me help you up," Ric said and reached his hand to me. He pulled me up slowly. "You look beautiful this morning."

I tilted my head to the side and furrowed my brows. He must have wanted something. Or maybe he'd done something. I decided to shrug my suspicion off and thanked him for his compliment. We needed to start moving if we wanted to reach Jake.

Ric encouraged us to push through lunch, and it wasn't long after noon that I made out Jake's wagon in the distance. He'd paused to enjoy some pickled eggs, and at the sight of our group, he gathered his reins and rode back to meet us halfway. His shotgun still looked to be his closest friend, and the liquid in his jar of hard boiled eggs sloshed over the side as he slowed his wagon.

Jake jumped down, and his spring bench squealed with delight.

"Well, I'll be," Jake exclaimed with a grin at the sight of Ric and me. "I'm as pleased as a pup with two tails to run into y'all. That nugget y'all left me was too generous."

He inspected our party with his hands on his hips. First, he took in the large family. He reach up to grab his jar and handed the eggs to Anson, encouraging them to eat. Then his eyes landed on Della. Jake straightened his shirt and squared his shoulders.

"You were the generous one," I replied, and stepped in the way of his line of sight to Della. "And we could surely use your help now. We're headed to Fort Smith for supplies."

"It is serendipitous we found each other," Jake said with a little more refinement than I'd heard him speak with before. "I'm headed to Fort Smith, and I'd be delighted if you good people would join me."

He tipped his hat in Della's direction, and I could have sworn she blushed at his gesture.

We traveled two days together before we rode into town. Della sat with Jacob at the front of his wagon most of the time, and Anson's wife and children piled into the back. Every now and then, Ric or I would excuse ourselves and shift to explore the trail ahead. We had no desire to stay at Fort Smith for long, but when we arrived, everyone else was excited to be in the hustle and bustle of town.

It was the first week of November, and it would be impossible to get through the mountains if we waited much longer. We knew the Rockies would be covered in snow by the first of December, and our journey to the falls would be physically demanding. It would be freezing. In addition to supplies, we would need blankets and skins to stay warm.

I had one gold nugget left, and the rest of our trading would have to be done with red gold. The idea of using the red gold scared me, because if Trudeau caught news of it, he'd come asking questions. We didn't have the luxury of time, so we had to make a decision about how to proceed in a day or two. Otherwise, we may not make it back to the settlement at all.

"Anson, have you considered our invitation?" Ric asked between spoonfuls of stew.

The magic-wielding cowboy nodded his head. He flattened his mustache out with a hand, covering his mouth. I couldn't tell if he was still considering it or avoiding giving us his answer. So I shoved some stew in my mouth and waited for his answer.

"Whatever you decide, it should be what you think is best for your family," Ric encouraged his new friend, and patted his back.

Anson scraped the bottom of his tin bowl with his spoon, and said, "Since you put it that way, I should shoot straight with ya and admit I have reservations. I mean, I don't want you thinking we don't appreciate everything you've done for us. But my ancestors haven't had much luck establishing towns."

The problem wasn't the Corey family or the Kasun pack, but it was supernaturals and humans trying to control each other. I couldn't argue with Anson, because he'd lost some of his loved ones in Salem, and he almost lost the rest of them in St. Louis. Trudeau would have killed them all to get what he wanted.

"If you don't go with us, you have to let us help you somehow," I reasoned, and pulled out a few of the red gold nuggets. "You'll have to be careful trading with these so Trudeau doesn't find you."

Anson started to shake his head, refusing the gift.

"You must take them," Ric encouraged sternly. "It's the only way we'll be able to move on without you in good conscience."

I leaned forward with my hand outstretched. Anson was hesitant, but he finally took them. The red gold sandwiched between our palms glowed. I pulled away, and the shining copper color dulled.

"What was that?" Della asked, sitting down next to me.

"What was what?" Jake asked from behind her. "I missed it."

"Oh, nothing," I answered. "We were just discussing plans to move on tomorrow, but Anson and his crew are thinking about sticking around here."

"Well, I'll be replenishing my inventory, since you bought everything including my wagon," Jake said, rolling his eyes teasingly, like he'd been put out by it.

The rest of us chuckled, but Jake couldn't take his eyes off Della when she smiled. He'd been doting on her since they met. Della was cautious, even shy, but I could tell she'd taken a liking to Jake, too.

Ric started talking to Jake about possible trails we could take and the weather, so I took the opportunity to check in with Della.

"Della," I called softly, trying to broach the topic gently. "I know you've always wanted to explore the continent. And you're more than welcome to travel with us to the Rockies. It's just, I was thinking, if Jake has to restock, he'll be setting out for places you've dreamed of visiting."

"That's true," she agreed bashfully, "but I'll have to join life forces with a tree soon."

"You will, but maybe instead of picking any old tree you could find the tree you were meant to be with." I winked at her and glanced at Jake, hoping she caught my meaning.

"After meeting Jake, I don't think any old tree will ever do," Della admitted and tucked a strand of hair behind her ear.

At the sound of his name or simply the sound of Della's voice, Jake perked up and gave Della his full attention. "Did you need me?" he asked.

She just smiled and nodded.

THE FIRST WEEK of traveling through Arkansas Territory was a breeze compared to the following two weeks. The temperatures in the mountains were thirty degrees cooler, and the air was thinner. Our wagon held together as we drove through creeks and around plateaus. The horses were tired, but we were careful not to work them too hard.

The first week of December we arrived in Kasun Pack territory, and a dusting of snow covered the frozen ground. I'd expected to be ankle-deep in the powder. As we approached the settlement, the Gregs waited for us at the tree line, having been on patrol.

"Gaby, Ric," Helena called out in surprise at the sight of us. "It is so good to see you both. We weren't sure if you'd make it back."

"Why do you say that?" I asked, and grinned at Ric.

Helena shrugged and bit her bottom lip. Her mate, Boris, answered in a gruff voice, "We thought you were dead."

"Oh, well, I'm not," I said, nervous about what we could be walking into if everyone thought I'd died in St. Louis. "How have things been here?"

"Miserable," Boris answered honestly.

"Interesting," Helena said at the same time, trying to soften the blow.

Ric and I laughed. Things hadn't changed that much while we were gone. There were definitely a few pack members pushing the boundaries I'd set. And we found out the whole pack felt my absence as alpha like Ric had after I was shot. It seemed, for the past four weeks, the Novaks and Horvats had given everyone a glimpse of what their lives would be like if I weren't alpha.

So when we pulled the wagon in front of our cabin, we were welcomed by most of the pack with hugs and kind words. They were genuinely happy to see us, and the pile of supplies gave everyone hope we'd survive the winter months.

Once everyone went back to their cabins, Ric and I decided to take a walk. We'd bundled up, and as we made the trek to the falls, I appreciated everything familiar about the canyon we called home.

A cold mist stung my cheeks as we walked around the pool at the bottom of the falls. I paused to take it all in, and Ric came behind me and wrapped his arms around my shoulders. I took a deep breath, and the cold, damp air burned inside my lungs.

"You did it," Ric said, proud of me.

"No, *we* did it," I replied, and turned to face him. Ric pulled me closer, and I no longer thought of the brisk air or magical water. I only thought of him. I tilted my chin up and pressed my lips to his.

EPILOGUE

1860

"The End," I whispered, and pressed a kiss to Conall's forehead. His blinks started growing longer after I told him Trudeau was shot. And he fell asleep around the part when Jake joined back up with us, but I couldn't not finish.

"I think I like your version better." Ric winked at me as he tucked Conall's quilt under his legs. "But since he fell asleep, you could have described that kiss in more detail."

I swatted at Ric's arm playfully, and said, "The true story is way better than that pack of lies you've been telling him."

We tiptoed out of the room, and once in the hallway, Ric turned to face me. He leaned down and wrapped his arms around me. I ran my fingers through his wavy, black hair and noticed a smudge of dirt under his ear. I tried to wipe it away, but it wouldn't budge.

"You still have dirt all over you," I said with furrowed brows, examining his neck and arms for more.

"I know a way to fix that," Ric grinned and scooped me up, startling me. He carried me through the kitchen, where pots of water were being heated on the stove. He set me down in front of the back door and asked, "It's not too late for a bath, is it?"

~

We hope you enjoyed this story in the Legends of Havenwood Falls series featuring a variety of supernatural creatures. The series is a collaborative effort by multiple authors.

Books in the historical Legends of Havenwood Falls series:

Lost in Time by Tish Thawer
Dawn of the Witch Hunters by Morgan Wylie
Redemption's End by Eric R. Asher
Trapped Within a Wish by Brynn Myers
Blood and Damnation by Belinda Boring
Fated Beginnings by E.J. Fechenda
Emeline by Katie M. John
Released From a Curse by Brynn Myers
A Pack of Lies by Kallie Ross
Kiss the Ashes by Desiree Lafawn
Hidden Truths by Colleen Nye
War and Retribution by Belinda Boring
Changing Fate by Char Webster

Also try the signature New Adult/Adult series, Havenwood Falls, and the YA series, Havenwood Falls High
Stay up to date at www.HavenwoodFalls.com

Subscribe to our reader group and receive free stories and more!

ABOUT THE AUTHOR

Writing unique adventures with heart.

Kallie Ross has a passion for writing that has become an adventure in itself. She desires to create unique young adult fiction that incorporates legend, conjecture, fantasy, and conviction.

In addition to loving her life as a writer, Kallie adores being a wife, mother, friend, and teacher. She began her creative journey with books, a blog, a podcast, and lots of caffeine. Ross never imagined her own adventure would be filled with so many wonderful people or words!

KallieRoss.com

@KallieRoss {Instagram & Twitter}

Kallie Ross Books {Facebook}

ACKNOWLEDGMENTS

Thank you, Kristie Cook, for trusting me with this *legend*. Ric Kasun is a pillar in the Havenwood Falls community and writing a small piece of his history has been a blast. I couldn't have finished this story without Gaby Robbins's friendship. She is just as inspirational as Gaby Kasun, and definitely more fierce when it comes to her family and friends. Jessica Gibson was also a huge support and encouragement.

My family is always supportive of my writing, and I am truly grateful for that blessing. Whether I'm hashing out an outline over breakfast or talking through a scene in car line, my husband and kids always speak into my storytelling.

Lastly, I want to thank the Havenwood Falls readers. Your enthusiasm for this world keeps me dreaming up stories and writing them down. Thank you!

AN EXCERPT

~ A Legends of Havenwood Falls Novella ~

HAVENWOOD FALLS LEGENDS

KISS THE ASHES

DESIREE LAFAWN

Kiss the Ashes (A Legends of Havenwood Falls Novella) by Desiree Lafawn

Mocked, ridiculed, and sentenced to death, seven-year-old River is saved from the noose when the Sisters McNee find her. They take her to their home in Havenwood Falls, a place for people like her to live safely, without fear of persecution. But what if the threat to their safety is River herself?

Her fire-maiden origins are a mystery. One a child has no hope of explaining. Then one futuristic vision from a well-respected member of the community seals her fate.

Flames.

Chaos.

Complete destruction.

Sixteen years later, River has come of age in the era of prosperity, prohibition, and ragtime music—and even as an adult, she still hates her power, resolute to never use it again. She tries to stay under the radar, but there is no hiding from the penetrating eyes of Jonas Pederson. Despite repeated warnings that she is dangerous, he won't stop pursuing her until she understands that he can easily survive her flames—even if he needs to show her his own well-protected secret.

It might be too late for River, though, when a threat from the past ignites that horrible vision.

Flames.

Chaos.

Destruction.

In the end, it will all be ashes.

KISS THE ASHES

I would never get used to hard-soled shoes even as an adult, but as a girl of seven I hated them. I'd much rather have gone barefoot, but the teachers in Carlisle were adamant the children properly dress themselves at all times. Dressed according to their standards, anyway. Our parents stood opposed even as the soldiers dragged us from the reservation.

"Who are you to take our children?" they cried out, unable to do more than shake their fists and stomp their feet; our once proud nation reduced to servants of a government foreign to us. A government so hell-bent on erasing our existence they uprooted the native children and forced them into boarding schools to learn the English way. Eliminate the savages and teach the children to be productive members of society.

Kill the Indian. Save the man.

Even now, many years later and grown, I have trouble wrapping my mind around the thought process that led to the exodus of the children—the reeducation process. But that had happened. And the history books will more than likely gloss it over the more time marches on, but I will never forget being five years old and plucked from the small plot of land I considered my home.

Parents wept.

But not my parents. They died of the great sickness a year before. I had no parents to hold me in their arms as the soldiers came and separated us. No one fought for me, so when the time came to leave— aside from dragging my heels in the dirt—nothing stopped the soldiers from putting me on the wagon, squeezing me up against the rows of other crying, terrified children.

But I was different. If they knew how different, would they have placed me with the other children? Would they have taken me? There was no way to know, and I wouldn't explain because I had learned long ago that *my* kind of different was best kept hidden. Even from my own people.

So to the Carlisle Indian Industrial School I went, sandwiched in with many other children from mixed tribes, all learning to speak English and change everything about themselves. The administration beat the students who cried, and the angry, rebellious ones received a harsher punishment. One so severe, we feared talking about it amongst ourselves—because those students left without warning and didn't come back. But I didn't cry, and I didn't rebel. I obeyed, because I knew no other way. And there I lived for two years, suffering at the hands of my oppressors under the guise of spiritual cleansing until the summer of my seventh year.

I made a mistake.

It was playtime in the yard. That short time of day between morning chores and evening chores when there was a small sliver of space to remember that we were just children. It was my favorite time, and every chance I thought I could get away with it, I'd chuck my shoes under the shade of a white oak tree and curl my toes in the grass. Not running, not moving, just standing in place, anchored to the earth. Eyes closed, I stood under the tree with my arms raised out to the sides, feeling the wind above and below me.

The Great Thunder is near, I thought to myself, smelling the rain on the wind. *I wonder what mischief the Thunder Boys will be up to tonight.*

The Great Thunder and his sons were a myth, and I dared not speak of it out loud, not when the teachers could hear. Speaking the stories of my people was forbidden and the punishment severe. But since no one controlled what went on in my head, I would think as I pleased.

"Come back here, Thomas," a voice shouted angrily, interrupting my peaceful moment. "You've stolen the bread; we know you have. Come receive your punishment."

A small brown blur came running across the packed dirt yard, and children of various ages stopped mid-play to see the boy running with the bit of bread locked in his fist. He came to a screeching halt about fifteen feet from where I stood, under my oak tree, and facing off like a boxer, he scowled at his aggressor.

I recognized the boy from my old village. I remembered when his mother had clung to him and the soldiers yanked him, only a year younger than myself, from her grieving arms. They'd given him a new name when he'd come to this school, just as they'd done me, but I knew his real name was Wesa. I knew because his mother had screamed it to the sky as they had taken away the children.

Wesa. Two years he'd been here, knowing the rules. And still he stole the bread.

Oh, Wesa, what will happen to you now?

Thomas now, no longer Wesa, stood in front of the man who'd been so aggressively calling his name. His cotton button-down shirt had come untucked from his plain brown breeches while chasing the boy, and he stood, panting, mouth drawn down in a formidable frown.

"Thomas. You've stolen food. Accept the punishment." The man's expression was stern, his eyes hard and unfeeling.

Wesa fidgeted before opening his hand to show the small bit of bread clutched in his fist. "But I'm so hungry, Mr. Crane." He looked at the food, his eyes wet and his lower lip trembling. "Please, I didn't want to steal, but I'm so hungry."

Sorrow gripped my heart for him. My stomach often felt hollow from the slim allotment of rations we were each given per day. And he was so young. *Poor Wesa.* Mr. Crane's features relaxed, and I breathed an inaudible sigh of relief. Mr. Crane was not a very nice man by nature, but I'd never *seen* him hurt any of the students. The same couldn't be said for other teachers. Several of them seemed to only be working at the boarding school because they loved tormenting children, seeking reasons to dole out discipline.

Mr. Crane just always had a sour look on his face, and even though he always smelled like whiskey, I'd never seen him raise his hand in anger.

"Bring it, Thomas." Mr. Crane raised his hand and beckoned Thomas closer. Two tears snaked down the small boy's cheeks, but the will of the older man won, and the younger of the two made slow shuffling steps across the packed dirt of the yard, head hanging low in defeat. Eyes so downcast he didn't see the blow coming and didn't even get to react. My seven-year-old self could do nothing but watch openmouthed at the violence that unfolded.

The cuff on the side of his six-year-old head lifted him straight off the ground and onto his back where he lay, a sad pile of arms and legs in the dirt.

"Thieves are beaten, Thomas," Mr. Crane said calmly, standing over the small boy on the ground too stunned to even react as the older man plucked the bread from his now slack grip. He grimaced and crumbled the small loaf with one hand until it was nothing but crumbs drifting to the ground. I mourned the loss of the food myself, hand drifting to my empty stomach. Now no one would get to eat it.

"If we let you do it, then everyone would think it entitled them to more than we give them, boy. You aren't special. None of you are. But if you're so hungry, you can eat your bread in the mud like an animal. Are you an animal, Thomas?" Mr. Crane's face twisted into something monstrous, and he stepped on the small pile of bread crumbs with his dusty brown shoe. "Go on, Thomas; eat it if you're hungry. This is good enough for you."

The small boy looked up from his place on the ground, afraid to move. More tears fell down his face, his little shoulders shaking with fear—or pain—maybe both. He made no move toward the pile in the dirt and crumbs, and still I stood in place, caught inside the vision with no way out. Mr. Crane sneered at him, his eyes a window to the depths of an ugly soul. Without warning, Mr. Crane's leg shot out, and his dirty brown shoe connected with the small boy's legs, lifting him up a few inches and sending him spinning farther in the dirt. Wesa— or Thomas, as they called him—lay on his back, clutching his side and crying. He made no move to get to his feet.

The air no longer smelled of rain. Instead, the wind carried the scent of burning. Similar to that of the blaze we gathered around when we had our own land, where the warriors told the tales of the hunt and the women sang their songs and cooked the meat. It was the smell of the fatwood just sparking, smoky and warm but not yet blistering. It was a small fire, but with enough tending it would become a great blaze, hot enough to sear anything placed before it. The breeze tickled my skin and moved the stray hairs that stuck out of my braids around my face. I didn't know where the wind had come from, but it did nothing to cool the aching itch marching up and down my skin, nor the anger that was bubbling just below the surface.

Mr. Crane was hurting Wesa—and no one was doing a thing to stop it.

He was a small boy, not so different from myself, who was just hungry. We all were, and that was a fact, but he was only six and didn't have as much of a grasp of self-control, even after two years in their Anglo prison. But Mr. Crane would make an example out of him regardless. The older man bore down on the child, his face as red as his facial hair, a grim smile plastered on his face.

He's happy. My inner thoughts echoed the stark reality. Even as a young child, I still understood. *He wants to hurt Wesa.*

But Wesa was so small, he couldn't take much more. Still no one in the yard moved. All those small faces looked on with fear in their eyes. No one would stand up for Wesa; no one could. Everyone knew what the punishment for rebellion was. I had seen the stone markings before —set up in the woods a short bit away from the school. That's where rebellion led you—to your very own stone marking in the dirt.

But even so, watching Mr. Crane as he reached the spot where he had kicked the young boy and hauled him back to his feet by his close-cropped hair had me gritting my teeth, the taste of bile and ash in my throat. He cocked back his fist and hit Wesa once; the impact split the skin on his chin and blood spurted out. Wesa cried. The smoke in the air stung my eyes, and my voice was that of a stranger croaking out of a throat lined with rocks and silt.

"No."

I wasn't loud enough. Mr. Crane didn't hear me, or at least pretended he didn't as he shook the boy until his feet left the ground, and he hung there in his master's hands, limp as an animal removed from a trap. "Come, Thomas, to punishment with you."

To punishment. As if the six-year-old hadn't been through enough. There was nowhere that Mr. Crane would take him that could be any improvement, and I doubted Wesa could even walk by himself. Blood poured from that angry cut on his face, and the crimson trail dripping from his tiny chin matched the hue of my blistering rage.

I found my voice.

"No." The heated breeze carried the word farther this time. This time Mr. Crane heard me, and his head snapped up, his eyes zeroing in on me from where he stood a short distance away. His mouth dropped open, but he didn't release his hold on the small boy.

"Mary, what are you doing?" *Mary.* That was my new name. I wasn't supposed to think of myself as River anymore, but sometimes I forgot. Times like now, when the atrocity I had just witnessed placed me somewhere outside of myself—outside of my safety nets and away from right and wrong.

I was just so *angry.*

Uncertainty graced Mr. Crane's face, and he took a small step back. I didn't want him to take a step back. I wanted him to let go of Wesa.

"No. You let him go. You hurt him—you're a bad man." The air snapped and crackled around me, and my braids rose and fell in this new heated breeze before unraveling completely. My long tresses danced in the angry wind.

"What are you doing?" the older man whispered, his eyes no longer narrow and cruel, but wide and fearful. "What are you—? Stay back. Stay away—"

But I didn't stay away. I couldn't, because Mr. Crane still had his meaty hand fisted in Wesa's short dark hair and was dragging him backward across the ground. Rage burned in my belly. He was a bad man. He hurt Wesa. He needed to be punished.

The ground I stood on cracked beneath my feet, the air so hot, the dirt released what little moisture it had and hardened like wood. The small bit of grass I'd curled my toes in earlier incinerated as if it had never been. I barely noticed. The heat. The smell. The acidic swell burning and churning deep in my belly—all were secondary to my rage as I looked at the man who had beaten a small boy to near unconsciousness.

"Drop him." The words blasted out of my mouth with ferocity, and Mr. Crane complied without thinking. Wesa just lay there, crumpled where he fell. The only movement in the entire yard was the myriad of small heads swiveling to look from Mr. Crane to me. The same look of horror that had been focused on Mr. Crane now moved to me. I didn't care.

I couldn't see any of them anymore. All I could see was the form of the man in front of me, the one who had such blackness in his soul, he could beat a child with a smile on his face. I only had eyes for him. Two other teachers had come into the yard by now—Mr. Weisman and Mrs. Crane. They had come out to see what was going on, I was sure, but I couldn't count on either of them to help in this situation. No, I'd witnessed their punishments before. No help would come from any of the adults in this building. I'd need to take care of them myself.

"What on earth is going on out here? Oh—" Mrs. Crane's sentence ended in a bloodcurdling shriek. "Mary! It's witchcraft! Savage witchcraft!"

I ignored her. I was far too focused on the backward steps of Mr. Crane as he tried to put as much space between the two of us as possible. Mr. Weisman had no such sense of self-preservation, and he marched to where I stood, circumventing Wesa on the ground as if he was nothing more than a puddle of dirty water. He almost made it in time to stop me. Almost.

I felt the graze of his fingers on my arm before I opened my mouth to scream. Dry, cracked lips pulled back as far as I was able, but no sound escaped. I spoke no words because I had none to give. But I had something else. That which I had been hiding for as long as I could remember. That twisting ache in my guts I had spent years learning to ignore, or at least keep hidden from everyone around me. My parents had taught me that, if not much else. Hide it away or bad things would happen.

Well, I'd hidden it all this time, and bad things still happened. There was no need to hide it anymore, so I let the mangled ropes of burning fury snake their way out of the depths of my body and erupt from my mouth in a single blast of heat and flame. I might not have any words to exorcise my rage, but I did have my fire.

Purchase *Kiss the Ashes* where books are sold.

www.ingramcontent.com/pod-product-compliance
Lightning Source LLC
Chambersburg PA
CBHW020512260626
47156CB00006B/1982